PAST
THE
LINE

By Jack Probyn

CLIFF EDGE
PRESS

ISBN: 978-1-80520-026-0

First Edition

Visit Jack Probyn's website at www.jackprobynbooks.com.

For Grandad.

MEET JAKE TANNER

Born: 28.03.1985

Height: 6'1"

Weight: 190lbs/86kg/13.5 stone

Physical Description: Brown hair, close shaven beard, brown eyes, slim athletic build

Education: Upper Second Class Honours in Psychology from the University College London (UCL)

Interests: When Jake isn't protecting lives and finding those responsible for taking them, Jake enjoys motorsports — particularly F1

Family: Mother, older sister, younger brother. His father died in a car accident when Jake was fifteen

Relationship Status: Currently in a relationship with Elizabeth Tanner, and he doesn't see that changing, ever

| DAY 1 |

CHAPTER 1

ENVELOPING EMBRACE

For many, family was everything. But for Erica Haversham, that wasn't the case. She despised hers with vehemence and indignation. She hated the way they treated her. The way they acted around her. The way they made her feel. The way they belittled her. They were nothing but a bunch of insignificant, supercilious, no-good bastards who'd ostracised her for too long.

But now, in the same way the seasons rolled from one to the next, it was time for all that to change.

The air inside the car buffeted and pulsated in time with the heavy bass. The vibrations tingled her skin, arousing the hairs on her arms and legs. The seats and dashboard were pitch black, save for the blue and red strips of light lining the footwell and door frame. Like driving in a spaceship.

Beside her was Dylan; strong, powerful, beautiful Dylan. Pumping himself up to the music, beating his fingers on the steering wheel, swerving the car left and right as the female singer's voice rose and fell. Thrashing his head back and forth as the song approached the bridge. And then, when the bridge finally finished, he launched himself into the finale: the rap.

What they say they don't know they do
What they say they can't see ain't true
Whether I believe you, the result's always the same: I'm fucking come for
you

Erica joined in, citing the lyrics verbatim. The result of days' worth of work in the music studio, fine-tuning the lyrics, the beat, the bassline, the melody and the role of the backing singer. The result of both hers and Dylan's efforts in making the song a worldwide success. One day.

As soon as it had finished, Dylan turned the volume down and swerved the car to the left, narrowly avoiding a bollard in the middle of the road. They were only two minutes away.

'What d'ya think?' he asked, turning to face her, one hand placed on the steering wheel while the other rested against the centre console. The epitome of cool. 'Good, eh?'

She smiled at him with glee. 'You know I love it, D.'

They continued down a secluded and remote street of East London until they arrived at a junction. Dylan switched the indicator on to signal a left turn, but Erica told him to head in the opposite direction.

'Trust me,' she said, pointing to the right. 'It'll be easier for us to get away.'

'But—'

'Trust me, Dylan. Please. I know what I'm doing.'

Dylan tapped the front pocket of his hoodie and said, with a wink, 'So do I.'

When Erica didn't respond, he placed his hand on her leg and squeezed. 'Everything'll be calm, aight? I got you.'

His touch roused the parts of her that were no longer innocent. His hands were soft, yet strong, sensitive. They had the power to make her feel things she'd never known were possible. When she was around them, she felt secure, safe, a cub under the stoic protection of its mother. And in light of what they were about to do, they made her feel unstoppable – even if the gravity of their decisions hadn't quite hit her yet.

A few minutes later, they pulled up outside a row of terraced houses in a quaint residential street. Small blocks of yellow light punctured the building like holes in a grater.

Erica leant over Dylan's lap, ran her hand teasingly up his thigh to his crotch and glanced up at the house. The curtains were pulled across the living-room window, and the only other light in the front of the building was the bedroom on the third floor.

You little shit. Her body tensed, and she dug her nails into Dylan's thigh without meaning to.

The man grimaced and placed his hand on the small of her back, on the brief flash of skin on display where her top had ridden up. 'Relax,' he said. 'Don't stress. Please.' Then he reached into his hoodie pocket and produced a small plastic bag; inside was a handful of white pills. 'Think you need a little pick-me-up, don't you?'

Without hesitation, Erica snatched the bag from Dylan, rummaged through the contents, found the first ecstasy tablet her fingers could get hold of and placed it on the palm of her hand. Using her acrylic nails, she split the pill in half and attempted to crush it into a fine powder.

'What the fuck you doing?' Dylan asked.

'I…'

'Just swallow it. You'll be off your tits before you know it.'

Not wanting to upset him, Erica did as she was told and placed the MDMA on her tongue. The reaction started at once, the tablet bubbling and fizzing on the surface, rapidly filling her mouth with the chemicals that would soon consume her entire body. She closed her mouth and dry swallowed, grimacing as she flushed the taste down her throat.

'Ready?' Dylan asked, pinching her cheeks with both hands.

'Time to face the music,' she said and stepped out of the car.

The humidity in the spring air had plummeted, replaced by an ominous chill that swept through the streets. The atmosphere was calm, untouched, unstirred like a sleeping baby. A dark and premonitory omen of what was to come.

As she rounded the front of Dylan's BMW, the moon bounced off the bonnet and blinded her. In her drug-induced state, she thought it looked like a giant football.

Ignoring it, she stumbled onto the pavement and climbed up a small flight of steps towards the front door. She retrieved her keys from the back pocket of her jeans and plunged the largest one into the door, her hands trembling with a combination of fear, ecstasy, and adrenaline. The sharp sound of the lock falling out of place amplified in her head, like the heavy bassline that continued to reverberate around her skull. Her senses ran wild and screamed at her from every angle.

The euphoria was kicking in. Faster than usual, she noted. Perhaps exacerbated by the splinter of fear creaking through the woodwork of her skin. Finally the door opened, and the crack sealed itself shut. The smell of recently cooked macaroni cheese – her favourite – wafted through the corridor and climbed her nostrils. She delighted in the scent and continued deeper into the house. At the end of the corridor lay the kitchen, and to her immediate left was the living room.

She advanced towards the kitchen. As she approached the threshold, the sound of a tap running and cutlery and plates ricocheting on the metal sink – a sound she'd been otherwise oblivious to – stopped suddenly.

'Erica!' Rupert Haversham screamed, throwing a sponge into the sink and spinning round to face her. The rest of his oversized body eventually caught up. 'Where've you been? We've been worried sick.'

'I'm fine.'

'Why didn't you tell anyone where you were?'

Before Erica responded, a figure appeared in the door frame to her left. Helena Haversham, Rupert's second wife.

Helena the Whore.

Helena the Homewrecker.

Helena, Erica's nemesis.

'Oh, Erica!' Helena screeched. The woman rushed towards her, flung herself over Erica's shoulders and squeezed with the false affection of a stepmother who cared more about her latest nail appointment than helping with her new daughter's science homework. 'I was *so* worried about you.'

Helena the Whore with the fake tits and teeth.

Helena the Whore with the skinny waist and perfect hair.

By now the drugs were fully making their way around Erica's system and she was entering what Dylan liked to call The Verisimilitude Phase. The fourteen-letter word was one that he'd learnt on a TV programme once and, after misinterpreting the meaning, had prescribed to be one of the side effects of ecstasy. The side effect that rendered the user with a slippery tongue capable of sharing their innermost and heavily guarded secrets as easily as a beaver building a dam.

But before she was able to unleash her tirade of vehemence, something distracted Helena, and she pushed Erica away and retreated.

'What is *he* doing here?' she asked, wrapping her cashmere cardigan tightly around her body, concealing the cleavage revealed by her low-cut top.

Erica spun on the spot, looked at Dylan, and then turned her attention back to Helena.

'*I* invited him,' Erica said with as much disdain as she could manage.

'I want him out of this house,' Rupert interjected, pointing at Dylan with a soap brush, flinging water and bubbles onto the floor.

'He has every right to be here!'

'Not without my say-so. He's no good for—'

'I can speak for myself, yo.' Dylan sauntered towards the granite island in the centre of the kitchen as though he owned the place and kept his hands submerged in his hoodie pocket.

As he passed, he gave her a quick blink.

The call to action.

'I can't be in here with him,' Helena said, then she waved her hand in the air dismissively and turned her back on the conversation. 'I won't speak to you until he's gone.'

Erica copied Dylan and placed her hand inside her hoodie pocket. Her fingers tightened around the item in there. She followed and slipped through the door before it closed, paying no heed to her father's cries.

Helena the Whore stormed through the dining room, through another door and into the living room, where she jumped onto the white seven-seater sofa, folded her legs onto the cushion and cast her attention to the TV that hung above the fireplace. Then she grabbed the remote and switched the channel to a home-shopping network. Oblivious to Erica behind her, edging closer, silent, graceful.

Like the leaves of autumn slowly dying.

Erica tightened her grip around the six-inch blade in her pocket until her knuckles whitened and her palm turned sweaty. For a very brief moment – and it was very brief, for it was only a flickering glance – Erica hesitated and contemplated her actions.

She asked herself: did she want to do this?

Yes.

Did she love the woman in front of her?

No.

Helena the fucking homewrecker whore with the big tits and the perfect teeth and the perfect smile and the perfect figure deserved everything she got.

Did she want Helena to be a part of her life anymore?

No.

The final one was toughest to answer: did she have it in her to do this?

There was only one way to find out.

Erica's body shook with adrenaline and excitement as she entered the Euphoria Phase. The rest of her body tingled as she pulled the blade from her pocket and stepped closer to Helena – closer to the chestnut-brown hair that Erica had always envied for looking so beautiful, even on her worst day. Closer to the stupid bitch who'd strolled into their lives and completely ruined everything. Closer to the woman who'd stolen her dad from her and manipulated him into making her life a complete misery.

From behind, Erica grabbed Helena's forehead, yanked it backward, opening up her airways, and slashed the blade across her throat, slicing cleanly into her carotid artery. A mist of blood projected into the air, showering Helena's legs and soiling the luxury sofa cushions and carpet in an explosion of red.

Erica glanced down at Helena's wild eyes. They were as white as the moon outside, and there was a pain behind them. Tears formed in the corners and eventually ran down her tilted forehead. Her arms flailed around, attempting to throw Erica off her, but her efforts were misguided, none of them making contact. By now, the letter-box hole in Helena's throat was overflowing with blood, running down her top and into her stomach.

As she watched over her stepmother, the guardian angel preparing to take her into the seven levels of hell, Erica wondered what the whore was thinking. Had she been shackled with guilt and loathing at having destroyed a happy family? Or had she been distracted by the disappointment of missing out on her husband's credit card forever more, of not being able to experience all the nice things he could afford for her?

Where she was going, she would never be able to experience nice things again.

Helena opened her mouth. Erica placed her hand over it and stifled the woman's final few gasps. Then she bent down beside Helena's head and whispered, 'You were never welcome in this house.'

And then, just like that, Helena lay perfectly still, calm, oddly serene.

Erica hovered over her stepmother, trying to comprehend how she felt. *What* she felt. The short answer was simple – nothing. Not even a morsel of guilt. The lines between reality and fiction, existence and death, had been blurred thanks to the waves of ecstasy rolling over her again and again, pulling her deeper, deeper.

And she didn't want them to stop.

She wanted to ride and ride and—

A sound came from the kitchen, shocking her back to the room. Erica swivelled on the spot and headed towards the noise, wiping the blade clean with the inside nook of her elbow.

As she entered, she froze in the door frame. Right in front of her was Rupert, Daddy, her hero, bent over the kitchen countertop. Slowly falling to the tiled floor, one hand clinging to the counter's edge, while the other clung to what remained of his existence. Dylan stood beside him, repeatedly punching the blade into Rupert's stomach and ribs and arms and legs and crotch and neck and head, making his way around the man's entire body until, like a wild gazelle that had been brought down by a lion, Rupert eventually breathed his last breath and collapsed to the floor.

What surprised Erica the most was that neither of them had put up a fight. They had been weak, defenceless, almost afraid to retaliate. For that very reason, they deserved to die – a minor consolation for the guilt she knew that she would no doubt feel later on. Weakness would hold no place in her life from now on. Not if she was going to survive the next few days.

'You good?' Dylan asked, panting. 'Helena?'

Erica nodded. 'She's—'

Something moved in the corner of Erica's field of vision. The movement came from the doorway to her right, leading into the corridor. She turned.

Froze.

Standing in the door frame, clutching a blanket against her chest and a teddy bear under her arm, was Felicity, her four-year-old sister.

'Ecky,' she whispered, her nickname for Erica.

'What are you doing awake, Fleck? You're supposed to be asleep.'

'What's going on?'

'We're playing a grown-up game. Now go back to bed.'

Felicity's eyes dropped down on Erica's body. 'What's that?' She pointed at the blade in Erica's hand.

'It's a dangerous toy. It's for adults to play with. I… I want you to go back to bed now, please.'

She was rapidly sobering up. No longer were her fingertips vibrating with the ferocious beat of her heart. No longer were her ears echoing every sound around her. And the longer she stood there, she knew, the harder she would fall into the impending comedown.

'You take me?' Felicity asked, holding her hand out.

Erica opened her mouth, but a lump caught in her throat. She swallowed and sniffled, stifled the growing tears in her eyes. Shaking her head, she said, 'I'm sorry, Fleck, but I can't. I've got some… I've got some *adult* things to do. Dylan…' She sniffed – hard. 'Dylan can take you. He'll take really good care of you. Do you remember Dylan?'

'Yeah. Mummy said he's a bad man.'

Helena the Brainwasher.

'He's not a bad man. He's a part of the family. Do you want him to read you a bedtime story?'

'OK,' Felicity said, nodding. As soon as she finished, she rubbed the sleep from her eyes.

Before Dylan turned to face Felicity, he handed Erica the knife and looked her in the eyes. 'Leave it with me,' he said. 'Find your dad's car keys. And— Shit.'

'What?'

'The CCTV – is it turned off?'

Erica shook her head. After working with some of the biggest criminals in the country, her dad had thought it best to secure the premises and arm every corner of the house with twenty-four-hour surveillance. Not for the safety of his family, but for the safety of his documents and the work he was conducting. Rival gang members, psychotic killers and any other stranger could wander in off the street and abduct them, and he wouldn't have lost a minute of sleep over it. But when it came to his work and the security of his professional standing as the best defence barrister in London, that was where he drew the line.

For many, family was everything.

'Find the CCTV and destroy it,' Dylan ordered. Then he shuffled towards Felicity, placed his arm around her shoulders, and escorted her out of the kitchen.

'Night, Ecky. Love you,' Felicity called behind her.

Erica opened her mouth to speak, but the words were too heavy. She waited until they were upstairs before she moved again and raced to the other side of the kitchen, through a playroom and into another room to the right – Rupert's office. A bookshelf as tall as the wall ran across one length of the room. On the other side was an exercise bike. In all the years her father had owned it, she'd only ever known him to use it once. Twice maximum. At the end of the room was her father's desk. Resting atop it was a small computer monitor with rolling footage of the security cameras around the house.

Erica advanced towards the computer.

Experience from her teenage years had taught her how to erase certain pieces of footage from the cameras. Like the time she'd come home drunk from a party in the middle of a field when she was thirteen. Like the first time Dylan stayed over and left in the morning with no one knowing.

It was easy when you knew how.

Erica awoke the computer, logged into the CCTV software and scrolled back to the footage from six hours ago. She highlighted the gap between then and now, and pressed DELETE on the keyboard. Just like that, the footage was gone, lost into the ether.

Using her sleeve as a cloth, Erica wiped the keyboard and mouse clean of her fingerprints, grabbed Rupert's car keys from the pen pot on his desk, then hurried back into the kitchen.

By the time she returned to the hallway, Dylan was already on the bottom step of the staircase.

She paused at the sight of him, her body paralysed with shock.

'Did you...? Is she...?'

'I was kind,' Dylan said. There was nothing in his expression that suggested he'd just murdered two people in cold blood. 'Did you get the keys?'

Erica held them in the air.

'And the footage?'

'Deleted and removed from the hard drive.'

He leant forward and kissed her. 'I'm proud of you. Now come on – let's get the fuck outta here.'

They left the house and split up; Dylan taking his own car while Erica raced towards Rupert's Mercedes.

'Remember what I told you?' he asked.

'Put it in gear. Find the biting point. Easy on the accelerator.'

'That's my girl.'

'See you at the house?'

'See you at the house.'

She unlocked the car, started the engine, and sped away. As she roared down the road, she fought the urge to turn back and face the house where she'd grown up. Where she'd fostered many happy memories. Where she'd hoped that many more would come. But there was no way she could turn back now. She and Dylan shared a bond, a connection like no other. Her body – and soul – had crossed the point of no return directly into his enveloping embrace.

Dylan's blood raced around his body, fuelling the adrenaline in his cells. He increased the volume on the stereo and blasted his song. He screamed. Yelled. Pounded on the steering column. The song drowning out his noise.

He'd done it. And now he felt fucking euphoric. Like nothing in the world could stop him. Like he could take on anyone and anything.

And then he remembered he had a job to do. A call to make.

Dylan placed his phone on the dashboard, unlocked it, and dialled the number.

The song suddenly stopped and was replaced by the sound of ringing.

Brmph-brmph. Brmph-brmph. Brmph-brmph.

Eventually, on the fourth ring, the other line answered.

'Yes?' came the calm, soothing voice.

'It's me.'

'Is it done?'

'It's done. All of them.'

'And Erica?'

'Coming back to the flat with me.'

'Very well. You know what you have to do next.'

The line went dead.

CHAPTER 2

GOOD NEWS

Henry Matheson had been looking forward to tonight all week. Casino night. The only time he and some of the other acquaintances he'd made in Wandsworth, one of Her Majesty's finest, could put their money where their mouths were and relax. The night where turf wars and rivalries were left at the door.

And tonight, Henry had the luxury of hosting it in his cell.

With him was Andrew Bennett, one of the men Henry had heard about growing up. The man had owned almost all the gun trade in and out of South London, and it was rumoured he'd been the one selling weapons to the Irish and British during the Troubles. Both parties were willing to pay whatever it cost, and Andrew Bennett was more than happy to oblige them. Convicted of terrorism offences shortly after, the sixty-one-year-old was serving his fifteenth year of his twenty-nine-year sentence.

Beside him, with his jumper pulled up to his chin, was Reggie Mings, a complete nutjob who, despite never having been tested for it, possessed all the qualities of a sociopath. Severely unhinged and slightly deranged, he'd been arrested for the armed robbery of an entire high street. Jumping from shop to shop, his spree on the small road in Leicester had resulted in three fatalities and sixteen casualties. After a quick hostage negotiation, the police had eventually thrown him into the back of a police van and convicted him ten months later. He, too, was serving a life sentence. Year ten, with a lot more to go. But he'd resigned himself to his fate soon after his arrival and was notorious around the prison for re-enacting his initial crime: charging into inmate's cells and robbing them while beating the shit out of them. He didn't gain anything by doing it. No respect, no leniency on his sentence – he simply did it for the fun of hurting people.

The last member of the group was Roger Silverwood, a man in his seventies who'd originally been convicted of robbery but since his arrival in prison had developed a taste for blood and desensitised knuckles. Only supposed to serve a five stretch, he'd added an extra twenty-five years to his sentence for beating someone to death in their cell. When asked why he'd done it, he responded with: 'Because he looked at me funny.' But everyone on the spur knew it was because the two had known each other on the outside, and the victim had bragged about sleeping with Roger's wife behind his back. Whether or not true, Roger didn't care. It was a matter of principle. And soon thereafter, everyone quickly learnt the importance of keeping Roger's wife out of any and all discussion, no matter where they were in the prison.

Henry Matheson, on the other hand, was the newest addition to the small knot of acquaintances, and by extension the prison. Before his sentencing, he'd been involved in an altercation with a former inmate. And for the first time in his life, Henry had come off worse: a ruptured anus, which still caused him immeasurable amounts of pain; a dozen holes in his stomach that made him look like a punctured jacket potato ready for cooking in the microwave; and a torso of burnt and raised skin that looked like an ordnance survey of the Alps. But the worst injury of them all had been the Glasgow Grin. The scars on his face stretched from the sides of his mouth to the middle of his cheeks. Eating was a task, and talking not much better. If he wasn't careful, saliva would dribble from his lips like he was a baby. Following the incident, a decision had been made to separate him from the rest of the prison population, and so he'd been transferred to Wandsworth.

Sadly, however, upon his arrival, one thing had become abundantly clear to Henry: he was at the bottom of the pecking order. In Belmarsh, Henry had owned the prison, the prisoners, the guards and just about everyone else in it. He was the king, the king responsible for facilitating everyone's habits and trading favours for commodities. But here, he was on the lowest rung. A nobody. Those accolades were instead given to the country's finest: serial killers, and the likes of Andrew, Reggie and Roger. But none of them were on the same level as the Albanian and Romanian gangs that occupied more than half the prison. Because of the increasing epidemic of prison overpopulation, two of the biggest competitors in the drug trade had been thrown into the boiling pot.

And now Henry had been thrown into the mix, too.

'Your turn,' Archie told him calmly. His entire disposition belied the insanity and complexities of his working mind. 'You gotta lay eeva a six or a nine.'

'Thanks for the lesson.' Henry thumbed through his cards and set down a six of hearts. 'When are we gonna talk about business?'

'What business?' Andrew Bennett asked. A cigarette dangled from his mouth, and wisps of smoke clawed into the air. The top of the cigarette jostled and shook as he spoke.

'Like getting me out of this fucking place,' Henry said defiantly, the arrogance and cockiness of his youth oozing through his ego. But deep down he was afraid, afraid for his life; the animals at the bottom of the food chain were always the first to go.

A chorus of laughter erupted from the men, the noise spilling out of the doorway and into the spur.

'Fuck off!'

'You're dreaming, kid!'

'You got more chance of Devlin giving you a successful sex change,' Roger said.

Devlin Cooper was a former award-winning tattoo artist responsible for stabbing a client repeatedly with a tattoo needle; he was the closest thing they had to a surgeon in the prison.

'You're stuck here for life.'

Henry joined in the laughter, keeping up appearances. 'In that case, I'm gonna have to see about getting me a couple of porno mags or something. I'm gonna need something else to look at for the next thirty years.'

Another chorus, another appearance maintained. Then it died down just as quickly. Almost as volatile as the four men's tempers.

It was Henry's turn again, and he laid down the four of diamonds. 'What's this I'm hearing about more Hellbanianz coming in?' he asked.

'Ain't much else to hear,' Reggie responded. 'Last I heard, there was a big bust-up down in Winchester and a dozen of them are coming in. The feds are finally doing something right.'

Andrew, Reggie and Roger were from a different class of criminal. At some point in their lifetime, each had had an involvement in the drug trade, but back in their days, it had been more relaxed and there had been a certain element of cricket about it. Now, however, there was a new breed of dealer on the streets. One who settled feuds and rivalries at the end of a bullet rather than the end of a fist. Henry had been part of that new wave of criminal – and as a result, he was very lucky to be sitting at the table with these gentlemen, let alone be respected by them. He suspected there was a hint of xenophobia and racism behind their approval. But when it came to it, he was nowhere near as ruthless as the Hellbanianz, the Albanians' self-appointed moniker, or the Romanians. Not only had they been driving down the price of drugs for the past five years, they'd also wiped out several members of Henry's gang, the E11. They were like rats, rapidly infesting the towns and villages, spreading their diseases and running everyone out of town. And now they were occupying the prisons, a popular and fruitful revenue stream.

'I think I'm gonna need some protection,' Henry said, a lump caught in his throat. The words came as a surprise to himself.

His name was on the tip of his enemies' lips, and his days of casino nights and quiet breakfasts, lunches and dinners were quickly becoming numbered. Somehow he'd avoided a hiding, but he didn't know how much longer his luck would last; he was the zebra, a beacon of black and white amid the dreary grey of the prison uniform, and there were only so many times he could avoid a mauling from the lion.

Bottom of the food chain.

'If that's what you want, Hen…' Andrew removed the cigarette from his mouth, flicked the excess ash onto the concrete floor, and took a drag. He inhaled heavily, filling his lungs with the toxic chemicals, and eventually exhaled, billowing a cloud of smoke across the pile of cards in the centre of the bed. 'Then you know what you gotta do.'

Before Henry could think about it, his mobile phone rang. He removed it from his tracksuit pocket and glanced at the screen – Dylan calling ahead of schedule. *Vrrmph. Vrrmph.* The phone vibrated.

Henry held his finger aloft, silencing the men in the room.

'Yes?'

'It's me,' Dylan replied. He sounded exasperated, his breathing wheezy.

'Is it done?'

'It's done. All of them.'

'And Erica?'

'Coming back to the flat with me.'

Henry paused a moment. He nodded.

'Very well. You know what you have to do next.'

He rang off and placed the phone on his knee, then returned his attention to the card game. He was momentarily unaware of what was going on, and what had happened in the twenty seconds he'd been on the phone. And he was only slightly aware that he was smiling.

'Good news?' Roger asked.

A smile yawned across Henry's face. 'Guess you could say that.'

CHAPTER 3

BLACK 24

One of the things Jake Tanner missed about having his wife Elizabeth around the house, more than most, was her cooking. Despite never having studied professionally, she could create the most beautiful and delicious infusions from the meagre scraps and rations they had lying around the house. It wasn't until she was gone that he realised how much he depended on her to cook a decent meal, something worth spending time on and enjoying. Instead, for the past few months, he'd been reliant on his own abilities, which stretched as far as anyone in his position. A piece of toast with a smattering of egg lightly sprinkled with pepper was one of the most delectable feasts he'd had the pleasure of making himself.

That was as exciting as it got.

Except for this evening.

This evening was different. This evening he'd get to experience good food. Proper food.

Food worth eating.

Food worth enjoying.

The only downside was the company he'd be forced to share it with: Martha Clarke, his mother-in-law. The owner of the house that Elizabeth and his two girls, Maisie and Ellie, had called home for the past twelve weeks. Jake didn't mind spending time with *them* – in fact, it was the very thing he wanted more than anything else in the world – but the less he was near his children's grandmother, the better.

After arriving early from work – something Elizabeth had always insisted he was incapable of doing when their marriage wasn't a mess – he slipped out of the kitchen into the living room, where he found his daughters. Maisie was seated on the sofa, reading a book, while Ellie was colouring in with a varying assortment of crayons.

As he stepped into the room, the girls offered him no notice, no invitation to play or hug or even sit down beside them.

A stranger to his own family.

'Careful you don't get anything on the carpet,' he said, perching himself on the edge of the sofa next to Ellie.

'Daddy!' Ellie yelled. As soon as she laid eyes on him, she leapt up and gave him a brief hug before quickly returning her attention to her drawings.

For the first time in a while, all thought of work and the stresses of the past few weeks disappeared from his mind, and he focused on the present. He looked over at his eldest. 'How was nursery today, Mais?'

'It was OK. Miss Arrowsmith gave me a hug.'

'Why? Were you sad?'

'Yes.'

Jake lifted himself to his feet, picked up Maisie from the sofa and sat down, setting her on his lap. She continued to read her book.

'What was making you sad, sweetie?' Jake asked, his mind whirring. He conjured images of another child bullying her, followed by more images of him storming down to the school, prepared to punish the child himself. Or the parents.

Fucking parents.

It was always the parents.

Maisie turned, her eyes a wide pool of innocence. 'When are we coming home, Daddy?'

It hadn't occurred to him that the distance between himself and Elizabeth had permeated through the malleable innocence of childhood. Perhaps he'd been naïve to think that they were oblivious to the realities of their parents' matrimonial turmoil.

Following the Matheson enquiry, the death of Assistant Commissioner Richard Candy and the personal attack on their finances, Jake's and Elizabeth's relationship had deteriorated. At first, things had seemed to be getting back on track, their marriage continuing with half-truths and a few white lies. But the straw that had broken the camel's back was when Elizabeth had discovered the news about his infidelity. The kiss that Jake and Stephanie, a former colleague, had shared one drunken night in a Premier Inn in the middle of Birmingham.

Now, she'd moved out, severed nearly all communication and taken the kids with her.

The childcare remained her job, while the mortgage, the bills and other expenses remained his.

So, in reality, it was as though nothing had changed at all.

Except *everything* had.

'Maisie,' Jake began, cautious on how to approach the topic. 'You know that Mummy and Daddy love you very much. And it's—'

'Jake! Maisie! Ellie! Dinner's ready,' Elizabeth called from the kitchen.

Saved by the bell.

Maybe there really was someone looking over him, even if it hadn't felt that way recently.

'Come on, girls – it's time to eat.'

Jake dropped Maisie to the floor, grabbed Ellie from the carpet and carried her to the kitchen, with Maisie trailing behind, holding his hand. In the open plan dining room, Elizabeth standing on her toes, reaching high into a cupboard, while Martha was on the other side of the kitchen, tipping ladles of spaghetti Bolognese into white china bowls. It was in that moment that Jake felt as though he were home, as though everything was back to normal again, as though the events of the past few months hadn't taken place at all and that it had just been a dream.

A dream that had turned into a nightmare.

'Jake,' Martha called, and immediately the feeling was crushed. 'Get the girls set up at the table. I don't want their food to get cold.'

And you think I do?

Begrudgingly, he did as he was told and found his seat at the table beside Maisie. A few seconds later, Martha handed the plates round, serving the girls first, then Elizabeth, then herself, and then Jake. He thanked her, sprinkled an extra serving of Parmesan on top, and grabbed his knife and fork just as Elizabeth finally sat down.

'Looks delicious, hun,' Jake said, glancing up at his wife and then down at his food again. 'Probably the best meal I've had in a long time.'

'Are you not eating properly?' Elizabeth asked before she shovelled a forkful of food into her mouth.

'Now and then. By the time I get home, it's too late to cook anything substantial, so I just have a couple of packets of crisps – or a ready meal – and that sorts me just fine.'

'They're not good for you, Jake. You need a proper diet.'

'I'm trying.'

'Like you are with everything else?' Martha said derisively, making no effort to hide the contempt in her voice.

'Pardon?'

'Mum, *leave* it,' Elizabeth insisted.

Martha wiped the side of her mouth with a napkin and set it on her leg. 'It's been three months since Alan died, and you've seen us – what? – only once before tonight. Do you really care that little?'

Here we go. Jake readied himself for an assault. They were commonplace whenever his and Martha's paths crossed. But since Alan's passing, following a failed kidney transplant, Jake had struggled to remain civil and an upholder of the peace. It was about time they had an overdue argument. But then he realised where he was, and whose company he was in.

Tonight was a special night for several reasons. Best not ruin it.

'Things are complicated,' Jake said, tightening his grip around his dinner knife.

'You're entitled to your days off – there's nothing stopping you from making an appearance.'

Jake considered for a moment. And then it dawned on him.

'You don't know, do you?' he asked.

'Know what?'

As he was about to open his mouth and explain to Martha what had really caused their separation, Elizabeth's eyes flared, imploring him to remain quiet. He did – and scooped another load of mince onto his fork. 'I don't think this is a conversation we should be having in front of the children.'

'I have a right to know.'

'And I said *no*. It isn't appropriate for dinner. Afterwards, maybe, but not right now. I suggest we talk about something else,' Jake said, hoping the forkful of food he'd just shoved into his mouth signalled the end of the conversation.

To his surprise, Martha backed down. He didn't like shouting at people or speaking to them sternly – especially when it was family – but he was tired of allowing her to dictate conversations and people's emotions.

'Have you heard anything from Rupert?' Elizabeth asked. She was in the middle of helping Ellie focus and pay attention to her food.

'I saw him today,' Jake replied.

'And?'

Jake hesitated, looked into her eyes, and shook his head. 'I'm sorry, Liz.'

Elizabeth dropped the spoon on Ellie's plate and sank into her chair. Her brow furrowed, and she glanced at her food with a lost, vacant stare.

'I'm sorry, hun,' Jake repeated.

'Is there nothing we can do to convince him?'

'I tried.'

'Do you want me to speak to him?' Martha interrupted.

When both Jake and Elizabeth looked at her in mild disbelief, she continued, 'He and I worked together. He helped us with Detson.' She was referring to the tower-block fire that had taken place several years before due to unsafe cladding and a faulty hairdryer. The word was synonymous with the night hundreds of families had lost their lives as the fire spread rapidly throughout every facet of the building, and the subsequent government cover-up that had left them bereft and homeless.

Martha was the housing minister in charge of the decision and the one who'd received the biggest flak afterwards. Yet had still managed to keep her job.

'Why haven't you said anything before?' Jake asked.

Martha shrugged. Jake was soon beginning to realise that the more time he spent with her, the more he found out.

'So it seems we're just a family full of lies.'

'What's that supposed to mean?' Martha asked.

'Jake, *please*,' Elizabeth implored.

But he continued regardless.

'If you must know,' he began, 'Liz kicked herself out of the house a few months ago. Not because of whatever reason she gave you, but because she found out something that I had been trying my hardest to keep from her – not because I was trying to hide it from her maliciously, but because I was trying to protect her. Cliché, I know, but here we are.' He spoke to Martha, but his attention was solely focused on Elizabeth. 'A couple of months ago, while I was investigating Henry Matheson, I took a short trip to Birmingham with a colleague. Stephanie. We stayed in a hotel overnight, got drunk and then we kissed. It was a mistake, a stupid, terrible mistake, and there isn't a day goes by where I don't think about what I did to hurt you, Liz.'

Silence ensued, save for the sounds of delight and the clattering of cutlery on crockery coming from Maisie and Ellie. By now, Martha had set her knife and fork down and was gently dabbing at the sides of her mouth with her napkin. Jake prepared his defences for an attack.

'Was this before or after what happened to Elizabeth?' she asked with an air of calm around her that unsettled him.

'After. And it kills me I can't be here with her while she's going through it all.'

'She has the girls. And she has me.'

'Is that necessary? Does she really need *you*? The Elizabeth I know is a strong and powerful woman who won't let anything like this faze her. She's perfectly capable of looking after Ellie and Maisie. She's been fine since they were born, so what's changed? Other than the fact that it might be soothing your ego slightly, or filling in the hole that Alan left after he passed…'

Another moment of silence descended upon the table. Jake reflected on what he'd said. Did he feel out of line? Maybe. Did he feel guilty? Not really. Did he regret what he said? Yes. But they were his feelings, and they had spent too long inside him to stay there any longer.

'I think it's about time we all started being honest with one another in this family,' he added, delivering the final blow to the jaw with a clean right hook. 'And I've said my piece.'

Martha's expression remained closed and impassive, a barricade in front of the castle. But Jake knew, deep down, deep beneath those walls, a fire raged throughout the castle. She began to sweat as she struggled to maintain her composure.

'And I think it's time for you to leave,' Martha said, her voice stern and authoritative.

'Mum, no, you can't. Let him stay.' Elizabeth placed her hand on Martha's arm.

'It's fine.' Jake lifted himself out of his chair and set his napkin down on the table. 'I can handle it.'

Jake kissed the girls on the head and said goodbye, grabbed his things and then left. Maisie and Ellie called after him, but he continued regardless. He couldn't lose face in front of Martha, not if he wanted her to have any respect for him further down the line when all of this was over.

On the drive home, his mind wandered in and out of reality like a drunk walking in and out of an off-licence, thinking about what the future might hold for their relationship. He adored Elizabeth and the girls more than anything in the—

Was that true?

He considered for a moment. The whole reason they were separated was due to a combination of things. But at the front of it all was his obsession – and, dare he admit it, *addiction* – to work. What had happened with Stephanie was a direct result of that. Too many other officers in the force had suffered similar infidelity horror stories. Too many officers were addicted to the job. It was an obsession, and once it had a grip on you, it didn't let go.

Yes, there was nothing he wouldn't do for his kids and his family and his marriage. But, equally, there was nothing he wouldn't do for his career. Perhaps it was time to think about someone else for a change.

Before he knew it, he was home, parked on the side of the road, and walking towards the front door. He fumbled the key in his hands, then slotted it into the lock. When he made to swing the door open, he was met with resistance. The pile of shoes on the other side of the door. The mountain of bills and junk mail and newspapers that had formed over the past few weeks. The overflowing refuse bags that had missed the last collection and needed a new home in the local landfill.

Jake leant into the door, easing the mess out of the way, then waded through the corridor and into the kitchen. A skyscraper of dirty, unwashed plates rested next to the sink; beside it was a tower of plastic microwaveable meal and takeaway cartons waiting to be dropped into a refuse bag.

The recycle cycle.

Jake grabbed a dirty glass, ambled towards the fridge and poured himself a Foster's. As the cold fluid descended his throat, he stopped and gazed around the kitchen, searching for something in particular.

Eventually, he found it. Somehow in a different place to where he remembered leaving it. When he lifted the laptop lid, the screen illuminated on the last internet page he'd been on before he'd left the house that morning. And he was still logged in.

As he perused through the dashboard, he realised there were four Champions League matches on in less than ten minutes. He glanced at the top right of the screen, saw his balance was at £23.52, and placed a series of bets. Barcelona to win. Chelsea to draw. Both teams to score. Final score for each game. First goal scorer.

In a matter of seconds, he was down to his last £1.52, so he turned his attention to something more immediate. Something that would satisfy his urges. Something that he could enjoy watching. Roulette.

Jake hopped over to the live casino screen and gambled the rest of the money on black twenty-four. He clapped his hands in the air as soon as the bet had been confirmed and waited. His heart beat in time with the countdown clock, ticking down until the next spin.

Ticking…

Beating…

And then it began.

He watched the smartly – yet seductively – dressed woman throw the ball into the wheel. It bounced and rolled until eventually…

'Yes!'

Black twenty-four.

He'd won, and when he refreshed the screen, an extra £53.20 had deposited into his account.

Elated, Jake downed his beer, grabbed the rest of the six-pack from the fridge and strapped himself in. It was going to be another exciting night. A profitable one too, he hoped.

In the weeks that he'd delved into the world of online gambling, he'd managed to burn through over a thousand pounds – more money than he owned in any of his bank accounts. His monthly outgoings chewed into what was left of his salary, and so he was relying on borrowed money – and borrowed time. He didn't know the exact figures because he didn't need to. There was a light at the end of the tunnel.

And that fifty pounds was just the beginning.

CHAPTER 4

NINE LIVES

A long, monotonous vibrating sound roused him from his deep sleep. Eyes half closed, he ignored it and rolled over to the other side of the bed, mistaking the noise for his own snoring.

But the vibrating continued.

Jake opened his eyes blearily, blinking the ambient light that filtered in through the curtains into existence. Then he slowly rolled from Elizabeth's side of the bed onto his own. The movement was gentle, considered, but it was enough to send the world into a spin, waves of delirium rolling and rolling and rolling over him.

The alcohol was still very much in his system, working its way through his liver. Excited by the football bets and the rolling symbols of the online arcades, one beer had turned into two. Two into four. And then before he knew it, there was a bottle of Jack Daniel's in his hand, keeping him company while he couldn't afford to keep the heating on.

Jake pinched the bridge of his nose and closed his eyes. Groaned.

On the bedside table, the phone continued to ring. But as he reached across for it, the call finished. That was the ninth missed call in the last twenty minutes. And they were all from the same person.

DCI Darryl Hughes, his manager.

'Ah, shit,' Jake whispered to himself as he unlocked the phone.

Nine missed calls. No voicemails. This was serious. Jake knew that meant Darryl expected him to call back as soon as he could.

Jake rested his arm on the pillow for support. His eyes trailed away from the harsh illumination of the screen and focused on the bottle of water he'd had the foresight to place on the bedside table. The cold liquid soothed his parched throat and quenched some of his unending thirst.

Setting the bottle back on the table, he returned his attention to the phone, tapped to return the last call, set it on loudspeaker and waited.

Within a few seconds, Darryl answered.

'Guv,' Jake said, massaging the side of his head, hoping that, by keeping his brain moving, the words wouldn't stumble out of his mouth. 'Sorry I missed your call.'

'*Calls*, Jake. Nine times – and you are nothing like a cat. I'd be very surprised if you had any lives left. I hope whatever it was you were doing was worth it.'

Jake remained silent.

'And I hope you've finished it too,' Darryl finished.

'Is it bad?' Jake asked, even though he already knew the answer.

'We've got a triple.'

'Who?'

'I think it's best you get down here.'

Jake swallowed. 'Where to?'

There was a long pause.

'Rupert Haversham's house. I trust you have the address?'

He did. And only because he'd been there a few hours earlier.

Jake checked the time. It was a few minutes to midnight.

How could he have drunk so much in such a short space of time? It was a miracle he was awake.

Begrudgingly, he said, 'I'll be there as soon as I can.'

CHAPTER 5

FIVE GUESSES

Rupert Haversham's street looked like the middle of a disco. Police cars were dotted up and down the middle of the road, their blue lights pulsating a sense of curiosity and hysteria onto the residents. An ambulance was parked immediately outside the front door, and a pair of paramedics were attending an elderly woman on the back of the van. Beside it, situated in the middle of the street, was a forensics van. A group of SOCOs – scenes of crime officers – huddled by the boot, clad in white, ferrying equipment in and out of the property like a line of working ants. Fencing them all in was the outer cordon, where a crowd of camera crews and reporters hovered eagerly.

'Excuse me?'

Jake sighed. He'd made it all of three feet from his car before being accosted.

Harassing him tonight was a young female journalist, whose short black hair and leather jacket reminded him of the lead singer of a punk band he used to listen to in the nineties, with the tattoos to match. A less attractive version.

'Yes?'

'What can you tell us about the crime scene?'

'I know as much as you do. You see this?' He pointed to his car. 'I've *literally* just got here. Give me some time.'

The woman hesitated a moment. Eventually, recognition registered on her face. 'You're Detective Tanner, aren't you?'

'Last time I checked. Now if you'll excuse me, I have to catch the bad guys.'

He was in no mood for a media interview or questioning of any sort. He'd had too many in the wake of Richard Candy's death. Unsurprisingly, the media had gone into a frenzy as soon as the news broke that the head of the corrupt police syndicate known as The Cabal was the assistant commissioner, one of the most highly revered and respected roles in the entire organisation. And Jake had been the one to watch him die. Naturally, everyone wanted to know his thoughts and his side of events but didn't care to hear that he was saving it all for a book a ghost writer would one day pen.

Jake ignored the reporter and ducked under the outer cordon. Then he signed his name and scribbled his initials, the purpose of his visit and the time, shocked at the fact they had passed him a tablet on which to complete his information. It seemed that, slowly but surely, the Major Investigation Team at Bow Green had scrapped the archaic, analogue ways of doing things and were finally entering the twenty-first century. It was a cleaner, more durable and more effective form of logging information.

Next Jake strode towards Rupert Haversham's house. The buildings and cars and people surrounding him swayed and spun as he approached. The dizziness still treated him abhorrently, and he sensed an incipient headache, more vengeful and spiteful than any he'd had before. Karma. Sadly, the takeaway coffee from the en-route McDonald's drive-through was doing little to abate his nausea.

On the way to the house, he wandered past the elderly woman being given the once-over at the back of the ambulance and moved towards the knot of officers who, in his drink-addled brain, looked vaguely like his colleagues. Huddled together, the three of them discussing quietly.

'Evening,' he said to them, forcing a convincing smile. 'Or is it morning?'

DCI Darryl Hughes opened his mouth to speak but then looked down at Jake's hand and pointed to the coffee. 'It's irrelevant when you're *this* late.'

'Sorry, guv,' Jake said. 'Figured it was going to be a long one.' He took another sip of coffee. 'So what do we have tonight? Death by immolation? Decapitation this time? Or something completely bonkers?'

Darryl took a step closer. Inches separated them, and Jake was able to smell an insipid stench on his boss's breath that suggested he hadn't brushed his teeth before leaving. Having said that, neither had Jake.

'I called you *nine* times,' Darryl said, his eyes locked on Jake's. They moved left and right. Jake tried to keep up with them but lost track. 'What have you been doing?'

'Sorry, guv. I was asleep. The girls've been tiring me out.'

Darryl sniffed, and then his gaze dropped to the ground. It remained there a few seconds before he eventually lifted his head.

'How long's it been going on for, Jake?' He spoke softly, quietly, almost a whisper.

Jake felt inclined to respond the same way. 'What do you mean?' He took another sip of coffee and swirled the liquid around in the cup, stirring the soot at the bottom.

'The drinking.'

'I only got this about ten minutes ago. At the drive-through by—'

'That's not what I meant, and you know it. You were drinking. I can smell it on you. How much have you had?'

'Darryl…'

'If I pull out a breathalyser on you, am I going to like the result?'

Probably not, Jake thought, but kept that response to himself.

'Jesus Christ, Jake,' Darryl continued. 'I put my fucking neck on the line for you. Do you know how many strings I had to pull, how many arses I had to lick in order for you to stay with us? People don't forget about the kind of shit you pulled. The Cabal might be dead, but that doesn't mean everything to do with him has gone along with him.'

Jake paused. Contemplated. Deliberated over what to say. For a long while, he stared into Darryl's eyes. The *shit* that Darryl was referring to had been a constant thorn in Jake's side, and a constant source of paranoia and unparalleled stress. On the day that Assistant Commissioner Richard Candy had died, Jake had forced Stephanie, his then-colleague, into covering up the gunshot that had killed one of The Cabal's men. Later analysis and testing at the forensic lab had determined that Stephanie had indeed pulled the trigger, contrary to their statement, and proven that someone somewhere was lying. After coming clean to Darryl in a safe and private environment (which Jake hadn't been too keen on, given how little he felt he could trust the man at the time), the two of them had left it to Darryl to tidy.

Stephanie had claimed self-defence, and given the nature of the incident – the largest investigation into police corruption in the force's history – the last thing the Crown Prosecution Service wanted was another example of corruption amongst the ranks, especially involving someone who happened to be a former member of the Independent Police Complaints Commission, and so they'd dropped all charges.

Darryl had, true to his character, come good on his promise.

'It was only a few cans, guv.'

Jake looked up at the expression of a man who didn't believe a single word of what he'd just said, but was too considerate of the surroundings to say anything about it.

'Just…' Darryl sighed – long, deep. 'Just don't make me regret my decision to keep you on.'

As soon as Darryl finished, Poojah Singh, the team's pathologist, appeared. She removed the mask from her mouth and, as she spoke, shot a small sideways glance at Jake. She gave the all-clear and said that the house was ready for them to enter. Darryl thanked her and ordered the team to suit up. Within seconds, Jake found himself a white forensic suit, complete with booties and double gloves. Once ready, he finished the last of his coffee and followed the rest of the team into the house.

'Anyone want to tell me what we've got?' Jake asked.

DC Ashley Rivers twisted to face him, a look of scorn burning holes in him. 'I'm sure you can use your imagination.'

That was the problem. He didn't want to. Partly because he didn't want it to impact or soil his own personal dealings with Rupert. And partly because he knew that, if he did, it would inevitably mean that he was about to launch himself into another investigation where he didn't want to discover the outcome.

The Cabal might be dead, but that doesn't mean everything to do with him has gone along with him.

Jake crossed the threshold into the house. For some reason, it felt oddly different to when he'd visited earlier in the afternoon. Something was out of place.

A flurry of SOCOs continued to hustle and move and pace about the corridors. At the end of one, by the kitchen, Poojah turned around and addressed them.

'Right, guys,' she began. 'We've already lifted DNA and fingerprints from the bodies, but there are a few things I think you'll find interesting. Come with me.'

With that enigmatic declaration, Poojah turned her back on them and showed them into the kitchen. As he followed, Jake felt like he was on a school trip to a museum or an aquarium, bewildered and amazed by all the sights.

The sight he eventually saw, however, wasn't one that a twenty-seven-year-old Jake Tanner was able to stomach, let alone a seven-year-old Jake Tanner.

A puddle of blood the size of a bath mat drenched the floor. Amidst it, Rupert Haversham lay on his back, eyes open, the light overhead reflecting on the milky gloss that covered them. His clothes had now dampened and were sodden with the very liquid that had kept him alive only hours before. Several red blotches adorned the same white shirt he'd been in when Jake had seen him, like acne on a teenager's face.

'What's with the gloves?' Jake asked, nodding at Rupert's yellow hands.

'The tap was running when we got here. My inclination would be that he was doing the washing-up,' Poojah replied. 'That's body number one. Body number two is this way.'

Poojah then led them into the living room. There, with her eyes rolled into the back of her head, was Helena Haversham. A thick red racing line ran across the circumference of her neck, and her arms were spread out wide, almost Christ-like. In his mind, Jake tried to piece together what had happened. The series of events that had led up to their deaths. But he had nothing. It was a lot for him to take in. Not just because it was another murder investigation, but because of the inconvenient implications it would have on Elizabeth's case.

In the room's background, the TV – tuned to a shopping channel – continued to play. A woman who looked remarkably like Helena was trying to shift a rowing machine, while dressed in gym leggings and a crop top, at a reduced price of £199.

'I can't believe people still buy this sort of shit,' DS Brendan Lafferty remarked.

'That's what someone who secretly buys from these things would say,' Jake replied, smirking to himself behind the mask.

'Enough,' Darryl replied calmly, silencing them both with immediate effect. 'What's next, Poojah?'

'Upstairs.'

As she started off, Jake called out, 'Hold on. Question.' He pointed to Helena's neck. 'Was the same blade used to kill them both?'

Poojah shook her head. 'Couldn't say for certain right now. There don't appear to be any missing knives from the rack.'

'And there's nothing in the sink being washed up?'

'No – we checked.'

As he left the room, Jake gave one last look into Helena's eyes and switched off the TV with the remote that lay beside her. She had been kind to him when he'd visited. Sympathetic. Friendly.

The entire family had. Which meant…

He prepared himself for what else was to come.

For *who* else was to come.

Erica Haversham's bedroom looked out onto the street below. A flat-screen TV hung from the wall. In the far-right corner of the room was an en-suite bathroom, and immediately behind Jake was a walk-in wardrobe. Beneath the window was a make-up table missing the make-up.

Erica's double bed was pushed against the wall on the left-hand side. In it lay a small body.

The sight made Jake's stomach tighten.

Felicity… No…

Images of Maisie flashed and burnt in his mind. The two girls were the same age, same height, same build. They had the same innocence, the same ebullience, the same mannerisms, the same excitement about the smallest things. The same love and enjoyment for life.

The duvet had been thrown from her body, and a pillow drowned her head. Her little arm dangled from the side of the bed. Pale, chalky.

'She couldn't have put up much of a fight,' Poojah said, as if voicing her internal thoughts.

'Whose room is this?' Brendan asked.

'Erica Haversham's,' Jake replied without realising he'd said anything. 'His eldest daughter. She's just finished her first year of college. She's into the arts.'

As soon as he finished, everyone turned to face him and gave him a look, as if to say, 'How do *you* know?' Jake felt an immediate obligation to explain himself.

'When you've been investigating Rupert Haversham as much as I have, you begin to learn about the family as if they're your friends.'

Ashley shook her head. 'You might want to rethink what you consider a friend, Tanner.'

'Any sign of her in the house?' Jake asked. 'Or are we going to find her body stuffed in a cupboard somewhere?'

'We've not found her yet,' Poojah responded.

Darryl took control of the conversation again and gestured towards Felicity. 'Is there anything else we need to know?'

It sounded like Poojah was smirking underneath her mask. 'I'll book the PM for first thing in the morning. But you might be pleased to know that the SOCOs found a fingerprint on the pillow.'

Pleased wasn't the right word. Relieved, yes. Relieved that the case was now fractionally easier.

'Let's hope it comes back with something positive,' someone replied behind him.

Jake was unable to break his gaze from Felicity's little hand. There was nail varnish painted onto her little nails. When he'd seen it earlier, he'd told her it made her look pretty. She'd replied with an ethereal smile and a polite thank you before hurrying off to Erica's bedroom, the place where she no doubt spent all her time idolising her sister.

No one had anything else to say. Dead children always had a way of silencing even the most hardened officers – especially those who carried the burden of experience. The clutch of officers drifted out of the room. But as they exited, Ashley froze and pointed to the ceiling. Buried in the corner was a tiny black box, with a small light flickering inside.

'What's that?'

'I'll give you five guesses.' Jake nudged past her, closer to the device. It cleared his head by five feet, just out of reach.

'What do they need CCTV for?' Ashley continued.

Jake found himself slowly beginning to sober up, and as a result, the synapses in his brain started to fire up again, producing more and more sarcasm.

'I would imagine it's because he didn't want to get broken into. Or, worse, in the event of his being murdered, they might be able to use the footage to find the killer – or killers,' Jake retorted.

His expression was met with muted, unimpressed stares.

'Poojah, we need that footage seized as evidence and sent for investigation as soon as possible please,' Darryl said, then addressed Jake, Brendan and Ashley. 'Sorry, guys, but it's going to be a long one. Call whoever you need to and let them know you won't be back for a while. Get back to the station and I'll see you there. The witness who found the body's ready to make a statement.'

| DAY 2 |

CHAPTER 6

TOLD YOU SO

With the mood Darryl was in, Jake had half expected his punishment for his late arrival to be taking the witness statement. Instead, he'd been given a task much more tedious: watching DS Brendan Lafferty take the witness statement from behind a screen.

A big *fuck you*.

And a big *thank you*.

Jake hated being a benchwarmer. Behind the scenes. It made him feel inferior. As though his monumental effort and hard work in uncovering the identity of The Cabal had been for nothing. Like he was a spent prostitute lying on the bed – the powers that be had got what they came for and slipped out the back door without giving him an afterthought.

Fuck you, so long and thanks for the shag.

Although, he couldn't deny he was intrigued to see the detective sergeant in action.

The door opened behind him, startling him. He twisted in the seat and watched who entered.

It was Alison, a member of the digital intelligence team they'd recently hired. She was fresh in the force – and fresh out of university – and eager to prove herself to Darryl and the rest of the team. Including Jake. In her hand she held a plastic cup of coffee.

'Here you are. Just what the doctor ordered,' she said to him as she set it down.

'I'm glad I'm not the only one who recognises the distinction between a cool guy and a physician.' Jake grabbed the cup and allowed the heat to warm his hands.

'What?'

Jake sighed inwardly. 'Never mind.' And he turned his attention to the interview.

Alison soon got the hint and left.

He took a sip of coffee, grimaced as the burning liquid scorched his tongue, and then set the cup down. On the computer monitor, Brendan had just entered the interview room, pulled a chair out from beneath the table, and sat down.

Nothing about the witness, sixty-four-year-old Margaret Humphries, suggested she should be treated as a suspect. Her slight frame. The thin cardigan wrapped around her body. The glasses that hung off her nose. Her thin blonde hair, which was streaked with bolts of grey. And there was no plausible scenario he could conceive where she would be able to overpower two fully grown adults, brutally murder them both with a knife and then suffocate a small infant. It was a ludicrous waste of time to think otherwise.

Yet, if there was anything that his investigations into The Cabal had taught him, it was that it was always the person you least expected.

'Thank you for joining us,' Brendan began after finishing the formalities. His voice was tinny over the computer speakers. 'Hopefully this won't take much longer than it needs to.'

'I certainly hope not.'

'Would you please explain what you saw before you called the emergency services?'

'Two dead bodies. Rupert and then Helena. They were lying there in their own blood.'

'And what inspired you to enter their house?'

'I was coming back from walking the dog. At first I saw Rupert's car was gone – which isn't strange because he's always coming and going at various points in the evening – but then, when I noticed that the front door had been left open, that was when I started to panic.'

'And so you went inside the house?'

'Yes.'

'And then what, please?'

'I called the police.'

'What exactly is your relationship with the victims?'

Margaret hesitated a moment before responding.

'I've been their neighbour for twenty-odd years. You lose track after ten.'

'So you know the family pretty well?'

'I suppose as well as anyone knows their neighbours, yes. It wasn't as though we had dinner parties together or went on days out. But...' Margaret stopped and then began to sob. She pulled a tissue from within her sleeve and dabbed underneath her eye.

She spluttered and hyperventilated as she spoke. 'I've... I've just realised... Where are the girls?'

'They...'

'Has something happened to them as well?'

'Sorry, Margaret, but Felicity's body was discovered in Erica's bedroom—'

Margaret gasped. She threw her hand to her mouth, and then, as the hyperventilating continued, moved it down to her throat.

'We're currently unable to locate Erica Haversham,' Brendan continued.

'Boyfriend,' Margaret struggled between gasps. 'She – has – a – boyfriend.'

'Who?' Brendan interrupted. 'Do you know his name?'

Margaret continued to struggle for breath. Brendan reached across the table and handed her the cup of water that lay a few inches out of reach.

'Have some of this, Margaret – it might make you feel better,' he said.

Jake's eyes widened, and he leant closer to the screen. *She doesn't need the water, you idiot. She needs medical help.*

Brendan inched the cup closer to her on the table, but it was useless; by now her gasps had become so frequent that it was as if she were inhaling for one continuous breath. When he finally realised something was wrong, Brendan stood up but immediately stopped, frozen in a half-stand. He teetered on the edge of action and remained there, like a child's toy that had finished winding down. Meanwhile, Margaret continued to gasp, gasp, gasp.

Jake couldn't watch any longer. He rushed out of the room, along the corridor, skipping a leaflet that had fallen to the floor, and burst into the interview room.

At his sudden entrance, Brendan's gaze shot towards him, eyes wild with fear. Jake paid him little heed and hurried across to Margaret.

By now, one hand clutched her chest, and the other was wrapped around the arm of the chair. Jake approached her, felt her pulse and yelled at his colleague, who remained idle.

'Move! Get some help!' he barked at Brendan.

It wasn't until he used an expletive, a language that Brendan understood, that the man finally moved. Within seconds, he was in the hall, screaming up and down for medical help.

Jake returned his attention to Margaret. He – and the rest of the police force – were trained in first aid. Up to a point. It had always been on his to-do list to develop his training and benefit from it in situations such as this, but he'd never been able to afford the time.

The door burst open again, smashing into the adjacent wall. Two paramedics fell into the room and surrounded Margaret. Jake took it upon himself to step away and let them get to work, watching as he retreated to a safe distance at the back of the room. The paramedics swiftly attended Margret and within a few seconds were carrying her out of the room in a wheelchair, pumping oxygen into her mouth. Jake and Brendan followed through the building until she was lumbered into the back of the ambulance.

'It's a miracle they were here when we needed them,' Ashley, who had been in the custody suite when the commotion started, said. 'Should someone go with her?'

'Well volunteered,' Jake said with a facetious smirk. 'It'll be better if you're there as well. You know, female to female.'

'Will you let Darryl know?'

Jake said that he would and waved Ashley goodbye.

He and Brendan headed back to the interview room, Brendan shaking his head and sighing deeply. Jake shut the interview-room door behind him and placed a firm hand on Brendan's arm.

'You good?' he asked.

The Irishman avoided Jake's gaze for as long as possible, until Jake squeezed harder and he eventually relented.

'I… I… I knew I shouldn't have done it.'

'Done what?'

'The interview. Before we went in, she said she wasn't feeling one hundred per cent up to it. I just… I just thought she was a bit shaken up, that's all.'

Jake sighed in disbelief. 'Did you get her checked over by a nurse or someone?'

'The paramedics had already cleared her and said she was fine.'

Clearly, she wasn't.

'What did she say to you exactly?' Jake asked.

'Her… her chest hurt. Again, I just thought it was the adrenaline of the situation.'

'Jesus, Bren…' Jake ran his fingers through his hair.

In the past few weeks, Brendan had gradually returned to full-time work. When he'd stumbled upon the apparent suicide of Roland Lewandowski, the team's digital forensic specialist and all-round tech wizard, he'd suffered from severe stress and anxiety. And ever since his return, his performance and quality of work had been below standard.

'Did she say anything to anyone else?' Jake asked.

'Only me. What shall I do, Jake?'

'You need to calm down. You've been under a lot of stress recently, and this isn't going to help. You've done nothing wrong – remember that. The paramedics should never have released her if her chest was hurting.'

But the truth was that Brendan had been in the wrong. And so had Darryl. They all had a duty of care over anyone in the building at any time, and the chief inspector had trusted Brendan to conduct the witness statement professionally and safely.

Brendan had failed.

And Jake couldn't help but feel a little smug about it.

Fuck you, so long, thanks for the shag and told you so.

CHAPTER 7

REPEATED CONTACT

As soon as the kettle finished its boil, Jake poured the steaming hot water into his mug and stirred until the instant mocha mixture had dissolved. As he set the spoon in the sink, a figure arrived in the kitchen.

'You're here early,' she said. She carried a Tesco supermarket bag in one hand and her phone in the other.

'We never left,' Jake replied, realising at once who it was. 'What time is it out there?'

'Nearly eight.'

'Jesus. The lights are so bright it's looked like broad daylight in here since midnight.'

'That long?' Lindsay Gray, the building's facilities manager, remarked. Today she was wearing a simple yet subtle grey suit that made her look both smart and casual. But the real focus of the outfit was the diamond earrings sparkling beneath the light. Jake thought he recognised them but then realised that sort of jewellery all looked the same.

Smiling, she set her bag on the counter and rummaged through the contents. 'Juicy one?'

'You could say that. Triple murder.'

'Extra juicy.' She pulled out a bag of biscuits and offered him one. 'Jaffa Cake?'

'No thanks. It was someone you knew as well.'

'*What*?'

'Not personally. I didn't mean it like that. I mean... you've probably heard the name before.'

'Who?'

'Rupert Haversham.'

At the mention of that name, Lindsay's lips parted, and her expression changed. It was as if she was looking through him. Her skin turned pale, as though the wind had just been punched from her lungs. As though she had just been told that she had months to live.

'I… I…'

'I didn't realise you were that close with him.'

Something in Lindsay changed, and she snapped to. Shaking her head, she replied, 'I wasn't. We weren't. It's never nice when an old name you knew dies. I spent a lot of time working with him when I was a DC. This was *years* ago, and – and I probably shouldn't be telling you this – but he asked me out once. Obviously, I told him no. I was happily married and not looking for anything. I think he was just lonely. Back then, he was on the good side. But after his wife died, I think things changed for him.'

'Either that or it was your rejection.'

Jake hadn't known about Rupert's first wife, Karen, though he'd met Helena. It was funny – in recent weeks he'd felt like he'd grown close to the man, bonded by a mutual desire to put Glen, the man who'd sexually assaulted Elizabeth, six feet under. Rupert had explained to Jake that Helena had gone through something similar, and that the best justice for it was a worthy sentence and a strike on the criminal record. It wasn't much of a bond, but it was enough to make Jake feel like he knew the man. Except now, the small revelations that there had been a first wife, and that Rupert had once been on the good side made him feel as though he didn't know the man at all.

Lindsay moved about the kitchen and grabbed a mug from the cupboard. 'You guys making any headway?'

'Not much. Just waiting for everything to come back to us now.'

In the past few hours, Jake and Darryl had submitted warrants and requests for various ANPR hits on Rupert Haversham's car, a warrant for all call and text history from Rupert's phone, as well as a warrant for access to his financial accounts. It was the one aspect of the job that he hated the most. Waiting, wagging his finger in the air.

'Any leads?'

Jake shrugged. 'One of Haversham's daughters is unaccounted for. There's a boyfriend we're looking into. Nothing's come back on him yet.'

'Well, I'm sure you'll find him. Although, you're going to need a couple more bodies out there. You're looking pretty sparse. The office could do with a shake-up.'

'You mean you don't long to see my face every time you come in?' Jake chuckled and then it turned into a long overdue yawn.

'Oh, Jake,' she said after he'd finished stretching his jaw. 'You know, I think you're the son I never had.'

Lindsay pinched his cheek and wiggled the excess skin from side to side. Jake smirked playfully, said goodbye, and then left the kitchen. By now, the mug had cooled and the water inside had turned tepid.

As Jake moved across the office towards his desk, Brendan entered the room. Their eyes locked and Brendan froze. His hands were wrapped around his Starbucks mug – the one he'd insisted on carrying about his person ever since his return to work. A look of sorrow and regret swirled around his eyes.

Jake was the first to make a move. He pulled his chair away from his desk and sat down, the computer and partition behind it blocking him from view of the rest of the office. Then he logged into his computer and opened his inbox. The first thing he noticed was the number of emails he'd received in the last twenty minutes. Fifty-six. More than he received on a busy day in the office.

Sipping his coffee, Jake sifted through the emails, purging the unnecessary ones and saving the important ones for later. As he reached halfway, he stumbled upon one that made him pause and then smile as he read the header. He scrolled to the bottom of the email and opened the attachment. In front of him was a complete list of Rupert Haversham's call history from the past three months. Thousands of lines of information he needed to sift through.

Lucky me.

Before he could begin, the buzzing sound of the office door echoed around the room and Ashley sauntered in. Jake leapt out of his seat and hurried over.

'Any news?' he asked, accosting her before she settled in properly. 'How's she doing?'

'Minor heart attack. But she's stable now. They're going to keep her in for a few days, monitor her condition.'

Jake breathed a heavy sigh of relief.

'Did she say anything about *me*?' Brendan stuttered quietly from the other side of the office.

'She was in the middle of having a heart attack. She didn't say anything about anything. And I imagine we're the least of her problems right now.'

Jake returned to his desk. Now he could focus on the mountain of data he had in front of him without that cloud of uncertainty about Margaret looming overhead.

For the next twenty minutes, he waded through the information. The majority of the calls Rupert made were to his family, home phone, or close business associates. But there was a frequent anomaly that stuck out to Jake. It was an unfamiliar number. Neither a house phone nor a mobile. And it was frequent too. Weekly. Same day. Same time.

Jake's mind started to wander. And one name in particular immediately screamed out at him.

But first, he needed to confirm his suspicions.

He copy and pasted the number into the Police National Computer database and hit return.

As the result appeared on his screen, Jake sighed and lowered himself into his chair. His suspicions had been correct.

In the past three months, Rupert Haversham had made repeated contact with HMP Wandsworth. The new home of East London's biggest crime lord, Henry Matheson. And the last time the two had spoken on the phone was a few hours before Rupert and his family had been murdered. Had Henry given the order shortly after the call? Or had it been part of a wider plan all along?

There was only one way Jake could know for certain: he grabbed his desk phone and dialled Wandsworth. He needed to speak with Henry Matheson. Urgently.

CHAPTER 8

BIRMINGHAM '99

The queue moved slowly, his fellow inmates more focused on their conversations than a desire to eat. Henry was starving, his stomach growling furiously. Back at Belmarsh, he'd been first in line at breakfast, lunch and dinner. He'd even had his pick of the food – and everyone else's. Feared, revered, they bowed down to him. But now he was stuck at the back of the queue, like a shmuck flying economy class.

Used to the first-class lifestyle for too long, he now yearned for it to return.

The queue moved down the conveyor belt a few feet, and he grabbed his plastic tray. Many a head had been bruised and assaulted beneath the force of one of those in his hands, and as he stood there behind Terrence Claiborne, a low-level fraudster, he became overwhelmed by the impulse to crack it over the man's skull.

Work his way up the food chain. All the way to the top. Where he deserved to be.

Just as he lifted the tray behind the man's head, he felt it get yanked away from him. Panicked by a potential guard behind him, Henry spun on the spot.

But standing in front of him was Boris Romanov, the leader of the Romanian gang. Behind him was his army of olive-skinned henchmen, looking like one of the world's worst boy bands. Most of them were slight, skinny, nothing to look at. But what they lacked in size, they more than made up for in agility.

Henry didn't see the lunch tray smashing him round the face; the first thing he knew about the attack was the cold floor.

'Fucking hell,' he whined, clutching his forehead. 'That hurt.'

He wasn't afraid of them. Not in a one-on-one situation, at least.

But when he was alone, surrounded by a dozen of them, in a prison where the guards turned their backs as easily as they turned keys in cell doors, he felt his arse cheeks clench.

'You're nothing, Matheson,' Boris hissed, his accent thick. 'We shit over you and your gang. The E11 is nothing anymore. It is finished.'

Henry picked himself up off the ground and squared up to the man, consumed by adrenaline and rage. Nobody dissed him and the E11. It was his baby, his precious, the thing he'd devoted his life to upholding. Blasphemy against the E11 was a death wish.

Yet for a long while he said nothing -- just stared ferociously into the man's eyes.

'Watch your step, Matheson,' Boris began. 'Otherwise you might trip and land on something sharp.'

The Romanian, followed by each member of his crew, barged past Matheson and took his place in the queue. By the time he got to the front of the line, he was left with the scraps. Yesterday's breakfast and last week's fruit.

It tasted the way it looked.

He sat in the corner of the canteen, alone with his thoughts, while the Romanians hijacked a table and chatted loudly in their native language. It was like a scene from a high school comedy, with the different cliques situated around the different tables. Except there was nothing humorous about the situation at all. Not even his friends from the casino night were brave enough to offer him a seat at their table; they couldn't afford to be seen fraternising with him.

There was only one man who could.

The shark of the prison, the overseer of the ocean. And if Henry wanted to climb up the food chain, he would have to become the innocent remora, swimming underneath.

His name was James Longstaff, and he had been a prisoner for nearly forty years. He was serving an entire life sentence for the murder of six individuals. His shopping list of other offences included extortion, money laundering, racketeering, GBH, manslaughter, drug trafficking, human trafficking and sex trafficking. He was one conviction away from completing the set. But what was most surprising about James Longstaff was that the majority of his crimes had been committed while in prison. From the stories Henry had heard, Longstaff saw the place as his home, his temple, his palace. And so whenever someone – or a group of people – came into his temple, guns blazing, thinking they had dominion over it, Longstaff was prepared to do anything to protect it.

Henry approached his cell and knocked, interrupting the man from making a cup of tea.

'At last,' Longstaff said, placing the spoon face down on the surface, 'someone with the courtesy to knock. The rest of these fuckers just waltz in like they own the place.'

Despite being in his mid-sixties, Longstaff looked stronger and more robust than most men in the prison.

Henry hovered in the doorway, caught by nerves. Eventually, he summoned the courage to step forward and extend his hand. 'Henry,' he began. 'Henry Matheson.'

Longstaff glanced down at his hand disparagingly.

'I know who you are, but don't get too ahead of yourself, kid. It'll take a lot more than knocking on my door to get yourself one of those.'

The kettle finished boiling. Longstaff poured the liquid into the cup and stirred. 'Did you come to tell me your name or did you want anything in particular?'

Henry eventually lowered his hand and wiped the back of his nose with it. 'I... Erm... I heard that—'

'Shouldn't listen to everything you hear, pal. Sometimes it means you end up worse than me.'

Henry chuckled awkwardly and then continued. 'I'm looking for something.'

'Well, you ain't gonna find it in here. If the screws can't, then neither can a little pissant like you.'

'I was talking about *protection*.'

That word gave Longstaff a cause to stop. He set the spoon down and shuffled closer. 'You've got the wrong man,' he said calmly. 'There are plenty of other people in this prison that will be happy to supply you with whatever you want. I'm sure if you ask around, you might be able to sell that sweet little arse for it.'

'I'm not selling anything to anyone. I'd rather die before I do that.'

'Why else are you here, then?'

'From what I hear, you're having a spot of bother with some Romanians and Albanians.'

'We all are, kid,' Longstaff replied. 'You included.'

'Two forces are better than one.'

'So you've gone from wanting protection to wanting a partnership. You can't have both.'

'A partnership. I want a partnership.'

Longstaff considered a moment. 'If that's the case, then there are some things you need to know. You may have been a big man outside, but you're not in the outside world anymore. There are different rules in here, different ecosystems. You're a very small fish compared to some of the sharks that roam these waters. I'm the fisherman who decides whether or not to catch them. So you do whatever I say when I say it. Understood?'

'Absolutely.'

A partnership, an alliance, was better than nothing. In the history of all the world wars, very few had been won alone.

'Wait here for a second. I need to fetch something.'

Longstaff shuffled past him, out of the cell, and headed down the stairs. He returned a minute later, carrying a wad of notes in his hand.

'What's that?'

'Consider it a down payment. It's all yours if you agree to do something for me.'

'What?'

'The Romanians and Albanians are a problem for you, right? What do we do with problems? We get rid of them. If you're serious about this partnership, I need you to deal with this problem.'

'Alone?'

'A shark swims alone for miles across the ocean and will attack anything it can find, sometimes animals larger than itself, whereas shoals of fish swim in groups and flee the shark when they see it. Which one are you, Henry?'

I'm the motherfucking shark.

He swam against the tide of traffic, making his way to his destination: Boris Romanov's cell. The man frequently shared the cell for ninety per cent of the day with his gang. And when they weren't all together in his cell, they usually occupied the entire east wing on the twos.

Henry had spent the past twenty minutes scouting Boris's cell, keeping a watchful eye on post-breakfast proceedings. The Romanians had spent most of that time talking with one another, playing card games, betting with each other and shouting in their mother tongue. Until thirty seconds ago, when the commotion Henry had caused disturbed them.

In preparation for the task, Henry had taken the money from Longstaff and bribed a couple of inmates to start a fight. One to keep his hands clean from any trouble – much like himself – Henry knew Boris would stay well away. And true to his character, Boris had indeed stayed behind.

A sitting duck.

A beached whale.

Henry was going in for the strike.

In his hands, he carried a blanket that had been doused in bleach. Droplets of the pungent liquid dripped onto the concrete as he hurried along the twos towards Boris's cell. There he found the man holding a magazine, looking proud of himself – as though he'd just taken a shit with the door open.

Henry lunged at him, catching him off guard. The force of his attack sent Boris sprawling into the wall, where his head collided with the concrete. Acting on the element of surprise, Henry rolled him onto his front, straddled the man's legs, and pinned his ankles to the ground. Then he removed Boris's shoes and socks and wrapped the blanket around his feet. The smell of bleach overpowered the stench of shit and piss. Boris eventually came to, but Henry was too strong for him.

And too quick.

By the time Boris had realised what was going on, the blaze engulfed his feet and had already started melting his flesh. He let out a tremendous roar, dampened by the sounds of cheers and cries coming from the commotion on the other side of the wing.

Wanting to waste no time, Henry hurried out of the cell and sprinted back to his own. Adrenaline bubbled in his blood, and his heartbeat raced. With Boris out of action for the foreseeable future, the Romanians' presence in the prison would dwindle, and Henry could climb higher up the chain.

All that remained were the Albanians.

When he returned to his cell, he removed his phone from the mattress and opened his messages. He quickly drafted a note to one of his contacts and hit send. As he was about to switch the phone off, a notification rolled down the top of the screen – a notification from *Kingdom of Empires*.

Since Richard Candy's death, he'd forgotten to delete the game.

Curious, he tapped the notification and entered his inbox. Sitting at the top was a message from LG540.

'Impossible,' he whispered to himself.

Moving to the bed, Henry kicked off his shoes and started a conversation.

LG540: I know what you did.
E11Geezers: UR meant 2 b dead.
LG540: Why did you do it?
E11Geezers: Problems need fixing.
LG540: He wasn't a problem for me. And now you've given me one to fix.
E11Geezers: UVE survived in the past.
LG540: This is different.

There was a long pause until he received another message.

LG540: Who did it?
E11Geezers: Y do u want the name?
LG540: Was it Dylan?

Henry paused. How did this person know who Dylan was? Dylan was a recluse, a junky, a nobody. He only ventured into daylight to steal money for drugs. And then he would slip back into his hole for another twelve hours, at least. He received another response.

LG540: I know Dylan was close to the Havershams. You made it that way, didn't you? Perhaps we can come to some sort of agreement.

Just as Henry was about to respond, a figure appeared in the door frame. It was Carmichaels, Henry's least favourite prison guard. He looked unimpressed – more so about life than being in Henry's cell –

and folded his arms across his chest.

'Oi, Matheson,' he began. 'With me.'

'Are we going on an adventure?' Henry asked, surreptitiously hiding the phone under his pillow.

'You've got a visitor waiting for you.'

'Outside of visiting hours? It must be my lucky day. Like Birmingham '99. You know what I mean?'

CHAPTER 9

VOLDEMORT

'Hello, Henry.'

It was only the second time Jake had seen the man he'd put in prison since the day of the verdict, but he was still frightened of the scars on the man's face. The injuries were hideous and reminded Jake that no one was safe, that even the mightiest could fall.

'Jake,' Henry replied. He sank into the back of the plastic chair and placed his feet on top of the table. Despite the injuries, he was still as defiant as ever. Jake suspected it was an act.

'Did I catch you at a bad time? You're all out of breath.'

'It's because I'm so excited to see you, Jake. But I must admit, I wasn't expecting you so soon. Missing me already?'

Jake smirked. 'You're all I think about.'

'I bet that's the truth as well, isn't it?'

Jake didn't reply.

'I get that a lot. It's not good for my ego.'

'We wouldn't want it to get any bigger.'

'You're the one responsible for making it as big as it is. You made me famous. You put my name and face all over the TV.'

Before it turned into the physical representation of a dried prune.

'Do you know how many letters I get from people on the outside every week?'

Jake scratched the scar on the side of his face. 'No, but I'm sure you're going to tell me, anyway.'

'Fifty-three. Give or take a few rogue death threats from previous partners wishing me a few wonderful remaining days. But the bulk of them are my fans, my lovers. Some of them are people I've never met. Some of them are people I've slept with, and only now have they come to realise how much of a good thing they're missing out on. I've even had a few marriage proposals.' Henry looked about the room, paying little attention to Jake.

Jake had expected the man's ego would run the show, but he hadn't expected it to be as prominent as it was. Henry was making himself out to be a hero, a sex god in the eyes of superficial and lonely women seeking the ultimate bad boy.

Like he was some modern-day serial-killer hero.

'Is that supposed to impress me?'

'I can tell by that little smirk on your face that you'd like a piece of my action at some point in your life. Everyone does, even if they're too afraid to admit it. The freedom. The respect. We've all got our evil sides, Jake. No matter how hard you try to suppress it, one day it's just… all going to come flooding out.'

Henry slowly tilted forward on his chair, studying Jake, and then he smiled, although with the Glasgow Grin stretching across his face it was difficult to discern. 'You've already found *your* evil though, haven't you? I've seen that look before. You'd be surprised how many police officers – and how many of the guys in here – have gone through the same thing. The black bags. The sleepless nights. The change in complexion. The unkempt hair. The bloodshot eyes. The out-of-character acceptance of bribery. The out-of-character acceptance to sit up, roll over and turn bent. But you haven't gone that far yet, have you?'

Jake chose not to answer the rhetorical question.

'No,' Henry continued. 'That's not the Jake Tanner way. He would never turn his back on the service that he's dedicated so many years of his life to. He's given everything to it. He's willing to put himself *and* it before everything else he cares about, isn't he?'

Henry paused a beat, dragged his feet off the table and manoeuvred himself into a comfortable position in his chair, just out of arm's reach. 'So let me ask you, Jake… what's got a hold of you and won't let go? Drinking? Drugs? Porn? I can get you—'

Henry hesitated again. This time his expression changed. His eyes widened, and as he smiled, the heavily scarred burns on his face lifted and creased his skin. It was clear to see the injury didn't affect his ability to be a complete wanker.

'It's none of those. It's another one… I can… Gambling?' Henry clapped, the harsh sound reverberating around the small room and bouncing around Jake's eardrums.

'Gambling?' Henry repeated and, shaking his head derisively, continued, 'Jake, Jake, Jake. I never thought it would get that bad for you. Especially since you've been struggling all your life with shitty finances. Imagine what it would have been like if you'd joined me. You wouldn't have needed to worry about money again.'

'But then I'd be stuck in here.'

'You think that would be a problem? When you're connected to as big a legend throughout these walls as me, you wouldn't need to worry about a thing.'

Henry held his finger in the air, pausing their conversation. He bent down to his side, removed his shoe and produced a wad of cash a few centimetres thick. Jake estimated there was over £500's worth of notes in his hands.

Not only was Henry Matheson a sex god, he was also a psychic – and a rich one at that.

'That can't be good for your posture,' Jake said, stifling a smirk. 'Or do you have the same in the other shoe?'

'I want you to have it.' Henry extended his arm across the table and dropped the pile on the table. 'Buy Elizabeth something nice. Or maybe you can treat yourself to a particular horse or dog. I might know a few fixers in that part of the world that could sort you out with a big payday. Some people will do anything if you've got a bit of dirt on them.'

In the time that Henry had been speaking, Jake had been unable to pull his gaze from the money. His eyes counted the notes in front of him – £460. Close to his original estimate. But it was still more than he had in any of his remaining bank accounts.

For a moment, he contemplated picking it up, putting it in his pocket and then forgetting about it. It would be enough to feed him for another few weeks, pay some of the mortgage, cover the bills. It wouldn't last him long, but it would at least last him longer than it would if he gambled it away. But there was no guarantee he would do any of that. A voice inside his head told him to bet it all on red, while the logical voice implored him to leave it there on the table and walk away.

Jake reached across the desk, scooped the money in his hands, and slid it closer to his chest.

'I know what we'll do,' he began. 'We'll play a little game. I'll ask you a few questions, and depending on your answers, your money will either survive or it won't.'

'You really aren't much fun, are you?'

Jake picked up a twenty and held it in his fingers. 'First question: what's your involvement in Rupert Haversham's murder?'

'He's dead?' Henry asked, sounding unsurprised.

'Weren't you expecting to find out yet?' Jake ripped the twenty in half and grabbed another one. This time a fifty.

'The walls talk in this place. Word flies around. But this is the first I've heard of it.'

'Who did you order to kill him and his family?'

'What makes you think it was me?'

Jake ripped the fifty. Henry's expression remained placid. The only thing that moved on his face were his eyes as they flickered between the money and Jake.

He picked up another twenty. 'I can do this all day,' he remarked.

'Until you run out of money. You know, you should really think about what you're saying before you say it. Makes you look quite inept as a police officer.'

Jake ripped the note. This time out of spite. He found it even more satisfying.

'I know he's been calling you in the past few weeks. I know the last time you spoke to him was yesterday, hours before he died. What were you talking to him about? What were you discussing?'

Henry pursed his lips. 'Not much. He was just telling me about his kids, how they're getting on, how they're surviving.'

Another question unanswered, another note torn in two.

'You two are friends again, then? Even if he's the one responsible for putting you in here?'

'Maybe it's part of our next master plan.'

Jake lowered the note in his hand and listened, intrigued. 'What's that?'

'Can't tell you just yet, Jake. That'll ruin the surprise.' Henry rested his elbows on the edge of the table. 'You know, I don't care if you rip up the money – I've got plenty more where it came from. But what I won't stand for is that you think it's OK to accuse me of murdering a close friend of mine, someone I've known for a very long time. Not to mention, you've not told me what I'm being questioned with, if I'm being charged, what evidence you've got against me. I've been through this process enough times now to know when somebody's not done something properly. And this looks like one of those times, Detective. With that money in your hand, anyone would think you're one step away from being bent.'

Jake opened his mouth, but the words died on his tongue. It would be foolish for him to believe everything Henry was saying, but there was a seed of doubt and reservation that had planted itself in his mind.

'There's also one vital thing you're forgetting,' Henry said after adjusting the chain around his neck.

'Oh yeah?'

'Have you considered the possibility that there's still a certain someone else involved in all of this?'

'Who?'

'You know who.'

'Spell it out for me.'

'Voldemort. He Who Must Not Be Named…' Henry paused. 'The Cabal. Still out there, trotting about as if there's nothing wrong.'

'Impossible,' Jake said, shaking his head.

CHAPTER 10

OPERATION THEMIS

The Cabal's breathing was steady, rhythmic, untoward. They checked the time – 4:52 p.m. The height of the afternoon. The limbo period when the shift patterns in Bow Green were changing. Officers coming and going, the building caught in a flux.

Sitting in the car, The Cabal stroked the steering wheel, waited until the time reached 4:55 p.m. and then left, grabbing the evidence bag on the chair beside them. They sauntered across the car park, into the entrance and past the reception desk, waving politely as they passed.

'Afternoon,' the officer behind the desk said, getting ready to finish his shift.

'Afternoon,' came the cheery and vibrant response with a smile and a dip of the head.

The first rule of blending in was making yourself seen. The human brain was programmed to notice anomalies, signs of threat and danger, so if The Cabal gave anyone any reason to suspect something untoward, that was the end of it.

On the other hand, it was important to keep human contact – and, more importantly, the number of witnesses – to a minimum.

A fine and sometimes precarious balance.

A balance they'd mastered.

Skulking along the corridor, keeping their head down, The Cabal weaved deeper into the building, until eventually arriving at the forensic lab at the back of Bow Green.

The Cabal scanned a key card at the entrance, waited until the light above the scanner flashed green and then entered. A dense wall of chilled air confronted them upon entry and continued until they meandered their way through a series of corridors, following the signs on the wall. After a few minutes of traversing the stairs and finding the right location, The Cabal came to a stop in a corridor on the third floor. The artificial lights brightly illuminated the dark-blue carpets and scuffed cream walls. On the right-hand side were the investigation labs. On the left were the evidence lock-ups.

The Cabal ducked into the first room on the left and closed the door carefully. Breathed a sigh of relief.

The evidence room was empty, save for the humming of the air-conditioning unit in the background. Reaching from the floor to the ceiling were rows of shelving units, alphabetised in descending order, each letter corresponding to the name of the investigation. And the title appointed to Rupert Haversham's death had just been announced: Operation Themis.

The Cabal searched for the shelf labelled T.

A few seconds later, they found it: the evidence bags taken from Rupert, Helena and Felicity's crime scenes. DNA. Fingerprints. Hair follicles. Blood samples. It was all there. Waiting to be sent off to the external forensic examination team. And it was all there for the taking.

The Cabal reached into the evidence bag in their hand and swapped the pieces of evidence found at the crime scene. Four pieces in total. One for each strand of identification method: hair, saliva, skin and fingerprints.

Within a few minutes, it was done.

And in a few hours' time, when the forensic team started to investigate the evidence, they – along with the rest of the station – would be surprised at the outcome.

CHAPTER 11

BE MY CABALLERO

The most profound and disturbing phrase echoed in Jake's mind.

The Cabal.

Still out there, trotting about as if there's nothing wrong.

Jake had tossed the idea that The Cabal could still be alive about in his head but knew it to be impossible. The Cabal was dead. Jake had watched him plummet fifty feet to the floor and land on his neck.

And ever since there had been reduced activity – no Henry Matheson, no more human trafficking, no more threats to his family, life or career. Nothing to suggest that he was under threat at any point. In fact, it had made a pleasant change.

But Rupert Haversham's death gave him cause for concern… What if he'd got it all wrong? What if the wrong man had died?

The more he thought about it, the more it made sense. Rupert Haversham was one of The Cabal's closest confidants, the one person who knew exactly what they were up to; where, when, and who else was involved. Rupert Haversham was the oracle who knew too much. And someone had wanted him silenced.

And succeeded.

This won't go away, Jake. And there will be nothing you can do until you find The Cabal.

Before he was able to dwell on it further, his mobile rang. Jake plugged the device into the car's audio system and pressed play. Owing to his Austin Mini Cooper's old age, it was aeons behind the technological advances most cars of today possessed. Fortunately, some genius somewhere had allowed those who insisted on living in the past to catch up and dip at least a toe in the pool of today's technology. And Jake felt that more than anything with the cassette adaptor, which enabled him to listen to music and answer telephone calls through the dashboard.

Past and future. Analogue and digital. Symbiotic at last.

'This is Jake,' he declared when he answered the call.

'Where are you, Tanner?' Darryl's voice echoed around the vehicle.

'I'm driving, guv. On my way back from Wandsworth.' Jake turned his attention to the changing zebra-crossing lights in front of him. He eased the car to a stop, grabbed his water bottle from the centre console and drank, flushing the liquid down his throat.

'Anything you need to tell me?' Darryl asked.

'Just thought I'd speak to Henry Matheson. I'm convinced he's got his part to play in this.'

'Evidence?'

'His entire life is evidence,' Jake retorted. He attempted to chuckle, to lighten the mood, to get one from Darryl, but when there was no reaction from his boss, he answered properly. 'Haversham's phone records indicate that he's made several calls to a Wandsworth prison number. I just wanted to see what Henry knew.'

'Without consulting me?'

'It was in an unofficial capacity, sir,' Jake replied.

The lights changed in front of him and he eased his foot down on the accelerator, pulling away.

Darryl sighed heavily through the phone. 'That's no excuse. This case has blown up right now. I've got a Gold Group meeting later on to discuss how we're going to deal with it. Haversham was a public figure, and a friend to many of the people you call sir and ma'am. They will want this dealt with in the swiftest, most convenient manner.'

Have you considered the possibility that there's still a certain someone else involved in all of this?

In the distance, towering above the horizon, was a block of flats. Jake placed his forearms on the steering wheel and leant forward, gazing up at them. As he observed the buildings, his stomach rumbled, and an idea popped into his head.

'Guv, I'm going to need a favour.'

'You're rapidly running out of those.'

'It's an important one.'

'They always are.'

'What are the chances you'll be able to work your magic and get me a directed surveillance warrant for the Cosgrove Estate before sundown?'

Darryl hesitated. Jake's stomach rumbled again.

On his left, fast approaching, was a lay-by next to an off-licence, a nail salon, a dog-grooming parlour and a few other shops. Jake indicated, slowed and parked outside the off-licence.

'If you can present me with some solid evidence, then you've got yourself a warrant.'

'Two words. *The*. And *Cabal*.'

'I've got two more words for you: *he's… dead*.'

52

'Or so we thought.'

'You can't be serious? That was all put to bed. Since Candy's death there hasn't been a peep from anyone, anywhere.'

Until now.

'I didn't want to believe it at first, guv, but Henry Matheson seems to think The Cabal's still out there. Even if Matheson's leading us down the garden path, I don't think it's something we should discount. There was something in the way he looked at me, something that made him look… frightened. I think he might have been telling the truth.'

'Don't start Stockholming him,' Darryl said, followed by another heavy sigh. 'But I suppose you're right. If I ignore you and you turn out to be wrong, dealing with you then will be worse than if I leave it.'

Another sigh, the pain in his voice coming through the dashboard. 'Leave it with me. I'll speak to the Home Office. See what I can do.'

'Hero,' Jake thanked his manager and then switched off the engine, disconnecting the call. Last night's disagreement forgotten.

Grabbing his phone from the dash, Jake stepped out of the car and hurried to the off-licence. He was greeted with a sickly sweet smell that emanated from the bay of assorted pick 'n' mix he'd once adored as a child. Too many times he'd returned home from school with bags of them stuffed into his pockets, and even more stuffed into his mouth. One time, his mum had told him that his blood would turn to sugar and that he would turn into a giant sweet if he didn't stop eating so many. Since then, Jake had never picked up another bag. It wasn't the bacteria or germs of everyone who'd ever breathed or touched them that scared him; it was his mum's horror story.

Along the left-hand side of the shop was a refrigeration unit. Jake grabbed himself a Pepsi, a chicken-and-sweetcorn sandwich and a packet of Walkers crisps. With the ensemble of food in his hands, he meandered towards the cash desk. As he set the food down, his stomach rumbled loudly.

'That was my stomach,' Jake said with a smirk. 'Not my arse.'

His juvenile attempt at humour landed in vain on the shop clerk, who took the items from him and scanned them through the till. A few seconds later, Jake flashed his card, paid for it and then left.

As he rounded the front of the car, juggling the food in one hand and reaching for the door handle with the other, something to his right caught his eye. It was blue. Dark blue, to be precise. The colour should have elicited calm and ease throughout his body. Instead, it invoked excitement and adrenaline – the things he'd come to love from his favourite gambling shop.

At first, when he'd pulled into the lay-by, he'd missed it. Perhaps it was subliminal. Perhaps his unconsciousness had disregarded it because he was on shift. Or perhaps it was because he was so focused on food that his mind had painted over it.

But now that he had his food…

Jake threw the meal deal into the car and then quickly hurried towards the bookies, skipping onto the pavement as he went.

One bet. That was all. A quick punt on a horse. Or maybe a trixie on the greyhounds. Or maybe the Japanese J1 League had kicked off…

Inside, the thick and obtrusive stench of scented air spray crawled down his throat. It was obvious that it had been used to drown out the fetid smell of body odour and alcohol that seeped through the pores of every patron inside, but all it could do was making him gag and cough.

Jake made a quick count. Three like-minded men in total.

The bookies was narrow and extended twenty feet. There was a row of casino machines to his left, a wall of TVs and the listings for horse races and football matches on his right, and in the centre of it all was an assortment of chairs. Varying seats. Varying heights. Varying degrees of sanitation. At the back of the room was the cash desk where Jake hoped, very shortly, he'd be collecting his winnings.

But before he could do anything, something disguised as concern entered his mind. He thumbed his pockets, checked his clothing, and made sure there was nothing obvious about his person that suggested he was a police officer.

A gambling cop… Oh, the Directorate of Professional Standards would have a field day.

Deciding that he was safe, Jake straightened his tie and moved towards the TV screens. He grabbed a betting slip and stepped backward, casting his eye up at the information on the corkboards and TV for the races.

'Need a hand, geez?' a man asked beside him. He was young, a similar age to Jake, dressed in a grey-and-white Adidas tracksuit, and wore gold chains around his wrist and neck.

Jake considered himself an expert on horse racing. He'd picked four winners out of his past twenty bets, a ratio of one in five. And with those statistics, he could have been making a living out of it – if only the odds he'd won at were worth writing home about. But when it came to greyhounds, he was especially lost. His criteria was the following: the comical value of the dog's name and how good the odds looked. Any less than a slight chuckle on the humour scale wasn't worth trying. Nine times out of ten, his criteria lost.

Not so good a ratio.

'Depends what you're offering,' Jake said, eyeing the man up and down.

'You like the 'orses or the dogs?'

'Football.'

'Don't get none of that this time of day. So you've either got to choose the 'orses or the dogs. Ain't no point betting on any of the other shit. Ain't nobody watched tennis or cricket in years.'

The man exuded cheap cologne with every movement of his body. It was as though he'd doused himself in it after he'd woken up to excuse not having a shower.

'What's your preferred choice?' Jake asked, suddenly realising that the things he was saying and the way he was saying them made him look out of place.

'I like the 'orses, geez. I ain't half bad at 'em either.'

'Any suggestions?'

The man stopped bouncing from side to side and extended his hand. ''Arry,' he said.

Jake assumed there was an H attached to the beginning of his name, but decided not to say anything.

'Jake,' he replied, shaking the man's hand.

'I ain't seen you round here before. You new?'

'First time.'

'I can tell. You don't look like a man who knows 'is way round a bookies.' Harry hesitated for a moment. 'You ain't no pig though, are ya? Dressed in that suit and all that?'

Jake smirked and shook his head. 'Nah. I work in an office nearby. Insurance. Wanted to get this in before I go home to the missus.'

'Ain't that the truth.' Harry immediately turned his attention to the TV. On the screen, a race was just about to end. Harry perched himself on the end of his seat, and as the race reached its final stages, he drew nearer and nearer to the TV, pumping his fist higher and harder into the air, until a few seconds later, a horse won and he screamed, 'Come on you beauty!' kissing the betting slip and hurrying towards the booth to collect his winnings. After a short while, he returned with over a hundred pounds in his hands.

Jake eyed the money surreptitiously.

One in five.

'Nice one, fella. You'll have to gimme some tips,' he said.

Without responding, Harry returned his attention to the TV screen again. The next race was in less than two minutes. Jake had under a hundred seconds to pick a horse and bet on it. He surveyed the line-up. Their names. Their odds. Their form. Their jersey colours. Their jockeys.

It was like building a car – all the pieces of information could be built into one machine, but the overall success of the machine was down to the driver, and how nicely they drove it.

'ThirdTimeLucky,' Harry said.

Jake continued to scan the names.

'No,' he said politely. 'I've got my eye on another one.'

'What?'

Jake said nothing, turned and rushed towards the booth. The woman behind it chewed maliciously on a piece of gum, as though she was afraid someone was going to take it out of her mouth without permission, and the only way to stop them was by chewing so hard she might bite their hand off.

'Be My Caballero,' Jake began. 'Twenty quid. Twenty-five to one. Doncaster. Next race.'

He scrambled for his Visa, slotted it into the card machine and entered his PIN, the clock ticking away in the background of his mind.

He beat his foot up and down as he waited, eyes fixated on the screen.

DECLINED, read the response.

'*What*?' Jake gasped. He must have used the last of his remaining money on the meal deal.

The most expensive lunch ever.

Frantic, he reached inside his wallet and searched for any notes, any change he may have had.

None.

As he sighed and turned to head back to Harry, an arm lunged into view.

'This one's on me, geez,' Harry said, baring a golden tooth Jake hadn't noticed before.

Jake opened his mouth to protest but was shot down.

The teller took the money from Harry and processed the bet. Jake's adrenaline pumped as he watched the horses begin. Thirteen in total, racing around a four-furlong track. For most of the race, Be My Caballero was faltering behind, hanging as far back as fourth and fifth. But when the first and second positions jumped and fell on the landing, Be My Caballero pounded into first place.

Jake clenched his fist and cheered a little. 'Come on! Come on! Come on!'

When Be My Caballero crossed the finish line, Jake erupted, jumped into the air and punched his fist high.

'You son of a bitch!' Harry screamed along with him, congratulating him by slapping him on the back.

With euphoria coursing through his body, Jake sprinted across to the booth, collected the winnings of £500, and hurried back to Harry.

One in five.

'Thought you said this was your first time?'

'Beginner's luck,' Jake lied. Although there had been some element of truth in it.

It was after all his first time in a bookies.

He counted through the money, split the winnings in half and handed one half to Harry.

'Nah, mate,' the man said. 'You keep it.'

'I insist.'

Eventually, after a few more pushbacks, Harry conceded defeat and accepted half the earnings.

Jake was delighted with himself. The first time he'd won a substantial amount of money gambling. He just hoped that it was a sure sign of things to come.

CHAPTER 12

UP IN FLAMES

In the time they'd been working together, Jake had never known Darryl to come through on a promise so quickly. Somehow, he'd managed to extradite the surveillance warrant through the courts and give it to Jake, fully approved and signed off, within a few hours.

The only problem now was that he was lumbered with DS Brendan Lafferty for the evening. Since his return to work, Jake had spent very little time catching up with Brendan, so what better opportunity than being confined to a metal box for several hours.

The Cosgrove Estate – commonly referred to as The Pit amongst the policing community – was a terrifying and dangerous place. In the few instances that Jake had been there, he'd felt vulnerable, as though he was being watched from every angle, and every angle was working out a way to dispose of him.

Tonight was no different.

On his lap, he held the Canon DSLR camera he'd found on a shelf in Elizabeth's wardrobe. One of her spares. Usually, he would have asked permission, but… things had changed. Besides, it was better to ask for forgiveness than permission.

'What time is it?' Jake asked, staring at the two tower blocks that dominated the estate.

'Half two.'

'Jesus. These people don't sleep, do they?'

The buildings, with the square holes cut into their sides, looked like giant cheese graters. Giant, breathing, conscious cheese graters. In the distance, the repetitive din of music reverberated around the estate.

Jake yawned and eased himself into his chair. He was shattered. He and Brendan had both had less than five hours' sleep in the past two days, and his body was beginning to feel the effects of it. Not even the high of winning £250 could keep him awake – and so far, it had only been the desire to return and place another bet first thing in the morning that had kept him going.

Jake reached for a cup of cold coffee in the door and drank. He grimaced at the taste and set it back down.

'I've got a couple of Red Bulls in the back if you want? I thought we'd need some supplies for the long night ahead. Fail to prepare, prepare to fail and all that.'

There was a nervousness in Brendan's voice. He lifted his Starbucks cup to his lips, tilted the bottle upwards and gasped excitably after he'd finished. Jake eyed the cup, casting his mind back to the first time he'd seen it. Had it been before or after Roland's death?

He couldn't remember.

'I used to know someone who drank from a cup like that,' he started.

'Oh yeah?'

'Yeah. You've heard of him. Liam Greene.'

'The former DCI?'

'The very same,' Jake replied with a slight dip of the head. 'And I think he had the same problem as you.'

'What… What problem?'

'That…' Jake pointed to the flask.

'You've lost me.'

'Yesterday. With Margaret. You fucked up. I swear I could smell alcohol on your breath.' A pause. 'When did it start? After Roland…? Is that why you've been off sick this long? I'm not a genius, and I'm fairly sure it doesn't take one either to work out what you've got in there.'

Brendan placed the cup between his legs, rested one hand on the steering wheel and the other on the centre console. 'You wouldn't believe me if I told you.'

'You haven't told me, so how will we know?'

Brendan hesitated again. This time for an even longer moment. Jake used the brief opportunity to do a recce of the estate: there had been no change, and the streets were still as empty as before.

Clearing his throat, Brendan began: 'What happened with Margaret was a horrendous mistake. I'm still beating myself up about it. But it was a one-off. I *was* inebriated. That time. That one time. And it won't happen again.'

'I've heard that before.'

Brendan sighed, grabbed the flask, unscrewed the lid and shoved it under Jake's nose. 'Sniff it, you idiot.'

Jake didn't need to hover his nose above the lid to know what was in it. The powerful stench of energy drink climbed Jake's nostrils and clawed its way down his throat, making him gag.

'Why are you showing me this?' he asked.

'I've been living off this every day. It's like an addiction.'

Jake shook his head in disbelief. 'Right, now *you've* lost *me*. Care to explain, or are you just going to leave me feeling like a lost child here?'

'It's difficult. And long.'

'We're not going anywhere.'

'I mean, right...' A sharp inhale, followed by a sharp exhale. Like a footballer readying himself for a free kick. 'When I was younger, I used to drink. A lot. From the age of about sixteen or seventeen, I was on a destructive path. Horrible. I hated everyone, and even more, I hated myself. It was the worst time of my life. But then I got off the stuff. And when I was going through it all, I realised I needed a daily reminder of my alcoholism. Something that embodied my drinking.'

Brendan waggled the cup in the air. '*This* is my daily reminder. Every time I look at it, I'm reminded of the pain I went through, the hurt, the ache, the suffering I put my family through – I even drove my dad into a stroke. He got so stressed out by it all. For years I was good, staying away from it, but then I slipped into old habits when Roland died. I'd never seen the bottom of so many empty bottles. But then... I had a sort of premonition, a telling-off by some divine spirit. I'm not usually one for believing in ghosts, but it happened. Scout's honour.'

'What did they say?' Jake asked, unsure who 'they' were.

'They told me I was only going to get one chance at this game of life, and that I was throwing it away with every drink.'

Sensing the atmosphere in the car needed raising a few notches, Jake asked, 'Are you sure you weren't watching *Rocky* or something?'

Brendan managed a chuckle, but it was weak. 'It's a long road to recovery. Margaret was an example of one of the potholes in the road along the way, but I'm getting there one day at a time. With the help of my caffeine and sugar, and my daily reminder, I should be able to get there.'

One day at a time.

'Does Darryl know?'

'He's aware and is keeping an eye on me. He's experienced it in his—'

A sound outside distracted them both.

'What was that?' Brendan asked.

It was the sound of a glass bottle smashing. The moment Jake heard it, his senses switched on and he became hyperaware. He turned on the camera and leant forward, his eyes scanning the horizon like a bird of prey. The nearest street light was over fifty yards away, and in front of them was a row of cars. On the right-hand side of the street, a figure on a BMX appeared with a hood pulled over their head. The bike weaved in and out of the markings on the road, edging closer and closer. Closer and closer.

'What is going—?'

Jake cut Brendan off by holding his hand in front of the man's face.

As the figure neared, their features became ever darker. Jake raised the camera, snapped several photographs of the individual, and then sank low into his seat as the biker rode past, panting, his pulse racing.

As soon as the biker was out of the way, Jake focused his attention on the wing mirror and watched the biker continue their path towards the end of the street, still weaving in and out.

False alarm.

'Is that normal around here?' Brendan asked.

As Jake glanced back at Brendan to respond, something caught his eye. Over Brendan's right shoulder, reflected in his wing mirror, was a giant ball of flame erupting from a vodka bottle, thrown by a figure clad in black, whose only discernible features were the outline of the clothes they were wearing.

Jake opened his mouth, but he was too late.

The window beside Brendan smashed and caved in. Glass rained down on them both, lacerating their cheeks and forearms. Then the bottle of flames came in. A swirling mass of orange and yellow engulfed the dashboard, spreading across the width of the window in an instant. A searing, impenetrable heat, combined with paralysing fear, pinned Jake to his chair. Screams filled the car as Brendan thrashed his arms in the air, grappling for anything that would free them; he'd been blinded by the blood that streamed down his face.

Panicking, Jake punched his seat belt, felt relief as it gave way, and swiftly removed Brendan's. Opening his door with one hand, Jake grabbed his colleague's shoulder with the other and dragged the man free from the burning blaze.

By now, the flames licked the windows and ceiling of the car, singeing the hairs on his head and arms. Brendan cried and wailed as Jake dropped him onto the concrete, his hands clawing at his eyes and face.

Jake stood up straight and darted his gaze up and down the street, searching for their attackers.

There, thirty feet away, standing underneath a street lamp, was one of them. Jake didn't know how many there were but he was sure it was several. A well organised and planned attack.

The figure, covered from head to toe in black, slowly removed their hoodie, revealing a vindictive, malevolent smile. The message behind it was simple: stay away.

A voice bellowed from the beyond, and the attacker bolted, disappearing off into the estate. Lost to the concrete maze.

Wasting no more time, Jake turned his attention back to the burning wreckage. The flames had reached the energy drinks in the back seat, and the sickly sweet smell of burning plastic wafted through the air. Meanwhile, on the ground, Brendan continued to scream. Wriggling, writhing, holding his face.

Jake dropped by his side and dialled 999.

'This is Detective Jake Tanner of Stratford CID. A petrol bomb's just been thrown in our car. Requesting immediate fire and ambulance support to the Cosgrove Estate.'

CHAPTER 13

IN COLD BLOOD

Gold Group meetings comprised the most senior officers from every department within the Met's Frontline Policing branch, from the superintendents to the commanders – and in this particular instance, all the way to the top with the assistant commissioner. In a way, they were a smaller-scale version of the COBRA meetings the Prime Minister and various other government heads attended. And Darryl despised them. Sometimes, though more often than not, the meetings were just an opportunity for his colleagues to show off their ego and rise a little higher than everyone else in a dick-swinging contest. The internal politics were bullshit, and Darryl always came away feeling like they had discussed nothing productive or made any progress at all.

It was probably one of the reasons Richard Candy had managed to get away with as much as he had for as long as he had.

Tonight's Gold Group meeting was no different. With the only exception that it was being held at Bow Green for the first time.

Sitting around the table was an assortment of faces Darryl had grown accustomed to seeing in the couple of years he'd been with the Major Investigation Team: Harrison Bramley, the director of the Met's legal service; Mark Haydon, the Commander of Specialist Crime; Anika Montague from the Crown Prosecution Service; Nigel Winterbottom, the director of media and communications; and DCS Erica Dane, from West Ham police station.

An A–Z of some of the most respected officers in the organisation.

The only problem was more and more of their faces were changing thanks to Jake's ongoing investigations into The Cabal. Most notably, the assistant commissioner. Sitting directly opposite him was a woman he'd only met twice since her appointment. Rebecca Marlow.

And on both occasions she'd always worn the same thing – her police uniform, replete with epaulettes and cap. Her glasses sat atop the bridge of her nose and reflected the artificial light overhead, and she wore a bronze bracelet around her wrist that she twisted absent-mindedly as she listened.

Rebecca reached across the table, grabbed the flask Darryl had prepared and poured the tepid water into her mug.

She took a sip, giving nothing away in her expression.

'Perfect temperature,' she said, and set the mug down. 'Thanks for coming tonight. I appreciate it's short notice and that you're not able to spend time with loved ones. I also appreciate that this is the first time some of you are meeting me. And the reason for this meeting is twofold: to introduce myself, because we're all going to be working really closely together over the foreseeable future, and to also discuss the latest developments we've had in the Rupert Haversham case.'

Darryl stifled a snigger. There were certain things he agreed with and certain things he didn't. For instance, when it came to hosting a high-level command meeting about the murder of one of the country's top defence lawyers within twenty-four hours of his death, while the investigation into the rape and death of an innocent young woman remained at the bottom of the pile.

That was when he began to question motives.

Why one life over another?

Perhaps tonight he was going to find out.

'Darryl,' Rebecca continued, 'you're working on the case at the moment. What do you see as the biggest threat to security right now?'

'What security?'

'National security.'

And there it was. The value of this one specific life over another.

'We don't foresee any national security threat,' he replied bluntly. 'The biggest threat Rupert Haversham posed was in defending Henry Matheson, and he's going to be behind bars for the rest of his life.'

There was a long pause. Rebecca stopped twirling her bracelet and set her hands on the table, palms down.

'I'm going to be frank for a moment, if you'll let me, Darryl, as there's no easy way for me to say this. However, have you considered the possibility that someone within your team is too close to the case?'

'Excuse me?' Darryl said plainly. His brow, eyes, cheeks, lips all dropped. 'I will vouch for all of my officers. They put in more work than anyone I've ever worked with.'

'That has no impact on what I'm saying.'

'Then perhaps you're going to need to explain it to me.'

'Jake Tanner,' Rebecca said flatly, then reached inside her briefcase and produced a series of papers housed in a brown Manila folder. She cleared her throat. 'After extensively reading through all the reports and witness statements and prosecution files on your predecessor DCI Liam Greene, DCI Helen Clements, DS Martin Radcliffe and, most recently, *my* predecessor, Assistant Commissioner Richard Candy, there seems to be one commonality between them all.'

'That's because he's the one who caught them. Quicker and better than anyone in the DPS or IPCC. The man has worked himself tirelessly in uncovering The Cabal, and no doubt his mental and physical health has deteriorated as a result.'

'And yet he's the common denominator, solving the riddles alone with no help. You've previously admitted yourself that you've had very little to do in the arrests of these individuals.'

'It's called modesty.'

'And the same can be said for their trials, too.'

'Are you putting me on trial now?'

Rebecca offered him a faint smirk, one that wasn't meant for him but for herself – and it filled him with rage.

'No, Darryl, you're not. But I'd like you to consider removing Jake from the investigation into Haversham's death.'

'No.'

'It has come to my attention that he may, in fact, be the person responsible for everything he's attempted to prosecute. The armed robberies. The drug smuggling. The human trafficking. Is it entirely unreasonable to suggest that the reason he's locked away these officers is because they were suspicious of him, because they were aware of his secrets, they were aware of his *real* identity? Has it not crossed your mind that he may in fact be using them as a scapegoat to maintain his identity, like he's living in a real-life version of *Fight Club*?'

Darryl burst into a single fit of laughter, unable to stop himself. 'Categorically not,' he said after controlling himself. 'I detest the insinuation. Detective Constable Jake Tanner is a stand-up officer, a role model. And any department would be lucky to have him. He'd put his life on the line to put an end to The Cabal's reign of terror. Richard Candy was able to infiltrate and propagate his corruption throughout almost every recess of the Specialist Crimes Command because he had the influence and the means to do so. How is it possible that Jake Tanner, a low-level detective constable, would be able to accomplish that without the same platform?'

'Perhaps he used Candy to facilitate it,' Mark Haydon said.

Darryl shot him a look, and the man retreated, instantly regretting his decision to enter the conversation.

Darryl sighed heavily, regaining his composure until he breathed through his nose and mouth.

'Excuse me,' he said politely. 'I need to go to the bathroom. We can continue this discussion in a minute.'

Darryl climbed out of his chair without waiting for a response and left the room. Furious, he stormed along the corridor into the main office. As he arrived, he gasped and jumped out of his skin. There he found Sandy Matthews, the senior SOCO responsible for submitting evidence for external examination.

'Jesus bloody hell,' he cried, holding his chest. 'What are you doing here this late?'

'Sorry, guv. I didn't mean to startle you.'

'Are you waiting for me?'

She nodded slowly. 'There's something you need to see. Can we discuss this in your office?'

Darryl glanced back at the Major Incident Room and then at Sandy. 'I can only give you a couple of minutes.'

They entered his office.

'Well…' he began.

Sandy looked down at the floor. It was a while before she responded, her prolonged silence filling Darryl with dread.

'What is it, Sandy?' he insisted.

'Fingerprints, guv. I've got some.' She produced a folder from behind her back and held it in the air. 'You know we found those fingerprints across Helena Haversham's neck, Rupert Haversham's clothes and the pillow that was used to murder Felicity Haversham?'

Darryl nodded.

'Well, I ran them through Ident1, and… we got a hit.'

Darryl smiled. 'Brilliant. Fantastic. Have you shared it with the team?'

'That's the problem, sir. I can't.'

'Why not?'

'Because… because they're Jake's fingerprints, guv.'

'Impossible,' Darryl replied instinctively. He hadn't allowed the words to compute in his mind. Like a terrifying diagnosis, he *couldn't* allow them to. 'Why haven't his prints been ruled out? It's standard procedure.'

'I wish that was the case, sir. But the prints were already lifted before you and the team set foot in the house. And you were with him the entire time – did you see him touch a single thing?'

He hadn't.

'So what are you saying: Jake killed all three of them and then returned to the crime scene with us to gloat over his efforts?'

'I'm just relaying the evidence back to you, sir. You're the one who comes up with hypotheses. But from the evidence, it suggests that, yes, Jake Tanner murdered all three of the Haversham family members in cold blood.'

CHAPTER 14

THAT DAY

The bright light from the fridge blinded Elizabeth and painted the rest of the kitchen a moonlit white, softly tinted with a hint of yellow. She reached inside and retrieved the half-drunk carton of milk, unscrewed the lid and emptied the contents into a bottle for Ellie.

It was beginning to look like another restless night – the third in the space of five days – and as she shuffled her feet sleepily across the floor towards the microwave, she wondered how much of it was down to Jake's absence in their lives. His actions on that night were unforgivable. But was he *really* the one to blame? Ever since Jake had first lazily mentioned Stephanie's name in a conversation, she'd known that Stephanie the Saint, Stephanie the Hero, was as trustworthy as a politician. She was a woman, and Jake was an attractive man. But then… there was the way he talked about her, too. The same way he'd spoken about Elizabeth to his friends and family when they'd first started going out. The excitable intonations in his voice. The adoration he held for her evident in the things he said, that beaming smile on his face.

Did he really have feelings for her, or was it just a platonic friendship that had been abused by one party and not the other? Was she really overthinking everything?

The microwave *binged!* and brought her out of her thoughts. She hadn't realised it, but she'd placed the bottle of milk in the microwave and turned it on for thirty seconds. Working on autopilot again.

And she continued in the same way: staring out the window, looking out onto the garden as she closed the microwave and screwed the lid on top of the bottle. Usually, her mind would be vacant, empty, but the severe sleep deprivation – *Or is it anxiety?* – was having an adverse effect on her and rousing the demons of paranoia to the fore of her mind.

Just as she was about to leave the kitchen, a noise came from outside in the garden. On a typical night, she would have ignored it; the garden backed on to a golf course and their particular plot of land was frequented by lost stag-do members and late-night partygoers. But something about the noise concerned Elizabeth. It was hushed, quiet, almost deliberate.

Clenching the milk bottle in her hand, Elizabeth stalked closer to the window. As her stomach came into contact with the cold surface of the countertop, her skin turned to gooseflesh.

She held her breath as she gazed through her own reflection in the window. And then she heard the sound again.

Hushed, quiet, deliberate.

A stifled cough.

Placing her hand on the surface for support, she leant forward until her face hovered a few inches from the glass. Her hand scavenged for the small fruit knife she'd washed and dried before going to bed. Years spent with Jake in the police force had taught her to prepare for the worst. No amount of action was an overreaction if it involved the safety of loved ones and other family members. Her children were her first priority, and she was the feisty lioness on the front line doing everything she could to protect them, even if there was nothing to worry about.

The moment you get a chance, call the police.

Then there was another sound. This time more distinct. The sound of a piece of wood snapping… the sound of a fence panel buckling at the other end of the garden. The sound of a figure breaking into the property.

Elizabeth, her autopilot switching into a defensive setting she didn't know she had, decided to investigate. Clutching the blade in one hand and the bottle of milk in the other, she shuffled sideways towards the back door and opened it using her elbow. The midnight chill clung to her face and hands and legs as she stepped onto the patio and moved closer to the grass that stretched to the bottom of the garden. In the distance, the golf course was brilliantly lit and music emanated from it. For a moment, she thought she was wrong – that the disturbance had indeed been some of the partygoers who frequented the course's social nights.

But then, as she stepped onto the grass, she realised she couldn't have been more wrong.

Behind her, the security lights illuminated and bathed the garden in a deep yellow hue that melted into the green and created a hint of lime. In front of her, twenty feet away, partially hidden behind the tree in the centre of the garden, was a blacked-out figure, features hidden behind a dark hoodie. Elizabeth didn't need to see his features to be able to work out who it was; she already knew.

She raised the bottle of milk in the air, keeping the knife by her leg, concealed. 'Get out of my garden,' she said, her voice trembling. Her chest heaved and her arms shook. 'You've got twenty seconds.'

Elizabeth started counting.

Twenty. Nineteen. Eighteen.

The trespasser showed no signs of moving.

She took a step closer, hoping it would deter the man.

She was wrong.

He stepped out from behind the tree and into the light, his features illuminated beneath the shadow of his hoodie.

'What are you doing here, Glen?' she asked, raising her voice slightly. It was just loud enough for him to hear, but not so loud that it would rouse her mother or anyone else. Yet.

'I just… I've been thinking about you.' Glen took another step forward, gradually coming towards her the way death approaches all of us. 'I wanted to see you.'

Elizabeth retreated slowly on the grass, shuffling backward.

'I told you not to come anywhere near me,' she said. 'And I told you what would happen if you did.'

Glen shook his head. As he stepped further into the light, Elizabeth noticed something strapped around his shoulder. It was his camera – the same one he'd used to photograph her on the set.

'You won't hurt me, Elizabeth. I know you – you don't want to do that. Please.'

Another step.

Elizabeth's throat closed and she struggled to speak. Something caught in her mouth.

'I've lost my job. I can't pay my bills, my rent. I have nothing. But… I have *you*.'

Ten feet separated them now. Elizabeth was unable to tear her eyes away from the camera. She thought of the images he must've been taking of her while she was in her nightdress. She thought of how long he'd been there and what other sorts of images he might have taken of her in the past few weeks – when she was getting changed in the bedroom, making dinner in the kitchen, enjoying it in the dining room. And there were those lingerie shots that she'd been unable to force him to delete. The bikini shots, the little-black-dress shots. And she didn't even want to begin to imagine how many he had of other women on there too.

'You want to see?' Glen asked, gesturing to the camera on his hip. 'You look so beautiful when you're half asleep.'

'How long have you been out here?'

'Long enough.'

'Get the fuck out of my garden!' she hissed, throwing the bottle of milk at him. Now her body filled with rage, her mind filled with fire – as though she could take on this piece of shit with a blade of grass and still be able to beat him.

Glen ducked the assault and advanced towards her. Before she was even aware of it, he was within a metre of her, holding the camera in his hands and flicking through the library.

'I've got one of you in my favourite angles.' He paused. 'Where is it…?'

Elizabeth stared at him in disbelief. She wanted to react, to retaliate, to lash out, to assault him, to make sure he understood to never return, but the fear of his being so close to her paralysed her entire body. She didn't know what she would do if he touched her, kitchen knife or not. He'd done it once before, and that was enough to make her shudder every time someone else tried to – Jake included.

'Get away from me,' she whimpered. 'Get away from me now.'

'Don't you want to see it?' he asked, beaming with an eerie smile that elicited flashbacks of *that* day.

'GET AWAY FROM ME!' she roared in his face. Her voice sounded demonic and echoed across the garden, all the way up to the country club.

Before Glen could react, she lunged at him. Wildly thrashing the blade in the air, she swung it at his hands and arms. She made a connection twice. On the back of one hand and then on his camera.

Glen cried out in shock, yanked his hand away and dropped the camera to the ground.

Elizabeth continued to attack him, advancing with every swing of her arm. Adrenaline now consumed her, squashing and burying any fear that threatened to delay her.

'Elizabeth!' came a scream from the house.

Glen's eyes flickered over Elizabeth's shoulder, and at the sight of Martha, he turned his back on her and sprinted towards the end of the garden, clutching the back of his hand. He disappeared into the darkness of the golf course a few seconds later.

As soon as he was out of sight, Elizabeth dropped to her knees and let the knife fall from her grasp to rest atop the dew-laden blades of grass. She sobbed quietly, staring at the camera that lay by her side. Martha rushed across to her, wrapped her arm around her daughter and held her there, silent, neither of them saying anything. Neither of them needing to say anything.

After she'd calmed down, Martha hurried into the house, grabbed a plastic bag and decanted the blade and camera into it before sealing them shut with an elastic band.

'Do you want me to call the police?' Martha asked, bending to Elizabeth's side, holding a bag in each arm. 'Do you want me to call Jake?'

Elizabeth contemplated for a moment.

'No. He doesn't need to know. Not yet.'

CHAPTER 15

BACK TO THE BEGINNING

Whipps Cross University Hospital in Leyton, North East London, was fast becoming a second home for Jake. In the three years that he'd been a member of MIT, he'd visited the hospital for a variety of reasons. When Elizabeth had been pregnant with Ellie. To visit DC Pete Garrison, an old colleague, after his severe car crash. To rush to the aid of Lewis Coyne, a former member of Matheson's gang, the E11. And most recently, when he'd been admitted for a check-up after the final showdown with Richard Candy.

He'd been given the once-over then, and he was being given one now.

Jake was seated on a hard plastic mattress that squeaked every time he breathed. In front of him was a nurse, frantically rushing to his aid. In her hand, she held several sachets of liquid and bandages. Clipped to his finger was a SATs reader, communicating with the machine to his left.

'Honestly, you don't have to do any of this. I'm fine,' he said, feeling rather stoic. He had no idea what time it was – time had become an illusion since he'd been waiting alone in A&E – but the adrenaline in his body was keeping him from falling asleep. No need for coffee, energy drinks, extreme doses of sugar – just the high-octane thrill of a petrol bomb being hurled through your car window. 'If I was in any serious pain or danger, I would've felt it by now.'

'Nobody likes a hero,' the nurse told him as she tore open the sachet, discarded the contents onto the bed, delicately lifted his arm and began to daub the burns on the back of his hand and forearm. His skin tingled, and a series of loci pain points pricked his arm, moving up and down as the nurse administered the medicine. Jake winced and flexed his tendons to alleviate the pain.

The nurse stopped and looked up at him. 'Not so brave now, are you?'

He hated the smug smirk with which she said it, and supposed that it was her *why*, the reason she continued to do the job so few wanted to do: so she could knock the idiotic and brazen down a peg or two.

Or in Jake's particular case, ten.

The nurse finished with one arm and turned her attention to the other. In the attack, amidst the swirling frenzy of the flames, Jake had tried to pick up Elizabeth's camera, lost in the footwell. In the process, he'd singed several hairs and scorched the tips of his fingers. Pain continued to throb and swell with the beating of his heart. Looking down at his limbs, he surveyed the damage caused by the blaze. What he couldn't see was the extent of the damage on his face. His hair. His forehead. His eyes. His nose. His cheeks. The tingling sensation that swarmed the right side of his face wasn't a positive sign.

'How does it look?' Jake asked, pointing to his cheek.

'Not that bad. Just a first degree. You might have a little swelling, but nothing to worry about. You're lucky. It could have been much worse.' The nurse opened another sachet and dabbed at his forehead, then made her way down his face. As she did so, they locked eyes several times. An intimate moment.

'When can I see my colleague?' he asked.

'Not for a while. His burns were severe. Third degree in several places. You said he was literally on fire, right?'

'I don't think I used the term "literally", but yes, he was on fire.'

She shot him a derisive look (this time it was *he* who'd knocked *her* down a peg) and then continued. 'Chances are he's going to be under for a couple of hours, and out of action longer than that. Depending on the severity of the burns, they may have to do a skin graft.'

An image flashed in Jake's mind, transporting him to the back of the ambulance. Brendan lying down, screaming. Trying to roll out of the gurney and claw at his face. Trying to tear away the pain, while the paramedic tried to help him, pin him to the bed, soothe him, calm him. And all Jake could do was watch from the sidelines and smell the thick, rancid aroma of charred flesh. It had a taste that, once in his throat, stayed there.

Even two hours later, it remained.

The nurse clicked her fingers in front of his face, bringing him back to the present. 'All done,' she said, picking up her rubbish. 'I'd give it a few hours until you're ready to go. But if you're that eager, I'll speak with a doctor and see what we can do.'

'Is that it? We're all finished?'

'Count yourself lucky.'

Jake did. He could only begin to imagine the immeasurable pain and suffering Brendan was experiencing. The thought of the attack made him angry. He replayed the events in his mind. The kid on the bike. The decoy. The orange ball of flames. The smashing window. The firebomb thrown into the car. The rapid rush and spread of the flames as they licked and crawled and danced. The sweltering, blistering heat. The adrenaline as he came face to face with their attacker – the face he'd now committed to memory.

As he sat there, alone in the hospital room, he pondered. Being there made him feel uneasy. They weren't the nicest of places on a good day, but his recent experiences had been worse than traumatising. It was, of course, the last place Jake had seen Alan Clarke, his father-in-law, alive, before the man had been put under the knife for a kidney operation. In fact, the room he was in right now reminded Jake of Alan's.

The operation had gone well. They'd operated and swapped over the kidney and stitched him back up again. But only a few hours later, his body had developed a severe infection and had started to reject the kidney. Then came seizures, fever, vomiting, followed by a brief stint in a coma, before he sadly passed away.

Meanwhile, Jake had been nowhere to be seen.

Instead, he had been focusing on work while his father-in-law was in a—

Coma.

An idea flashed into his mind.

Unplugging his finger from the SATs reader, Jake jumped off the bed, paused at the door, glanced up and down the corridor and hurried back the way he'd come. He made his way down to the nearest reception desk and waited in line.

When it was his turn, he idled up to the counter and placed his hands against the edge of the surface.

'I was wondering where I might find a friend of mine. Peter Garrison,' Jake asked. A thin film of sweat formed on his back.

'I'm afraid it's no longer visiting hours, sir.'

'With the greatest of respect,' Jake began, 'he's in a coma. It's not like we're going to be singing and dancing and waking the whole ward up. I'm a colleague of his. I wanted to see how he's doing.'

Before the woman could protest any more, Jake flashed his warrant card. The nurse sighed and typed the name into the computer.

'Intensive care unit,' she said. 'First floor. Ward E. Room thirteen.'

Eventually, after traversing the myriad corridors and getting lost a handful of times, Jake found the right place and barged through the double doors of Ward E on the first floor. As he meandered down a long corridor, his head pivoted left and right, counting down the room numbers.

He stopped outside number thirteen. On his left was the door. On the right, stretching across the rest of the room, was a window. Jake shuffled closer to the glass. There, on the other side, attached to numerous machines, and with cords and tubes attached to his wrists, was Pete Garrison, the man whom Jake had admired most during his early years at MIT. The man whose life had been taken away from him months before he was due to retire.

Jake studied him. His greying hair. The skin that sagged on his jowls. The steady rise and fall of his chest. The skinny, wiry skeleton that was all that remained of him. A lump swelled in Jake's throat.

He watched a nurse wrap the bed sheet tighter around Garrison's body, tucking him in for the night.

Once she was finished, she collected a sheet of paper and headed out of the room. It wasn't until she closed the door that she noticed Jake. At the sight of him, she let out a small whimper and clutched her chest.

'Oh,' she said, stepping away from the door. 'I'm sorry. Is it you tonight?'

'Excuse me?'

'Are you visiting tonight?'

'No, I was told—' He paused and removed his warrant card again.

As the nurse's eyes fell on the ID, they widened and her cheeks rouged. 'O-Oh, I'm sorry,' she began, stammering. 'Is there... is there an issue? Is something wrong?'

'I was told visiting hours were finished. Why would you think I was here for visiting?'

'There's just, um... usually, there's... um...'

'Take your time,' Jake said, attempting to disarm her nerves with a smile. 'You're not in trouble or anything.'

The nurse chuckled nervously and breathed, composing herself. 'Sorry. It's been a long day. I'm just about to finish my shift, and I thought you were someone else. Pete never gets any visitors during the day, but there's always one person who comes at this time of night – just before I'm about to go home. I let them come in and spend some time with him outside of hours. I know I'm not supposed to, but she says it's the only time she can come.'

She? Jake thought. His gaze entered the room and fell on a packet of digestive biscuits half opened on the bedside table. Pete's favourite. Even in the hospital, he had a pack by his side.

'She always brings them. Sometimes she leaves them for the rest of the team, sometimes she sits there eating them all herself.'

'Who is she?'

'No idea. Never cared to ask. Ever since his wife stopped coming, he doesn't have anyone to visit him.'

In the weeks following Garrison's accident, while the doctors and experts conducted their tests to determine the reasons for the coma and the extent of his injuries, his wife Patricia had stopped visiting. Perhaps she couldn't deal with the stress. Perhaps she couldn't bear to see her husband chained to a bed. Or perhaps she was so afraid of the uncertainty of looking after him once he'd finally woken up that she'd given up before it had even started. Their relationship hadn't been great. Jake had heard many horror stories in their evenings down the pub. But how could she leave him like this, alone? She had taken the coward's way out, and for that, she didn't deserve Garrison.

'Did you used to work with him?' the nurse asked to fill the void.

Jake nodded. 'Only for a couple of months before his accident. How's he doing? Any signs of coming round soon?'

'There's no way of knowing. We just have to wait and see. But he looks like a kind soul. He'll pull through.'

'Yeah,' Jake said, 'I hope so.'

It was funny to him how, in matters of life and death, respect was always paid to the good things someone had done in life, and how nobody ever focused on the bad. He supposed it was all to do with seeing the light amidst the darkness. That somehow everyone was redeemable. But what if they'd been a terrible person? What if they'd never done anything for anyone else and only ever thought of themselves?

And what would people say about Jake at his *own* funeral? That he'd been a shitty husband. A terrible father. A bad police officer. Because sometimes, no matter how much he tried to convince others and himself of the contrary, he always felt like he *was* those things. The demons and pernicious thoughts in his mind convinced him it was so, as they picked out his faults and flaws.

Sure, Garrison had been a bad man; he'd been part of a corrupt cell within the police, but there were fifty-four years' worth of his life before that where he had been a good, kind, gentle being. And that was what Jake supposed he should focus on in his own life. The times before the tough, before things began to fall apart, so he could remodel his behaviour and way of life on the previous version of himself.

So he could go back to the beginning.

Nobody deserved to be in Garrison's position, no matter what they'd done, because they hadn't always been bad. The light shone in the dark. And Jake was sensing his own coming through.

'Yes,' Jake said, muttering to himself as he continued to stare at Garrison. 'Yes, he will get through this.'

CHAPTER 16

PERPETUAL ORGASM

Dylan's body pulsed and swayed. His hands in the air, numb, feeling as though they were no longer attached to his body. The beer in his hand felt even lighter, almost weightless, and for a brief second, he wasn't sure it was still there. He gave himself a shock as soon as he opened his eyes to check: in his hallucinogenic state, his arms had turned to octopus tentacles, and his fingers into suction cups, waving and flying in the air. By now, his extensive experience with narcotics had prepared him for the unexpected, so he closed his eyes and indulged himself in the effects of the chemicals surging through his system.

If he was arrested right now and asked what he'd taken, he wouldn't be able to answer. The list was too long. The drugs were so good that they all coalesced into one giant dose of euphoria. MDMA. Cocaine. Ketamine. Mushrooms. LSD. And the final cherry on the top of his drug cake, marijuana. Sweet, sweet, *sweet* Mary J. The joint dangled from his lips and felt like an extension of his tongue, like the prongs at the end of a snake's tongue.

Dylan continued to dance and sway around the smoke-filled room, trying to keep to the beat as much as possible. He was listening to a pirate radio station that blasted illegal and uncopyrighted songs into the dead of night. Garage. House. Drum 'n' bass. Hip hop. Rap. Every type of music he adored.

The signal came from somewhere in the estate, and, occasionally while he was severely under the influence, he'd set out on an adventure to find the mythical source of the sound. The Cosgrove Estate had its very own Bilbo Baggins. What would he do when he found it? Hug each and every one of the hosts and beg them to play his song? Their listener numbers must have been in the millions, if not tens of millions, he was sure. It could be his lucky break. All he needed was someone to take a step of faith in the right direction and play his music. His life's greatest achievement.

With the help of Rupert Haversham's incoming life insurance money, it would give him the kickstart, the impetus to his career that he so desperately needed. Henry Matheson had promised that he'd arrange the money and all the dealings for both of them. And then, soon after, he'd be selling copies by the millions, earning platinum rewards, making collaborations with some of the best in the business and selling out headline acts at festivals. The dream was finally coming true in his mind.

A tear formed in his eye as he thought about it. He stopped dancing, lowered his hands, and opened his eyes. Somehow, he'd ended up on the other side of the room by the window that looked out upon the Cosgrove Estate. His reflection stared back at him, startling him. In the time that he'd been dancing, he'd completely forgotten he was wearing his lucky hat – the hat his dad had given him before he went to the shops and never came back.

Society told him he should have hated his dad, and by extension, the hat. But that wasn't possible. Not when his dad had been the one to introduce him to music. From the first time his dad had played the hard-hitting beats and rhymes of the NWA, to the time he came home with a drum set for Dylan to smash and test to within breaking point, Dylan had known that music was the career he wanted. It might not have been in his blood or his DNA, but it was in his heart.

He cast his eye out upon the estate beneath him. He recognised Reece Enfield riding around on his bike, circling the lamp post and the basketball hoop in the centre of the grounds. He could also see dozens of empty plastic bottles littering the concrete.

The flat was in a similar state, though those bottles were slightly different. He turned away from the window and glanced down at the bottles on the floor. At Henry Matheson's legacy and drug empire.

Many years ago, to combat the heightened police presence on the estate, Henry had introduced a new means of dealing drugs. Soft-drink bottles, split into three sections. Top. Middle. Bottom. The top and bottom contained the soft drink, and the middle section – hidden behind the plastic labelling – contained whatever drugs had been ordered. It was an ingenious solution, and one that many held in high regard, Dylan included.

In the past twenty-four hours, Dylan and Erica had pumped a cocktail of different drugs into their systems. All except one.

'Dylan,' Erica whispered. She struggled to talk as she lay on the sofa with her arm dangling over the side, an empty can of beer a few inches from her fingers.

'You good?' he asked her, perching himself on the other end of the sofa.

'I don't feel well.'

'It's fine,' he replied. 'You just have to let yourself go. Let yourself get into it. Ride it out. Relax and let it take over.'

'But…'

Before Dylan could react, a barely audible knock came from the door. His eyes widened and his head snapped towards the source of the noise, his body turning rigid and his breath echoing in his ear. He paused. Waited. Listened.

The knock came again, this time louder.

Keeping his eyes locked on the door, he rose out of the chair, grabbed the kitchen knife from the small treadle table by the door and pressed it against his back. Using his other hand, he pulled the door open carefully. It opened a few inches, restricted by the chain keeping it in place. Dylan peered through the small gap and locked eyes with the knocker.

It was one of the estate's youngers, a kid half his age and half his size.

The kid flicked his head upwards and kissed his teeth. 'Turn that shit off, man. Ain't nobody wanna hear that this time of night. Who even is it?'

'It's me.'

'Don't take this the wrong way, bruv, but it's wank. Hope you ain't gonna do it some more.'

Dylan scowled at the kid. 'What do you want?'

In response, the kid pulled his arm from behind his back to reveal a bottle of Fanta Orange in his hand.

'Courtesy of Henry Matheson,' the kid replied. 'He sends his regards. Oh, and he also said to stay the fuck indoors and turn this shit off.'

'He said that?' Dylan asked as he took the bottle.

'Most of it, yeah. I made up the last bit. Seriously, though, turn this shit off. My mum's tryna sleep. She got an exam tomorrow, and if you keep her up any longer, the next time I come back, I ain't gonna be bringing a plastic bottle.'

The kid made a gun sign with his fingers, made a popping sound with his mouth, and then walked off.

'Prick,' Dylan scoffed under his breath as he closed the door.

Then he moved across the room and slumped onto the sofa, forgetting to move Erica's legs. He unscrewed the top half of the bottle and handed her the Fanta; she opened the drink blearily and poured it down her throat. Then he unscrewed the middle section and held it in the air in high anticipation. Carefully, he peeled back the label.

Inside were two small bags of heroin that glistened in the light.

A deep grin rose on Dylan's face. Without saying anything, he propelled himself off the sofa and raced to the kitchen sink. Beside the basin was a half-empty box of cornflakes. Beside that was a small ornate plate decorated with blue flowers. Sitting on it was a lighter, a charred and blackened spoon, a shoelace and a syringe. Plate in hand, he scurried back to Erica.

'What're you doing?'

'I got something that's going to blow your mind, girl. Trust me.'

'What?'

'Heroin.'

'Dylan, I don't want…' Her eyes closed and then gradually reopened again. 'That's the bad one, isn't it?'

'Only when you've never done it before.' He was sweating profusely now, his excitement rising like a phoenix. 'Once you've had some of this, you'll never want to try anything else ever again. It's like fucking gold dust.'

Dylan leapt off the floor, switched the music off, and jumped back down by Erica's head. His mind was sobering up and beginning to work on autopilot. He'd only ever had the pleasure of experiencing heroin on a few occasions – partly because it was difficult to source nowadays, thanks to the Albanians and Romanians controlling that side of the market, and partly because he'd tried to let himself only ever have it as a treat – but when it came to preparing the drug for consumption, he was a pro.

Dylan decanted the yellowed powdery contents into the spoon, ignited the lighter, and held the flame underneath the spoon. Within seconds, the heroin bubbled and sizzled until it became a dark brown liquid. Dipping the syringe into the liquid, Dylan extended the plunger, drawing in the heroin. Then he grabbed Erica's arm, tied the lace around her bicep, and tightened. As he slapped the vein into prominence, and wiped the needle clean of dust with his thumb and forefinger, he prodded it into Erica's vein and depressed.

At first, she struggled and attempted to defend herself, but it was no use. She was too weak and spaced out to do anything about it.

'Relax,' he said. 'Just let it come over you. Ride it until you run out of steam.'

Slowly, he pulled the needle from her arm and repeated the process for himself. By the time he'd sucked up what little remained on the spoon, Erica's eyes were already rolling in the back of her head. A smile grew on her face and she groaned gently as she slipped into catharsis.

Dylan cleaned the syringe with his finger again before plunging it into his arm. It took less than a second for the chemicals to take hold of him. He gasped, clenched every muscle in his body, and relaxed against the side of the sofa. The feeling of pure euphoria, unlike anything the rest of the drugs in his system could deliver, consumed his entire being. His skin pricked and crawled as the hairs on his arms stood on end, and he shuddered, as if he was experiencing a perpetual orgasm.

'Wow…' he said and turned to Erica.

A special occasion required a special moment between them.

But there was a problem.

A blanket of white covered her eyes and her mouth dangled open, spittle and phlegm dribbling down her chin. Her breathing was light, and the pulse in her neck was non-existent.

'Erica,' Dylan whispered, clawing at her face. 'Erica.'

But it was no use. By the time he twisted to face her, the drugs in his body took hold of him and dragged him down into the abyss. The world turned black before his head hit the carpet.

| DAY 3 |

CHAPTER 17

CHARGED

The early morning sun crept over the horizon as the taxi pulled into Bow Green car park. The driver slowed to a stop in the space furthest from the entrance and ended the journey. Thirteen quid. Jake reached into his pocket, produced the wad of money he'd won the day before and slipped the man a twenty. Then he waited for his change impatiently, tapping his feet on the floor of the car. He was nervous. Not because he was worried the cabbie might keep his change, or that the consequences of discharging himself early from the hospital might catch up with him, but because Darryl had sounded worried over the phone. There was something that couldn't wait, which meant that there was either a development in the case or something was wrong. Regardless, Jake needed to be there; even the minutest detail could lead them closer to the killer, closer to The Cabal.

As he took the change from the driver and exited the vehicle, his thoughts spun into a complex and dizzying web of debilitating paranoia.

When he entered the foyer, Darryl was already waiting for him, a stroke of solemnity painted across his face.

'Morning, guv,' Jake said, trying to add a semblance of joy to his voice.

Darryl lifted his head, glanced through Jake and then started towards the stairs without a word. Bemused, Jake followed a few feet behind until they came to their second home on the third floor.

'Guv…' Jake called after Darryl. 'Everything all right?'

Darryl came to a sudden stop outside one of the briefing rooms and pointed inside. 'Take a seat please, Jake.'

Jake hesitated in the door frame, bounced his gaze between Darryl and the room several times, and then ducked his head as he entered.

He took it upon himself to find a chair.

A few seconds later, Darryl shut the door gently and sat opposite, knitting his hands together, sitting bolt upright.

'Why do I get the impression this isn't going to be a nice catch-up asking how Brendan and I are feeling?'

Beside Darryl were a few sheets of paper. He reached for them, overturned them, and then rolled them into a tube.

'How is Brendan?' he asked after some time, his voice devoid of emotion.

'In a bad way.'

'What happened to him?'

'Third-degree burns on his face and arms. They ended up having to do a skin graft. They operated overnight.'

'Goodness.' Darryl hesitated and broke Jake's eye contact. 'Sounds horrendous.'

Jake wasn't sure what he was supposed to say to that. Nor was he entirely sure why Darryl's reaction was so placid and bland.

'Why am I in here, guv?'

Darryl unrolled the tube of papers and slid a sheet across. Jake reached for it and started reading. His skin turned cold as his eyes fell over the words. He read them again and then reread them for a third time.

Setting the sheet on the table, he said, 'What's the problem? Thought our prints are supposed to be removed from the equation.'

'They are.'

'So why are none of you being put on trial?'

'Because our prints weren't found all over the crime scene, Jake.'

At that moment, Jake was transported back to Old Manor House, a foster home for teenagers and children who'd suffered trauma in their life – the death of a relative, most commonly. He'd been spending the afternoon with Lewis Coyne, a former member of Henry Matheson's gang, when he'd received a text message from an unknown number, explaining who The Cabal was.

The one you want is D.

Jake had thought that had stood for Dick Candy. Now he wasn't so sure.

'Am I being put on trial?'

'How else do you explain it? Ninety-five per cent print coverage, Jake. It's almost as if you made them that obvious on purpose.'

'Are you listening to yourself right now?' Jake snapped, jumping on the defensive. He didn't know how the fingerprints had got there, but he sure as hell wasn't going to stand for this interrogation.

'First, you didn't pick up my call. Second, you arrived late. Third, you had alcohol all over your breath. It's got some of the alarm bells ringing, Jake, I must admit. Tell me where you were between the hours of 8 p.m. and 11 p.m. on Wednesday.'

Jake sighed, rolled his eyes and muttered under his breath in disbelief. He couldn't believe what was happening. It was unfathomable. Unbelievable. History repeating itself for a third time.

'Am I being charged?'

'You want to go down that route?'

'I think you need to make a decision.'

Darryl looked down at the table, deep in thought. Battling with his personal connection to Jake and his professional one to the job. He stroked his lip with his thumb and forefinger.

The tension infuriated Jake. He hadn't slept in over forty-eight hours, and he hadn't eaten a proper meal in over twelve. And his wires were becoming rapidly shorter and more fried with every passing second.

Eventually Darryl cleared his throat and lifted his head to look at Jake.

'Jake Tanner, I am arresting you for the murders of Helena Haversham, Rupert Haversham and Felicity Haversham. You do not have to say anything. But it may harm your defence if you do not mention when questioned something which you later rely on in court. Anything you do say may be given in evidence.'

CHAPTER 18

SITUATION

Jake flushed cold. A lump swelled in his throat. And it felt like the four walls surrounding him were rapidly closing in, knives and blades and spears and sharp wooden sticks protruding from the surfaces, ready to impale him. Nausea quickly rolled over him and disappeared like a fighter jet streaming overhead. Was this it? Could this really be happening? The end of his career. The end of his marriage. The end of his life as he'd known it. The end of his financial struggles too…?

Darryl cleared his throat again and pressed the button on the recorder. After the harsh buzzing sound finished, he began.

'Interview commenced at 10:33 a.m. Present is Detective Chief Inspector Darryl Hughes. Being interviewed is Jake Tanner. Please state your name for the tape.'

'*Detective Constable* Jake Tanner,' he said, taking any win he could get.

'Before we begin, I would like to remind you of your rights. You do not have to say anything. You have the right to legal advice – which you may ask for at any time throughout the interview process. And you have the right to make a phone call to notify someone that you're here. Would you like to action any of these?'

Jake shook his head. 'Not yet.'

Darryl cleared his throat again. 'Thank you for confirming,' he said. 'Where were you on the night of thirteenth April?'

Jumping in at the deep end already, are we?

'At my mother-in-law's.'

'All evening?'

'Most of it.'

'Can you remember what time you left?'

'I think it might have been at about nine o'clock.'

'And where did you go after that?'

'Home.'

'Did you drive?'

'I'd had a couple of beers and was feeling inebriated. It would have been irresponsible of me to get behind the wheel. Elizabeth drove instead,' he lied. He didn't want Darryl to know his home life was currently a mess – that Elizabeth had all but left him.

'Elizabeth?' Darryl asked, pretending as though he didn't know who Jake was referring to.

'My *wife*.' He leant closer to the microphone on the recorder, keeping his eyes fixed on Darryl. 'E-L-I-Z-A-B-E-T-H. And she is my wife. W-I-F-E. Just to avoid any further confusion.'

Darryl scowled at Jake malevolently, but he paid it little heed. It was barbaric to think that he was being interviewed in connection with these murders. He'd given everything he had to finding The Cabal and the people behind his empire, and now he was being treated as a suspect.

The Cabal. Still out there, trotting about as if there's nothing wrong.

D for Darryl.

'Thank you for that, Jake. What were you doing for the rest of the evening, after you'd come home from your mother-in-law's?'

'I carried on drinking.'

'Feeling festive? Celebrating anything?'

'Not that it's relevant, but yes.'

'Oh?'

'Like I said, it's not relevant.'

The interview process was one of the elements of the job Jake adored the most. The battle of egos, the battle for information. Chipping away at the suspect's usually hardened exterior. Each interview and suspect represented a mountain to climb. At first they started out tough, the elements fighting back, but after he got into the groove of it and his head above the clouds, he was usually at the top in no time. After all, everyone had something they were eager to reveal, a confession to make – especially the horrible bastards who slaughtered and murdered innocent individuals for no reason. They did so because it satisfied their ego, and all that did was make it easier for Jake to get to the top, like a gust of fortuitous wind blowing him all the way. Yet, during his tenure with the police, he'd never come across his Mount Everest. The pinnacle of his career.

But for his boss, a man whose experience outshone Jake's two to one, he was going to make sure he was Darryl's Everest. And there would be no handy gusts of winds to get him to the top.

'Do you have any relationship or have you ever had any interaction with Rupert Haversham?' Darryl continued.

Jake shook his head. 'Only when I've been opposite him in an interview room like you and I are now. That's the most intimate we've been.'

'So you've never seen him nor spent any time with him outside of a professional capacity?'

Jake hesitated. Raised his eyebrow. What did Darryl know? And then he realised the CCTV footage inside the house would incriminate him for being there hours before their death. Did they have access to it already? He didn't want them to find it. He didn't want to have to explain why he'd hidden his partnership with Rupert from Darryl; that he'd been fraternising with the enemy; that they might begin to suspect he was The Cabal; that his home life had a black mark against it. They could never find out.

'Jake?'

'No,' he replied without thinking. 'Never met up with him – or any other member of his family – outside of my professional capacity.'

'Do you have any idea what might have happened to Erica Haversham?'

'Are you asking me in a professional capacity or as a suspect?'

Darryl relaxed into the back of his chair, shuffled and then stammered. 'He… I… You…' He cleared his throat and continued. 'On the night in question, I tried to call you several times. You missed nine of them. What were you doing at that time which forced you to miss my calls?'

'Sleeping. All that beer'd got to me. I fell asleep on the couch. Elizabeth left me there and went to bed shortly after I'd conked out.'

Darryl paused, looked down at the sheets of paper as though they would inspire his next question, and then scratched his ear.

'So,' he began. 'You say you were drunk on the night of the murders?'

'Yes.'

'And you didn't stop drinking until just before you'd fallen asleep at…?'

'Ten p.m.'

'So, Jake, were you not, when attending the crime scene at approximately midnight, driving under the influence of alcohol? A severe offence in anyone's eyes, let alone a police officer's.'

Jake sighed and swore under his breath. He'd fallen for that one hook, line and sinker.

'It's impossible to know without having done a breath test. One man's drunk is another man's sober – especially for someone who doesn't drink that frequently.'

'So why were you drinking in the first place? Special occasion?'

Jake knew what Darryl was trying to get at. But he wasn't going to give it to him.

'Like I said, not relevant. Fabricate this as much as you want, but I didn't do it. I did not kill Rupert, Helena or Felicity Haversham, and I have no idea where Erica might be, either. And you know it too. You know this is as far-fetched as that time I was accused of colluding with The Crimsons and getting them out of prison. Call Elizabeth, ask her to come in for a statement. Treat her as a suspect too.' He knew she would cover for him, regardless of what was going on between them at the moment. 'God knows we haven't got enough going on, so why not add this little piece of shit to the mixture.'

'Jake, you—'

'And I want to know who supplied you with those fingerprints. I've been set up.'

'That's the first time I think you've denied your fingerprints being there,' Darryl replied. 'What made you change your mind.'

'The fact that they're ninety-five per cent accurate. Nobody leaves fingerprints that perfect unless they've been placed on purpose. Perhaps, for example, when police officers have to give their prints so they can be ruled out of any further investigations.'

Darryl stared at Jake for a long moment. There was something in the man's eyes – a glimmer, a reflection – that said he knew it was all bullshit but couldn't rule it out. The evidence was conclusive.

'Am I still a police officer?' Jake asked.

Darryl pursed his lips before responding. 'Following the evidence given to me, at this time I am charging you with one offence related to Section 5 of the Road Traffic Act 1988 for driving under the influence. For now, however, I will not be charging you with the murders of Rupert, Helena and Felicity Haversham, but we will keep you in custody until we believe we have sufficient evidence.'

A crippling knot, as strong as the tide, formed in Jake's stomach. The sensation rippled and swayed up and down his body, into his chest, throat, then back down to his gut, where it settled in his arse. He felt like he was going to throw up and shit himself at the same time. In all the years, in all the allegations that had been thrown at him, his career had never been undone by any of them. But now... now it was his own mistake that had created his downfall.

'An escorting officer will take you to the custody suite where you will be formally charged and placed in a cell. You will remain there until we either charge you further or release you on bail.'

'Guv, no. Don't do this. You can't.'

'I'm sorry, Jake.'

With that, Darryl terminated the interview, removed the disk from the recorder, and grabbed the papers on the desk. He slammed the recording device shut and started out of the room.

'You know someone's been after me for ages. You know someone's been out to get me for years now! You know it!'

Darryl stopped at the door and turned to face Jake. 'Richard Candy's dead, Jake. You can't use that as an excuse anymore.'

'You're wrong. Yes, Candy is dead. But The Cabal isn't. The Cabal's still out there, and I can prove it.'

Darryl depressed the handle and opened the door. Before leaving, he remarked: 'Get some sleep, Jake. You look like you could use it.'

It was funny. Jake had spent years trying to put bent coppers behind bars. And now he was becoming one of them. The thing he'd fought so hard to destroy. The thing he'd fought so hard to scare out of the police service. And, for the first time in his life, he wished Liam was back. That his old, bent boss was still a part of the team. Because if there was one thing his old bent boss could do, it was get him out of this clusterfuck of a situation.

CHAPTER 19

TARNISH

The images on the TV screen moved rapidly, but Elizabeth paid them no attention. Her mind was elsewhere, blank, an empty canvas of thought waiting for the next torrent of fear and images of *him* to appear, only for it to reset and happen again. And again. And again. On repeat, like it had been for the past few hours. In fact, she didn't know how long she'd been sitting there. She was vaguely aware that it could have been the entire night, but equally, it could have only been thirty minutes. Time was no longer a construct or reality that she found herself situated in. She was both in and around her body, floating, hovering, suffering.

A knock came at the living-room door. She heard it but chose to ignore it. She already knew who it was, and she already knew her mother would come into the room regardless of whether she granted her permission or not.

'I made you a coffee,' Martha said, entering the living room with a steaming mug in her hand. 'There's also a tea in the kitchen if you'd prefer that.'

'Neither,' Elizabeth replied, keeping her eyes fixed on the TV.

At that moment, she became acutely aware of what she was watching. A cartoon programme. Animated. Something to do with superheroes and dogs dressed as humans. She groaned internally and struggled to break her eyes from the screen. Same shit, different day. There was no escape from it. Every morning. Every single fucking morning.

'I checked on the girls,' her mother began. 'They're still sleeping. I didn't want to wake them. I don't think we should send them to nursery today. I think they should stay here.'

'They go.'

'Liz, you're not—'

'They're my daughters.'

'And I'm only doing what's best for—'

'I said they're going to nursery!' Elizabeth bellowed at her mother. It was an innate, maternal reaction. A raw anger and aggression that disappeared as soon as the final syllable had left her lips. Calmly, she said: 'I'm not paying a grand a month for them to sit at home and skive off.'

'Skive off? They're a bit young for that.'

'I'll take them.'

'No. You need to rest. I'll get the girls ready and take them out for a little drive. Give them some fresh air and a change of scenery.'

'They're not fucking dogs.' Her mother had outstayed her welcome, and the longer she remained, the shorter Elizabeth's fuse would be.

'Yes. You're right. Of course.'

Martha moved closer to her and sat beside her on the sofa. Elizabeth scrunched her knees into her chest and wrapped her arms around them, shrinking herself into a human ball.

'I didn't mean to upset you, Liz. But I'm worried about you.'

'I'm an adult.'

'But you shouldn't have to be going through this alone.'

'Like I said. Adult.'

'You're missing the point, darling. Nobody should have to go through this.'

'But I have, Mum, haven't I? I *have* gone through this. And I keep going through it. And I keep going through it. And I keep going through it. Again. And again. And again. And again. Every second of every minute, I relive in my mind what that man did to me. I relive where he tried to touch me. What he tried to do to me. His body on top of mine. His weight. His smell. His sweaty hands. His disgusting breath. I see the smirk on his face every time I close my eyes. I'm scared to sleep because that's when I'm most vulnerable, that's when I'm afraid he might do it again, and again, and again, and again, and —'

Martha placed a hand on Elizabeth's arm, instantly shutting her off like she'd pressed a switch. She hadn't realised it, but she was rocking back and forth on the sofa. Tears had formed in her eyes and distorted her vision. Everything had become a blur.

Without saying anything, Martha enveloped Elizabeth in her arms, clutching her tightly against her body.

Her mother's warmth instantly radiated through her and transported her back twenty years to when she was a child, bawling her eyes out after she'd fallen from a tree and cut her knee. The warm and tender embrace of a mother, the only person in the world who could make everything bright again and banish the darkness away. Elizabeth never wanted to leave it. But she also realised that if she could give her girls the same feeling of love and protection that her mother gave her, then she would consider herself a good mum responsible for a good job well done.

What should have been a beautiful moment was beautifully interrupted.

The doorbell sounded in the distance. Elizabeth jumped and shook with fear, clinging to her mum's knitted cardigan.

'It's fine,' Martha said. 'It's OK. Everything's OK. I'll open it. I'll be right back.'

Tentatively, Martha eased herself off the sofa and shuffled towards the front door. Elizabeth lowered her legs to the floor and listened. She heard voices but was unable to discern what was said. Too far away, too hushed, too secretive. Then the door closed and she waited.

A few seconds later, her mum appeared in the door frame.

'Who was it?'

Elizabeth had her answer a fraction of a second later: two uniformed police officers entered behind her mother. At the sight of them, she leapt out of her chair, only one thing in her mind.

'Oh my God. Is it Jake? Has something happened to him? Is he all right?'

'Liz. Honey. This isn't about him.' She turned to the officers. 'I called them. They're here to talk to you.'

Elizabeth's throat tightened. This was worse, much worse. For a split second, she hoped that something had happened to Jake just so that she wouldn't have to go through this and experience everything again. She wasn't sure if she could relive it for the fifteenth time in one day.

'I... I...'

How could her mother betray her like this, after she'd told her explicitly not to call the police? She didn't feel angry; she felt scared. Scared that her attacker was behind them. That he was going to come out and assault her again. That it would be even worse than the first time. That he was going to kill her.

'Mrs Tanner,' the officer closest to her mother began, taking a small step forward. He introduced himself as PC Davies and his colleague as PC Albrighton. 'Your mother informed us you needed to make a statement about an assault.'

Elizabeth scowled at her mother and tried to open her mouth, but nothing happened. Ever since Jake had first joined the police force, she'd taken a keen interest in the ins and outs of the rules, the procedures, the technicalities, and she'd even gone so far as to ask for advice and best practices on making statements and the interview process. At first, it had just been a bit of fun, an intriguing way to pass the time. But then, as Jake delved deeper into the deplorable world of police corruption and drug dealers and death, she became more aware that, one day, she might need to make a statement about something in order to protect her husband. Yet at no point had she prepared herself to give a statement about something that had happened to her.

Despite all the training Jake had given her, her mind turned white, devoid of everything he'd once told her.

'I have nothing to say,' she said.

'Elizabeth, don't be stupid, please. You have to report this man. These people want to help you,' Martha implored. 'We have to make sure he doesn't do this to anyone else.'

Elizabeth wasn't sure that was possible.

'Nothing happened,' she said. 'It's already being dealt with. Don't worry. Jake's on top of it all.'

'We might be able to assist whatever it is your husband's taking care of,' PC Albrighton said.

'How do you know my husband?'

'We're aware of DC Tanner's position and who he is. He's branded as something of a hero amongst many in the service. But for some… not so much.' Albrighton pivoted on the spot and shared a knowing glance with PC Davies.

At once, alarm bells sounded inside Elizabeth's head. Jake had a notoriety, yes. But that was in Stratford. She was in Croydon. The two locations were worlds apart in terms of London and crime rates, so how did they know who Jake was so readily? As part of her training, Jake had taught her the ABC method. It was simple: assume nothing, believe nothing, challenge everything.

And Elizabeth was going to do exactly that.

'I'd like you to leave, please,' she said, folding her arms across her chest.

'Liz, don't do this,' Martha began, stepping closer towards her. 'You're making a—'

'Gentlemen,' Elizabeth started, ignoring her mother. 'I appreciate the time and effort you've made, but right now I would like you to leave. There are some more discussions I need to have with my husband. There's nothing you can do that he can't, and right now I don't feel comfortable having you in this house.'

PC Albrighton's face remained taciturn. He pocketed the notebook and pen she hadn't seen him remove and then started out of the house.

'Thank you for your time,' he said, hovering by the door just as he was about to leave. 'But Mrs Tanner – and I hope you don't mind my saying this – your husband is a brilliant detective, but just because he deals with corrupt and bent coppers doesn't mean you need to tarnish us all with the same brush. We're good guys too. Not everyone is like the people your husband puts away. I hope you remember that the next time you need us.'

And then he was gone. Elizabeth stared into the space he'd just been. His words had slapped her across the face and made her realise something deeper than she wanted: not everyone was like Liam Greene, Drew Richmond, Elliot Bridger, Pete Garrison, Helen Clements, Martin Radcliffe, Richard Candy. Not everyone was a bad egg, looking to corrupt others for their own personal and financial gain.

Before she was able to think of anything else, she was distracted by her phone ringing.

She answered.

'Is it Jake?'

'Hey, Liz. It's Darryl.'

'Is it Jake?'

'I'm going to need you to come down to the station as soon as you can, please.'

'Is it Jake?'

'I can't say too much at the moment, Liz. And I really don't want to be made to say it over the phone. But he's safe. I just need you to come down to the station ASAP. It's urgent.'

CHAPTER 20

FLOWERS

Just over an hour later, Elizabeth stormed into Bow Green. The car journey there had been filled with even more anxiety and despair, and for over half of it, she was sure she hadn't focused on the road at all.

As she hurried through the foyer towards the reception desk, she caught a whiff of her body odour. She hadn't showered, and she'd been sweating during the night. Not to mention she'd neglected to brush her teeth before leaving the house. But she didn't care. She just felt sorry for whoever had to deal with her.

'My husband. Jake Tanner. Where is he?'

Before the officer behind the desk could respond, Darryl appeared out the corner of her eye.

'Thanks for coming.'

'Are you going to tell me what's going on?'

'I'm afraid not yet. Would you mind coming with me, please?'

Reluctantly, Elizabeth followed him into a small room of similar size to her mum's bathroom. It had a desk and two chairs positioned opposite one another in the centre, and in the middle of the desk was a recording device. In the top corner of the room was a camera, a small red light flashing intermittently, signalling to her that it was on and fully functional.

'Why do I get the impression that this isn't going to be a cheerful conversation?' Elizabeth asked as she rounded the table and pulled out a chair.

She sensed her mind already putting its defences up. The hours of training with Jake were about to come in handy again. Oddly, she felt more prepared for this than she had back at the house.

'I'm not sure how much you're aware of, Elizabeth, but two nights ago, Rupert Haversham and his family were murdered. They were brutally stabbed to death and we believe one of his daughters is missing.'

Darryl paused for effect, but she gave nothing away in her expression, even though she felt appalled at the news.

'As part of our investigation, we conducted a sweep of the crime scenes and surrounding areas. We found fingerprints on or around all three bodies. They were a direct match to your husband's.'

'What do you need me for?'

'Pardon?'

'What do you need me here for, Darryl? Am I being arrested for something? Am I under caution? Am I a witness to something that Jake didn't do? What am I doing here?'

'I need you to confirm where you were on Wednesday.'

'At my mother's house.'

'Why?'

'We fancied a catch-up.'

'Celebrating anything fancy?'

'Did we need to be?'

'And where was Jake?'

'With me. And my mother. And my two girls. Having a wonderful dinner together.'

'What happened after you'd finished dinner?'

'We left. I can't remember what time it was. Must've been about nine. It was getting late, and we had to put the kids to bed,' she responded without even thinking. It was as though her response was innate, as though Jake had telepathically told her what to say.

'What can you tell me about Jake's demeanour that night?'

She shrugged. 'He was fine. Excitable and lively because he'd had a few to drink. We got home and then we fell asleep because we were shattered.'

No matter what had happened between the two of them in recent months – the lies, the betrayal, the affair – she'd concluded long ago that Jake was her husband, and that he was the man she loved. And, as she'd promised all those years ago, he was the man she would protect and hold, for he was still a decent human being, and an even greater father.

'And, to the best of your recollection,' Darryl continued, 'does Jake know, or has Jake ever mentioned, Rupert Haversham's name to you?'

'Sometimes he tells me about the cases he's working on and, sure, that name's sprung up a few times. But other than that, no.'

That was a lie. Jake did know Rupert. And so did she. But she wasn't going to tell Darryl that. She didn't want him to know that Rupert was investigating her sexual assault case. She didn't want him to know that Jake had been to see Rupert at her request on the day he'd died.

'If you don't mind my asking,' Darryl continued, sniffling, 'is everything all right at home? Is there anything that I should know about on a professional level that might impact Jake's performance?'

She shook her head, offended by the insinuation. 'Jake's a very proud man, Darryl. You should know that by now. He wouldn't tell you his mum had just died if he knew it was going to get in the way of his work. He wouldn't even tell me. He puts his work above everything else, and you know it. He pushes himself too hard and puts in far too much for very little back – and this is how he's being treated for it? I thought you of all people would understand and appreciate that about him. What happened to ABC? Is it not part of your responsibility to challenge everything you see? Why aren't you challenging *this*? You know Jake isn't capable of this. Someone's done this to him – someone's putting him in the frame for murder.'

Darryl knitted his fingers together and wore the embarrassed look of a child. A middle-aged man reduced to a single figure. Without meaning to, she'd just concluded the interview.

'Where is he?' she asked. 'I want to see him.'

'He's in a cell. But don't worry, he's being given the presidential treatment. The doctors said he needed to rest, so he's got a nice bed.'

'Doctors?' Elizabeth snapped. 'Doctors? What are you talking about, "*doctors*"?'

Darryl hesitated for a long while. Then cleared his throat. 'You don't know? He hasn't told you?'

'You're scaring me, Darryl. What's going on?'

'Jake was involved in a car incident. Down by the Cosgrove Estate. Someone threw a petrol bomb inside the car and blew it up.'

'Oh my God,' Elizabeth whispered. Her lips moved, but nothing but air came out. 'Is he… Is he…'

'He didn't tell you?' Darryl asked, with the glimmer of a smirk on his face.

'He… he… he doesn't like to wake me and the kids unless it's really urgent.'

Darryl nodded in reluctant acceptance of her response and opened the door. In silence, the two of them wandered through a myriad of brilliantly lit corridors, down a flight of stairs and into the custody cells.

Lying on the bed at the back of one of them was her husband. The man that had kept last night's events from her.

That makes two of us.

With one arm resting behind his head, propping his neck up like a pillow, the other lying by his side covered in bandages, he looked relaxed. White pieces of fabric had been placed over his face and the lower half of his neck.

As soon as the door opened, he rolled off the bed and rushed towards Elizabeth. The three-week scruff on his face prickled and chafed her skin as he buried his head into her neck. He hugged her tightly – more tightly than he had in the past year – and to her surprise, she hugged him back with the same vigour and adoration. The events of the past few months disappeared, and it was just the two of them again, on their own, delighting in a pure moment with one another. Elizabeth's body tingled, and she pulled away, kissing him on the lips and stroking his hair.

'I'll give you two a second,' Darryl said, starting out of the room. 'Sounds like you've got some catching up to do.'

'Wait,' Jake called after him. 'What's happening? Am I done? Are you letting me out?'

Darryl pursed his lips. 'I've got some paperwork to fill out.'

With that, he left and closed the door behind him.

As soon as the door slammed shut, rage washed over her, the last few moments of intimacy disappearing as though they'd never existed. Before Jake could open his mouth, she slapped him on the cheek. The connection was half-hearted, but she hoped her intentions were clear.

'What was that for?'

'You've got some explaining to do. When were you going to tell me about Rupert? When were you going to tell me about the petrol bomb? Eh? I just had to lie through my teeth to make sure nothing happens to you.'

'Liz, I can explain,' Jake said, holding his hands up in defence.

She folded her arms across her chest. 'I'm waiting.'

'It's complicated…'

'Please tell me you had nothing to do with it.'

'Are you genuinely asking me that?'

'How am I supposed to know the truth anymore? I haven't seen you since you stormed out of my mum's. I have no idea what you've been doing since then. For all I know, you could have gone to Rupert's and killed them all.'

'What did you say? What did you tell Darryl?' Jake paced from side to side, running his fingers through his hair.

'Nothing. I told him nothing. I hope I was right to, Jake.'

'Yes. Of course you were. I have no idea how my prints were found at the scene, I'm telling you. Somebody put them there, I'm sure. But Darryl, in true Darryl fashion, wouldn't believe it.'

'I said the same thing. I told him you were being framed.'

Jake stopped abruptly, his face beaming. He placed his hands round her hips and leant in for a kiss on the lips, but she pulled away and gave him a cheek instead.

'I knew I could rely on you. That training came in handy, didn't it?'

Of course it had, but she wasn't about to give him the satisfaction of knowing that.

'How's your face?' she asked. 'It looks bad.'

'It's fine. Stings now and then. Brendan was a lot worse. He's still in A&E now. Doctors were operating on him. Third-degree burns all over his face and head and arms.'

Elizabeth glanced down at the floor solemnly. Images of Brendan flashed into her mind. Of the time they'd all celebrated Jake's birthday round their house; of the time Brendan had dropped Jake off in the early hours of the morning following someone's leaving do; of how he smiled at almost everything and at any point during the day.

She looked up at Jake. 'I'll send him a card and some flowers.'

'I'm sure he'd like that.'

'I'm not bringing the kids to see you. I don't think they should see you with all these bandages on your face. Can you wait until they come off?'

Jake dipped his head. 'If you want me to, yes.'

'Have you got enough food and drink at home? Enough to sustain you?' Before she gave Jake a chance to answer, she continued. 'Don't worry about it – I'll go to the shops and buy you some bits.'

'You don't have to…'

'Put your ego aside for a minute and let me do this for you. It might be the last time I ever offer.' She fought to suppress a smile.

Just as Jake was about to respond again, the door opened with a sharp piercing noise behind her.

'Good news, kid,' Darryl said, standing in the door frame. 'You're good to go.'

CHAPTER 21

SPEAK OF THE DEVIL

When he finally returned to his desk, twenty minutes later, Jake slumped into his chair, stretched his legs and yawned. The soft padding – which until this point he'd deemed one of the most uncomfortable materials he'd ever had the misfortune of sitting on – massaged and relaxed his vertebrae, easing the tension in his lower back and neck. Leaps and bounds ahead of the solid mattress he'd been forced to lie on in the cell. From that moment on, he would never take an uncomfortable chair for granted.

Jake yawned again and decided to make himself a coffee. As he lifted himself out of his chair, he realised how sparse the office was. No Brendan. No Darryl. No Ashley. Just him and Alison, the detective constable who'd recently joined them, and a handful of other DCs in the team.

The kitchen was even quieter, which surprised him because it was usually the hub of entertainment, socialising, gossip. The place where, for a few minutes, they could come and switch off and discuss normal things like the latest episode of *Game of Thrones* or the last season of *Breaking Bad*. Little things to remind them they were human beings, rather than robots numbed to the horror and pernicious behaviours of the depraved and wicked.

'Good morning, stranger,' came a voice from the other side of the kitchen. 'What happened to your face?'

Lindsay Gray stepped into the room carrying a brown paper bag and rushed towards him. In her late fifties, she was old enough to be his mother, and sometimes he treated her like that, using her as an impartial sounding board for advice and guidance. But now she insisted on inspecting his hands and face, scrupulously analysing the extent of his injuries.

'What the hell happened?'

'It's nothing to worry about,' he said. 'Brendan's worse off. He's in Whipps Cross now.'

'Were you there with him?'

Jake dropped his gaze to the floor. 'Yeah,' he replied slowly.

Lindsay moved across the kitchen and returned her attention to the bag. 'Have you got any idea who did it to you?'

'Not exactly. But we were at The Pit. It was just another one of Henry Matheson's men carrying out his dirty work, I suppose.' Jake spoke as though there was no life left in him – no emotion, no passion, no excitement, nothing. A part of him hoped Lindsay would pick up on it.

'You just need to be careful out there.'

'Where's everyone else? Hardly anyone here.'

'I don't know, but I went for a walk and brought breakfast back with me. You want some?'

Jake moved to the kettle and switched it on. Then he realised there was no water in it. His mind wandered as he hovered the kettle under the sink.

'Jake,' Lindsay called. 'Jake.'

Eventually, he came to and saw her holding an all-butter croissant in her hands. Jake's stomach rumbled at the sight of it.

'If you wouldn't mind,' he said, realising what she'd asked him.

He stalked across the room, took a packet from her and returned to the cupboards, where he grabbed himself a mug and filled it with coffee powder.

'Jake,' Lindsay insisted, appearing by his side. 'Is everything all right? Is there anything else going on? You can talk to me, you know.'

'I just…' He recced the kitchen, made sure it was safe and that there was nobody listening, and then continued. 'The past few weeks I've just been feeling so alone, so isolated. I hate it. Now Brendan's in hospital. Ashley's doing her own thing – kissing up to Darryl at every given opportunity. And Darryl's been making it his life's mission to make me suffer. I haven't slept properly in weeks. Elizabeth doesn't live with me anymore, so I've got no one to talk to when I get back from work. No kids either. Just me and the TV. And even then I'm too restless to focus on it at all. It's just…' Jake paused. 'I'm struggling.'

The words he'd bottled up and kept locked away, now released, lifted a mountain of despair from his body and pulled him into the air where, for the first time in a long time, he felt able to breathe again.

Lindsay placed a hand on his arm and squeezed, smiling affectionately at him. 'Have you asked about taking some time off? Give yourself some time to sort your headspace, work everything out?'

'I can't. Things are too manic here. Especially with us being a man down too. Work keeps me busy, and I worry I'd be too bored at home.'

'If you work yourself too much though, Jake,' Lindsay began, 'you won't make it to the end to see this through. And you know it.

Nobody'll praise you for trying to act like the hero when one isn't needed. And this place certainly isn't going to give you the recognition and adoration you deserve. You think about yourself for a change. I've been in this job long enough to realise that those who make themselves known are the ones who suffer the most. Sounds backward, I know. But when people in positions of power see your name more and more frequently, they panic. They get jealous. They get worried about the up and comer rising through the ranks. Then they play dirty against you.'

You can say that again.

D for Darryl…

Speak of the devil and he shall appear.

The chief inspector stood in the doorway, looking proud of himself. 'Ah, here you are,' he said to Jake. 'There's something I need to discuss with you.'

'What now?'

'Erica Haversham. It's now been over forty-eight hours and there's still no sign of her from any of her friends or teachers or family members. We are now classifying her as a missing person. Which means both MIT and MisPers will be working together on this case.'

CHAPTER 22

STEPHANIE THE SAINT

Elizabeth inserted her house key with an enormous amount of trepidation. It was the first time she'd been home in three months. Three months since she'd picked up everything she and the kids needed. And she didn't know what to expect. What sort of condition had Jake left the house in? A part of her – a small part admittedly – expected him to have cleaned and tidied and kept it in pristine condition. But then she realised how well she knew her husband; that, if it weren't for her, it wouldn't be tidy, and the mug she'd accidentally left on the kitchen counter would still be there three months on.

She twisted the key, opened the door and made to step inside. But the door stopped halfway, blocked by something behind it. She peered it round and gasped, dropping the small bag of provisions she'd bought him to the floor.

'Oh, Jake,' she whispered as she kicked the piles of newspaper and junk mail and letters to the side, forging a path through her house.

Once inside, she stormed down the corridor and into the kitchen. Her estimations about her husband had been completely accurate. The house was a mess. A catastrophe. Worse, Jake was a mess. How could he have let it get this bad? Dirt and dried food and drink stains swamped the surfaces. Plates and cutlery overflowed from the sink. The bin was full, with tins of beer and oven meals placed neatly on top of one another in a pile beside it. Her once immaculate house – the one she'd spent her mornings and afternoons cleaning laboriously – was nothing short of a landfill site. And the man she loved was responsible.

She didn't even know where to begin.

But then something caught her eye – the laptop on the table to her left. The lid was half-closed, and resting atop the keyboard was a letter. As though it was meant to be hidden. Elizabeth didn't need to read the letter to know what it was likely about. In the past few years, ever since Maisie had been born, they'd been plagued with penalty notices, default payments, rising bills and charges on all of their accounts. They weren't poor, but they were by no means rich either.

In the months that they'd been apart, Jake had called her to discuss some of the incoming bills and work out a strategy of how they were going to pay them back. Either he hadn't followed through on his word, or these were fresh ones he hadn't told her about. To her it seemed funny that, despite their temporary separation, there was still one thing keeping them in contact with one another. It wasn't the girls. It wasn't their love for one another. No, it was the little pieces of paper in her purse and the numbers in her bank account. She hated that a part of their relationship's downfall had been over the one thing they'd both sworn to care little about when they'd first got together. They'd been students – having no money was second nature to them – and they'd managed to get by then, so what was different now? Yes, they had the girls, but everything had been fine before…

Elizabeth lifted the laptop screen, and the pixels illuminated, the login page flashing up. She took the letter and read the header. It was from the bank, notifying Jake that he was in his overdraft – and rapidly running out of money in there.

'Jake…' she whispered. 'What are you doing?'

Before she allowed her mind to dwell on it further, she pulled the chair out from beneath the table and sat down. She entered Jake's laptop password, set the letter on the table, and waited.

A few seconds later, a picture of the family appeared. Smiling, happy, enjoying better times in front of the snow-capped mountains of the Scottish Highlands, with a rare sighting of the Northern Lights overhead, whipping and swaying in their ephemeral green and turquoise. A flicker rose on her lips. It had only been five months ago, but it felt like a year. It had been a simpler, happier time.

She moved the cursor to the bottom of the screen and opened Google Chrome.

The tabs had still been left open, and as soon as the application launched, Elizabeth's eyes widened. In front of her was the gambling site she'd caught him on previously. The site that had caused such a disruption in their marriage the first time round.

'You arsehole,' she said as she moved the cursor and hovered it over Jake's profile.

The bank balance appeared and showed her there were no funds in the account. Then she moved to the betting history tab in the top right of the screen. The page refreshed and showed a list of all the bets Jake had placed in the past three weeks. Her body turned cold as her eyes fell over the numbers. In the space of a few days, he'd burnt through over a thousand pounds on horses, football matches, roulette tables, and even cricket. And yet he hadn't made any of their money back.

Fury swelled within her.

On the kitchen counter, their landline started to ring. It shocked her, but after realising what it was, she ignored it. If it was important, they'd call back or leave a message.

Focusing her attention back on the laptop, Elizabeth removed her mobile and started snapping photographs of the account. Jake needed to admit there was a problem. And he needed help from a professional.

Because he sure as fuck isn't going to listen to anything I tell him.

A combination of emotions roared through her body, too many at once for her to channel and focus on.

But then the decision was made for her.

Anger.

The telephone stopped ringing and the automation system told the caller to leave a message after the tone.

The tone sounded. The message began.

'Hey, Jake.'

Elizabeth recognised the voice instantly.

Anger turned into fury, then into resentment.

'It's me, Steph. Listen – I know you're probably at work or still in the hospital, but I wanted to send you my regards. I heard about what happened with Brendan and I wanted to make sure you were OK.'

A long pause. Elizabeth lifted her head and glared at the machine, shooting daggers at it.

'Listen,' Stephanie eventually continued, 'I miss you. I know I shouldn't be telling you this after what happened. But I hate the way things have been between us. That night was a mistake – we both know that. And I don't think we should let that—'

She leapt out of the chair and pounced on the telephone, snapping it out of the cradle and unleashing a torrent of fire and fury at Stephanie on the other end.

'You've got some nerve calling here, you bitch. What gives you the right to call my home? You destroyed this family once, and I won't let you destroy it again, you whore. The next time you call, I will look for you and I will find you. Stay out of our fucking lives.'

Stephanie the Saint.

Stephanie the Shitbag.

Elizabeth gripped the phone in her hands. Clenched it until she felt the plastic creak and give way. Then she slammed it down on the cradle. Again. And again. And again. Until shards of plastic flew across the surface.

In one final act of aggression, she launched the telephone down the corridor, splintering it into a dozen pieces. Then she punched the kitchen counter with the palm of her hand and screamed until her lungs and throat ached.

CHAPTER 23

KEEP YOUR ENEMIES CLOSE

An inexplicable, unrelenting pressure squeezed Jake's head continuously until stars began to swim in his vision. It reminded him of the times his sister used to throw him to the floor and sit on his skull, punching the rest of his incapacitated body into submission until he ceded control of the TV remote. She had been a few years older and almost double his size at that age, and she used to bounce on his head as if he were a space orb.

This time was no different. The tension. The pressure. The pulsating throbbing in the back and front of his skull.

The past forty-eight hours were finally catching up with him. He hadn't slept. His body ached. And his mind felt fatigued.

Jake closed his eyes and rested his forehead on his keyboard. Rich, vibrant colours of yellow and orange battered him from all sides, encompassing him in a deadly duvet of death. He was inside the car again. Reliving the events of the previous night.

Brendan's face appeared in his mind. Happy. Jovial. Then solemn and pensive. And then the bottle had been thrown in. And then the fire had spread across the dashboard. And then the flames had burnt and scarred them both. The stinging. The searing heat. The panic. The claustrophobia. The—

A loud noise sounded in the office, mercifully bringing Jake out of his nightmare. He craned his head over the computer monitor and witnessed Lindsay picking up a stapler from the floor. Returning his attention back to the letters on his keyboard, Jake wiped a film of sweat clean from his forehead and took a sip from the week-old water bottle on his desk.

It was all too much.

He needed fresh air. He needed to do something physical. Take his mind off it all.

But he couldn't afford to spend time away from the investigation. Erica Haversham was still missing, and they were no closer to finding her. The front runner on the suspect list was her boyfriend, but he was proving difficult to locate. And so the killer – or killers – remained at large.

Which reminded him...

Our prints weren't found all over the crime scene, Jake.

Anger rose through him, and he hurried away from his desk, bottle in hand, down to the forensic laboratory. By the time he arrived, the bottle was empty. He discarded it inside a bin and scanned his key card to the building. Only those with special permission were granted access to the building, and after months of nagging, Jake had been granted it by Darryl's predecessor, Liam Greene.

After letting himself in, he meandered through more corridors until he found what he was looking for: Sandy Matthews. She and her team had a designated laboratory where they were responsible for conducting preliminary investigations and preparing evidence before it was sent off to an external laboratory for further forensic examination. If anything was going to happen to the evidence, it would be here.

'Jake,' she said as she swung the door open. She looked startled to see him. 'Is it important? I'm busy.'

Without saying anything, Jake barged past her and stormed into the room.

'What are you doing? You can't just waltz in here whenever you like.'

Jake stopped in the centre of the room. His frustration had reached boiling point and was now bubbling over.

'I need to talk with you,' he said as calmly as he could manage.

Realising it wasn't worth a full-blown argument, Sandy closed the door, brushed herself down and wandered towards him. 'I have a calendar for a reason. You can send me a meeting invite whenever you feel like it.'

'Then why did you close the door?'

Sandy sighed and removed her glasses from her forehead. 'What do you want, Jake?'

'Those fingerprints. Where did you get them from?'

'You mean *your* fingerprints? I found them on the bodies. I shouldn't be discussing this with you. Are you being treated as a suspect?'

'Not anymore,' Jake said, folding his arms across his chest. It was difficult not to sound smug, but then he realised he shouldn't have to sound smug about not being a suspect in a murder investigation in the first place. 'Darryl's dismissed them because I've got an alibi. So how did my prints get on the bodies?'

Sandy's eyes widened, and she looked at him, stunned. 'Do you want me to look into my crystal ball?'

'That's not what I'm saying.'

'Then what do you want from me? My team just find the evidence, sort it and send it off for external examination. We do nothing beyond that.'

Jake sighed and glanced down at the floor. His mind was a mess, frayed, battered. He didn't know what to believe anymore. Back when he had Liam and Drew and Garrison on the team, he'd known where he stood: at the bottom of a corrupt food chain. Back then he'd been oblivious to everything, to all the goings-on behind the scenes, to the corruption that had poisoned three decent police officers. But now he was painfully aware – and suspicious – of what really happened within the police service. A part of him wanted to go back to the good old days where he was naïve to it all, so he wouldn't have to deal with all the stress and the grief of trying to out bent cops. But now that he had notoriety – a certain reputation within the service – it was too late. Jake was stuck in the wormhole of trying to do what was right, and the only people following him were the ones trying to silence him.

'Who has access to the building?' he asked.

'Anyone with permission. Me, the rest of my team and anyone above superintendent.'

D for Darryl.

'And me.'

'How?'

'Liam. I begged him for approval.'

'Have you seen him recently?' Sandy asked, the aggression in her voice dissipating like the sea retreating from the shore.

Jake shook his head.

'From what I hear, he's not in a good way. The cancer's back and is eating the last of him. Doctors have told him he's got a few weeks left.'

'I didn't know you were friends with him.'

'I'm not. I'm just telling you what I heard. You should visit.'

Before Jake could answer, his mobile rang. He silenced her by holding his finger in her face as he answered the call.

'Yes, guv?'

'Where are you? We've just received reports of an abandoned Mercedes parked outside a field in North London. Descriptions match Rupert Haversham's missing car. We're running the number plate through the ringer as we speak. I'll send you the address and I'll meet you there. Nice little chance to redeem yourself. And I want you somewhere I can keep an eye on you. Don't let me down again, Jake.'

D for Darryl keeping him abreast of the information.

D for Darryl for keeping him close.

Friends… Enemies…

Don't let me down again, Jake.

CHAPTER 24

TERRIBLE STUFF

Nancy Cartwright, Governor of HMP Wandsworth, was a woman in her early sixties who looked like she'd spent longer than prescribed on the tanning bed. Either that or she'd just returned from a long holiday in the sun. Somewhere less bleak and grey than dreary London. She was smartly dressed in a dark grey suit, and her hair was cut short. Behind the thin veil of make-up, her wrinkles were beginning to show, and Henry wondered how quickly they'd advanced since she'd started working for the prison service. In his last prison, he'd known the governor very well: meeting him several times to discuss his behaviour and bribery. But as for Nancy Cartwright, he'd only ever met her on a few occasions. This was their first incident-related meeting. A momentous occasion.

Which required a momentous performance if he was going to impress.

The incident in question was the assault on Boris Romanov. Shortly after he had been found screaming in his cell, the screws had started rounding up the prisoners one by one and bringing them in for questioning. Someone somewhere was bound to know something, but so far nobody had said a word. Partly because Henry had been discreet and inconspicuous, and the number of witness could be counted on one hand. And partly because James Longstaff had exercised his influence on those few witnesses.

The Romanians and Albanians were certain it was Henry, but with no evidence or solid eyewitness accounts, he was in the clear.

Just like the good old days.

'I'd like to start this meeting by asking you a very simple question, Henry,' Nancy said. Her voice was soft, and because he didn't hear many women's voices that often now, he found it oddly seductive and imagined her wearing a dominatrix outfit in a red room. 'Do you know anything about what happened to Boris Romanov in his cell?'

'No.'

He couldn't shake the image. Red leather. Spandex.

'Guards reported seeing you with a bottle of bleach in your hands moments before the incident.'

A whip. Some chains.

'Wasn't me, ma'am. Ain't nothing to do with me.'

'They also reported that they could smell the bleach on your hands and clothes. Do you know anything about that?'

Crack!

'Maybe someone had just cleaned the place. That stuff's quite strong, you know.'

Nancy paused and looked down at the notes on her desk. A gentle cough erupted from the prison officer standing guard by the door behind him. Henry had forgotten the man was present, but now that he remembered, he thought maybe he could join in.

A dominatrix, a prison officer and a prisoner, all bundled into one mass of skin and limbs. A wicked fantasy for a wicked man.

'Do you know Boris Romanov?' Nancy continued.

'Not personally. I try to keep myself to myself.'

'Your record would suggest otherwise. In fact, if your record is anything to go by, this is right up your street.'

Henry tried to look offended. 'I'm a changed man, ma'am. I just wanna do my time as easily as possible.'

'So making an allegiance with James Longstaff is your way of achieving that, is it?'

Henry hesitated. She was talking about things that she had no right to know about. How could she have found out so soon? Had Longstaff snitched on him or had someone overheard and ratted them out?

He decided to end this fantasy before she started asking questions he might give away the answers to.

'Do you have any proof it was me?' he asked.

'Is that you confessing?'

'The opposite. I want to get out of here and go back to my cell.'

'For an easy life?'

'Right. An easy life.'

Where he could imagine himself having sex with people his own age.

'Do you have any forensics?' Henry asked.

No response.

'And you don't have any eyewitnesses either?'

No response.

'And you don't have any evidence to suggest it was me, other than your fanatical theories?'

No response.

Henry tutted, shaking his head. 'Well, shit. I hope you find the guy who did this, I really do. But if we're done here, I'd like to go back to my cell.'

Nancy glanced up at the prison officer, flicked her eyes, and immediately disregarded Henry, returning her attention to the notes in front of her. Before he knew it, Henry was being lifted out of the chair and escorted out of the room.

When they came to the door, he stopped and called back, 'I forgot to ask: how is Boris? Were his injuries severe?'

Nancy offered him a moment of her attention. 'His feet suffered third-degree burns. He's lucky they're not having to be amputated.'

'Terrible stuff,' Henry said as he was ushered out. 'Terrible stuff indeed.'

CHAPTER 25

TWO THORNS

Dylan's head pounded so hard it felt like he'd gone the full twelve rounds with Muhammad Ali, Mike Tyson, Tyson Fury and all the other heavyweight champions of the world at once. The unending squeezing sensation was making him feel sick, and it sent the world spinning in a carousel of grey and white, save for the sporadic interjection of green and red from Erica's hoodie.

The past thirty hours – which had felt like three hundred – were a blur. A mirage of euphoria. A perfect and beautiful chance to forget and ignore what they'd done. But that had all come crashing back to earth as soon as Dylan realised Erica was still on the sofa. Unconscious. Unmoving. Her breathing shallow.

Dylan pressed the back of his hand against her forehead again. Cold. Almost freezing. Almost devoid of life. Then he moved his finger down to her neck. There he found a pulse, but it was faint. Very faint. Dylan had only ever experienced a pulse that faint – his little brother, Ricky – a few years ago, and the outcome had been severe. To this day, it still haunted him. And he couldn't begin to imagine what it would be like if the same thing happened again.

'You fucking idiot, Dyl,' he chided himself. He'd gone overboard. The heroin had been the final nudge over the edge. He'd given her too much. Now she was dying.

And it was all his fault.

Dylan's chest rose and fell. His breathing quickened, and he started to hyperventilate. Panicking, thrashing his arms around, he searched the flat for his mobile phone. He leapt across the room, throwing pizza boxes and plastic bottles onto the floor, soiling the carpet as he went. Then he returned to the living room, rolled Erica onto her back, and removed the pillows and cushions from beneath her.

There, buried beneath a cushion, was his mobile. He yanked it free and dialled Henry's number. If anyone would know what to do, it would be him.

The phone rang and rang and rang, and then went straight through to voicemail.

'Come on. Come on. Come on.'

Dylan tried again. Still nothing.

A third time.

A fourth.

'What the fuck do you want?' Henry hissed down the phone, eventually. 'I thought I told you to wait until I called.'

'Erica,' he babbled. 'Erica. Erica. She's... she's not... she's not breathing.'

'What have you given her?'

'Everything.'

'Which includes?'

Dylan told him.

'How much heroin?'

'More than... more than me.'

'You fucking idiot. What did you do that for? You know she's a virgin.'

'I... I... She said she wanted it.'

'Don't lie to me.' Henry sighed. 'Once again, I have to fix your mistakes. Useless cunt.'

'Hen, what do I do? Is she going to die?'

'If she dies, or if anything happens to her, I'm making sure you don't get a single fucking penny of Haversham's inheritance.'

No. Not the inheritance. Anything but the inheritance.

'*Please*, Hen. Tell me... I need to know. What do I do?'

Henry sighed again. 'Right, this is what I want you to do: I want you to go into the cupboard, yeah?'

'Yeah?'

'And in that cupboard, do you still have that gun I gave you?'

'Yeah?'

'Right. Well, I want you to shoot yourself in the fucking head with it. I'm done with you, Dylan. You're a useless sack of shit, so why don't you do us all a favour and load two bullets in there for good measure.'

The line went dead before Dylan could respond. He hovered the phone before his face, staring at the screen, at Henry's name, anger boiling in the pit of his stomach, rapidly rising through him like smoke through a chimney. Then he threw the device against the wall. The tiny burner phone split in two. Dylan jumped across the room to it, lifted his leg and then stamped on it repeatedly until the plastic screen splintered and buckled under the weight of his feet. Saliva dribbled from his mouth and down his chin in his frenzied state.

That bastard. That fucking bastard. It suddenly became apparent that there was no inheritance, there was no music career. Henry had just used him to get to Rupert and his family. Dylan had been a pawn in Henry's game. And now that he'd fulfilled his part of the operation, he was surplus to requirements.

You're a useless sack of shit…

With their trust for one another gone, so too was their loyalty. And Dylan sensed a long-overdue, generous dose of karma coming Henry's way, for he had access to a wealth of knowledge. The phone conversations. The text messages. The instructions. The gun in his cupboard. All of which could incriminate Henry and exonerate himself for the murder of the Havershams.

But then he realised that would be a terrible idea. Instead, he needed to do something else. Make it more personal. Hit Henry where it hurt him the most. But where?

Before Dylan could give it any more thought, a noise distracted him. The sound of spluttering. Coughing – Erica choking life back into her veins.

Dylan spun on the spot and rushed over to her. Her head had lolled to the side, and long droplets of saliva dangled from her mouth and stroked the carpet.

'Erica! Are you OK?' he yelled. 'Thank God you're alive. I thought I'd—'

'Where am I?'

'One of Matheson's empty flats. Cosgrove Estate. Remember?'

'What did you do to me?' Erica groaned as she rolled herself onto her back and stared skyward. Her eyes were bloodshot, and her pupils were still the size of dinner plates.

'I…' He paused. 'I didn't do anything. *You* told me you wanted the drugs. I said you didn't need that much, but you told me you wanted it, anyway. I tried to stop you, but you wouldn't listen.'

Erica's eyes moved like glaciers to look at him. Her expression was plain, and the light overhead reflected the deathly white of her skin.

'Really?' she asked. 'I… I don't remember.'

'Did you enjoy it?'

That was the crucial question.

The only question.

A smirk grew on Erica's face. 'I still am.'

Henry paced about his cell, the rapid movements gradually dissipating the anger in his blood.

Dylan.

Dylan, Dylan, Dylan.

Dylan had always been the wild card in his operation to get revenge on Rupert Haversham and The Cabal. The young man was a liability, a massive coke-head whose addiction consumed his entire life. But he was also the easiest to prey on, the most vulnerable. And as soon as Henry had heard about his chance encounter with Erica, he had overlooked the flaws and seen the immense possibilities.

A spy infiltrating the Kremlin.

Cosying up to the barrister and manipulating the daughter to kill her entire family.

In fairness to him, he'd done a good job. But now, with the constant barrage of phone calls and text messages begging for the fake inheritance he'd been promised, Henry knew that Dylan would soon become a problem. A thorn in his side riddled with infection. But not only was Dylan a problem, Erica also posed a worrying threat.

She knew just as much as he, and if Dylan didn't kill her through his love of drugs – or torture her by making her listen to that shit he called music – then that equalled two thorns in his side.

Two thorns, two potentially lethal infections.

Henry stopped pacing, found his phone and loaded *Kingdom of Empires*.

He found the chat with LG540 and typed a message.

I've got an idea that I need to run by you. Tell me what you think about this…

CHAPTER 26

NURSE WARREN

Jake stepped out of the car and into the early afternoon sunlight. He and Darryl were in one of London's lungs beside Hollow Pond, a large basin of water home to several species of ducks and geese. In the distance was the murky skyline of Central London, hazy and covered in a low cloud. The Shard pierced through the skyline, like a splinter protruding from the rest of the city.

On the outskirts of the park, sitting neatly amidst a row of cars, was Rupert Haversham's abandoned Mercedes. The vehicle had been spotted by a runner who'd tripped on the kerb and clattered into the back of the car, spraining his ankle in the process. Fortunately for the runner, Whipps Cross Hospital was round the corner, and he'd been able to hobble to safety. It wasn't until he'd later seen the news that he'd recognised the number plate and called it in.

Between them, and with the help of two uniformed officers, Jake and Darryl had set up a perimeter around the car. The area was a crime scene, and the wider the perimeter, the better. Darryl donned a pair of blue forensic gloves. Jake hurried back to Darryl's Volvo and found a pair for himself. Within seconds, the pores on his palms opened and secreted sweat. He could almost taste the smell of them already. He grimaced.

'You start at the back, I'll start at the front,' Darryl instructed, then turned his attention to the glove compartment.

Jake was always tentative whenever he opened the boot of an abandoned car. In the past, he'd encountered a series of weird and horrible things inside them. Drugs, money, a young boy who'd fallen foul to a childish prank. And most recently, a dead body – the life of a young adult of similar age to him stolen from the world so soon.

He hoped history wouldn't repeat itself. That he wouldn't find the disintegrating remains of Erica Haversham in the confined space.

Muscles taut, one hand clenched, he placed his other hand under the boot's release catch and pulled.

As soon as the boot opened, Jake jumped back several paces and breathed a bittersweet, heavy sigh of relief. The boot was empty, which meant no dead body. But it also meant Erica was still out there, potentially alive somewhere. He tried not to think what sort of condition she might be in. Beaten. Bruised. Tortured. Raped. Burnt alive. Dosed full of drugs. Buried in a concrete tomb. Jake was all too familiar with Henry Matheson and The Cabal's methods of killing people.

Jake returned his attention to the boot. All that was inside was a briefcase and a series of folders and papers spread loosely across the carpeted flooring. Jake reached for the briefcase, positioned it in the centre of the carpet, and then opened it. Inside was a series of legal documents and email printouts between Rupert and several of his clients. As he scanned them, a passage stood out to him:

Dear Miss Cipriano,
Apologies for the delay in getting back to you, but it's taking me a little longer to find the files you requested. As far as I'm aware, there's nothing to suggest —

The email continued onto the next page. But the sequence was out of order as the documents had become loose during a drive. And as Jake turned the sheet, he noticed something.

His email address.
jake.tanner308@gmail.com

His more professional one, rather than the immature one he'd set up as a teenager. But what was it doing in there?

And then he remembered: Rupert Haversham was a fastidious man who made copies of documents and emails and other pieces of information for his cases in triplicate – except, it seemed, when it came to The Cabal and keeping those secrets hidden from the police.

The logical part of his brain told him Rupert was just being cautious, while the cautious part told him Rupert was saving the case notes for blackmail further down the line.

Either way, it was curtains closed for Jake if anyone found it.

Jake peered round the side of the car at Darryl. The man was busying himself with the pockets in the car door. Jake ducked his head back into the boot, grabbed the papers with his name on them, and leafed through them quickly. The printouts were of his and Rupert's email chains regarding Elizabeth's sexual harassment case – the one nobody except for Rupert, himself and Elizabeth knew about. And now nobody else ever would: in front of him were the three copies Rupert had produced. Safe in his possession. A myth.

Just as Darryl shut the driver's door, Jake folded the letters in three and stuffed them into his blazer pocket. Out of sight. And out of mind.

Except they weren't out of his mind. Not by a long way. In fact, as he closed his blazer, he thought about his meeting with Rupert. The small room in his house he called an office. The two computer monitors. The CCTV footage on the right-hand side on a continuous reel. The printer beneath it. The lever-arch folders on the floor... Was there anything else with Jake's name on it that would incriminate him? They'd only discussed a few things on email before Rupert invited him over...

And then he remembered. He'd been invited to sign a contract and to discuss fees. His name, as well as Elizabeth's, would be on those documents. But where would they be?

In the house.

In the lever-arch files.

And, of course, a digital copy would be sitting on Rupert's hard drive.

There was no doubt in his mind about that. Jake had even watched him scan it in and upload it.

But wait. Something wasn't right.

Jake cast his mind back to their meeting. He'd wandered into the office, sat next to Rupert, and then signed the physical copy of the agreement. *And then what? And then what happened? He... he... he...*

Yes! That was it. Rupert had scanned the document into his printer, and was about to upload it to his hard drive and print another copy when Helena had interrupted them, saying she needed to speak to her husband. Then, when he'd returned, he'd asked Jake to leave, as there was something else he needed to take care of. They would need to reschedule.

Maybe he forgot about it, Jake thought, fear beginning to surge through his body. The only thing connecting him and Rupert Haversham, the thing that also proved he'd lied and perverted the course of justice, was sitting in the middle of Rupert Haversham's office printer. Jake just hoped it was still there.

But then the more immediate problem presented itself: how to get it.

'Earth to Jake,' a voice called. It sounded distant, but as he realised who was speaking, he came crashing back to the planet. 'What have you seen?'

'Rupert's work. Stuff with some clients from a few years ago. I recognise a few of the names – could have come in handy when we were putting them away.'

Darryl's expression dropped. 'Not if it's legal privilege.'

Jake rolled his eyes. 'If only you were as good at understanding sarcasm as you are at reminding me of the processes and procedures every five seconds, we might get on a little better. Don't you think?'

Darryl's lips parted. He looked as though he wanted to say something, but then thought better of it.

'I'll let you know if I find anything else,' Jake said, hoping that Darryl would take the hint and wander away.

For the next hour, Jake and Darryl scrutinised and inspected the entire car, making notes and highlighting certain areas they wanted forensics to focus on. The outcome was disappointing. There was nothing in there that told them what they wanted to know – at least, nothing visible to the naked eye. There was no blood. No hair. No fingerprints that they could see. All they could do was wait until the forensics team arrived, and then wait for *those* results.

The painstaking and laborious process, everybody! And now for our next trick, we take six days to complete a job that, with enough manpower, resources and funding, could be done in six hours.

'Right,' Darryl began, 'back to the office?'

'Yeah, sure,' Jake said reluctantly.

Then his mobile rang. He felt the vibrations against his leg.

Jake answered the call without looking at the screen.

'Hello?' he began.

'Hi. I was wondering if I could speak with Jake Tanner please?'

'Speaking.'

'Oh, er, hi. This is Nurse Warren calling from Whipps Cross. One of my colleagues met you last night. I was just… I was just ringing to let you know that Peter Garrison is out of his coma and is ready for you to come and visit whenever the time suits you.'

CHAPTER 27

TOOLS

It took a lot for Henry Matheson to turn angry. His job at the top of his empire required him to remain level-headed and calm as much as possible. But that had been back when he'd had an army of youngers and elders willing to shot his food for him. Decisions he made did not have an immediate impact on him; any repercussions usually took a while to travel upstream. The same rules had applied during his time in Belmarsh. But here… here was different.

The impact of his actions was swift and immediate.

And he'd already had his first taste.

Earlier that afternoon, following his questioning from the governor, he'd returned to his cell to find it turned over. Everything inside flipped, his possessions stolen. Including the money Longstaff had given him.

'Who the fuck did this?' he'd asked his cellmate, a soppy, wet-behind-the-ears twenty-five-year-old doing a three stretch for putting someone in a coma while drink driving.

'Dunno. I ain't see nothing.'

Course he hadn't. Selective sight, along with selective hearing, was commonplace in prison. Almost as commonplace as the drugs he was being forced to sell.

Having decided that his cellmate was less than useless. Henry had stormed towards James Longstaff's cell, where he'd found the man sitting on his bed completing a crossword puzzle. Alone. The radio playing in the background.

'You seen what they done to my cell?' Henry had asked.

'Should I have?' Longstaff had kept his attention maintained on the puzzle.

'They've fucking flipped it. Stolen everything. I've got nothing left.'

'Who?'

'The fuck do you think?'

'That'll probably be because you haven't paid your dues.'

'Excuse me? I thought we were in partnership. You're providing me with protection. I've already done what you asked.'

Longstaff had made Henry wait while he completed a section of the crossword.

Eventually, he'd replied, 'I think you misunderstand me, Henry. Your protection lasted for one day and one day only. If you want to live out the rest of your days here at peace, then you're going to have to earn it.'

'By working for you every day?'

'Yep.'

'Some fucking partnership that is,' he'd said, then realised that if he didn't want his feet burnt to a crisp, he didn't have a choice. Reluctantly, he'd asked: 'What do you need me to do?'

The answer was currently in Henry's hand. The plastic bag of spice was slicked with his sweat. It had been a long time since he'd last handled drugs. Usually accustomed to someone else doing it for him, he didn't know how to act, how to behave.

Cool was the answer. Relaxed. Calm. And *not* like he was about to shoot the president or commit a terrorist act.

He was in his cell, waiting for the buyer to slip in and then back out again. Quick, simple. No fuss, no stress. Except Henry didn't feel relaxed at all. If he was caught, he was at risk of adding to his sentence and possibly spending time in isolation. If he was caught, he would lose out on tomorrow's protection. And the day after that. And the day after.

If he was caught, the guards would paint a target on his back, their trigger fingers hovering over the bullseye every moment of the day.

James Longstaff had lied to him and betrayed him. The man had manipulated and reassured him into thinking he was safe when the opposite was true.

Was this how Dylan felt? Was this how all his other youngers and workers had felt when he'd failed to come through on a promise?

Tough, yes. But the difference between him and his youngers was that he was far more experienced and determined to do something about it. If he was in a hole, he possessed the tools to get himself out. Not everyone did.

After an agonising and paranoid twenty-minute wait, the buyer eventually turned up. Henry didn't recognise him, and he didn't want to either; he just wanted it done and dusted. In and out.

The man slipped into the cell, hand extended, money at the ready. As Henry went to shake it, they exchanged the items, and then the inmate left.

In and out in a matter of seconds.

Which, despite the fear surrounding the situation, gave Henry an idea.

CHAPTER 28

IMPETUS

In Jake's humble opinion, Pete 'McVitie's' Garrison had been an arsehole for most his career. In fact, Jake was certain the man had been an arsehole for his entire life. But he was MIT's arsehole, and Jake missed him dearly. He didn't know the exact figure, but it was close to five hundred days since Garrison had been locked in the prison of his mind, trapped in a cornucopia of unconsciousness, elicited by a reckless act of betrayal. It had taken Jake a long time to process, but now he was glad that the man who'd put him there – their old colleague and friend, Drew Richmond – was dead.

Garrison's 'accident' had been a dark part in Jake's life. But those days were behind him. Everyone involved in that saga was either dead or in prison. Drew was dead. Danny Cipriano was dead. Michael Cipriano was dead. Georgiy Ivanov, aka The Farmer, a highly decorated and professional contract killer, was in prison. Nigel Clayton had died of a brain haemorrhage. Martin Radcliffe had killed himself while in prison. And, finally, Liam was also in prison. The list was so long that he wasn't sure if he'd missed anyone out or not.

Jake didn't know why, but as he stood on the other side of the glass, staring at his friend in the hospital room, he felt oddly at ease about the future and what it might bring. As though Garrison was the symbol of calm and reflection that Jake had been missing in his life since the man had stepped out of it. Perhaps it was something paternal between the two of them that Jake hadn't realised before. Perhaps it was just because he saw elements of his father in Garrison.

The hospital-room door opened, and standing in front of him was the nurse who'd just been attending to Garrison. It was mid-afternoon, and on the other side of the window, looking out on the horizon from Garrison's room, was the London skyline: The Shard,

Canary Wharf, The Gherkin, the hubbub and bustle of modern life. None of that mattered in here, in the hospital. Jake wanted to focus his undivided attention on his friend for the next hour or two – or until he was told to leave by the nursing team.

'He's ready for you now,' the nurse told him, placing a comforting hand on his arm.

'How's he doing?' Jake asked with a lump in his throat. He swayed from side to side on the balls of his feet.

The nurse turned her head and glanced at Garrison, who lay upright in his bed, focusing his attention on an apple. 'He's... he's not the same as he was. He's... When he woke up, he had no recollection of where he was or how he got there. There's some indication of memory loss, but he appears to be showing signs of familiarity with certain things. As soon as he saw the biscuits beside his bed, he devoured them.'

'He's going to love these then,' Jake said as he held aloft the packet of digestives he'd bought from the convenience store in the hospital foyer. 'Does he remember anyone's names? Family members, friends, colleagues?'

The nurse shook her head. 'We've not got that far yet. The doctor's booked him in for some brain scans this evening. We'll know more about his condition when the results come back.'

Jake smiled awkwardly, thanked the nurse for her help, and then stepped up to the door. Only a few inches stood between him and Garrison, but it felt like miles. The door handle felt as though it weighed a tonne and would require his full body weight to shift it, and the biscuits in his hands strained his arms. Then Jake thought about what he was going to do as soon as he set foot through the door. What was he going to say? How much was he going to ask? How much could he ask? How much did Garrison remember?

There was only one way to find out.

Grinding his teeth, Jake lowered the door handle and entered. Garrison was still sitting upright, but now he chewed slowly on his apple, staring into the bedsheets.

'Hey Pete,' Jake said as he moved across the room towards the nearest chair. 'Good to see you again.'

'Are you a doctor?'

Jake smirked even though those four little words struck an unexpected chord in him. 'Sorry, pal. I'm not a doctor. But I'm an old friend. Jake Tanner.'

'Do I know you?'

Another four words. Another chord struck.

Jake didn't know how much more he'd be able to take of this already.

'We worked together, Pete, remember? Major Investigation Team. Bow Green. I'm the little detective constable who liked to drink piss whenever we went to the pub.' Jake pulled the seat furthest away from Garrison out and sat.

When no response came from his old colleague, Jake continued, 'I brought you a packet of biscuits. Digestives. Your favourite.'

As soon as Jake held them aloft, Garrison's eyes beamed and he leant forward to snatch them.

'Try not to eat them all at once,' Jake said, feigning a chuckle. 'Although you've been asleep for a long time – maybe you could do with the calories. And I'm sure it beats eating hospital food. Nobody should have to eat food that bad.'

Jake continued speaking, but it was useless. Garrison's attention had waned and was now focused entirely on the biscuits in his mouth.

'The nurses in here are good, aren't they?' Jake asked, trying to fill the void with small talk. 'Are they looking after you, making sure you're catered for? You always were a little bit of a diva in the office.'

No response.

'Do you remember the office, Pete? It's not changed much since you've been gone. There are a lot of new faces though. Liam isn't there anymore. Neither's Drew. Do you remember those two, Pete?'

At the mention of both names, Garrison dropped the biscuits on his lap and stared at Jake, his expression blank.

'They were our colleagues. Do you remember them?'

Blank.

'What about what happened to you? Do you remember the accident?'

Blank again.

This time, Jake tried to push it one step further, hoping for a response or any sign that Garrison knew what he was talking about.

'What about… what about The Cabal, Pete? Do you remember that name? The Cabal.'

Without warning, Garrison shrieked, his shrill cry piercing the air. 'Nurse! Nurse!' he screamed, then launched the biscuit packet at Jake. One of the biscuits flew from the pack and crashed onto the floor.

'Nurse!' Garrison screamed again, this time louder. 'Nurse! Nurse! Nurse!'

Then he lunged across the bed, grabbed the emergency panel, and prodded the summon button repeatedly.

'Nurse! Nurse! Nurse!' Garrison continued to scream until his voice turned hoarse.

He ripped the white sheet from his bed and launched it at Jake. Then he started to remove the plugs and drips and tubes that were connected to his body.

Jake watched on in horror, paralysed in his chair. He didn't know what to do. What he *could* do. He'd been the one to start the episode. He was the reason Garrison was acting like this. He was the one who'd taken it too far too soon.

A second later, a band of two nurses burst into the room and rushed to Garrison's side. The one who Jake had spoken to a few minutes earlier placed her hands on Garrison's shoulders in an attempt to stabilise him and calm him. But it made everything worse.

'Nurse! Nurse! Nurse!' he continued to scream. 'Get him out of here! Please. Nurse! Nurse! Get him out!'

Paralysis clung to Jake like a baby monkey around its mother's neck, pinning him there, holding him against his will. He wanted to leave, he wanted to bolt out of the room – but he couldn't. Something was holding him back. Fear. Guilt. Shame. He didn't know, but he didn't want to cause Garrison any more suffering and upset than he already had.

The second nurse stepped in front of him.

'Excuse me, sir,' she said, already placing a hand on him. 'I'm going to have to ask you to leave.'

Jake didn't need telling twice; the woman had given him the impetus he needed to stretch his legs and hurry out of there.

As soon as the door closed behind him, he staggered to the ground, brought his knees to his chest, and rested his head in his arms.

What had he done?

CHAPTER 29

M

By the time he got home it was dark. Dejected and defeated, Jake threw his house keys into the clay pot by the front door, then kicked his shoes off and wandered through the corridor, dragging his heels on the floor and his knuckles against the wall. Garrison was still on his mind, and had been ever since he'd left the hospital. The drive back had been long, monotonous, and filled with fresh images of his former colleague. Snapshots of their interaction playing on repeat. Jake felt sick with guilt, the contents of his stomach moments away from making a return visit.

But before he could think about it any further, something caught his attention.

The kitchen had been tidied. The tins of beer, the plastic microwaveable-meal trays, the leftover food on the plates, the dishes in the sink – they'd all been cleaned away. And he'd been able to enter the house unhindered by the detritus that had been gathering behind the front door.

Elizabeth. Of course she'd been the one responsible. Elizabeth the wife. Elizabeth the mother. Elizabeth the woman who demonstrated a never-ending love for him. Not only had she lied to the police to protect him, but she'd also stuck with him while everything else was going on. Proof that she did still love him, that their marriage wasn't completely over, that it was worth saving, that perhaps one day, in the not too distant future, she and the kids would move back in.

Things were *all right*. Not good, but not bad. Getting better. Like most things, it would just take time. But if there was one thing Jake wasn't very good at, it was patience.

He ran his hand across the kitchen surface, his fingers tingling as he registered its smoothness. And then something to his left caught his eye. It was a sheet of paper resting atop his closed laptop.

Funny, he didn't remember closing it.

Maybe…

Shit. Elizabeth must have opened the laptop. But how could he blame her? She had every right to be curious after what she'd done for him today. Not to mention the fact they hadn't seen each other properly in weeks, and she hadn't been home for longer. It was only fair that she be interested to see how much time he'd been spending on porn or things he shouldn't.

Like online gambling websites.

'Fuck, fuck, fuck.'

Frantically, he snatched at the piece of paper and thumbed it open until the words on the page came into view. Written in red, indelible ink, the colour of blood, they screamed at him.

I know about the gambling. I know about the debt. Oh and Stephanie left you a lovely little message by the way, but I picked it up for you so you wouldn't have to. You're welcome.

Don't call or talk to me again. Stay out of our lives, you piece of shit.

Jake's body turned numb. Paralysis wrapped itself around him and squeezed him tightly, asphyxiating the oxygen in his brain. He stood there, staring blankly at the document as if he'd forgotten how to breathe. A chill swarmed him, climbed around his face and then down his throat. The hairs on his neck and back stood on end. Now he really wanted to be sick. But there was something holding him back. Impenetrable, unmovable.

Being caught on porn would have been better than this.

At that moment, Jake wanted to crawl into a ball and cry. It had been a long time since he'd needed to cry, and even longer since he'd actually shed a tear. It was an alien sensation to him. One that wasn't reserved for men like him, the providers, the alpha males. The ones who always wanted to be in control. Because if he cried, it signified he *wasn't* in control.

And if he didn't have that, then what did he have?

Instead of allowing the floodgates of despair and disappointment to open, his mind returned to its debilitating and destructive thoughts. Reminding himself that *he* was the issue. That *he* was the reason they were in this position. Their marriage had become a failure because of *him*. No one else was to blame except for *Jake Tanner*. The shitty husband. The even shittier father. The man who couldn't provide for his family, even though he'd convinced himself during every waking moment that that was what he was fighting for. He was a fraud, a disgrace, a despicable person.

An overwhelming sense of rage began to swell inside him, biting into every fibre of his being and spreading its poison through him. Before long, it had consumed everything else and altered his state of mind.

His life was in a paroxysm of chaos – his career, his friendships, his marriage, his family. And right now the only thing that wasn't, the only thing that he could say with a degree of certainty was in order, was the kitchen. It was clean, tidy, the complete antithesis of everything else.

How fucking sad was that?

So what harm would it do to add a little bit more chaos?

Jake clenched his fist and brought it down on the kitchen table like a hammer. He tore Elizabeth's note into a dozen pieces, kicked the table leg, picked up a chair and launched it at the living-room door, then turned his attention to the island in the centre of the room, grabbed the fruit bowl, smashed it down on the surface and launched an apple at the wall, then an orange, then a pear. Then he rounded the island, opened the cutlery drawer, scooped knives and forks and spoons into his hands and threw them blindly in the direction of the windows that opened into the garden. Jake paid little heed to the damage he was causing and tore through the rest of the kitchen until, a few minutes later, he was finished. Worn out. And had run out of things to destroy. At the end he simply stood there, panting, surveying the destruction he'd caused, like Hitler surveying Europe.

It was carnage, and he had no intention of tidying it up. In fact, he couldn't bear to stay in the house anymore. It reminded him too much of Elizabeth and the girls, too much of the hurt he'd caused. And what made it worse was the photo of the four of them he'd decided to leave unscathed on the kitchen countertop, sitting there like Switzerland. Unharmed and independent of any turmoil.

Jake needed to get out of there. For a long while. For a drive.

The street lights outside illuminated his car with a deep orange hue. He paced towards it, yanked the door open and slid in, slamming it shut behind him. He placed his hands on the steering wheel and massaged it up and down.

Paused. Thought.

What was he doing? What was he going to do? He had nowhere to go. Nobody to see. Nothing to do. So why was he being such a wanker? His reaction was incredulous. He needed to calm down, sort his shit out and move on. Just like he had done in the past, and just like he always would do.

Be a fucking adult about it, you silly cunt.

Yes, he was going through a tough phase, but there was always someone else going through a lot worse. He had a lot to be grateful for, and he needed to be appreciative of that. He needed to focus on the positives rather than the negatives. He'd been in a rut before – and had managed to get himself out of it then. And he was going to do the same now.

He recalled the breathing exercises his therapist had given him following the avalanche that had almost killed him a few years ago. In through the nose. Hold. One. Two. Three. Four. Out through the mouth. Hold. One. Two. Three. Four.

After several attempts, the fog in his mind cleared, and he began to think clearly, more succinctly, rationally. The anger and resentment in his blood dissipated and flowed out of his system, and before long, he was calm again.

Jake closed his eyes and rested his head against the headrest. The sudden urge to sleep washed over him.

As he yawned and stretched his arms, his mobile phone vibrated, bolting him awake.

'Elizabeth?' he hoped, reaching into his pocket.

Wrong. It was an unknown number. Perhaps it was the hospital notifying him he couldn't see Garrison anymore. Perhaps it was Henry Matheson telling him he was coming after Jake and everyone he loved. Perhaps it was The Cabal telling him the exact same thing.

The Cabal's still alive.

Trotting about...

D for Darryl.

Tentatively, Jake unlocked his mobile and opened the message.

You don't know me but you will soon. There's a funeral being held on Sunday at Croydon Crematorium. I think you should be there. I'll be in touch with more information soon. M.

Jake scanned through the message again a second time. And then a third. On the fourth, he was still none the wiser about who it was from, what it was about, or why it had been sent to him. At first he'd thought it had been sent by mistake, and a relative of the deceased somewhere had missed out, but the first line had perplexed him.

Intrigued him.

You don't know me but you will soon.

M.

M, M, M. He repeated the letter in his head, trying to think of all the people he knew beginning with M.

Martha? Unlikely. She had his number, and he already knew her...

No, this was someone else. Someone—

And then it struck him. Could it be The Cabal? Rousing him somehow, flushing him out into the open. Making him attend his own funeral.

Or was it someone who was going to lead him directly to the answers he'd been searching so long and so hard for?

| DAY 4 |

CHAPTER 30

BRAVE

Darkness suffocated the light from the room, suspending Jake in a deep and cavernous void. He lay on his back, staring into the ceiling, hands laced across his chest, eyes focused on nothing – not even the street light from outside was strong enough to filter through the curtains. Elizabeth had purchased them when they'd first moved in as an attempt to help Jake get some deep sleep when he came home from a job. But the reality was that the very nature of his job required his mind to constantly be alert, receptive to even the slightest noise or movement, aware of everything that was going on around him. As a result, he was a very light sleeper. Except, as had already been proven, when he'd been drinking.

Jake rolled to the side and glanced at the digital alarm clock – 4:12 a.m. A couple of hours until he needed to be awake and ready for work. A couple of hours to get some sleep. But what was the point? If sleep had evaded him the entire night, it certainly wasn't going to make an appearance in the next two hours. And so, within a few seconds, he got out of bed. He shuffled along the carpet, strolled into the shower and less than ten minutes later was dressed and ready.

With a scalding-hot cup of coffee in hand, he ambled towards the car, slipped in and started the engine. Bathing the sleepy residential street in the soft glow of his headlights, he pulled away and started the long journey to Stratford on the other side of the city – with a slightly different destination in mind.

Erica Haversham was still missing. Had been for nearly seventy-two hours, and yet he and the team were still none the wiser where she might be. At this stage of the investigation, Jake would normally have been on it – working hard, numerous hours, following up lines of enquiries, doing everything he could to find her abductor. But in truth, he hadn't thought about her disappearance since Darryl had confirmed it. Instead, he'd been too focused on covering his tracks and dealing with his personal issues. What did that make him? A shitty and jaded detective who'd started to fall out of love with the job? Someone who'd been withered down to nothing but a man who turned up and did the bare minimum? This wasn't the Jake he knew himself to be. This wasn't the Tenacious Tanner everyone else knew him to be. Something needed to change, something needed to give. And as he'd lain there, staring into the blackness – a visual representation of his own mind at times – he'd come up with a solution.

The answer had been staring him in the face all this time.

If his theory was right, and Henry Matheson had indeed ordered the hit on Rupert Haversham and his family, then the likelihood of Erica being kept under the watchful eye of the E11 in the Cosgrove Estate was incredibly high. She was their insurance package. But for what? To make matters worse, their investigations had identified a boyfriend, Dylan Ayers, and several attempts had been made to contact the twenty-three-year-old, but none had succeeded. If Erica was in the Cosgrove Estate, then she was locked up somewhere in the myriad of flats and rooms within the two tower blocks. A piece of algae floating in the ocean. The best hiding place in the world.

Because they knew that no police officer was brave enough to enter the estate alone.

Well, they'd clearly never met Jake Tanner.

CHAPTER 31

KEEP WALKING

Less than an hour later, Jake was positioned over a hundred yards away from his target, hidden in the shadows behind a Ford Transit van. In the distance, a single street lamp illuminated the road on the north end of the estate. The bulb flickered intermittently like a star sparkling in the night, teasing the residents with its existence. Perfect for conducting drug deals beneath; less so if you were a young woman returning from shift alone. Up ahead, on the other side of the street, loitering on the corner, was a group of youths. One on a bike, leaning across the handlebars, playing on his phone. Another standing beside a letter box with her hands in her hoodie's front pocket. And a third individual sitting on the wall with their hood pulled over their face and their features mostly hidden. But what Jake could see, he recognised immediately.

It was the group from the other night. The ones he'd briefly considered chasing after they'd petrol bombed Brendan's car. Had it been a fortuitous circumstance, a piece of divine intervention, that they should be there at the same time he was, or had his subconscious delivered him there for a different reason? Either way, as soon as he spotted the individual responsible for the attack, all thoughts of Erica Haversham and her whereabouts evaporated from his mind. It was time to get even.

Even if he was alone and without support.

Jake lowered his car window a fraction. From previous experience at The Pit, he'd learnt that throughout the night, the residents in the estate were awake, alive and trying their best to make sure everyone else was as well. Except for now: 5 a.m. was the time that the party had historically stopped and all the residents had crashed into their own bed – or someone else's.

All except for the group hovering beneath the street light, their loud and obnoxious shouts of abuse to one another echoing up and down the walls. Jake strained his ears to listen to their conversation while he studied them intently.

'All I'm saying is,' one of them said, 'she ain't gonna last long in here. Give it a couple more days before she gets found out. And when that happens, I'm ducking, bruv. Dyl ain't gonna be able to keep her here for that much longer. He'll fuck up soon enough. I reckon he'll have run out of that smack I sold him the other day. The guy's a wasteman, fam.'

Jake wanted to stay and listen, but his impatience convinced him otherwise.

He closed the window, exited the car quietly, and then locked it. Whenever he set foot in The Pit, his body surged with the primal instinct to protect himself from every angle. But now, in the middle of the night, when the estate was at its relative quietest, he felt nothing like that.

Instead, he felt calm, relaxed, invincible.

He sauntered into the middle of the road and, keeping his hands in his pockets, wandered towards the group. As he drew nearer, he tightened his fists into hard balls.

Skin and bone versus a potential knife. Skin and bone versus a potential piece of lead.

The distance between them gradually reduced.

Thirty feet. Twenty-five. Twenty.

Then he stopped on the outskirts of the lamp's cone of light. Kept his hands in his pockets, his eyes maintained on the group.

It didn't take them long to react. The kid on the bike was first. Followed by the only female in the group. And then the leader in the hoodie.

The one he wanted.

They all turned to one another, their voices muffled and hushed. One of them gesticulated, and immediately the guard dog on the bike wheeled himself closer towards Jake.

He came to a stop in the centre of the road. A Mexican standoff between adult and teenager.

'You lost, fam?' Handlebars called.

Jake didn't respond.

'Oi! I said, are you lost, fam?'

Jake didn't respond.

The kid turned his attention to a glass bottle on the ground. He leant over, picked it up and held it in his hands. Jake estimated they were over fifteen feet away from one another, and he was certain his reactions were fast enough to jump out of the way if necessary.

Without warning, the kid propelled the bottle into the air. The remnants of its contents glistened under the light as it soared through its trajectory.

Jake eyed its path every step of the way; it landed five feet short of him and shattered into hundreds of pieces by his feet. A few shards struck his shoes and legs, but nothing serious enough to cause any harm.

A brief moment of silence ensued as both parties waited for the bottle's smash to finish echoing around the estate.

'I don't think you wanna be here, fam. You must be lost,' Handlebars said, leaning forward on his bike again.

'He's right, mate,' the petrol bomber said, jumping down from the wall. 'People who get lost round here sometimes don't make it back. I suggest you keep walking.'

Jake stared into Petrol Bomber's eyes. His face was exactly the same as he remembered it – except even uglier. The tightly curled black hair that dangled from his forehead in thick strands. The equally dark and cavernous eyes that seemed to absorb everything that looked into them. The thick shoulders. The gap between his teeth.

'Did you hear me, bruv? Keep walking.'

Jake opened his mouth to speak but decided against it. Reality sank in and he realised where he was and what he was doing. And what he was up against. Three against one. With the possibility they were armed. If he was going to do this, he was going to do it the right way, the smart way.

Without saying anything, Jake turned his back on the group and headed towards his car, keeping his senses finely tuned, anticipating a surprise attack while his back was turned.

'Fucking nonce,' Petrol Bomber called as he wandered away.

Jake returned to his car, slid into the driver's seat, and started the engine. With the headlights switched off, he turned in the road and drove away in the opposite direction.

CHAPTER 32

PLAYING WITH FIRE

Time, it suddenly dawned on him as he sat there in the front seat of his car, was no longer a constant. Nothing but a construct. He realised life didn't matter as much as he thought it did when everything was regulated by an invisible invention. Going to bed at a certain time. Getting up at a certain time. Getting to work, staying for a certain time, coming home. What if he just did what he wanted when he wanted? Refused to celebrate birthdays, anniversaries, any form of special occasion. Would he be free, or would he find himself shackled by another constraint his mind had fabricated? Maybe he should just live in the moment and hope to learn from it. He didn't know. But what he did know was that while patiently waiting for his attacker to become isolated and alone, his mind was becoming more and more unhinged. These were thoughts he'd never had in his life before, so where the fuck were they coming from?

He recalled something one of his lecturers had said during a seminar once: *Our minds are the greatest and most complex creations. Our everyday thoughts, occurrences, interactions and movements all feed into our subconscious and change the way we behave and act. This is how we create our sense of self. And without our sense of self, we're nothing.*

So what did that make him? He was dealing with criminals from the general public and those within the biggest police force in the country. Surrounding himself with their treachery, deceit, villainy every day. Was that who he would inevitably become? Was his sense of self folding and bending the wrong way?

He was reminded of the Nietzsche quote that his lecturer adored: *Whoever fights monsters should see to it that in the process he does not become a monster.*

Well, Jake was certain he was already halfway there. And he

sensed that as soon as he set eyes on the petrol bomber – the next *monster* – he might even stoop to another level. If it was all right for Liam and Drew and even Garrison to get away with it, not to mention all the others, then why couldn't he? Without his interference, they would have continued their corruption and illicit activities, and everything might have been different. He might have even joined them and worked his way up through their ranks. God only knew how much dirty money he could have made on the side. God only knew how much better his and Elizabeth's relationship would be without their financial struggles. He would have been able to buy his family nice things, afford for them to go on more trips, shower them with the things they *deserved*. But no, he had to ruin it for everyone, and now everything he loved and held dear to him had fallen apart and shattered into a hundred irreparable pieces.

Again, what did that make him? Was he really the hero or had he, through no fault other than his own, become the villain of his own story?

All because of time.

Existential crises such as this were a peculiar, unfamiliar and particularly frightening experience for Jake. He'd never had one before, that deep and profound sense of being overwhelmed, of having the world at your feet yet finding yourself at the bottom of it all. Minuscule, inconsequential, insignificant, confined to the finitude of life.

A life governed by time.

Before he was able to fall deeper into the abyss of his own mind, a figure in the distance yanked him away. The petrol bomber. Alone, heading out of the estate.

Bingo. Gotcha.

Jake switched on the engine, slipped the car into first and pulled out of the lay-by. Petrol Bomber swaggered in the middle of the road, bowling his shoulders from side to side, invincible in the face of machine versus man. One hand was in his hoodie pocket while the other was cradling a cigarette.

Jake poodled behind him in the car, keeping the headlights off. Maintaining a distance of fifty feet, he massaged the steering wheel in his hands, gripping it tighter now and then, until his knuckles whitened.

When Petrol Bomber finally noticed the car, he slowed, turned and gave Jake a defiant middle finger. In that moment, everything seemed to stop, and Jake was no longer DC Jake Tanner; instead he was a regular joe, a random stranger off the street, an aggrieved vigilante seeking justice and retribution on a despicable human being. He hovered his foot over the accelerator and contemplated mowing the man down in a hit and run.

The ultimate test of machine versus man. Where there was only one winner.

'The fuck you doing, fam?' Petrol Bomber shouted as Jake nudged closer.

He thought of the bottle.

He thought of the fire.

He thought of the pain.

He thought of Brendan.

Then he slammed his foot on the accelerator.

The engine roared beneath him, and the needle on the rev counter soared into the red zone. The sound of the screaming engine filled the car. But the attacker didn't move, remained standing.

Machine versus man.

Then Jake slammed his fist on the horn, the tone bouncing off the walls of the estate. After a few seconds, the petrol bomber eventually ceded and moved out of the way.

As soon as he stepped off the road, Jake sped off, circling his way around the entire estate until he pulled back into the same position a few seconds later.

Whoever fights monsters should see to it that in the process he does not become a monster.

If he was going to do this, he was going to do it the right way, the smart way.

Do it properly. Don't give him any reason to get away with it.

Grabbing his radio from the dashboard, Jake stepped out of the car and proceeded on foot. By now Petrol Bomber had only reached the other end of the road. Jake skulked along the pavement, clutching the radio tightly in his hands. He twisted the dial on the top of the device and changed the channel to match the radio frequency of the dispatch controller in the station.

'Lima-Golf-Two-Three, Lima-Golf-Two-Three,' he whispered into the microphone. 'This is Juliet-Tango-Four-Five, over.'

'Juliet-Tango-Four-Five, this is Lima-Golf-Two-Three, reading you, over.'

'Lima-Golf, requesting immediate operational support, over.'

Jake reached the end of the road and turned left.

'Copy that, Juliet-Tango. What's your location, over?'

'The Cosgrove Estate. Currently heading east on Waterden Road. Send two operational units. Suspect could be armed and is considered dangerous. I'm in pursuit now. IC3 male, wearing a black hoodie with grey jogging bottoms. Currently holding a cigarette. Approach approved. Immediate response required. No blue light or siren. Get them to come in flying low, over.'

'Understood Juliet-Tango-Four-Five. Two EMTs en route now. Approximate ETA two minutes, over.'

Two minutes too long, Jake thought as he called off.

A lot could happen in two minutes; he could lose the target, blow his cover, get mobbed and attacked by another petrol bomb.

In the world of policing, two minutes was an eternity.

Something needed to be done to ensure he didn't lose sight of his goal.

The suspect was on the other side of the road, cigarette in one hand, mobile phone in the other, pressed against the side of his face. Talking vibrantly, gesticulating wildly.

Jake crossed the road and increased his pace, counting down the time until the officers arrived. Counting down the time he had to get his revenge.

Whoever fights monsters should see to it that in the process he does not become a monster.

Fuck it. Brendan was lying in a hospital bed with life-changing injuries because of this bastard.

He was the real monster.

Jake clenched his hand into his fist and reduced the gap.

Ten feet. Eight. Five. Three. Two.

Jake whistled.

At once, the attacker spun round. Before the man was able to react, Jake landed a punch in the stomach just beneath the ribcage – the place it hurt the most. The man bent double and dropped the phone. As the petrol bomber leant forward, Jake jabbed him in the kidneys and kneed him in the stomach. The attacker yelped in pain and fell to the ground.

That's for Brendan, you sick bastard.

As soon as the man was on the ground, whimpering and holding his stomach, Jake sprinted away in the opposite direction, towards the end of a row of terraced houses. He skidded to a stop in an alleyway, gasping for breath. He smirked, laughed. He felt alive. Invigorated.

Was this the way Liam and Drew had felt for all those years? Crossing the thin blue line of right and wrong and stepping into unfettered territory?

Even though he knew it was wrong – *so* wrong – he would do it again. Justice had been served.

But now it was time to deliver a different type of justice on behalf of Brendan.

Less than ten seconds later, two liveried police cars sped past him. Jake peered round the entrance to the alleyway and watched them slow to a halt. Two officers quickly spilt out from the cars and rushed to the man on the ground, still clutching his stomach.

Jake hurried over.

'Just in time,' he said to the officers, flashing his warrant card to them.

'You the one who called it in?' one of the police constables asked.

'Yup.'

'Is this the suspect?'

Jake nodded. 'The very same. Found him like that. Think someone got to him just now.'

'What we arresting him for?' the other officer asked. He stood there with his hands in his chest pockets and a plastic coil connected to his ear. Jake wasn't sure whether he was being recorded, but experience had taught him to be cautious of whomever he was around, regardless.

'Lads, this man here assaulted one of our own. Put him in hospital with third-degree burns. Potentially put him out of a job too. Maybe we should take him down to the station and see how much he enjoys playing with fire.'

CHAPTER 33

BITE OF THE APPLE

The man's name was Leyton Cameron. Twenty-six. Five foot nine. Resident of The Pit. Member of the E11.

And after nearly an hour of making him sweat and consider his existence, he was ready for his interview.

The custody officer jingled as he walked and fumbled for the set of keys against his hip. He eventually found the right one and slotted it into the door. On the other side was Leyton, lying on the four-inch-thick mattress, using his arms as a pillow. Jake stepped into the cold room and gave the nod for the officer to close the door behind him.

'You've been a busy man,' Jake said, feigning a smile.

Leyton remained silent and continued to stare into the ceiling.

'You know,' Jake continued, 'we ran your prints through the database and a whole wealth of stuff came back on you.'

Still nothing.

Jake moved closer to Leyton, and as he came to a stop, he said, 'Maybe we should go and talk about it.'

Without warning, he grabbed Leyton by the jumper, ripped him out of the bed and threw him against the wall. Before Leyton was able to react, Jake gripped a piece of his hoodie and held him at arm's length, steadying him on his feet.

'Sorry about that,' Jake said sarcastically. 'I don't know my own strength sometimes.'

'The fuck you doing, cunt?' Leyton asked as he clenched his fist and hovered it around his midriff, preparing himself to launch an attack.

'You wouldn't be thinking about assaulting another police officer, would you? Not again. That'd be a very ill-advised thing to do.'

Leyton spat on the floor by Jake's feet. Jake glanced down at the concrete in disgust, and as he returned his attention to Leyton, he dropped his right shoulder and moved his arm towards Leyton's ribs, feigning an attack. He had no intention of punching Leyton – he'd already got that out of his system earlier – but nothing was going to stop him from wounding the man mentally.

'This is fucking police brutality,' Leyton remarked, his breathing heavy and raspy. 'You can't touch me like that! I want a fucking solicitor, you fuck-shit psychopath!'

Jake loosened his grip on Leyton's jumper and patted him down, smirking. 'You know, they call these cells The Screamers. Do you know why? Rumour has it that as soon as you spend over eight hours in here, you start to go mad. The walls start to talk to you. At first you don't think it's true – you just think you're going slightly crazy. But then, as the voices get louder and clearer, and you start to realise that nobody's talking back, *that's* when you begin to believe it. You've only been in here a half hour – but you already know exactly what I'm talking about, don't you?'

Leyton's face told Jake everything he needed to know. The regret and fear in his eyes. The lines in his face that disappeared as his expression fell into a frown. The colour that rushed from his cheeks as he realised that there was some element of truth to what Jake had said.

'I want my solicitor. I know my rights.'

'You have to be human for those to apply.'

Jake shoved Leyton towards the door. When they arrived at it, Jake banged on the metal latch and waited. 'We're just going for a quick chat – we don't need any solicitors present yet.'

When he'd first started working with Pete Garrison and Drew Richmond, Jake had never appreciated their brilliance. They were masters in intimidation, and he was proud to say he'd learnt a thing or two from them.

Like turning the air conditioning on in an already chilled room or only having one poorly powered light switched on overhead. Both methods were frowned upon and were immediate breaches of the PACE regulations he was governed by, but so was abusing the offender. Something he felt little to no remorse over. He'd already committed the worst offence there was, so what harm would a little gooseflesh and widened pupils cause?

'Sorry about the lights,' Jake said as he moved across the room and slammed a folder on the table. 'They've been playing up all week. We were supposed to get someone in to fix them but, well... that doesn't look like it's happened.'

'Can we move?'

Jake stared at Leyton blankly. 'Since when did you get to start calling the shots?'

'I know my rights.'

'Like I said earlier: you have to be human for those to apply.'

'It's freezing in here, man.' Leyton wrapped his arms around himself and massaged his shoulders for warmth.

'Thought your type was used to standing outside in the cold all day and all night?'

'Is there anywhere else we can go?'

Jake shrugged and shook his head. 'They're all busy. They're all in use.'

'It's seven o'clock in the fucking morning.'

Jake smirked. 'You're not the only one who stays awake past his bedtime, Leyton. There are a lot of fuckwits who think they're billy big bollocks out there. But you're not. None of you are. And none of you are above the law.'

A moment of silence fell between them. In his mind, Jake mapped out the route he wanted the conversation to follow: intimidation, confession, intimidation, confession, intimidation, followed by a final confession. He was sure there was a lot that the man before him should have been held accountable for, but hadn't been. And he was determined to get it out of him. But first and foremost he wanted to have fun with it, see how far he could push Leyton, what sort of things he could force on him and push him to confess to. Was it ethical? Fuck no. Was it morally right? Arguable. Was it going to alleviate some of the pain and suffering that he was feeling about Brendan? Yes. Some, but not all.

Jake decided to go for the jugular straight away.

He leant forward, opened the folder and removed the first document. Then he closed the folder and placed the sheet of paper on top. Delicate, composed. Signalling he was in charge of the interview.

'Do you know what this is?' he asked.

'No comment.'

'It's a report of the findings from your flat. That's right – we've already got the warrant, been inside and sifted through your belongings. We can work quickly when we put our minds to it. There was plenty in there that intrigued me, as I'm sure you can imagine.' Jake explained. 'Mostly because there's enough horse tranquilliser in your flat to knock out the entire ensemble of the Grand National. Now, if this were any other individual, I might assume they were keeping it for their horse farm or making a decent living out of selling it to farmers, but you're not, are you, Leyton? You're attempting to sell it – along with the kilograms of cocaine, MDMA, heroin and marijuana that we also found in the flat.'

'No comment.'

'It wasn't a question,' Jake snapped. 'But what shocked me the most is that there was a heap of Henry Matheson's old plastic bottles lying around the place. Now, you and I both know what those bottles are, so I'm not going to waste my time and explain them to you. So it begs the question: what are you doing with them? Hint: *this* is a question that requires an answer.'

'No comment.'

'Are you taking over the E11 and Henry Matheson's drug operation?'

'No comment.'

'Or are you minding it for him while he's in prison?'

'No comment.'

'You've met Henry Matheson before, haven't you? You know what he's capable of?'

Leyton didn't respond, which was answer enough.

'You've heard the stories. He's a dangerous man, even more dangerous when you get on the wrong side of him. I'd know... I mean, look what he told you to do to my friend.' Jake opened the folder again and pulled out an enlarged photo he'd taken of Brendan's wounds. 'But what did that gain you? A morsel of his respect? A higher position in the gang? I'm sure you've heard other stories about Henry, haven't you? The bloke he almost beat to death in prison. The time he convinced a fourteen-year-old to kill his best friend and his dad. But you already know about all of these, don't you? In fact, I bet you were there for some of them.'

No response.

'So what makes you think he won't do the same to you?'

'I ain't betrayed him,' Leyton retorted, rubbing his shoulders more violently.

'Not yet. There's still time, and there's still a lot more you need to tell me.'

'I ain't telling you shit.'

'I thought you might say that, so we've gone to the lengths of running your DNA through the systems. But I'll get back to that soon. First I want to know what you know.'

'About what?'

'Is Henry Matheson The Cabal?'

No response. No change in expression either. No pupil dilation. No sudden eye movement.

Time to move things along.

'With the evidence we've got on you, Leyton, you'll be going to prison for a very long time. Assault on a police officer. Arson. GBH. Intent to supply. And there are a few other things on there that I haven't mentioned.' Jake paused. 'Now, this can go one of two ways. If you tell me what I want to know, I can make things easier for you. I can make sure you don't end up in the same prison as Henry, and that you don't suffer the same fate as anyone else who's crossed his path in there. I can make sure you're protected. If you want to turn into a super grass, then I'm all for it.'

'What makes you think you can protect me?'

'Because Henry's net doesn't spread as wide as he thinks it does. Trust me. And when he falls, there will be no one to take his place.'

Leyton pursed his lips and hesitated. 'I want a lawyer.'

'Who? Rupert Haversham? If I had a pound for every time I'd

heard that name, I'd be richer than you. But you can't have him. He's dead. Him and his family were murdered. But you're already aware of that, aren't you? Maybe you even had something to do with it. What do you know about Rupert's murder and his daughter's abduction?'

'No comment.'

'Anyone mentioned anything to you or in passing?'

'No comment.'

'Seen anything that looks like a girl being kept against her will?'

'No comment.'

Jake dropped his head a fraction. Leyton was turning out to be a hard nut to crack; if only he'd had longer to train and learn from Drew and Garrison. He decided it was time to play his trump card. The one he'd been hesitant to use at first. But his state of mind had since altered – if he could pull it off, he would have all the information he needed.

'You know,' he began, 'I've often wondered what it's like for people living on the other side of the line. What sort of things they get up to. What manner of depraved activity. And I had my answer when I got the report from your DNA. It came up on an unsolved case a few years ago. I think you know the one I'm talking about.'

Jake paused for effect. Then he reached inside the folder and produced another sheet of paper. 'Does the name Rhiannon Webb mean anything to you, Leyton?'

At the mention of Rhiannon's name, Leyton's face dropped, and the colour drained from his cheeks.

'I think she was fourteen years old when you met her, wasn't she? Who did you pay to get yourself out of that one? Rupert? You slept with a fourteen-year-old, Leyton. I hope you appreciate the severity of that. And do you know what happens to those types of people in prison? They get beaten, assaulted, raped, sometimes even murdered. Does Henry know? I imagine he doesn't, otherwise he would have got rid of you a long time ago.'

Jake hesitated again. 'So… imagine a hypothetical situation for me. You're in the same prison as Henry. He finds out you've betrayed him by getting yourself arrested. And then, to add salt to the wounds, he finds out you're a nonce; he gets some of his new boys to come and find you; you're in your cell just chilling one day; they come in and shank you, cut you up, beat you, smash your head in, cover you in napalm. You're on the brink of death, but you wish they'd just kill you instead. It continues like this for weeks, months. The guards aren't going to do anything about it because they secretly agree with what's happening to you. You want to kill yourself, but they won't let you, so you put up with it until you become numb, and then they find new ways to make you hurt. Imagine that for the rest of your life. Would it really be worth keeping secrets from us now?'

Jake held his breath as he let his question hang in the air. This entire interview had been against everything he stood and fought for, but it was difficult to deny: stepping out of line just once, having a small bite of the apple, was as exhilarating as the rush he got every time he won big on the horses or football.

As exhilarating as catching the bad guys in the first place.

To his surprise, it didn't take long to get a response.

'Before I tell you anything about Erica and Rupert, I want some assurances. But anything else, I'll tell you. I'll tell you everything you need to know.'

CHAPTER 34

TRUCE

Things were on the up.

The shackles of anger and frustration had finally dissipated and left his body, and now he had a clear mind. Much clearer than it ever had been.

He'd spent the past hour lying on the bed in his cell, staring into the holes in the ceiling. Clearing his mind, thinking, planning, calculating.

As it turned out, his situation wasn't as dire as he'd first thought. In fact, he was in a fortuitous position. Namely because he had The Cabal right where he wanted him.

By the short and curlies.

After exchanging messages with the anonymous figure, Henry had learnt that Dylan and Erica posed a threat to The Cabal. Although vague on the details, Henry was almost certain it was because they had seen The Cabal's face or knew of his identity somehow. What this offered Henry was something that had become an alien concept to him in Wandsworth: leverage.

The same way James Longstaff was manipulating him to get what he wanted, Henry was going to manipulate The Cabal.

Leverage.

If he was at the bottom of the food chain, then The Cabal was the plankton he ate for breakfast, lunch and dinner.

And so the two of them had come up with a plan, a plan that largely consisted of Henry instructing The Cabal to do his bidding. Which made a nice change for once.

But first, he needed to make sure he got the rest of his ducks in a row. Starting off with entering the lion's den.

Armando Strakosha was the leader of the Hellbanianz. Taller and more physically imposing than their Romanian counterparts, they were also smarter and more intimidating. In just a handful of years, they had slashed the prices of heroin and various other drugs, and managed to occupy most of the east of England. They flew under the radar, and they conducted their business like Wall Street. Inside the prison, they stuck together in one large group, and finding one isolated from the rest of the pack was as likely as Henry getting released that afternoon – an impossibility. As such, he prepared himself for the very real possibility that he might get beaten and stabbed by a group of fifteen men.

All in the name of his business. All in the name of the E11.

Armando Strakosha was thirteen months into a three stretch, and his cell was on the threes, furthest away from the stairs. Spilling out of the small room were some of the other Hellbanianz, stone-faced, hair greased and slicked back. Fashion was important to them, and somehow they even managed to make the dull prison uniform look appealing.

Henry approached them.

He made it twenty feet from the cell before he was accosted by a man who looked as though he'd just left school.

'The fuck you do? You not wanted here. Go away.'

Henry tensed his body. Remained stern. 'I want to speak with Armando.'

'He not want speak with you.'

'Tell him I have a proposition for him. For *all* of you. A truce.'

The word didn't register in the man's limited vocabulary.

'Can I speak with him please?' Henry persisted.

The man placed a hand against his chest. Firm, solid, and Henry sensed a lot of power behind it, despite the young man's age. 'Wait here. I check.'

Henry waited patiently, and after a few seconds, the man returned. This time he was followed by an entourage of five other men, each seemingly taller than the last. Henry wondered how many he could take on if the occasion required it. But he very quickly realised the answer was zero. He'd have more luck proving his innocence to all the people he'd killed and betrayed in this life.

'All right, lads?' he started, trying to hide the anxiety in his voice. 'What we all doing out here?'

He found out when the young man grabbed him by the chest and squared up to him. Then the four men started frisking him, touching every inch of his body. As soon as they were happy he was clean, they each gave a nod and the man who'd stood behind ushered him into the cell.

The cell was cramped with eight thick bodies pressed against one another. Some had tried to spread about the room by sitting on the bunk beds and resting against a small cabinet, but it made little impact. They all hovered around the TV screen, watching a football game. A dense cloud of smoke hung in the air, but it was nothing compared to the acrid stench of the men's cologne that clung to the back of his throat like a bad cold. He stifled a cough until his chest hurt.

'All right, lads?'

The heads of everyone in the room turned to face him. All except one. Armando Strakosha.

The man was hidden from view, lost behind the forest of legs in front of him.

'You're crazier than I thought, Matheson.' His voice boomed around the room. He spoke much better English than the rest of his gang. 'But you're also fucking stupid. You better have a good reason for being here.'

Armando climbed out of the bed and stepped in front of the TV so he was in full view.

'I-I do,' Henry said, stammering beneath their intimidation. 'I have a truce for you. And I have a brilliant idea. One that's going to make both of us very, very wealthy.'

CHAPTER 35

MISSING MAJOR PERSONS CRIME

The tinny, unbearable sound of metal clinking against china rang in Jake's ears as he stirred the contents of his instant coffee in the mug. His mind had wandered off into a dreamlike state, devoid of any and all thought. A wasteland where he was left to roam free. He should've been happy that he'd managed to prise information out of Leyton Cameron, but instead it filled him with dread. The man had confirmed that Henry Matheson had ordered them to get rid of any and all police presence on the estate swiftly and efficiently. The attack on himself and Brendan wasn't personal – they were simply in the wrong place at the wrong time.

More importantly, Leyton had also confirmed that The Cabal was still out there. According to Leyton's version of events, The Cabal had reportedly made contact with Henry while he was in prison. As to what it was regarding, Leyton didn't know, but now he and the rest of the E11 were in charge of finding out who it was. Sadly, Leyton had no information for Jake to follow up on. 'This fucker just appears out of nowhere and then disappears again,' Leyton had said, and Jake had been inclined to agree with him.

But Leyton had remained tight-lipped when it came to Erica. The man had confessed to knowing where she was, but first he wanted assurances. The most prominent of which was that he wanted to be entered into the witness protection programme. And until then, he wasn't saying a thing. Jake had agreed to look into it for him, but he knew from experience that the process wasn't as easy as filling out a form, putting it into someone's in tray and wiping his hands of it. It was much more convoluted than that. And what made it even more difficult was the fact Leyton's statements so far had been obtained unlawfully and under the radar, and his subsequent statements would also be. It was at this point that Jake realised he needed a bent copper to wander back into his life for a brief moment. Someone like Bridger or Danika – both of whom had previous experience with that exact same thing.

Both of whom were dead.

A sound to his right distracted him.

'Morning,' Darryl said.

Jake turned to face his boss. 'Morning.'

'MIR three. Two minutes.'

'There was no memo.'

'I'm giving it to you now,' Darryl said and then left.

Jake chucked the spoon in the kitchen sink and then made his way to the Major Investigation Room. The room bustled with life, filled to the brim with chatter, energy and excitement from officers of both the Major Investigation Team and the Missing Persons Unit, who now shared the office floor. Standing at the head of the room were Darryl and DCI Hamilton, the senior officer in command of MPU. Jake slipped in and shuffled to the back of the room, joining the rest of the overflowing staff. He yawned and sipped his coffee, delighting as the bitter taste flushed down his throat.

A well-earned reward.

Though not as much of a reward as placing a bet.

'Christ, Jake,' a voice to his left said, 'you look like shit.'

It was Devon Patrick, the newest addition to Missing Persons. He'd joined the team from Essex Police, and in the short time Jake had known him – which had been less than a month – he'd grown to like the new recruit. He was outgoing and not afraid to say what he really thought.

Jake smirked. 'I *feel* like shit too.'

'Long night?'

'And a half.'

Before Devon could respond, Darryl held his hand in the air. Silence immediately fell on the room, and then he began.

'Morning everyone,' he said, 'trust you're all well. I'd like to start by welcoming you all to the new team. DCI Hamilton and I are tentatively calling it Missing Major Persons Crime. But I'm sure someone else can come up with something a little better. This is our first debrief since the announcement yesterday that MisPer would be joining us in Operation Themis.

'I must also add, before we begin properly, that I'm still waiting for some of your reports from yesterday.' Darryl shot Jake a side glance. 'If I'd had those on time, it would negate the need for me to have a little moan and whine about it. So please: on time. Without fail. You should all know what to do by now.'

Jake folded his arms and leant against the wall, sighing heavily through his nose. This was beginning to feel like a telling-off in school. He hadn't come here to be lectured; he'd come here to make a difference and change people's lives – to protect them – not to be treated like a fifteen-year-old.

'Now that's out the way,' Darryl continued. 'I think it's time for the lowdown. What's the latest on Erica Haversham's whereabouts?'

'Honestly, guv,' Devon said, raising his hand slightly, 'not a lot. We've submitted the evidence you found on Rupert Haversham's car to the lab and that should be coming back today or tomorrow with any luck.'

'We've been following up with some of the house-to-house enquiries along the street,' continued Hannah Ridley, another member of MPU. 'They all maintain they saw nothing.'

'Not true,' interrupted Devon. 'I spoke with someone who mentioned they saw a car pull up outside the house at the time of the murders. They saw two people exit, male and female, and when they looked again, both that car and Haversham's were missing.'

Darryl pondered a moment, deep in thought. 'Have we considered the possibility that Erica is involved in this somehow? And what about her boyfriend? For the moment, we're treating him as our number-one suspect. Do we have any update on him? His whereabouts? Living habits? Where he lives. Who he lives with.'

'Yes, guv,' Hannah said. 'He's a bit of a nomad, it would appear – he doesn't seem to live anywhere. His name's appeared on the PNC and NCIS database for some low-level drug crimes, but other than that, nothing. There was an address registered at the Cosgrove Estate, but when we visited, there was no answer, and no sign of it having been lived in for months. But intelligence suggests he's still on the estate. We asked a few of the neighbours and they seem to think they've seen his face around the place. Either he's squatting somewhere or living rent free in someone else's flat.'

Jake drifted off as his sleep-deprived mind wandered around the room.

Drifting, drifting, drifting…

Until his eyes landed on the printer in the corner of the room, and a thought hit him like a steam train: Rupert Haversham's printer. Their correspondence was still hiding in there. He'd completely forgotten about it until now. If Jake was going to destroy it, he'd need a legitimate reason for being at the crime scene, otherwise there was no way he'd be able to justify going to Rupert Haversham's house to collect it. He needed a plan.

Before he could think of one, the door opened. Sandra stepped in, apologised for interrupting, and then handed Darryl a folder. Darryl opened it and read the first few lines.

'We've got a positive fingerprint and DNA analysis on the evidence seized in Rupert Haversham's car,' he said. 'It matches Erica Haversham's.'

Bingo.

'Have we seized her computer?' Jake asked, taking the room by surprise.

'Why?' Darryl asked.

'The fingerprint could be circumstantial evidence,' he replied. 'You never know – Rupert might have let her drive the car in the past, for a bit of practice. We'd need something slightly more tangible. If we can seize her computer or tablet, we might be able to see if she and Dylan have been planning this thing together for a while.'

He was clutching at straws, but it was all he had.

'Would they be so stupid as to do that online?' Ashley Rivers asked. She sat on the opposite side of the room with her legs crossed and her glasses resting on her head.

You don't need to convince them all. Just one. Just one.

'They're kids,' he replied. 'Of course they are. They love social media… Facebook, Instagram, Twitter. Any of those platforms will have information on it.' He paused and turned to Darryl. 'I think I saw an iMac in Erica's room. If she's not said anything on social media to Dylan, then she'll have done it by iMessage. If she's got her iCloud synced up to her computer, you'll be able to read her text messages without having the phone.'

Darryl contemplated for a moment. He folded his arms, turned his back on the team, and scribbled the words DYLAN and COMPUTER on the whiteboard.

'All right,' he said, turning his attention back to Jake. 'That's in line with the hypothesis… Sounds like a plan. Come up with the warrant, get it approved, and then find the computer. Take some SOCOs with you. Make sure the evidence is as pristine as possible.'

Jake nodded. Round one to him.

Now that he'd got that out of the way, he was able to focus on the other matter at hand. The Cosgrove Estate.

This time, Jake raised his hand.

'Sorry, guv. Just a quick little thing to back up what Hannah's saying. Last night I arrested Leyton Cameron. He lives in the Cosgrove Estate. When I was there, I overheard one of his friends saying something that sounded very much like Erica was in the estate somewhere with Dylan. My guess would be one of Matheson's properties.'

Darryl hesitated for a moment, pursing his lips. 'Right, OK. Well, this is news to me. And I think the whole scenario needs explaining. Number one: what were you doing on the estate making an arrest? You were off duty.'

'I might have been off duty, guv, but I wasn't off the job.'

Darryl sighed and placed his hands on his hips. 'And you think to tell me this now?'

Jake shrugged. 'With respect, sir, it's only the second time I've seen you this morning.'

Darryl sighed again, and this time shook his head. 'All right. Fine. But I want to speak to you at the end of this meeting.'

I'd expect nothing less.

As Darryl turned his attention to the rest of the team, Devon piped up. 'There you go, guv. We've got them now.'

'Not necessarily,' DCI Hamilton said, stepping in. 'The Pit is massive. And Matheson owns about fifteen properties in his building alone, too many for us to be knocking on all the doors at once. As soon as they catch wind that we're there, they'll get out of there faster than you can say "fuck me, they're off".'

'What about surveillance?'

Hamilton shook his head. 'Time isn't on our side. I want the fastest possible solution.'

'Then how can we get to them?' Devon asked finally.

'We need to draw them out,' Ashley added. 'Like adding smoke to a wasps' nest. Maybe we should put an urgent call out on all social-media channels and TV stations, urging people to get in contact with us if they have any information. They'll see it and panic. If we monitor the estate closely, we'll catch them before they can say "fuck me, where'd they come from?".'

Everyone, including Darryl and DCI Hamilton, nodded in agreement.

'How quickly can we make that happen?' Darryl asked Hamilton.

'Within the hour,' the DCI replied.

Darryl clapped his hands together. 'Let's get to it then, team.'

At once, the room erupted. Everyone launched out of their seats and made for the door. As Jake reached for the handle, Darryl called back to him.

'Jake,' he said. 'Don't think I've forgotten about that word.'

CHAPTER 36

SUPERGRASS

Darryl eased the door shut and moved across the room, lowering the blinds and twisting them until it was just the two of them. Nobody allowed in. Nobody allowed out. Not without his say-so.

Whatever was coming his way was going to be heavy.

Jake retreated slightly into the centre of the room and leant against the back of a chair for emotional as well as physical support.

'I don't think you and I are getting along very well at the moment, Jake,' Darryl said. It was the understatement of the year. 'What else do I need to know?'

'About what, guv?'

Playing it innocent always worked. Most of the time.

'About everything. What do you think you were doing at The Pit last night? Alone. Without any support.'

Jake thought the answer to that was obvious, but decided against saying so.

'I'm sorry, guv,' he started, 'but I really don't see what the issue is. I took a dangerous criminal off the streets. Correction: I found the man responsible for putting Brendan in hospital. And you've decided you want to have a go at me for it? Forgive me, guv, but I don't see how that works out. Would you rather I just sit back and let the criminals of this city take it over once again?'

'Watch your tone, Jake.'

'Would you prefer I didn't do my job?'

'I told you to watch your tone.'

'And I told you that I'm just trying to do my job.' He hesitated a moment to steady his breathing. 'You know, there's been something on my mind. You've been gunning for me these past few days. Shooting me down at every angle, every turn. And if there's one thing

I've learnt in the job, it's when that begins to happen, it's usually for a reason.'

'I don't like what you're insinuating here, Jake. If you still want to have your job by the end of the day, you'd better be very careful about what you say next.'

D for Darryl…

The Cabal's still out there…

Trotting about…

Jake swallowed, then cleared his throat. He was on a train heading to destination warpath, and the train had no intention of stopping. 'I've been doing a bit of thinking – quite a lot of it lately, in fact. This morning, last night, when you arrested me… And do you know what I thought? It occurred to me that maybe there's a reason you've been against everything I've done so far during this investigation. Maybe I've been chasing *you* for the past four years and haven't realised it yet. Maybe I'm really close to finding out just exactly who *you* are. Arrived here from nowhere after Liam left so you could keep an eye on things. Always so close to the action, you knew what to avoid. Throwing Henry Matheson under the bus. Using Richard Candy as a scapegoat, as your number two. Killing Rupert Haversham and planting evidence against me to pin the murders on me. Now it's all adding up.'

Jake had been expecting a bigger reaction. Something explosive. Something that was going to tease Darryl into cracking his shell and revealing who he really was. But the opposite happened. He sauntered towards Jake, rested against the wall beside him, and placed his hands in his pockets.

'Sit,' he said.

Jake glanced down at the seat he was leaning against. 'I'd rather—'

'Sit,' Darryl insisted.

Tentatively, Jake rounded the chair and perched himself on the edge. He was potentially sitting a few feet from The Cabal – the person who'd made his life a misery for the past few years – so he should have been feeling nervous, afraid. But he wasn't. Jake had managed to whittle The Cabal down so that they were now on a level playing field, equals, and there was no more exercise of power and control that The Cabal had over him.

'So it *is* possible for you to follow instructions,' Darryl said sarcastically, edging closer. 'I'm going to be honest with you for a moment, Jake. You're probably not going to want to hear it, but tough shit. You've got a problem of some description – a vice that you can't shake no matter how much you want to. I can see it in your eyes, your face, your entire demeanour. That's why you're so tired. You look as though you haven't slept in days. You need to rest. I'm sure Elizabeth's been telling you the same thing. You're letting everything get to you. You're stressed to the limit and I don't want that. You're a stellar detective, and this force would be nothing without you. But I've seen it happen to many other detectives in the past: they become obsessed, too "job pissed", too consumed by the work they're doing. They obsess over it until they inevitably reach the point where it ruins their lives. And then there's no going back. That's when the problems begin. The addiction. The financial issues. The marital issues. Relationships start to fall apart. The depression kicks in. PTSD, and the rest of it... It's already become a part of your life. And I wouldn't be doing my job if I didn't do something about it. I have a duty of care over all of my employees, and I need to put your needs before everything else. Like I said, Jake, you're a good detective, and we can't afford to lose you.'

'So don't,' Jake said with an extreme air of ignorance and defiance about him. He hated being lectured. *Hated* it. He knew that he had a problem – he'd been the first one to realise it. And he didn't need other people reminding him of the fact that he was a fuck-up, somebody who'd let control of his own life slip. He was going to stop the gambling and everything else. For Elizabeth. For Maisie. For Ellie. It was just a shame that it had taken this long – and for Elizabeth to leave him – for him to realise, to look, to atone for his mistakes.

'Don't force me into a decision I don't want to make, Jake,' Darryl said after a long moment. 'I'm not who you think I am, so you can get that out of your head immediately.'

Jake wasn't going to roll over and lie down that easily. 'Prove it,' he said.

'Excuse me?'

'Prove it. Leyton Cameron is sitting down there in his holding cell, thinking he's about to be whisked away to the witness protection programme.'

'Why would he think that?'

'Because he agreed to give information in exchange for turning into a super grass and becoming another name on the list. I told him it was a done deal.'

Darryl scratched the back of his head in frustration. 'Why the fuck would you do that?'

'Because he says he knows where Erica Haversham is staying. I didn't want to say anything in front of everyone, but he's not talking until he knows he's going into witness protection.'

'You know it isn't that easy, Jake. You should have consulted me first.'

'Like I said, this is only the second time I've seen you this morning. Doing it this way means you can prove yourself to me. Make it happen – get Leyton into the witness protection programme without word leaking to anyone. I don't care how you do it, but just make it happen. Then we'll find Erica, and you can save the day. We're the only two people who know anything about this, so if anything happens to him, I'll know who to blame.'

Darryl nudged himself away from the wall and gradually moved towards the door, still scratching the back of his head. Jake watched his every move.

'And if I refuse?' he asked, placing his hands on the handle.

'You know what'll happen. We won't find Erica. And then I'll come for you like I came for everyone else. And I won't stop until I've found out the truth.'

Darryl looked to the floor, defeated, and then back up at Jake. 'Get back to work,' he said as he opened the door.

CHAPTER 37

GRANULE

The entire pressure of the world, the universe, and the ever-expanding cosmos pummelled on Dylan Ayers' head. The slightest movement pained him. His eyes. His arms. His fingers. His chest as it rose and fell. The mother of all comedowns was in full swing, and experience had taught him that he needed to simply ride it out, lie perfectly still on the floor and wait for the hours of turmoil and terror to pass. Although, with the way he was feeling, he wasn't so sure that would be possible. What if it didn't pass? What if he was trapped in this existential state of misery and fear and crisis for the rest of his life?

Blood surged through his body. His breathing increased, provoking more pain in his chest, and he gasped for air, attempting to find it in front of him, but there was nothing left. The room had been starved of oxygen and soon his lungs would do the same. He stared blankly into the ceiling, imagining his shitty and wasted life before he'd taken the copious amounts of drugs that were now flushing through his system.

He opened his mouth to scream, but there was nothing in his lungs, no air left in his body to accomplish the task.

Then he flailed his arms, regardless of the pain it brought with it.

'Hel— Gar— Hen— Pla—'

He was dying. Slowly, slowly dying. The first person ever to switch off the part of their brain that allowed them to—

Something slapped him across the face, and suddenly, everything returned to normal. His breathing. His heart rate. His movements.

'You're scaring me, Dyl,' Erica said. He felt her presence beside him. She touched his hand and massaged his arm with the gentle touch of a mother.

'It's fine. I'm fine. Just a comedown. You might need to do that now and then to bring me back. Put the telly on,' he ordered. 'That helps distract me as well.'

'Are you sure?' Erica said as she stood and moved towards the TV.

'Hundred per cent. I know what I'm doing. How are *you* feeling?'

'Fine,' Erica replied as she switched on the TV and searched for the remote. 'Why aren't I coming down?'

'Oh, you will. Just wait. You don't know when it's coming, but it'll come. So make the most of the high while you still got it. You ain't ever gonna want that baby to stop.'

Erica returned to his side after finding the remote, and as she flicked through the channels, Dylan became frustrated; the jarring sounds coming from the different channels pained his ears and his mind.

'Nickelodeon channel,' he told her. 'I need some SpongeBob.'

'What?'

'Don't judge me.'

'No…' she said. 'I meant *what?* The TV. Dylan… babe, why is your face on the news?'

Dylan shot up, heedless of the searing nausea in his gut, because there, right in front of him, was an enlarged mugshot from the time he was arrested for drug possession and intent to supply to a minor. Beside his face was Erica's, in all her youthful vibrancy and beauty. Her photo was one he didn't recognise -- perhaps it had been taken from her Facebook or somewhere in the family home.

Either way, the reality was the same: they were fucked.

'What are we going to do? Dylan. Dylan. Dylan. What are we going to do?'

Dylan stared at the screen, his mind devoid of thought. How was he supposed to know? He and Henry hadn't planned that far in advance. And after he'd destroyed his phone, there was no way of contacting him for advice.

'They're coming for us,' Erica said, hysterical. 'They're going to find us both. I don't want to go to prison.'

'Be quiet,' he told her, but when she continued to obsess and scream and shout, he eventually told her to shut the fuck up, otherwise he was going to call the police and hand her in himself. 'You stupid bitch. Relax. They've only just put our faces out. Nobody will have seen this yet. Especially in this area.'

'What do you think we should do?'

Because I'm such a fucking master at this…

He was barely able to tie his own shoelaces.

Dylan closed his eyes and tried to think. His mind was as black as the universe and gave him nothing in response, save for a few stars and flashing white lights millions of miles out of reach. Which meant there was only one solution: drugs. More drugs. He always did his best thinking when he was as high as the International Space Station.

Clambering to his feet, Dylan leapt for the baggies of ecstasy, cocaine and heroin on the coffee table, rummaged through the contents and rubbed the rest of the drugs into his gums. There was hardly anything left, but he wouldn't need a lot. Just a little pick-me-up to keep the juices in his brain flowing – and the ideas and good times a'coming.

Almost instantly he became more alert, more alive to the fact his face was on TV, and he began to pace from side to side, thinking, brainstorming, consolidating his thoughts. He didn't know the specifics of what was going on inside his head, but ideas were forming, convalescing, and things were taking shape. If only he'd had this much cognitive ability during school, he might have been able to make something of his life.

It didn't take long before he had a fully formed idea.

'Where's your phone?'

'In my bag. I switched it off like you told me to. I promise.'

Dylan pounced across the room, flipped her bag over, and spilt the contents to the floor. Then he rummaged through it all, searching for her device. Once he'd found it, he hurried over to her.

'I have an important task for you,' he said, waving the phone in her face. 'There's a girl on the estate. Naomi. She looks a lot like you. Same hair. Same height. Same body. Same build. Same eyes. She lives at 461.'

Erica stared at him blankly. To help her understand what he was asking of her, he turned his back on her and searched for the blade they'd used to kill Rupert and Helena. He found it on the kitchen counter, resting atop a chopping board. An everyday item they'd just used to cut a piece of chicken breast.

Erica retreated and scurried to the wall. 'Dylan, what the fuck are you doing?'

'It's for Naomi. Bring her here. Use the knife if you have to. Just make sure she ain't get away.'

Erica's wild eyes bounced between the blade and Dylan. Blade and Dylan. Blade and Dylan.

'The fuck you waiting for?' he snapped, shoving the handle into her fingers.

Reluctantly, Erica took it, fumbled and then dropped it. Bending down to retrieve it, she sobbed, 'D-D-Dylan… Dylan, I can't. What are you going to do with her?'

Dylan wiggled the phone in front of her face again. 'Facebook Live. Stream it. Whatever. Put her face on the Internet. Make her look like you, and then we'll use her to get a ransom. Pretend to kill her if we ain't get what we want.'

It was the best he could come up with.

Correction: the *only* thing he could come up with.

His mind was moving at over a hundred miles an hour, and if he was going to sustain this sort of cognitive thinking, he was going to need more drugs in his system.

'Why can't you come with me?' Erica asked.

Dylan shook his head. 'I gotta set it up. Make it look legit.'

'But what if she's not in, Dylan? What are we going to do then?'

'She'll be in,' Dylan replied, panting with excitement. 'That lazy bitch ain't left the house in weeks. Now get the fuck outta here and go.'

Tentatively, Erica pressed the blade against her chest and, looking like she was about to take part in some sort of religious massacre, ambled towards the door, shuffling her feet along the carpet.

Dylan watched her go, screaming at her internally. She had no sense of urgency. No realisation of the clusterfuck they were in and the desperate need to find a solution as soon as possible.

Once the door closed behind her, he bounded for the bedroom. In the time that she'd taken to leave the flat, Dylan had remembered one very important thing: he had an emergency supply of cocaine locked in the airing cupboard, hidden behind the boiler and network of pipes.

If the next hour was going to be a success, he was going to need every last granule.

CHAPTER 38

NAOMI

Erica's legs trembled under the additional weight of the knife in her hand. She didn't know what to do with it, where to put it, where to hide it. When she'd last held it the other day, she'd known exactly what to do, how to use it. Because of Dylan. When she was with him everything made sense, everything had a purpose. But now she was alone, a polar bear searching for its next meal, fighting for survival.

Now their faces were on TV, that was only going to become harder.

How could they have let it get this bad? The police weren't supposed to identify Dylan this quickly. From all the years she'd heard her father badmouthing the police, she'd gathered they were incompetent and incapable of finding anyone, even if they wandered into the police station and told them exactly who they were. Even Henry had told them it would be easy, that he'd be able to lead the investigation away from them for as long as possible. Unless... unless he'd betrayed them and thrown them under the bus by detailing their location to the entire police force.

No. That was a stupid thing to think. It was a fluke. The police had got lucky, and now they were going to have to deal with the consequences.

Fuck, her head was a mess. The walls and buildings were moving, melting, talking to her. Her eyes were still wide open, and her pulse had never been this high – not even when she'd competed at the regional 5km championships. The drugs were supposed to help numb the pain of slaughtering her family. Yet every time she closed her eyes, she saw them. Bleeding out on the sofa, in the kitchen. Their lives vacating their bodies. Sometimes the hallucinations and images were visceral, horrible, and frightened her to the core. But whenever she set eyes on Dylan, she was reminded she was safe. That he wouldn't do anything to hurt her. Dylan was, without a doubt, the best thing that had happened to her, and she couldn't let anything bad happen to him. To *them*. She trusted him completely, wholeheartedly. And she'd even give her life for his.

Her family already had done.

Fuck her parents. Fuck them all. It was their own fault they'd resented him, disapproved of him the moment they'd met him. It was their own fault they'd judged him for coming from the estate, for being 'lower' than them. All she'd wanted was for his music career to become a success. All she'd wanted was a few thousand pounds, so Dylan could invest it in recording equipment and getting himself signed to a record label. But they'd point-blank refused – and had committed themselves to a bloody death without even realising it.

Somehow, Erica's legs delivered her to flat 461, almost as if she knew instinctively where to find it.

With the blade pressed against her leg, she knocked on the door and waited. Paced from side to side, then turned her back on the flat.

She needed the element of surprise.

And as soon as the door opened, she had it.

Spinning around, Erica lunged at Naomi and held the blade against her neck. She pressed her unsuspecting victim against the wall and covered her mouth with her free hand. Something alien had come over her. Rage. Hunger. This was survival, and she was going to do everything possible to make sure they got out of this alive.

'Shut the fuck up and do exactly as I tell you,' Erica hissed into Naomi's face.

It was like staring into a mirror. The girl pinned against the wall was almost identical to her. The wide, thin eyebrows. The tall forehead. The narrow nose that flared with two large nostrils at the bottom. Even the curve in her lips was the same. It was uncanny.

'Do you understand?'

Naomi nodded, panting heavily.

'If you scream, I will kill you. If you try to run away, I will kill you. I just need to borrow you for a short while. After that, you'll be allowed to go.'

The look in Naomi's eyes told Erica that she didn't believe her. And for a moment, Erica wasn't sure she believed herself either. She had no idea what was going to happen to Naomi after they were finished with her… if they ever were. Would they just let her go or would they end up killing her too?

Another name on the list.

That was too much to think about right now. She was wasting time – time they didn't have. They could deal with that problem when they eventually came to it.

Tears welled in Naomi's eyes. Yet she remained calm. Her chest rose and fell gently, and she stood almost perfectly still. Erica liked to think she would have reacted the same if the situation was the other way round. Fortunately it wasn't, and she hoped she'd never have to find out.

'Come on. You're coming with me.'

CHAPTER 39

CRIME FICTION CRAP

Jake was under strict instructions to wait for the forensics team to arrive before he could even think about setting foot inside the Haversham family mansion. Had this been any other circumstance, he would have gone through on his own regardless, but because tensions were at an all-time high between himself and everyone else on the team, it wasn't worth the risk. Besides, Jake recognised the police constable stationed outside the house as the resident 'arsehole in uniform'. The man had been known to grass on a couple of other officers in the team for the tiniest things. Like forgetting to date the crime-scene-attendance log; not signing the log properly; forgetting to enter any information into the decision logs. He was a try-hard, a pissant, someone who had the shitty job of standing in the same spot for twelve hours a day until it was time for someone to take his place, yet felt like he was the king of all those above him. An overinflated ego for a slight, skinny man. If he wasn't careful, it would blow him away.

'Excuse me, sir,' the officer said, holding his hand out at Jake. 'This is an active crime scene. I'm going to have to ask you to leave.'

Of course he doesn't remember me. Self-centred prick.

'It's all right, Phil. You can put your truncheon and handcuffs away. I'm not into that kinky stuff,' Jake said, flashing his warrant card.

'Tanner. My apologies. Didn't recognise you.' Phil stood tall and puffed his chest out a little higher as soon as he recognised Jake.

'I'd like to keep it that way, thanks. Don't want people thinking I have any friends.' Jake enjoyed making conversations uncomfortable and awkward, especially with people he didn't like. 'I imagine you've been rushed off your feet standing here.'

Phil shrugged smugly. 'You'd be surprised. From what I hear, Haversham was a bit of a local celeb round these ends. We've had a lot of strangers and people claiming to be friends and family coming round here to see what's going on.'

'Good thing we're doing a good job of keeping the press out of it all, isn't it?'

'I don't give it long. If you ask me, we should have gone public with it sooner.'

I didn't ask you, but thanks for your concern.

'All hell would break loose if you were in charge, Phil,' Jake replied, placing his hands on his hips. 'Imagine the anarchy.'

'That reminds me,' Phil started. 'Some woman came by yesterday asking after you – said she recognised your face from all that TV work you did. Think she wanted to chat.'

'I'm a local celeb round this neck of the woods, Phil. She'll be asking to have my babies soon.'

Fortunately, Jake was saved from more mind-numbing chat by the arrival of a Volvo V60 outside the house. Two SOCOs alighted the vehicle and wandered up to them. One of them held a briefcase in their hands while the other was on their phone.

'What's this?' Jake asked. 'Didn't you get the memo? We're all supposed to be dressed in our uniform for the party.'

'Funny,' the SOCO carrying the briefcase said. He set the case on the pavement and removed three white oversuits, then handed one to Jake and another to his colleague.

'Is there something I need to know?' Phil asked.

'Didn't anybody tell you? We've come here to slaughter you and hide the remains,' Jake joked, but from the look on Phil's face, he didn't find it funny. Jake rolled his eyes, apologised for causing any offence and then explained the real reason they were there.

'I wasn't aware of this,' Phil responded.

'Well, now you are. Where do you want me to sign? On the back of the page? Your arm? Forehead?'

Phil scowled at him and pointed to the box on the document. Jake entered his details, the purpose of his visit, and then signed and dated it on the far right of the sheet. Then he sidestepped Phil and entered the house.

'You know what you're here for?' Jake asked as the SOCOs followed shortly behind him.

'Erica Haversham's computer,' Briefcase replied.

'Correct. And everything else that comes with it. Mouse. Keyboard. Memory sticks. Anything you can find.' Jake paused. 'Well, off you go then.'

'Aren't you coming with us?'

Jake shook his head. 'I was just told to stand here and look pretty while you guys did all the hard work. So I'll be waiting right here for you when you get back.'

The SOCOs shrugged as though it was a common occurrence,

pinched their face masks into position and climbed the stairs. As soon as they were out of sight and he could hear the sounds of them setting to work on the top floor, Jake shuffled to Rupert Haversham's office as quietly as possible and started opening the door. The hinges groaned and echoed throughout the house, so he opened it just wide enough for him to fit through and slid in. Without wasting any time, he hurried past the bookshelves and elliptical machine towards the printer in the far corner.

There, he crouched down and, using the sleeve of the oversuit as an extra layer of protection against his fingerprints, lifted the lid on the printer.

Nothing. Save his reflection in the glass scanner.

Fuck.

Where was the final copy of their agreement? Where could it have gone? He was adamant Rupert had placed it in there and then forgotten about it. Unless it had already been seized as evidence by one of the SOCOs?

Double fuck.

But wait, no, that couldn't be the case, otherwise Darryl would have jumped on his arse like an angry police dog as soon as he'd discovered Jake had been lying to him. No. No. No. It was somewhere else; he *needed* it to be somewhere else.

Where the fuck would it be?

Jake rose, took a step back, and closed his eyes. Transported himself back to the meeting. Rupert on the left. Himself on the right, sitting furthest away from the desk. Rupert leant across. Placed the document in the printer. Scanned it. And then…

There'd been a knock on the door. Helena, Rupert's wife. Standing there in her Lycra leggings and crop top. She'd just finished a session with her personal trainer. Apparently, it had been a difficult one; the beads of sweat on her face and chest were testament to that. She apologised and said she didn't mean to interrupt, then had asked to borrow her husband for a second. Jake had replied that it was OK.

Rupert had lifted himself out of his chair and a sound had come from behind Jake – the sound of the scanner lid opening – but he'd paid little attention to it and unashamedly admired Helena Haversham instead. She looked good for someone in her late forties.

Then Rupert had distracted him by explaining he'd be back in a second, and as soon as he'd left, Jake had returned his attention to the desk and the printer, swinging in the chair awkwardly while he waited.

But what was different about the image? There was something new which hadn't been there moments ago.

And then he remembered.

Jake opened his eyes and craned his neck to look at the shelf that hung above the computer monitors. His gaze searched the forest of folders and files until eventually it landed on a light pink folder. He pulled it down, paying extra attention to delicacy, lest the rest fall atop him.

A white sticker was attached to the front of the folder. *Sexual Harassment: Women.*

Jake wasn't sure he appreciated the colour coding, but he was more than grateful it was helping him now.

He opened the folder and held his breath, hands shaking as he leafed through the first couple of pages. Fortunately, the number of cases regarding Sexual Harassment: Women was relatively thin, so it didn't take him long to find it.

Mr Jake Isaac Tanner.

Mrs Elizabeth Isobel Tanner.

Then he heard footsteps, drawing closer, coming from upstairs. Each creak of the floorboards sent sharp daggers of paranoia up and down his spine.

Panicked, he tore the contract from the ring binder, folded it several times, and slipped it into his blazer pocket beneath the forensic suit. Slamming the folder shut with one hand, he zipped his suit up to his neck with the other. In the time that he'd taken to find the contract, the folders had fallen and leant against one another at an angle. He didn't have time to remember exactly where the pink one went, otherwise he was certain he'd be caught in the act.

'Detective Tanner?' called a concerned SOCO.

He ignored them and focused on the small – yet seemingly insurmountable – task of putting the folder back. After squeezing it between a yellow and green folder, he skipped backward into the centre of the room and pretended to look at the books, just as Briefcase entered the door. For a short while, Jake's life had been like a movie scene – except without the fame and the glory and the multimillion-pound pay cheque at the end of it.

'Detective?'

Jake snapped his gaze to the man standing in the doorway, feigning surprise.

'We've got everything we need,' the SOCO explained.

'Excellent.' He pointed to the books. 'You like to read?'

'Not particularly.'

'Neither do I,' Jake said, starting towards the investigator. 'Can't stand all that crime fiction crap, either. Hardly any of it's right. The bad guys always seem to get caught and the good guys get off unscathed.'

'They call it fiction for a reason.' The investigator smirked and stepped aside for Jake to pass.

Just as they entered the hallway, Jake's mobile vibrated. He unzipped himself and fished the device out of his pocket.

It was Darryl.

What now?

'Everything all right, guv?' Jake asked magnanimously as he answered the call.

'Jake, I need you to get down to The Pit ASAP. Dylan and Erica

Haversham have just gone live on social media. Dylan's threatening to kill Erica on the Internet.'

CHAPTER 40

SQUEEZING

'It's fucking simple, you fucking cretins,' Dylan hissed on the other side of the door. 'She ain't getting outta here alive until we get our money. A hundred grand. In tens.'

The last image Erica had of him, before she'd closed the front door, was of him holding the knife against Naomi's neck, standing in front of her mobile phone, which had been propped onto a makeshift stand.

They were livestreaming the horrid event on Erica's Facebook page, where all her friends and family – and hopefully the world's media – would be watching. Naomi was almost comatose, thanks to a combination of ecstasy they'd forced into her bloodstream from Dylan's secret stash followed by a punch to the head as soon as they'd realised the drugs were having the opposite effect – they needed her unconscious rather than bouncing off the walls. Meanwhile, Erica was under strict instructions to stay outside the flat and stand guard. It was too risky for her to be in the same space as him, just in case she came into shot or spoilt the façade they'd created.

Be a good girl and keep a lookout, will ya, babe? Will you be a good girl?

She paced from side to side, scratching her arms nervously until she no longer felt pain. Her fingernails ran over the razor-blade scars she'd given herself last year, before Dylan had entered her life. They were nothing but a blemish on her skin now, a distant memory of when times had been dark. But there was light in her life now. She loved him, and he loved her. And they were going to do everything together. They were going to become rich. They were going to follow Dylan's master plan.

'You've got twenty-four hours to give us our money!' Dylan screamed on the other side of the door. 'If you come anywhere near us, I'm going to kill her and then you'll be fucking sorry.'

Erica stopped pacing. Something in the distance had caught her eye. A black car pulled in and parked up outside the estate. And then another. *Holy shit.* Reality sank in. They'd arrived. But now she and Dylan had a lifeline; they were staying in one of the low-rises that looked out onto the estate, and she estimated they had a lifeline of a few minutes. The police wouldn't find them immediately, but it wouldn't be long until they did.

Erica spun on the spot, and as she placed her hand on the door handle, a figure appeared out the corner of her eye.

'Excuse me?' the figure asked, moving closer.

Erica tried to move, but couldn't. Her hand was frozen to the handle.

'I was wondering if you might be able to help me?'

Erica slowly tilted her head. Before she could get a clear look at the person's face, they lunged at her.

The person's arms wrapped around her body. In their hand, they held a piece of cloth and smothered it over her mouth. Erica gasped and clawed at the cloth and arm, begging for air to fill her lungs, but instead she was disorientated by the acrid taste and smell that filled her world.

Spinning, spinning.

She struggled, but her efforts were useless beneath her attacker's weight. Then her attacker's arm tightened around her neck, like a python slowly crushing its victim to death, and she felt her head pulsate and expand as if it was about to explode. Stars started to dance in her vision, erupting around the estate, leaking colour all over the walls and sky. Until a giant purple veil fell over her vision.

Squeezing, squeezing.

Her attacker's grip remained firm against her throat and the back of her neck, the chokehold doing exactly as prescribed.

Gradually, with each gasping breath, the purple veil darkened and obfuscated her surroundings.

Squeezing, squeezing.

'Easy does it,' a distant voice said, growing more distant with every second. 'I'm going to take good care of you. Don't worry.'

CHAPTER 41

STRATOSPHERE

The blistering sensation that coursed through his veins was bigger and better and more euphoric than any drug he could have injected himself with, smoked, snorted, or rubbed into his gums. It was otherworldly. Taking him to another planet, another solar system, another universe. Sending him into the barrenness of the cosmos.

Flashbacks of stabbing Rupert Haversham multiple times in the stomach and suffocating little Felicity Haversham raced through his mind. It had felt good, yes. A release, yes. But nothing as powerful as this. Killing the Haversham family had been a necessity, and because they were so wrapped in the fear and trepidation of it all, the show had been over too quickly. As a result, he hadn't been able to enjoy it as much as he'd hoped.

But this… this was different. Instead of taking another life, he was teasing it, balancing it on the edge of death or freedom. That balance gave him power – unimaginable amounts of power. He could certainly get used to this.

He pulled the knife away from Naomi's neck and pointed it at the camera.

'Any of you fuckers think you'll find us, you're wrong. You ain't never gonna find us.'

Naomi's head lolled to the side. By now, the drugs he'd found in his emergency stash were taking full effect and she was becoming a dead weight, gradually dropping into a comatose state. His left arm bore the brunt of it, and it was beginning to ache. His muscles weren't built for this; the heaviest thing he was used to lifting was the six-pack of energy drinks he used as an alternative whenever he got the munchies.

He shimmied her up to get better purchase around her waist and tried switching arms. But as he moved the blade from one hand to the other, he almost dropped her.

Eventually, he did it without issue.

That was better. The beautiful girl on the right, the beautiful blade on the left. Now he felt much stronger, much more in control. Except for his left arm, which still felt weak from the weight of her body.

But he couldn't lose face. There were people watching. Hundreds. Thousands. Maybe even hundreds of thousands. Think of what this could do to his career – it could send him into the stratosphere. He'd be famous after all this was over.

No inheritance? Didn't matter. He had brand deals and sponsorships coming his way. The lot.

He was going to be a millionaire, guided by his own delusions.

But there was a problem.

Without warning, Naomi's body convulsed. And then convulsed again. And again. Phlegm and spittle dribbled from her mouth, down her chin and onto her shirt.

As Dylan peered round her shoulder to have a look at her lopsided face, he lost hold of her. Her body only fell a few inches before he regained control, but it was enough time and distance for the edge of the blade to impale itself in her throat.

'Fuck!' he screamed. But it was already too late. As he panicked, he yanked the blade forward, tearing her throat in two, spilling fountains of blood onto the metal, his wrist, and her body.

Panicked, he dropped her and let her collapse to the floor. If she wasn't already dead from the drug overdose, then she was now.

Before he did anything else, Dylan grabbed the phone and launched it at the wall. The device remained solid, but the glass screen fractured into hundreds of splintered pieces. He bent down, stepped into the pool of blood that was now forming around Naomi's neck, and removed the blade that had become lodged between her oesophagus and bone.

He stared at her for a long time, feeling the raw power dissipate from his body. The furore and excitement were gone, along with his chances of becoming a millionaire.

Clutching the blade tightly in his grip, he sprinted towards the door and found the corridor empty.

Where the fuck's Erica?

This was fucked. *He* was fucked. He needed to evacuate immediately. He couldn't think about Erica right now – whether she'd popped round the corner or if she'd gone to get a drink from the off-licence. She'd deserted him and now it was time to desert her. Every man for himself.

Survival of the fittest.

Unable to process the last few minutes, Dylan turned and sprinted down the side of the building, jumped into the stairwell and skipped the steps two at a time. A few seconds later, he arrived at the bottom of the block, ran across the forecourt, and headed for the streets. But as he paced through the underpass beneath the building, an Austin Mini Cooper skidded to a halt on the other side of the road. A man dressed in a suit erupted from the car and chased after him, screaming into a radio.

Dylan pumped his legs and arms like his life depended on it.

CHAPTER 42

PUNCTURE

Jake prioritised his radio as he erupted from his Mini and chased after Dylan Ayers. They were of similar age, but Dylan's body was slighter, thinner, shorter, sportier. The young man's legs moved rapidly as he sprinted to the edge of the estate. Jake, lumbered with uncomfortable shoes that were in no appropriate state for running and his blazer flapping about by his arms and back, pursued a few yards behind.

'All units. All units. Suspect fleeing the Cosgrove Estate, heading west on Mortham Street.'

Before long, his breathing became heavy, exasperated, and he struggled to enunciate the words effectively. The months' worth of alcohol and ready meals were finally playing catch-up. And he knew that, soon enough, he wouldn't be able to speak at all – not unless he wanted to slow his pace and hand Dylan the advantage.

Although, as things stood, that was already the case. Dylan's skinny legs moved in a blur, and with every passing second, the distance between him and Jake grew. If Jake was going to stand any chance of catching up with him – before his lungs, heart and cardiovascular system gave up – then he was going to have to do it sooner rather than later.

They reached the end of Mortham Street. Dylan cut a right and headed north on Bridge Street, veering into the centre of the road. On the right-hand side was a neighbouring housing estate, with cars parked awkwardly on both sides of the street. Jake hoped Dylan didn't duck in there; otherwise, he would lose him through the myriad underpasses and alleyways. This concrete jungle was Dylan's playground, and Jake was in his territory.

Meanwhile, on the left-hand side, running alongside them, were seven lanes of railway track. Docklands Light Railway carriages shuttled past them in both directions, their wheels running smoothly over the tracks, creating a rhythm for Jake as he pumped his body.

Thck-dum. Thck-dum. Thck-dum.

By now, adrenaline surged through him, swallowing the fatigue and aches in his muscles and feet, his movements methodical, smooth. Left. Right. Left. Right. Breathe. Swing. Breathe. Swing.

Slowly, he was regaining ground on Dylan. But it still wasn't enough.

Jake was already beginning to sense what was happening – what Dylan's plan was. That the young man was heading straight towards Stratford High Street Underground station. If Jake lost him there, there would be no catching up with him.

'Juliet-Tango-Four-Five. Juliet-Tango-Four-Five,' the call came over the radio. 'This is Lima-Golf-Two-Three. Update your status.'

Jake slowed, held the radio to his mouth and gasped between breaths. 'North – on – Bridge – Street – High – Street – station.'

The sudden distraction, as much as it was good because it meant support was on the way, had had a negative effect. Rather than being numbed to the pain of sprinting, he became aware of what he was doing. Aware of the physical endurance he was suffering. And his brain became aware of the need to slow down and recover.

Jake couldn't let that happen.

In the distance, he heard sirens wailing. But they weren't close enough. He needed them to be on top of him, racing down Bridge Street.

Up ahead, a car hurtled towards them. Dylan veered onto the other side of the road, running alongside the railway lines. For a split second, Jake thought he was about to vault the walls and cross the tracks.

Before he allowed his mind to think too much about anything, Jake waited for the car to pass him, crossed the road, and continued ahead. The entrance to the Underground station was less than a hundred yards away.

Jake snapped his head to the left and saw a southbound train nearing the platform. The only thing standing in their path was a teenager pushing a pram. Dylan side jumped out of the way, and Jake followed suit, stumbling over an exposed tree root.

It was then, as he regained himself and as Dylan flailed his arms in the air to avoid the baby, that Jake realised the assailant was carrying a weapon in his hand. A blade. Six inches.

Maybe longer.

Was it the same murder weapon used to kill Rupert and Helena? Now wasn't the time to think about it.

Ten seconds later, they arrived at the Underground station. As they reached the entrance, a flurry of police cars turned up at the end of the road and skidded to a halt. Dylan made a sharp left turn into the station before any of the officers had alighted their vehicles.

Jake, now, was inches behind him. The young man was showing

signs of fatigue, but there was a determination in him to succeed – Jake supposed it was innate to all inhabitants of the Cosgrove Estate, regardless of their age and physical appearance.

Ahead, up on Platform 3, was the train Jake had spotted coming in, slowing down as it neared the platform. By the time it opened its doors, Dylan had reached the end of the bridge and arrived at the centre of the station. Jumping two steps at a time, Jake followed and kept an eye on the carriage doors, praying they would close in time.

Mercifully, as they both leapt onto the platform – Jake inches behind Dylan – the doors to the DLR train shut. Dylan collided with the metal carriage to pry the doors open with his fingers. But it was no use. Jake was on top of him before he could realise what was going on.

Sirens wailed in the distance. Screams and shouts pierced the tranquillity of the station, heavy footsteps echoing around the platform and bridge.

Jake tackled Dylan to the ground, rolling away from the soon-to-be-moving train. He landed on his back with his arms wrapped around Dylan. The man still held the knife in his hands, and the blade hacked at Jake's wrist. Sharp bolts of pain shot up his arms and hands. He flinched and released his grip.

Dylan took the opportunity and capitalised, rolling off Jake and readying himself for attack.

Wise to it, Jake grabbed Dylan's hands and the two of them fought for ownership of the blade – Jake fighting for his life, Dylan fighting for his escape.

The young man's weight crushed him, and he was slowly losing his strength, the tip of the blade getting closer and closer to his stomach.

Closer and closer.

He gritted his teeth and summoned every ounce of energy he could find. His muscles screamed in agony. The demonic look of determination in Dylan's eyes told him there was no way out. Jake was going to die. Stabbed in the stomach.

Closer and closer.

Then he felt the tip pierce his clothes.

Closer and closer.

Puncture the skin.

Before Dylan could inflict any more damage, the army of police officers rushed over and tackled him to the ground. The knife became dislodged from Jake's stomach and clattered to the ground.

He lay there on his back. His body numb. Paralysed. Only slightly aware of what had happened to him.

He moved his hand down his left side and touched the wound. His hands were covered in his own blood. His own blood!

And that was when reality sank in. The pain swelled in his body like a balloon, ready and waiting to burst.

Two uniformed officers jumped down by his side and placed pressure on the wound to staunch the blood flow. They were shouting at him, but he couldn't hear anything they were saying. Sound had become muted, silent, drowned out by the noise of his heart beating in his ear a hundred times a minute. An invisible weight pressed down on his chest. His pores opened up, and he began to sweat.

He was having an anxiety attack. The swathes of white were rolling over him as he stared into the sky, clawing at whatever oxygen his lungs could grab. The last thing Jake saw before he passed out was a commercial airliner cutting his field of vision in two.

CHAPTER 43

DOCTOR'S ORDERS

Something in Jake's brain triggered and startled him awake with a gasp, clawing for his next breath. His eyes burst open and, as soon as he realised he was no longer staring into the sky in the middle of Stratford High Street station – and that he was in fact staring into the plasterboard of a ceiling – his heart raced, and his skin became moist with a thin layer of sweat.

He was lying on a hospital bed. Beside him was an ECG monitor beeping monotonously next to his head, the sound echoing inside his skull.

Beep. Beep. Beep.

To his left was his darling Elizabeth. Sitting in a chair, her head slumped forward, resting against the pillow of her collarbone. As he stared at her, something innate roused her. Perhaps it was a maternal instinct. Perhaps it was because their love for one another was stronger than anything on a physical level. Whatever it was, it made her leap off the chair as soon as she realised he was awake.

'Are you OK? Oh, Jake, you foolish, foolish man. I've been worried sick about you. Everyone has. What have I told you about making sure you come home to the girls in one piece?'

Nice to see you too. He knew she was only saying those things because she was protective of him.

'One of these days I'll listen.'

'Do you know where you are?' Elizabeth asked, wrapping her hand in his and placing the other on his shoulder.

'I assume it's not Disneyland? Or if it is then is it Paris? I heard that's the shit one.'

Elizabeth's lips flickered, the start of a smile striking her face – but she soon stifled it. 'Now's not the time for jokes. This is serious.

You've been stabbed.'

Jake remembered it perfectly: jumping into Dylan before he boarded the train, falling to the platform, tussling on the ground, the blade penetrating his stomach, the officers rushing to his aid and arresting Dylan a few seconds too late. But it wasn't until she confirmed it for him that it became real. Up until that point he'd felt nothing – not even the slightest modicum of discomfort – but as soon as she'd said it, a vicious, searing pain swelled in his lower left abdomen. It hurt to breathe. He moved his hand to his stomach, but the pain was too intense.

'Maybe we need to get you more painkillers,' Elizabeth said, squeezing his hand. Like most wives, she didn't enjoy seeing him in any sort of suffering or discomfort.

'No,' he told her. 'It's fine. *I'm* fine. Just sit. Please. Take my mind off it.'

Jake, stoic as ever, winced as he tried to shuffle himself higher up the bed. Elizabeth attempted to help him but he told her no.

'How many fucking times do I have to say this, Jake? You – don't – always – have – to – be – the – fucking – hero. No one's going to judge you for accepting help. Not for the situation you're in.'

Jake rolled his head to the side and stared into her eyes. 'I know,' he replied. 'I know. I'm just… I'm just in shock.'

'So am I!' She reached for his hand and grabbed it gently. Her soft squeeze numbed the pain slightly. 'I've been worried sick. When Darryl told me you'd been injured, I thought it was a lie. I thought it was some sort of sick joke you guys play.' Tears of pain and fear – and perhaps a few tears of love and respect – began to swell in her eyes. 'Oh, Jake. Why did you chase after him if you knew he was carrying a knife?'

'I was doing my—'

'Don't you dare say it,' she interrupted. 'Don't you dare utter *that* word. You've put your life on the line for that job, Jake, and one of these days you're not going to come home. Something bad's going to happen to you and I don't want to be the one to tell the girls that their daddy's never coming back for dinner. You're only one more mistake away from making that a reality.'

Jake paused a moment. He wasn't sure whether she was referring to the stabbing or to what was going on in their personal lives.

The answer was in the phrase.

One more mistake away…

Solemnly, Jake replied, 'Listen, Liz. I can explain.'

'Don't. Just don't. Please. I don't want to talk about it. My mum's tidying up the house now. As soon as you're released, I'm taking you back where you belong – and you're going to *rest*.'

Jake smiled, but it wasn't the smile he wanted to give, and it wasn't the one she wanted to receive.

'I can't, Nelly. I have to go back to work.'

'Like fuck you do. What did I *just* say about being a hero?'

181

Jake sighed and turned his head away from her. For a moment he contemplated trying to explain it to her – that he needed to finish the investigation, that he needed to clear his name, that he finally needed to find out who was framing him and threatening to ruin his career – but then he thought better of it. She wouldn't understand. She had no idea what was going on at work. And that was his fault, his mistake. He'd kept her in the dark about it all, and now he'd made it more difficult for himself to open up to her and let her in. It was just a shame that it had taken a stab wound to the stomach for him to realise that. But he'd gone past the point of no return now. He was in the habit of lying and shielding her from the facts, so why start being honest now?

Slowly, he turned to face her. 'What did the doctors say?'

Elizabeth rubbed her eye and wiped away the tears from her cheek. 'They said that you're very lucky. So don't throw that luck away by being stupid. Less than an inch of the blade went in. They said it was more of a flesh wound than anything, so it missed your vital organs and you were protected by the layer of fat on your belly. All those ready meals and takeaways have done you some good, it would seem.'

If that wasn't a winning argument for having a takeaway once a week, he didn't know what was. Flesh wound or not, he would tell people he'd been stabbed. And that he had the scar to prove it.

'They've done some blood tests on you, but they want to do more. The police reckon the blade might have been used to kill Rupert and Helena, so they checked you for HIV.'

Jake's body went stiff. 'And?'

'Like I said, lucky. You've not come back with anything, but they want to keep you in a little longer.'

'Did they say how long?'

'A couple of days or so. You also have to wait for the stitches to heal, don't forget.'

Days? Jake didn't have days. There was no knowing what The Cabal could do in that time, what Henry Matheson could do in that time. Both organisations were working independently of one another, which meant there was no snake's head to sever that would kill the rest of the body. These were two deadly and venomous vipers, working on their own for their very own purposes – even if The Cabal's wasn't abundantly clear yet. And if he was going to mount investigations into both, against an invisible clock, he couldn't afford to take several days off.

Jake's gaze moved across the room and fell on Elizabeth's coat on the end of his bed.

'My clothes…' he began. 'Where are they? My blazer… where is it?'

'I don't know. I think the paramedics took it when they brought you here. Or the hospital disposed of it. I haven't seen them.'

'You need to find my blazer,' Jake replied, keeping his gaze on

Elizabeth's coat.

'Why?'

'I need you to find it. It has the contract we signed with Rupert.'

At the mention of the solicitor's name, Elizabeth's eyes widened.

'I took it from his house earlier and was going to burn it, but then… You need to find it, Liz. Make sure nobody sees it. I don't want to give anyone any more reason to suspect me of killing Rupert and his family.'

'I understand.' She nodded. 'Who can I speak to about it?'

'General procedure would dictate that—'

A knock came at the door. Elizabeth and Jake glanced over at once, fear etching its way onto Elizabeth's face. To calm her, he nodded, confirming that it was OK for her to open the door.

Standing on the other side was Darryl.

'I thought I heard voices,' he said as he entered the room. 'I can come back if you'd like?'

'Come in,' Jake affirmed.

'It's good to see you. The boys and girls back at the station have been worried sick.'

Jake smiled facetiously with the expression of someone who just wanted to hear what needed to be said and then move on.

'I just… I wanted to let you know that we've got Dylan in custody. You did a good job out there. I'm proud of you. The team is too. Without your bravery, Dylan would have escaped. I'll see to it you get a commendation for this.'

'I don't want a commendation,' Jake replied. 'A piece of paper won't change anything.'

'Erica Haversham's still missing,' Darryl said, moving the conversation along.

'How?'

'A girl was found dead inside one of Henry Matheson's old flats. But it wasn't Erica. You know the livestream they started? Turns out they'd abducted another girl to pose as Erica. I've watched it over a dozen times and her death looks like an accident, but we have no idea where Erica is now. She could be on the run. Afraid. Frightened. She could have been abducted again. Or, worse, she could have been killed and left somewhere.'

Jake sighed and stared into his feet at the end of the bed. His toes were filthy and in need of a clean.

'I can help find her,' Jake said. 'As soon as I'm out of here, I'll—'

'No you won't.' Elizabeth paced over to him, pointing at his face. 'You'll do no such thing.'

'Liz, I have—'

'If you go back to work, I'm leaving you.'

One more mistake…

'Liz, come on—' Jake turned to face Darryl, imploring him with a look to support him and convince her.

In response, Darryl raised his hands and stepped back. 'I'm

staying out of this one.'

'What?' Elizabeth cried. 'You're not going to do anything? So you're happy for him to come back and risk his life again?'

'No, that's not what— That's not entirely… I mean…' Darryl paused to compose himself. He lifted his head and looked at Jake. 'It's simple, mate. And I know it's not what you want to hear, but you're injured. We've got enough bodies on the ground who can solve this case. But right now, you need to put your body and your health first. Depending on the doctor's orders, I'm suspending you for the indefinite future. You need to rest.'

CHAPTER 44

VICODIN

The mantra was simple: keep your fingers clean while everyone else dirties theirs. It wasn't eloquent, but, after all, it was simple. And simplicity was the main reason she was at the top of the industry and had remained hidden, unseen and unidentified for so long.

But in the past few months, ever since Richard Candy, her second in command, her fall guy, had died, things had grown increasingly complex. Her entire empire had fallen. The human trafficking business was defunct and all the funds had been seized. The drugs business was now functioning without her overseeing operations – Henry Matheson was in charge and continuing to run things from inside prison. She had no pulling power, no stamp of authority; everyone who'd ever worked with her was either dead or in prison.

And neither of those two options were helpful to her.

No longer was she able to instruct her subordinates to carry out her dirty work. No longer was she able to keep the dirty cogs in her corruption machine free from her fingerprints. The game had changed. But like any entrepreneur and self-starter, she had improved, overcome and adapted. And she would continue to do so.

Henry thought he was so clever. Sure, she was wrapped around his little finger, telling her what to do, but she had plans of her own.

The lights inside Jake Tanner's house were on. There was a car parked outside the front, and she recognised it as Martha Clarke's. That bitch. Without realising it, she'd ruined the next part of the plan. Now she was going to have to deal with the problem in the back of her car another way. She hadn't wanted it to come to this, but it was necessary, if only temporary. The Cabal switched into reverse, turned in the road and headed home.

As she pulled up outside her house on the outskirts of London in

Essex, just within the circle of the M25, she made sure the street was deserted and the lights in the houses were switched off. It was 2 a.m., and there was no reason for most people to be awake. It was a weeknight, so the kids would be asleep, and the adults, if any, would be enjoying some alone time. The only risk she could foresee was Charles, the brain surgeon who lived a couple of houses down the road. On too many occasions, she'd bumped into him in the early hours of the morning as he came back from one of his gruelling thirteen-hour shifts. But she didn't need to worry about him too much; Charles was aware of the line of business she was in, even if she'd never told him explicitly.

After making sure the street was empty, she alighted the vehicle, moved to the rear of the car, and opened the boot. The small yellow light buried into the coving illuminated a frightened and sodden Erica Haversham. The young girl's clothes were damp with sweat, and there was a dark patch by her crotch where she'd soiled herself. The unmistakable smell of piss wafted through The Cabal's nostrils. *Poor little girl.*

As soon as the boot door opened, Erica cowered behind her arms, protecting her face from potential attack. The tape that she'd placed around Erica's mouth, hands and eyes had been shoddy, a hashed job, but it fulfilled its purpose.

She bent down to Erica's height. The girl groaned and moaned slightly as she came nearer.

'If you scream, I will make you wish you hadn't. Do you understand?'

Erica froze.

Slowly, she nodded.

Without saying anything else, The Cabal hooked her hand underneath Erica's arms and lifted her out of the boot. Supporting the girl's weight on hers, she shut the boot and dragged her to the front door.

Knocked, waited.

There in front of her was her husband, dressed in his pyjamas, with a cup of tea in one hand and a newspaper in the other. Several hours behind the rest of the country.

'Is it ready?' she asked as she crossed the threshold into her home.

'Just about,' he replied.

'I asked for it to be ready by the time I got here.'

'You said we'd never need to use it again.'

She shook her head in disbelief. 'I never said never.'

She shuffled Erica through the hallway and towards the stairs. Beneath them was a cupboard. She yanked it open and led Erica down to the basement. There, in the centre of the basement, was Erica's home for the foreseeable future.

She called it The Box. Five feet wide and eight feet deep, made of solid steel – ample space for Erica's tiny body. Carved into the door was a small hole, large enough for a plate to fit through, that only opened from the outside. There were no lights inside, no windows – except for a small hole in the top for ventilation.

There was no escape.

For the next few days at the very least, Erica would be submerged in total darkness. She wouldn't know what time it was. What day it was. Where she was. The darkness was going to become both her enemy and her friend.

The Cabal opened the door and thrust Erica inside. The girl stumbled and smashed her hip into the bed, let out a little whimper and cowered into the foetal position. Along the back wall was a single bed, with only a six-inch-thick mattress for support. On the right-hand side was a makeshift toilet connected to a pipe that led to a drain outside the house. And that was it. The bare essentials.

'Turn around,' she told Erica.

Slowly, the girl complied.

'This is home. You will be fed. You will be hydrated. You will not scream. You will not be able to do anything. You will never see our faces.'

She moved forward, grabbed the tape around Erica's mouth, and yanked it free.

'Do you understand?'

'Yes,' Erica replied, her voice weak.

Then she removed the tape around Erica's hands and eyes. As she stepped out of The Box, Erica remained staring ahead.

'I'm sorry it's come to this, Erica,' she said and then shut the door.

After the sound of the door slamming had finished echoing around the basement, the room was quickly filled with silence. It didn't take long for the noises to start. At first it started off as sniffling. Then it turned into a gentle, light sob.

The Cabal looked down at the floor and pinched the bridge of her nose. She meant what she'd said. It wasn't right. And it wasn't fair to Erica. But she had a job to do.

As The Cabal started up the stairs, she froze. Her husband was waiting for her at the top with his arms folded.

'We need to talk about this,' he said as he shut the door behind her.

'There's nothing to talk about, Dennis. It's done. I've had to do what I've had to do. It's only temporary.'

She moved into the kitchen, over to the sink, and started to wash up the dishes. She always found it helped clear her mind, the sounds of constant running water drowning out the noise in her head. Plus it helped hide the tears that were forming in the corners of her eyes.

'But what if—'

'Can you please just go with me on this one?' She switched off the tap in anger and dried her hands using a tea towel. 'Have we got enough Vicodin?'

'Enough for a couple of days, like you asked.'

'Good. Thank you. You *are* capable of doing what you're told then.'

She moved over to the wine rack, pulled herself together, poured a glass of wine, and then downed it. It had been a long time since she'd needed a drink.

'What happened out there?' Dennis asked, attempting to place a soft, comforting hand on her shoulder. But she was in no mood to receive it and shoved him away.

'You'll find out soon enough,' she responded.

'Was it Matheson?'

She set the glass down on the counter. It made a little *clink*.

'When isn't it about Matheson?' she replied, more a statement than a question.

A moment of solemn silence fell on them. She decided to fill it with the sound of her pouring more wine into the glass and drinking it – this time slower than the first.

'Did you do what I asked you to?' she said, setting the half-drunk glass on the countertop.

'Yes.'

'And?'

'Hari confirmed the shipment's coming in.'

'And?'

'A hundred kilos of heroin and cocaine. Stuffed in TV boxes.'

'He told me it was only fifty,' she said, more to herself than her husband. 'That cheeky shitbag.'

'It's all coming in one container.'

She sidled closer to her husband, forgetting entirely about her drink. 'Continue…'

'His side of the bargain is that he's being entrusted with the delivery. If it goes wrong, it's on his head and he pays the price.'

'A hundred kilograms of heroin and cocaine is a massive price.'

'Exactly, but if he can make it work, then he's getting a thirty per cent stake in the market. And the Romanians and Hellbanianz are promising to stay off his turf. From that point on, there's a truce.'

'And how do we fit into this?' she asked, thinking aloud again.

Henry Matheson's agreement completely shut her and her husband out of the deal. Before, back at the height of her empire, she'd been the one dictating the agreements with the competition, making sure that they stayed out of East London. That had given her control over the market, but with Henry now possessing all the bargaining power, she didn't have a leg to stand on.

'Did you ask when the shipment's coming in?'

'The same day Matheson told you.'

'At least we know he's not lying to us about that. But I still don't trust him.'

'Why?'

'Because this is Matheson we're talking about. He's always got a plan. And I want you to find out what it is. When I spoke to him the other day, he said he wanted you there to keep an eye on things, to make sure all went smoothly and that you report the truth to him –

apparently his guys like to embellish the facts if things go right, and hide them if they don't. I want you there in a different capacity. I want you to document the drug deal so that we can hand it into the police. That way they'll put everyone in his gang, the Romanians and also the Albanians, behind bars. Nobody will trust Matheson again, and once the dust has settled, we can pick things up again. But whatever you do, don't fuck it up. I've got to sort out Erica first.'

| DAY 5 |

CHAPTER 45

FUNERAL

It had taken Jake several hours to convince the nurses and doctors –
without Elizabeth present – that he was fine and ready to go home.
The last place he wanted to be was in the hospital. Not least because
he didn't like them, but because he was feeling much better, save for
the infrequent pain in his lower left abdomen when he stretched or
reached too far. After carrying out a few more tests, the doctors
eventually ceded and let Jake leave. Their last instructions to him had
been to rest and not exert himself too much. Which shouldn't be too
difficult now that he was about to become house-bound, anyway.

Jake thanked them for their help and then started out of the
hospital. Elizabeth was waiting for him by the entrance, holding a
bottle of water for him. After convincing her it was the doctors'
decision, and that he'd had no influence over it at all, she'd finally
come round to the idea of him being dismissed so soon.

'How are you feeling?' she asked as she gave him a kiss on the
cheek and wrapped her arm around him.

'Sore. But I'll live.'

They shuffled towards the car, slid in and drove home, the
morning sun shining brightly above them.

As they neared their home, Elizabeth disturbed the uncomfortable
silence between them.

'We need some rules, Jake,' she said.

'What kind of rules?'

'I need you to promise me a few things.'

'Pinky promise?'

'No. You've broken too many of those for it to mean anything now.
I just need you to promise me, for the kids.'

'What?'

'That you won't contact Stephanie *ever* again.'

'I never did in the first pl—' He stopped himself when he realised this line of response was going to get him nowhere. 'Yes. I promise. She's gone. I won't ever speak to her again.'

Tears formed in Elizabeth's eyes, yet she continued to focus on the road ahead. 'And the gambling as well. That needs to stop. I don't even want to know how much money you've burnt through doing that. How much you've put us all through with it. But it needs to stop. Right now.'

Jake turned to face her. He placed a hand on her leg and squeezed. 'I promise. I won't go anywhere near a gambling site or a bookies ever again.'

And, this time, he meant it. The past few days had put things into context for him. Here, right beside him, was a woman who had – at the beginning of their relationship – loved him unconditionally. But now, several years later, she was struggling to even look at him, let alone love him. And he was the one to blame. He was the one at fault. He was the one responsible for nearly ripping their family apart. And what made it worse was the fact that he was certain Elizabeth was only still with him because of the children. That hurt the most.

They finished their conversation as they pulled into the driveway. Slowly, Jake slipped out of the car and towards the house, moving gently to avoid any pain flare-ups. By the time he got to the door, Elizabeth was already in the kitchen, shuffling and moving things around.

'Mum came round last night,' she reminded him, calling back down the hall.

'She's done a wonderful job,' Jake replied as he hobbled along the corridor.

'She said it was like a bomb site when she got here. How could you have made it so messy in a day?'

Jake smirked, attempting to disarm her with some of the charm she'd fallen in love with.

'That's my bad. You know I've always been a bit of a slob.'

It didn't work.

Elizabeth said nothing. Instead, she turned her back on him, switched the kettle on, and told him to sit in the living room. She was making a cup of tea.

Jake did as instructed, but just as he was about to sit on the sofa, his phone chimed. For the past hour since they'd left the hospital, his mind had been devoid of any thought – work, Brendan, Darryl, Matheson, The Cabal.

But that all changed when he read the message.

More details, as promised
Deceased: Mark Murphy
Date: today
Time: 1200

Jake's eyes scanned the message again, and then for a third time.

'Oh my God,' he said the moment Elizabeth entered the living room, holding the mug of tea in her hand.

'What?'

'It's… I…' Jake tore his eyes from the screen and looked up at Elizabeth. 'Do you remember Mark Murphy?'

She shook her head. 'Remind me again.'

'Surrey police. The bent copper who was working with Bridger on The Crimsons case. Slept with Danika. Having an affair with Pemberton at the time. Disappeared into thin air without a trace.'

The look on her face suggested she didn't remember. 'What about him?' she asked anyway.

'He's dead.'

'Oh, that's terrible.'

'No, it's suspicious, is what it is. He already died. There was a funeral and everything.'

Elizabeth shrugged. 'Maybe you're getting confused with someone else.'

Jake didn't believe that. To prove his argument – and to settle the nagging voices in his head – he loaded the Internet on his phone and typed in Mark Murphy's name. The first hit on the search results was a *Daily Mail* piece. The title read HERO COP TRAGIC DEATH.

Jake read through the article.

On 13 November 2010, Detective Sergeant Mark Murphy was pronounced dead at the scene of a car crash. It is believed he was working undercover for Greater Manchester Police in a drugs bust.

DS Murphy's colleague and friend, DCS Matilda Hancock, described Murphy as 'an outstanding character, and an even better detective. Mark gave his life to the pursuit of criminals involved with drugs, and we will not let his death be in vain. We will, with the rest of the remaining resources and power that we have, continue with Mark's immeasurable work.'

It is clear to see how much of an impact DS Murphy's persona and appearance has had not only on his colleagues but also his friends and family as well.

The article then proceeded to show a few images from the funeral. Hundreds of people in attendance. And none of them were faces that Jake recognised.

Something was wrong. There were too many anomalies and holes in the story. It was the first Jake had heard of Murphy being involved with Greater Manchester Police. If he was running for his life from The Cabal, then why would he have joined GMP? He would have disappeared to the Scottish Highlands or somewhere no one else could find him. And then he replayed a sentence in his head: *Mark gave his life to the pursuit of criminals involved with drugs*.

He was even more certain that that wasn't just some sort of poetic sentence. There was no way that Murphy had dedicated his life to the pursuit of drug operations and drug busts. That was a lie. He was a bent cop on the run from an invisible enemy. But now he'd turned up again. Dead. Under even more mysterious circumstances. Why now? And what was with all the cloak-and-dagger?

Curiosity burnt within him. He wanted to know what was going on, *needed* to know what was going on.

Jake lifted himself out of his chair.

'Where are you going?'

'To get ready. I need to shower. I can smell myself.'

'Ready for what?'

'The funeral.'

'It's now?'

'At midday.'

'You're not going.'

'Liz, I have to.'

'Who said so?'

Jake hesitated, controlled himself.

'What if it was me?' Jake asked, playing with her emotions. 'What if I was being buried and nobody turned up?'

'Don't you dare say stuff like that. You know I dread the day that happens.'

'Answer the question, Liz.' Jake waited for a response; when one didn't come, he continued. 'Wouldn't you want everyone I'd ever worked with to be there so they could pay their respects?'

'The same ones trying to force you out?'

Jake opened his mouth but faltered. 'Regardless…' he eventually said. 'I know my ego would want them all there.'

'Sometimes you need to learn to put your ego aside and focus on what's important in life.'

Jake sighed. The conversation was going nowhere, and he was no closer to convincing her. Sadly, there were no medical experts he could call upon this time.

Looking down at the screen, he said, 'I'll only be gone a couple of hours. Max.'

Elizabeth folded her arms and scowled at him. 'Why do you do this?'

'What? Show mutual respect for a colleague and a friend? Despite what he's done – and what he did – he was still a human being. Now that he's dead, none of that other stuff matters.'

Elizabeth lifted her head, gazed into his eyes and for a moment they stared at one another. Her expression was impassive and gave nothing away, but there was a pain hidden deep within her eyes.

'Fine. Go to the funeral for all I care. I'll still be here when you eventually decide to come back. God knows why.'

CHAPTER 46

THIRTEEN HOURS

'Dylan! Dylan!'

The young man's head rolled to the side.

'Hey…' Darryl said, leaning across and giving him a gentle prod on the shoulder. But when there was no response, Darryl turned to Dylan's solicitor and asked, 'Is he all right? Does he need more time?'

The solicitor shrugged. Useless. Darryl had seen his type before. The on-call solicitors that were given to defendants when they didn't have a solicitor of their own. Some of them were excellent, formidable opponents who were willing to defend their client to the bitter end. And then there was the other pile. The loungers, the 'Just-Enoughs' as Darryl liked to call them. It was obvious they didn't want to be there. They didn't care about their client. They didn't care about what happened to them and where they ended up. All they were worried about was making life as easy as possible for themselves – and if that meant advising a defendant to plead guilty, then they weren't afraid to do so.

Darryl recognised the type immediately.

The solicitor gave Dylan a tap on the head and then a shake. Eventually, after several attempts, Dylan came to. His eyes opened half-heartedly, and his head lifted.

'Dylan, do you know where you are?'

'Somewhere I'd rather not be.'

Darryl cleared his throat before continuing. 'We're going to continue for the time being, but if your symptoms deteriorate, we're going to have to get you some medical treatment? Do you understand?'

Dylan nodded. His bloodshot eyes glistened crimson under the artificial light. After finding copious amounts of narcotics in his bloodstream, they'd given him some time to sleep it off and excrete from his system.

Clearly, that hadn't worked.

'As I was saying,' Darryl started. 'Where is Erica?'

'No comment.'

'When was the last time you saw her?'

'No comment.'

'Where did you last see her?'

'No comment.'

'Why did you kill Naomi, Dylan?'

'No comment.'

'Whose idea was it to livestream the event?'

'No comment.'

'Did you kill Erica before Naomi?'

'No comment.'

'Did Henry Matheson tell you to kill her?'

'No comment.'

'Did Henry Matheson tell you to kill all of them?'

'No comment.'

Darryl licked his lips. The on-call solicitor may not have cared about his client's well-being, but he'd cared enough to instruct him to give a 'no comment' interview. If it carried on this way, they would get nowhere. It was time to shake things up.

'On a scale of one to ten, how angry would you say you are right now?'

Dylan's face contorted with confusion.

'Nine? Five? Three?'

After a moment's hesitation, Dylan replied, 'The fuck you talking about?'

'I just want to know how angry you are. Were you angry when you killed Rupert and Helena and Felicity Haversham? Were you angry when you killed Erica Haversham? Were you angry when you slaughtered Naomi Rossitter?'

'You don't know what you're talking about, fam. I weren't angry.'

'What were you feeling?'

'I was fucking high, fam.' Dylan prodded the red scars and track marks on his forearm repeatedly.

'Were you also high when you killed Erica's family?'

'It ain't all me, you know. Erica did some of that shit, too.'

Finally. They were getting somewhere.

'What was she responsible for?'

'I ain't no snitch!' Dylan waved his hand in the air and brought it down on the table. 'Just like I ain't gonna snitch on Henry, either.'

'You don't owe him any loyalties, Dylan. You understand that, don't you?'

'Fuck you.'

Darryl leant forward and rested his arms against the table. He made sure to get as close to Dylan as possible without making it look awkward or like he was struggling.

'I bet he promised you the world, didn't he? That he'd make sure nothing happened to you. That he'd get you out of any difficult situation.' Darryl paused a beat. 'Well, you're in a difficult situation now, and the best hope you've got of getting any semblance of a good deal is sitting right next to you. Not looking good, is it?'

Dylan huffed and folded his arms tighter against his chest.

'You know what Rupert did, right? He was the one man Henry – and a whole host of murderers and criminals – relied upon. And you went and killed him. Now, the way I see it is, you can help us. You can tell us some pieces of information here and there, and we'll be able to work out some sort of lenient deal with the CPS or the judge.'

'I ain't no snitch.'

'So you've told us already. Not even if we gave you some security? I could speak with my seniors and we could make it happen.'

'I ain't no snitch,' Dylan echoed. This time, he leant forward and spat on the table. The yellowed globule of phlegm sat in the middle of the desk, glistening like a disco ball.

Darryl glanced at the spittle and then back up at Dylan. 'I'm extending this offer for the next thirty seconds. If you refuse it, it's gone forever.'

Dylan shrugged like a petulant, defiant child who'd just been caught but was adamant they'd done nothing wrong.

'I'm curious,' Darryl continued. 'You've spent some time with Henry Matheson before, haven't you? So you're aware of what the man is capable of. To him, you're just a loose end. And when you end up in prison, you're going to be a cornered, loose end with nowhere to go. Regardless of whether you've told the police anything or blabbed about what he told you to do, he's going to kill you – or, at the very least, seriously injure you – in order to teach you a lesson. He has his own agenda that he's kept you far removed from. You were just a tool, a pawn in his game. Think about that in the next five seconds before this offer expires.'

Five.

Dylan leant forward.

Four.

'I.'

Three.

'Ain't.'

Two.

'No.'

One.

'Snitch.'

Done.

Darryl exhaled a sigh of despair. He'd really thought Dylan would take the offer. Perhaps the young man wasn't as smart as he'd given him credit for. Dylan didn't know what was good for him, and if that was the case, then he deserved to rot in prison where he would undoubtedly spend the rest of his life.

Darryl closed the folder by his arm, terminated the interview, and told them it was time to go.

'Where?' Dylan asked.

'You're going back to your holding cell.'

'Why?'

Darryl checked his watch. 'Because we've still got another thirteen hours to charge you. And then you'll be on your way to prison.'

As Darryl stepped out of the room, he hoped that, in the next twelve hours and fifty-nine minutes, Dylan would change his mind.

CHAPTER 47

DOWN

In the deep recesses of Henry Matheson's brain, things began to happen and unfold. Things began to take change and manifest into ideas. Ideas began to morph into plans. Plans began to morph into fruition.

Slowly, the wheels in his colossal drug empire were turning again. The drugs, and more importantly his signature plastic bottles, were back on the streets and bringing in revenue, and for the first time ever, the competition was onside.

Following his meeting with Armando Strakosha, he and the Albanian had agreed to call a truce. In exchange for taking all the risk in bringing in the next lot of heroin and cocaine shipments – which left him vulnerable and open to arrest – Henry was allowed his corner of the market. Boris Romanov had also agreed to the deal from the confines of his hospital bed – with a little help from Armando.

There was no doubt in Henry's mind that the two were planning something against him; Boris had bowed and conceded too easily – the last thing he would have wanted was to agree a deal with the man who'd put him in hospital.

As a result, Henry thought it a good idea to plan something against them as well.

Things manifesting into ideas.

Ideas morphing into plans.

And now his plan was coming to fruition.

Every Sunday, between nine and midday, a select group of inmates were enrolled in a textiles initiative on the other side of the prison. A group of fourteen were offered the opportunity to create cushions, tea towels, tablecloths, bags. The initiative was designed to develop inmates' skills, provide them with a sense of purpose and desire to live a crime-free life.

Sadly for Henry Matheson, he simply saw it as an opportunity to exact his plan.

The constant whirring of sewing machines bounced around the walls. The fourteen prisoners were situated like American schoolchildren in the classroom, each working at their own bench, facing the front of the class.

Henry eased his foot off the pedal and brought the machine to a gradual halt. He'd just finished work on a textile gift card. The design he'd gone for today was a blue and pink rabbit, sitting in front of a backdrop of purple flowers. It had taken him the length of the session to complete.

When it eventually came to a close, Henry took his time to pack away – folding the leftover materials into a pile; tidying the cables at the back of the machine; placing his creation on the table at the back of the room as though the teacher would put it on display at parents' evening at a later date.

Before the session had begun, Henry had spoken with James Longstaff and organised a meeting. Everyone in the room, except for Armando Strakosha, was told to leave them behind, including the volunteer running the workshop, who'd been handed a pretty bribe to turn a blind eye. As it turned out, everyone was corruptible, even the good-hearted people seeking to make a difference in the world.

A few minutes after the teacher had called time, Armando and Henry remained. Armando pretended to busy himself with his machine. Henry approached him.

'How is the shipment coming along?' Armando asked.

'My guys are handling it.'

'I do not want to be let down.'

'None of us do. We're all relying on each other.'

Armando turned to him, his face stern. 'Some more than others.'

Henry switched it up. 'How you finding life in the joint? Missing your family?'

'Don't ask questions you know you're not going to get an answer to. It's dangerous for everyone involved.'

'What's life without a little danger?'

'Better than this shithole,' Armando replied.

'How's your wife and kids?' Henry asked. 'They must really hate not being able to see you every day.'

'I don't have kids.'

'No? I thought I heard through the grapevine that you did.'

'If I do, then I don't know about them.'

'Not even Amir and Alma? Three-year-old Alma must really be missing her dad by now.'

Armando's face dropped. His pupils dilated and his brows furrowed. His lips moved up and down, but nothing came out – only short, exasperated gasps of air.

Jeremiah's earlier reconnaissance mission had proven to be a success. Armando had a weakness, and now Henry knew exactly what it was.

'Oh, I'm sorry,' Henry continued, stepping closer to his new business partner. 'Did I say something out of line? I didn't mean to upset you.'

Armando remained in his chair, forced down by shock. 'Don't threaten me. It will not end well for you.'

Henry took another step, this time rolling the needle he'd taken from his machine in his hand.

'It's not a threat. I was just making conversation.'

Another step.

In his head, Henry counted down until it was time to attack.

'I think it's important we get to know each other.'

Three.

'Like, for instance, there's one thing you should know about me.'

Two.

'It's that I don't work well with others.'

One.

Henry swung his fist down onto the back of Armando's hand, burying the pin into his flesh and cartilage. The man screamed as the needle chipped at bone. Before he could react, Henry punched him in the jaw and slammed his head against the bloodied table. Again. And again. And again. Disorientated, Armando never saw the second punch coming, this time a right hook to the temple.

Then Henry turned his attention to the sewing machine. The big, weighty device offered several methods of torture. The only question was which one to choose first.

He opted for the device itself. Summoning all his strength, he lifted the machine and tried to slam it across Armando's face. But under its immense weight, Henry's grip slipped, and the device clattered into his victim's nose instead. A waterfall of blood now gushed from both nostrils, flooding down his jumper.

Henry dropped the machine onto the table, then turned his attention to the next method of inflicting pain: running the man's hand under the needle. Armando, completely incapacitated, was defenceless as Henry yanked his unharmed hand and shoved it beneath the device. He stamped his foot on the accelerator so the machine whirred into action and began rapidly perforating Armando's skin like it was the film on a ready-meal carton. Armando screamed, but there was no one there to hear him. Not even the souls of previous inmates left behind by the justice system.

Henry eased up on the accelerator and turned his attention to the final instrument of torture – the cable. He unplugged it, manipulated it in his hands and lunged for Armando's neck. Once he had purchase around the man's head, he spun him round and pulled it tightly, yanking him off the chair and onto the floor. Armando gasped and panted and clawed and kicked, but it didn't make a bit of difference.

Still holding the cable tight against his throat, Henry kicked him in the ribs and kidneys several times, no doubt rupturing some organs. There would be internal bleeding at the very least.

He was unrelenting.

And before long, Armando gave up fighting and his body fell limp. It was over.

Exasperated, Henry let go of the cable and let the man slump to the floor. Then he left. As the door gradually closed behind him, he was sure he heard the faint wheezing sound of someone struggling for what might be their last breath.

Down, but not dead.

CHAPTER 48

CAR CRASH

Jake was beginning to lose count of how many funerals he'd been to this year. The number was already too high. First, there'd been Roland Lewandowski's. His colleague and friend had been found dead in his flat on New Year's day, a bullet hole perfectly centred on his forehead. Then he and Elizabeth had attended his father-in-law's. Then there'd been Melania's small funeral, held for those who wanted to pay their respects before her body was returned to her family in Romania. And lastly, he'd attended Elliot Bridger's. The man had given his life for Jake, and the least he could do was be the only one there to say goodbye.

All of them were heartbreaking, all of them depressing. But the worst part about them was that they were all avoidable. If it hadn't been for him – and his war with The Cabal – nobody would have died.

The same was true for everyone else that had died in his life. But by and the large, the funeral he blamed himself the most for was his dad's. Jake had been fifteen when his father had died on the way to pick him up from a football match. He'd been involved in a car crash and had passed away en route to the hospital. The images and emotions he'd felt when his mum broke the news still lived with him. It was one of the hardest days he'd ever had to endure. Saying goodbye to his dad had hardened him to the realities of funerals and made him more mature in the face of death. They were painful and heartbreaking affairs, but Jake knew they would never be as tough as the one he'd faced when he was so young.

Jake pulled into the car park at Croydon Crematorium and drove into the first space he saw – although he was spoilt for choice. The car park was empty, save for the hearse and funeral directors in tow.

Jake paused to scan his surroundings before he switched off the engine and alighted from the vehicle.

The sun was shining overhead, but a blanket of thin cloud dropped an ominous shade of grey and a slight chill into the air.

Jake skulked along the car park, keeping his left hand in his trouser pocket and pressed his arm against his wound to alleviate some of the pain. Sitting in the car at a certain angle had flared up the hole in his stomach, which was beginning to feel tighter and tighter as the wound gradually healed. He was under strict instructions to keep movement to a minimum.

Soft orchestral music sounded from inside the building and reached his eardrums. Atop the roof, a chimney roared with smoke. Standing beside him in the doorway were two undertakers.

Jake checked his watch – 11:58 a.m.

'Is this… is this the right service?' Jake asked a female undertaker to his right. She had short brown hair that was shaved on the sides and longer on the top. Mascara adorned her eyes and her cheeks were blushed.

'For Mark Murphy?' the woman replied, smiling at him. She looked familiar, but Jake couldn't remember where from.

He nodded slowly.

'This is the right place.'

Jake wandered into the crematorium, peered around, and headed back out again.

'Where is everyone? I thought there would be more people here.'

That was wrong. What he meant was: he thought there would be at least *someone* else there. The small hall, filled with row upon row of seats, was empty.

The woman stared at him, still wearing that facetious smile on her face. 'Maybe they were all involved in a car crash with a busload of children on the M25.'

As soon as she said it, Jake froze – stunned, paralysed. For a long time, he stared at her, his mind awash with a myriad of thoughts.

A busload of children…

He recognised the phrase straight away. He remembered it vividly. That was the lie that Elliot Bridger had used to delay the bomb squad from getting to Candice Strachan's house during The Crimsons' final heist in Guildford. It was the clue that Jake had needed to realise that Bridger wasn't who he said he was, that he was bent and working against the police in trying to get The Crimsons out of the country. It was the phrase that had sparked the entire saga with The Cabal. And Mark Murphy had been in on it too.

But what did this woman have to do with it all? And how did she know that phrase?

'Excuse me, sir,' she said, breaking him out of his reverie. 'The procession is about to start. Would you care to enter?'

Stunned, Jake stammered and looked around at the undertakers like they were speaking a foreign language. Tentatively, he entered the crematorium and pulled out a chair in the middle of the room. He was surrounded by seats from every angle, and as he waited for the officiant to come out of their room, Jake felt suddenly very isolated and vulnerable. Almost as if he was about to find himself in the coffin entering the room very soon.

CHAPTER 49

PROOF

The funeral was over shortly after it had begun. The officiant had done his job and had said some nice things about Murphy, even though Jake was certain most of them weren't true. But he still paid his final respects to his former colleague and wandered around outside for a few minutes before heading back to the car.

The entire ordeal had been surreal. There was no explanation for anything. None of it made sense. There were no family members present, friends, former partners. Not even former service members. It was almost as if Mark Murphy had never existed and Jake was the only living person who remembered him.

Who cared enough about him to attend.

Maybe they were all involved in a car crash with a busload of children on the M25.

They. Who were 'they'? All the people that hadn't bothered to show up? Or all of Murphy's former associates from Surrey Police who were no longer with them.

That was a list he knew very well.

Danika Oblak.

Elliot Bridger.

Those were the two names that stuck out to Jake the most, like the moon on a clear summer's evening. And they were dead.

But there was someone else…

Jake shuffled in his seat, attempting to ease the pain in his stomach, and found his phone. He hoped he still had her mobile number and that it hadn't changed.

Jake let out a little gasp as he found what he was looking for. He composed himself and dialled, without knowing what he was going to say.

The phone rang and rang. Rang and rang. Rang and rang.
But there was no answer.
He tried again.
This time—
'Hello?'
Jake exhaled heavily as he heard her voice. 'Nicki? Nicki Pemberton? It's Jake. Jake Tanner.'
There was a long pause before he received a response.
'Good to hear from you, Jake. Although it's never a good thing when you call. I trust you're not going to ask for the impossible again. I can't deal with one more fuck-up.'
Jake felt a seed of guilt germinate in his gut. The last time they'd spoken had been during the middle of one of the country's largest murder investigations. A lorry container, filled with forty dead immigrants from all over the world, had turned up in a motorway service station on the M25. Organised by The Cabal and his clandestine network. Jake had persuaded Nicki to let him speak with the driver, in the hope it would lead him to The Cabal's identity. A decision which had proven costly for her career prospects and her position in the team, he was later informed.
'Nothing like that,' he said with confidence. 'This is a bit strange, and I'm not sure if you're aware, but DI Murphy died.'
'I know,' Pemberton replied bluntly. In the distance, it sounded as though she were at a playground; children were screaming and yelling at one another excitably. 'We buried him. I went to his funeral.'
'No…' Jake said, considering how to approach his next few words. 'I'm at his service now. In Croydon. We've just held a reception for him. But… there's nobody else here.'
A long silence fell between them. Then, after a short while, the sounds of screaming children gradually disappeared and were replaced with a slight echo, as though she'd moved into a private corridor.
'Don't call me again, Jake. I'm sorry.'
'What?'
'I can't help you. Mark's died twice now and I want to make sure nothing happens to me or my children.'
'No, wait!'
'You need to get yourself out of whatever you're in, Jake. You're in deep. Get yourself out before you end up like Mark.'
'Nicki…'
'I tried to help him, but he wouldn't listen. Don't make the same mistakes I did. It's a warning.'
'For what?' Jake screamed into the handset, trying to keep her on the line.
'I've said too much already.'
'Nicki, please. Tell me…'
'There are some things you don't know, and I don't want to be the one to tell you. But think about it: it's not every day somebody dies

twice, and it's not every day only one person attends a funeral. It's a signal that you'll be replacing him in that box. It's a tradition.'

Pemberton's words chilled Jake. But he wasn't about to let her go just yet. He had a dozen more questions that needed answering.

'A tradition? Tradition for who? Tradition for what?'

She hesitated. The sound of a toilet flushing echoed in Jake's ear.

'It's a tradition from The Cabal. I've heard of it before. Mark used to tell me when we were… well, you know. They've done it several times in the past, and they'll do it again.'

'But The Cabal's dead…' Jake said, playing his trump card in the poker tournament of this conversation. Both players held cards of information to their chest, and Jake was willing to bluff his way to the win by pretending he knew nothing.

'Here's your proof The Cabal is alive and kicking, Jake. Like I said, it's a warning. A tradition. You need to be careful. I stayed well away from that life as soon as I found out what Mark was involved with. I'm sorry, Jake. But I can't tell you any more.'

The line went dead. Slowly he lowered the phone away from his ear and placed it on his lap. His mind should have been working on overdrive. It should have been contemplating what she'd told him. He should have been thinking about the repercussions – what it meant for his safety, for Elizabeth's safety, for Maisie's, for Ellie's. But instead he needed answers.

What the fuck was Pemberton talking about? Why had there been a second funeral? What involvement did she have in The Cabal's network?

And then: was *she* The Cabal?

He needed to find answers.

And he knew just the man to help him.

CHAPTER 50

POETIC

In a former life, before he'd been stripped of his rank and credibility, Liam Greene had been a detective chief inspector – one of the highest-ranking roles within the police, sitting a few pegs below, in his own words, the big dogs who sat at the big tables.

Liam had never wanted to be a big dog, and he'd never wanted to sit at the big table. Being a DCI was the perfect position; it meant that he was senior enough to exercise corrupt control over everything he did, yet he was not so high up that he raised suspicion.

The Cabal's venom had filtered its way through every rank in the force. From DCI to DC. At the head of it all had been the assistant commissioner, Richard Candy. A man who had the power and persuasion of everyone beneath him to do the dirty work, so he remained out of sight and out of Jake's suspicions.

Like Liam's role, it had been the perfect cover-up.

But what if that's exactly what it was? The perfect cover, and Liam had pulled the wool over Jake's eyes for so long. Always protesting innocence and ignorance when it came to The Cabal's real identity. Being close to the action while inside prison, where he was already untouchable. Controlling everything from the confines of his cell in one of Her Majesty's finest.

Could Liam Greene, the man he'd once idolised and worshipped, be The Cabal?

Well, as Liam sauntered into the prison meeting room, Jake realised he was about to find out.

Except there was a problem.

The man opposite him wasn't the same one he'd known these past few years. The man before him was weak, skinny, frail, bald, his skin sagging loosely from his bones and muscles, and he looked thirty years Jake's senior – life gradually being sucked from him, as if by a leech whose hunger could never be sated.

Jake couldn't believe the difference in the three months since he'd last seen him.

'Not looking too good, am I?' Liam said as he struggled to pull himself closer to the table. 'But it's good to see you, old friend.'

Liam coughed hard, spluttering the contents of his throat and lungs into his hand and arm.

Jake opened his mouth to speak, but Liam beat him to it.

'You came at the right time,' he began, wiping his sleeve on his trousers. 'Five weeks. That's how much longer I can expect to live. Five more weeks. Doctors said it could be slightly more, but either way, I'm gonna die in this shithole alone.'

Jake's voice came out as a whisper. 'Liam… I'm so… I'm so sorry. I thought you were in remission?'

'I was. But then the bastard came back. With a vengeance, it would seem.'

Jake looked down at the table, unable to hold Liam's vacant glare.

'What brings you here then, pal?' Liam asked.

'Murphy.'

'Mark? Yeah, I know him. What about him?'

'He's dead.'

'Again? Seems unlikely.'

'Well I've just come from his funeral, so it's not that unlikely. I was the only one there.'

At that, Liam's deep, hollow eyes widened. He eased himself into the back of the chair and shook his head.

'What have you got yourself into?' he asked with the concern of a worried father.

'What do you mean?'

'Legend has it – although it's not much of a legend because I've witnessed it myself – that two funerals are a sign. Being invited to the second is a sign that The Cabal is going to kill you off next.'

Liam cleared his throat. 'Back in the nineties, when The Cabal was just starting out, they were betrayed by a lot of people. Criminals and police officers alike. When police officers, and by extension criminals, were caught grassing, The Cabal had them killed. Everyone – and I mean *everyone* back in those days – attended the funeral. Then, after the funeral had died down and things had moved on, if The Cabal found out someone else was grassing or posed a threat to their operations, they would send them another invitation for the same funeral. They'd be the only one to get it. It was a sign that they were next.'

'What did they do?'

'Well, they were scared shitless. So they either retired and ran or just kept their mouths shut. The third option was to join ranks, but you were never fully trusted by The Cabal if that's the route you took.'

Jake absorbed what Liam had said and did the calculations,

adding two and two together.

'Is that what you did?'

Liam nodded. 'After I found out Drew'd raped that girl and that Garrison had kept it quiet for him, I was ready to go to the DPS. But then I received a funeral invitation, and I realised what I was dealing with. So I stayed quiet. Ever since then, The Cabal never fully trusted me. Maybe that's why I was put in charge of those two fuckwits.'

'And that's why they turned on you?'

'Bingo.'

Jake sighed slowly. It was a lot to take in.

'So what does that mean for me?' he asked. 'What's going to happen to me?'

'It means you need to tread very fucking carefully. Now more than you ever have. You're either dangerously close to blowing the lid off everything, or you know something in particular The Cabal would rather you didn't. You just need to stay away from it all and keep quiet. Which is what I've been warning you this entire time.'

That was true. Right from the start, Liam had been protecting him, trying to get him to stop intervening with The Cabal's network. But that wasn't in his nature. He'd already caught The Cabal once – or at least who he'd thought was The Cabal – and he was more than willing to do it again. At any cost. He'd joined the police force to uphold right from wrong, to catch criminals – and The Cabal was the biggest catch of all. Stopping wasn't an option, not if he was so close to exposing their true identity. He would just have to be smart about it.

'I'll keep a low profile,' he suggested. 'Suppose it's a good thing I've been sidelined for the next couple of weeks.'

'How come?'

Jake leant back in his chair and pulled up his T-shirt, revealing the bandages and several layers of tape stuck to his stomach.

'Did The Cabal do that?' Liam asked as he peered over the table.

'Close. Some drug addict working for Henry Matheson.'

Jake then proceeded to give Liam the brief rundown on the Haversham murders, explaining how they'd been killed, who'd killed them, and that Erica was still missing. After he'd finished, Liam folded his arms and stroked the underside of his chin, deep in thought, pensive.

'So… let me get this right,' Liam began. 'You're stabbed less than twenty-four hours ago and you're already out of hospital carrying on with work?'

Jake nodded.

'I think we need to get your head checked over. That's not normal, pal. And I don't like it either. It's too dangerous. I'm hearing from a lot of voices in this place that Matheson's product is still making the rounds in The Pit. Pissing off a lot of the Albanians and Romanians, he is. I'm also hearing that something bigger is going on. And when The Cabal finds out, if they haven't already, then something even more monumental's going to happen.'

Jake's ears perked up. 'Are you sure they're not the same person?'

'Fuck no. They hated each other. Henry always wanted to do his own thing – which usually went against whatever The Cabal told him to do. They clashed occasionally, but I don't think Henry ever knew the real person he was dealing with. Yet he always toed the line, and The Cabal had the final say. But I think, after Candy died, Matheson assumed The Cabal was gone and that he could now bring back his empire.'

'Why would Matheson want to kill Rupert?'

Liam shrugged. 'Perhaps it was revenge for Rupert abandoning him at his trial. Henry had a lot of enemies, but Haversham had an even bigger pool to choose from. It would make no sense for The Cabal to assassinate Rupert and his family. I mean, Rupert was the reason their entire operation managed to stay out of the public eye. Haversham kept us out of prison as much as he could. But for some of us, there was nothing he could do.'

Jake paused a beat as he considered his next question.

'What's going down between Matheson and The Cabal?'

A smirk grew on Liam's face. 'I thought you'd have worked that one out by now. You've got the psychology degree. What happens when we're told we can't do what we want to do?'

'We want to do it even more…'

'And what is Henry Matheson known for?'

'Drug trafficking.'

'And what is The Cabal known for?'

'Drug trafficking, human trafficking, organised crime… the list goes on.'

'But with Matheson in prison, The Cabal's trying to fight for the strongholds in the Cosgrove Estate and on the docks. Except Matheson's not going to let that go so easily. Both of them are working on something big. And with Henry already beginning to show his hand by assassinating a high-profile lawyer while he's locked up inside, it's not going to take a genius to work out who's going to come out on top.'

Jake sat still for a moment, stunned. His mind worked overtime as he tried to absorb everything. He wished he'd brought a recorder in, but he hadn't had the foresight to realise the conversation would be so lucrative. He just hoped he'd remember it all, and that the extreme tiredness in his brain wouldn't hamper his memory.

'But,' Liam began after a while, 'like I said, you need to stay the fuck away. Back well off. That funeral was a warning. Listen to it.'

As soon as Liam finished speaking, he coughed again, this time spluttering blood on the table. As Jake watched his friend cough the contents of his lungs onto the table, a thought hit him.

'Garrison's awake,' he told Liam.

At that, Liam stopped. 'What did you say?'

'He woke up from his coma the other day.'

Liam glanced down at the table and then up at Jake. 'Poetic, isn't it? I'm about to be taken from this world and he's just entered back into it.'

CHAPTER 51

READY AND WAITING

Time was no longer a tangible thing to her. Constantly surrounded by darkness, she had no idea whether it was daytime or night-time, morning or evening. In the beginning, she'd tried to keep a log in her head somehow – using her body clock as a barometer – but that had been less than useless. She'd even tried straining her ears and listening for footsteps or signs from above that her captors were still awake. Nothing. Unless they spent every minute of the day asleep, she couldn't hear a thing.

The one thing she used to regulate the time, however, was food. Since she'd been cramped in the squalid conditions, she'd received what she assumed to be breakfast. It comprised three pieces of buttered bread and a plastic cup of orange juice. Still, she couldn't complain; it was just as easy for them to give her nothing.

But her body needed more than that. A lot more. By now, the drugs in her system had completely worn off. No longer was she hallucinating or riding a wave of euphoria that soared through her bloodstream. It didn't take long for the comedown to settle in and park itself next to her on the bed like an existential extension of herself, a shadow, a manifestation. The whole night it sat there talking to her, reminding her of all the bad things she'd done in life, making her regret everything she'd ever said or felt. It had been a restless night. And now she stank of sweat, thanks to her pores, which had spent the entire time excreting the drugs from her system.

She hated life.

She hated herself.

She'd been locked up inside this box for a reason. It was because she'd killed. This was her punishment. She deserved to die in the box – the voices in her head had told her so.

She was such a stupid, selfish little bitch. Such an arrogant, insolent child. Yes, she was a child. A spoilt brat who'd killed her own family because she hadn't got what she'd wanted. What was wrong with her? She should be dead instead of little Felicity.

How could she kill herself inside the box? She couldn't see anything, and the only opportunity she had was whenever her food was brought down to her and placed through the small hole in the wall. Maybe she could use the time between meals to survey her options. Maybe there was a piece of string she could use to tie around her neck. Or a sharp piece of metal she could use to slit her wrists. Or maybe she could starve herself – flush the bread down the toilet as soon as it came in. Yes, that way she could get away with not eating anything. She could get rid of her existence that way.

A slow, horrible suffering for a horrible and despicable girl. The least she deserved.

Before she was able to dedicate any more effort and thought to her plan, the basement door opened and the gentle sound of footsteps coming down the stairs eventually made it to her ears.

A few seconds later, there was a knock. The noise reverberated and amplified around the box.

Lunch.

Or was it dinner?

'Up,' came a man's voice – deep and gruff in a way that smacked of unconvincing acting. 'Are you up?'

Erica hesitated for a while. The voice was different to the one she recognised from last night and this morning. She couldn't place the female's voice, but she was certain she knew it from somewhere.

Where?

'Hey!' The man smacked on the wall with the palm of his hand. 'Are you awake?'

'Yes,' she replied weakly. 'I'm up.'

Without saying anything more, the man lowered the lid on the wall and slid a plate through the hole. Three slices of buttered bread and a packet of crisps. An upgrade from her previous meal.

Lunch.

'Take it,' the voice ordered.

For a while, Erica stood there contemplating it. She was hungry. Worse, she was ravenous. And she needed to eat something to satiate the cravings her body had for drugs. She wanted to eat it. But she couldn't. Not if she was going to starve herself. Fuck! Was she really so weak as to stumble on the first hurdle?

'Take it!' the man barked at her, kicking Erica into gear.

As she sauntered towards the square hole, she kept her eyes trained on the bread. Her mouth salivated and her lips moistened.

As she reached out her hand to take it, the man grabbed her. Still feeling the effects of the heroin, her reactions were too slow, and he yanked her towards him, slamming her into the wall.

'Don't disobey me like that again, you little stupid cunt,' he snarled. 'Otherwise I'll fucking make you regret it. You don't want the food, then I'll give you more and more until you don't know what to do with it all. Soon you won't know the smell of your own shit from the rotting food inside your prison.'

The man shoved the food inside, spilling it onto the floor, and slammed the window shut, suspending her in darkness again.

While her eyes adjusted to the darkness, she froze. Just like that, her master plan had been foiled. How could she starve herself if more and more food was funnelled into her prison? The temptation would be too great.

No. She needed a change of plan.

And she had an idea in mind. The last time she'd been spoken to like that was by her stepmother. That bitch. And she'd had the courage to slit that cow's throat with a knife; she could only begin to imagine what sort of damage she could do with her hands. Or maybe even her body.

He was a red-blooded male with urges, just like the rest of them. Just like Dylan. Urges that would be too great. Especially if he found her passed out naked on the bed.

Ready and waiting.

To spring the attack.

CHAPTER 52

EXPOSE

Never in all the years that he'd been married to Elizabeth had he ever felt so bad about telling the truth as much as he did on the way to Whipps Cross Hospital in Stratford. After he'd finished at the prison, Jake had received a call from the hospital, notifying him that Garrison was awake again and asking for him by name. Him. Jake. By name. The same man that had scared him only the other day. It didn't make sense, but he wasn't about to turn down an opportunity to meet an old friend and – hopefully – get some answers.

'It's Garrison. The hospital called me a moment ago. He's asking for me personally,' Jake explained.

'And your *children* are asking for you personally, Jake. Or have you forgotten about them?'

Jake sighed and rolled his eyes as he tore through the busy streets of London, overtaking cyclists and buses at every opportunity.

'You know I miss them. You know I'm happy that you're back. Please don't make this harder than it is, Elizabeth.'

He hated using her full name like that. The only time he ever did was when they were in the middle of an argument and he needed to make a point.

'When will you be home?'

'As soon as I can,' Jake replied.

He hung up before Elizabeth had a chance to find a hole in his response and moan about it.

Before he knew it, he was inside the hospital and waiting outside Garrison's room. Two nurses were busy attending to him. One of them held a clipboard in one hand and a pen in the other, while the other nurse set a tray of food down on Garrison's lap.

Jake waited patiently until the nurses were finished.

'Good to see you again,' the nurse from the other night said. 'Hopefully, he's a little more receptive than he was last time.'

Jake feigned a smile. It was the one thing he'd been dreading most about his visit. 'I suppose asking for me by name is a good thing, right?'

'Best sign we've seen yet. You're clear to go in whenever you want.' The nurse shut the door, then moved to the other end of the corridor, where she started talking with a colleague about the next patient who required her invaluable expertise.

For a long while, Jake stared at the door handle, willing himself to pull it. Five seconds. Ten. Twenty. Rooted to the floor in fear of history repeating itself. Aware of the dangers of his visit – both to his standing with Garrison and the effect it would have on the other man's mental health.

Eventually, after nearly a minute, Jake swallowed deeply and opened the door.

'Hello, bud,' he said, forcing a smile as he closed the door behind him. 'How you feeling? Nurses said you were getting better. Hope you haven't been giving them any grief?'

No response. Garrison remained in his bed, sitting upright, staring at Jake as he crossed the room.

Please don't freak out.

Jake pulled a chair away from his friend and sat.

'Did you bring any digestives this time?' Garrison asked delicately, their long-forgotten friendship coming through in his voice.

Those seven words shocked Jake. Garrison remembered!

'Unfortunately not, mate. I forgot this time. But next time I'll have some for you.'

'I might not wanna see you again,' Garrison joked, a small smirk growing on his face.

'Good luck trying to keep me away.'

Then Jake's eyes fell on the bedside table nearest to him. There was a packet of Hobnobs on the side already. He pointed to them. 'Where'd you get those from?'

Garrison grunted and shrugged.

'Can I have one?'

Jake received the same response. He took that to mean yes, so he nabbed one. As he stuffed it into his mouth, he continued, 'You know, Pete, I'm not sure if you're aware, but I'm sorry about your wife. It takes a real heartless bitch to leave you when you're like this.'

'Good riddance,' Garrison said nonchalantly. 'Best excuse ever.'

'The nurses told me you have a little friend come and see you every night. A girl. Who is she? Family? Friend? Former lover?'

Garrison didn't respond. Instead, he sat upright and threw the remote control at Jake. Within seconds, he started screaming for the nurses, his cries reaching fever pitch.

History repeating itself.

In an even shorter time, the nurses arrived and surrounded him, placating him with hushes and soft, gentle touches. The nurse Jake had spoken to only moments ago ushered him out of the room apologetically. Jake didn't blame them – he couldn't. They were just doing their job.

History repeating itself.

'Give it some time,' the nurse said as Jake entered the corridor. 'He'll come round, eventually.'

He knew she meant well, but it didn't make it hurt any less. For the next two minutes, Jake sauntered through the hospital corridors, making his way to the exit.

After he breached out into the open, he descended a small flight of steps and traversed the car park back to his car, feeling deflated.

But there was something wrong.

There was somebody standing beside his car.

The funeral director from Mark Murphy's service. And then he remembered where else he recognised her from: outside the Haversham crime scene. She'd been the journalist asking him annoying and incessant questions.

Jake approached with caution.

'I don't suppose it's a coincidence that we run into each other here, is it?' Jake asked as he arrived at his car. Fortunately, she was on the other side, and there was half a tonne of metal separating them. Just in case.

The woman lifted her head. Their eyes locked on one another.

'If you really want to find out what happened to Mark and what it's all about, I can help you. But I need you to trust me.' She removed something from her pocket and slid it across the roof. 'Meet me tonight. I'll text you the time and address. Come alone. I'll answer everything then. If you really want to expose The Cabal, you'll come.'

CHAPTER 53

LITTLE MORE TIME

Jake closed the door, kicked off his shoes and wandered through to the kitchen absent-mindedly, only half aware that he was in his own home. He didn't know what time it was, except that it was getting dark outside, which meant it had to be nearing half seven.

'Dinner's in the microwave,' Elizabeth told him as he entered the kitchen – just as she was about to leave with Ellie in her arms.

'Oh… OK. Thanks.'

Without saying anything else, he switched on the microwave and set his food to cook. While he waited, he stood with his hands on the kitchen counter, staring into the machine window as the plastic tray spun and spun.

Bing!

Dinner for one.

His stomach growling, he pulled the tray out, plopped it onto a plate and readied himself to eat dinner on his own while Elizabeth and the girls watched TV in the living room. It wasn't the hero's return he'd been expecting – nor was it one he ever thought he'd have to endure – but at least he had all his girls with him.

Home. Safe.

Before he allowed himself to dwell on thoughts of his marriage and relationship with his kids, he tucked into his dinner. Meatballs and pasta. Sub-par. The pasta was bland. The meatballs were bland. And the sauce was bland. But microwave meals had been his only comfort these past few months. He'd had so many that he'd been able to refine his palate to them, and now he could taste the minute differences between them all – which ones were too oily, which ones had too much salt in them, too much pepper, paprika, spinach. It was almost as if he'd become a connoisseur of shitty food.

The living-door room opened and Maisie wandered in. In her hands, she held a tablet and a plastic cup of water. She blanked Jake, as if he was part of the furniture, and made her way to the fridge. There, she pulled it open and poured herself a drink of juice, spilling the contents onto the wooden flooring.

'You want daddy to give you a hand with that, Mais?' Jake asked.

'No,' Maisie said as she focused her entire attention on the drink. 'I'm a big girl.'

A smirk grew on his face. Her innocence and sweetness were the biggest things he'd missed about her in recent months – that and the ability to hold her in his arms.

Deciding he wasn't going to listen to her, he climbed out of his seat, picked up her tablet, and wiped the juice clean from the floor.

'You've made a bit of a mess.'

'Grandma says you made a mess, too.'

Jake didn't need to be a genius to work out what Martha had been referring to. He placed his hand on her head and stroked.

'You shouldn't be listening to other people's conversations, sweetheart. Especially when they're adult conversations.'

'I didn't. Grandma told me when we were making biscuits the other day.'

'She said that?'

Maisie nodded and took a long sip from her cup.

Jake bit his tongue. Martha was no saint, either.

'How about you tell me the next time she says things like that. But she mustn't find out – it'll be our secret mission. OK?'

'OK, Daddy.'

After throwing the wet kitchen roll into the bin, he lifted Maisie into his arms, picked up her tablet and carried her towards the dining table. Then he placed her on his lap and unlocked the tablet. The screen loaded on an online game Maisie had been playing.

'What's this?' Jake asked her.

'*Kingdom of Empires*,' Maisie replied, still sipping her drink.

'What do you have to do?'

'Build kingdoms. Fight people.'

'Sounds a bit too dangerous for you. Does Mummy know you play this?'

Maisie nodded. 'She showed me how.'

Turns out neither of us is scoring highly on the parental responsibility leader board.

Jake wasn't too keen on his four-year-old daughter playing violent adventure games on the iPad, but it was becoming increasingly difficult to monitor her habits on the device, especially when she was always glued to it.

In his defence, that had been Elizabeth's domain for the past few months and she should have been paying more attention. Not that he was keeping a tally of course.

'Do you want to show Daddy how it works?'

Excited, Maisie set her cup on the table, took the tablet from him and started playing. Her movements were deft and slight as a magician, and her fingers and eyes as rapid as a professional. As if it were second nature to her – like brushing her teeth or going to the toilet. Within seconds, she'd managed to recruit a small army of archers, knights, and giants to her barracks; build several mills, bakers and houses for her residents; and fortify her surroundings with extra defences. Jake struggled to keep up with her as he watched. It was a more advanced game than he'd been expecting, but then Maisie was incredibly bright for her age.

And then, just as he was about to ask what something was, a message appeared in the top-right corner. From LG540.

'Who's that, Mais?'

'A friend.'

Now Jake became worried. Not only did he not want her being exposed to violence, he also didn't want her messaging people online. And vice versa. He knew all too well the realities of what happened when unsuspecting kids fell victim to the evil and sinister paedophiles that existed on these platforms. The traps they could fall into. The techniques used to manipulate them.

It made his skin crawl.

Jake snatched the tablet from her and opened the inbox. The message she'd just received from LG540 sat at the top.

Hello, how are you?

As he scrolled through the rest of the messages, he relaxed a little. There were over twenty in total, but they were all from the same online profile, and Maisie hadn't replied to a single one. None of them were too insidious or malicious; the majority of them asked the same question, seeking a response.

'You're a good girl,' he told her.

'Mummy told me not to message people I don't know.'

Elizabeth hadn't done such a poor job after all. He struck a mark off against her name on the tally.

As he passed the device back to her, his phone vibrated. After reading through the message a second and third time, he told Maisie to go back into the living room because he had a call to make. Then he pretended to be on the phone as she left. He gave it a few seconds before hanging up and entering the living room.

Elizabeth was sitting on the sofa watching the TV, stroking Ellie's hair while she slept.

Jake hurried to her side and kept his voice low.

'Hey,' he whispered, 'that was work. They need me in.'

'What? No.'

'It's about Dylan. He's refusing to talk.'

'You're meant to be off work.'

'They said he only wants to talk to me. There's not long left before they can charge him.'

Elizabeth understood the procedures better than any other civilian

222

he knew. She'd always been the first one to help him practice when he was revising for his exams, and she had a better memory than him. So he knew it would be pointless trying to lie to her about anything procedure related. She would see right through it.

Elizabeth exhaled a deep sigh. 'Fine. Whatever. I'm not bothered anymore. Go. Just go.'

As Jake leant in to give her a kiss, she pulled away. Hurt – but not nearly as much as she was – Jake headed back into the kitchen where he grabbed his things. When he'd first uttered his vows, he'd promised never to hurt her, to lie to her, to betray her.

But the reality was he'd done all of those things. And in the space of a few sentences. Martha was right – he had messed it up.

But he was doing it for their benefit. Getting rid of The Cabal would be the best thing to happen to all of them. If only they could see that what he was doing for them was for their own good.

If only they could give him a little more time.

CHAPTER 54

M

The address on the text message was a small house in the middle of a quaint cul-de-sac in Stratford. It had taken him the best part of an hour to drive there, worsened by the traffic as the city welcomed the evening's partygoers and couples searching for a night of debauchery, gluttony, and celebration. There were seven houses in the street, all of them identical. They were small, nondescript and unappealing, the roofs slanted and the tiles decrepit and falling apart. The house he was looking for – number thirty-nine – was the worst of them all. The front garden was overgrown, and the garden fences had bowed and buckled in the wind. Whoever the owner was – whether it was the funeral director herself or someone else – it was clear to see they didn't care much for the upkeep of the property.

Jake killed the engine and waited. Listened to the silence, straining his ears for any signs of disturbance or movement that seemed out of place. Way off in the distance was the hubbub of Stratford – cars on the A12, the dozens of trains coming and going from Stratford station, and the distant sound of police sirens. A city in harmony.

He stepped out of the car and wandered towards the house. Knocked on the door. Waited.

A few seconds later, it opened. In the past few hours, the woman from the funeral service had changed her appearance drastically. She'd ditched the waistcoat, trousers, blazer and tie for something a little more causal: a pair of black jeans that were ripped at the knees, an AC-DC T-shirt that Jake thought he'd seen in Primark one time and a set of thick round glasses. An earring dangled from her left earlobe and a series of studs were punched into the top of her ear. Her eyes were darkened with make-up, which emanated a youthful rebelliousness. Yet she looked older than him, though only by a few years.

Saying nothing, she stepped aside and allowed him to enter.

'Kitchen's on your right,' she said as he stepped inside. 'Would you like a tea? Coffee? Water?'

'Tea. Please. One sugar. No milk.'

The interior of the house, much to his surprise, was in complete contrast to the exterior – modern, well looked after, homely. So pretty he wondered whether she had another job as an interior designer.

A journalist. An undertaker. And now an interior designer. A woman of all trades.

Without his realising it, she'd finished making the tea and set his mug on the table in front of him. She'd left the bag in, with the string dangling over the side of the mug. Just the way he liked it.

'So…' she began. 'Where do you want to start?'

'Names are generally a good place. But you already know mine, so I guess that just leaves yours.'

The woman wrapped her hands around the mug and stared into the Earl Grey. 'You wouldn't believe me if I told you…' Tentatively, she shuffled towards the kitchen door. 'For you to truly understand, I have to show you. Follow me.'

Jake froze for a moment. He didn't feel comfortable, but he also didn't feel *un*comfortable. He didn't know what it was about this woman – perhaps it was her voice, her mannerisms – but something made him feel at ease, slightly relaxed. It was all the secrecy that put him on edge.

In the end, intrigue got the better of him, and he followed her into the hallway. On the left was a flight of stairs, directly ahead a living room and on the right a closed door. The woman stood beside it with her hand wrapped around the handle.

Jake's body tensed, preparing himself for what lay behind it.

The Cabal?

'Relax,' she told him. 'You're perfectly safe.'

I'll believe it when I feel it.

Jake gave a little grunt of approval. Then the woman nodded and opened the door, revealing an office space larger than the kitchen he'd just come from.

The room was dimly lit by a lamp in the corner of the room. Beside it was a desk with a computer and a mountain of files resting next to it. On the floor was a bin. On the left-hand side of the room was another lamp by a set of patio doors. Through the glass windows nothing else was visible except for thick foliage and trees – no windows from other houses that could look in, no other signs of life from the neighbours either. Immediately in front of the patio doors was a desk with more papers and folders and Post-it notes adorning the surface. But the thing that stood out most to Jake were the walls. In particular, the one to his immediate left.

More Post-it notes.

More sheets of paper.

But there were some subtle differences. There were photographs of people Jake recognised, photos of crime scenes, photos of criminals Jake had helped put away – Danny Cipriano, Michael Cipriano, Henry Matheson. For those that were dead, a large X had been crossed in the top right of their photograph, and connecting the hierarchy of names and faces were pieces of string. Jake's eyes climbed the pyramid. At the top of it all was a blank sheet of A4 paper with THE CABAL written in red pen.

Before him was a pyramid of bent coppers. A pyramid he'd helped construct and identify. The same pyramid that he'd built in his mind.

Jake turned to the woman. 'Who the hell are you?'

'Sit.'

Jake did as he was told, his interest having never been so high.

'Like I said, you're not going to believe me.'

'Just tell me.'

The woman looked down at her drink again and paused, contemplating. She sighed and breathed deeply.

'I've been following you for a long time,' she began. 'Ever since that day in Guildford with The Crimsons. That event put you on my radar.'

'What do The Crimsons have to do with this?'

She looked up at him. Her eyes were bloodshot and looked as though she'd been hiding tears behind them.

'My name is Michelle Cipriano. Danny, Michael and Luke Cipriano are my brothers. I'm the fourth member of the family.'

CHAPTER 55

UNENDING POSSIBILIES

'I could get used to seeing your face on a more frequent basis, ma'am,' Henry said to the governor.

'Sadly, I don't feel the same way about you.'

But he wasn't listening. A dozen thoughts were ripping around his head. The tentacles of his business were rapidly growing back, and he needed to keep control of them if he wanted to make his plan a success.

Although, by now, it may already be too late. The wheels had been set in motion, and so he needed the arms to be fully operational.

Following the incident with Armando, Henry had been kept in isolation, where he would remain for the foreseeable future. The governor had been away all day and had only just returned for their chat.

'Your behaviour in my prison has become increasingly unacceptable, Mr Matheson. And I will not tolerate it.'

Mr Matheson.

Oh God...

The image of Lycra and spandex returned, and a bulge swelled in his tracksuit bottoms.

'Have I been a bad boy?' he asked.

'You know you have.'

Please stop.

'Are you going to punish me?'

'Nothing would give me greater satisfaction.'

God, you're killing me.

The bulge continued to swell until it became solid, and there was no sparing the governor's blushes.

'What are you going to do to me?'

227

'As of now, you're staying in isolation until I can find a suitable transfer for you out of this prison. Until then, you are to have no contact with anyone from the prison, and I am suspending all privileges. You will eat three times a day on your own. You will sleep on your own. And you will get one hour exercise a day on your own. Do you understand?'

Henry understood perfectly.

The final few pieces of his plan were coming together nicely. Everything he could have asked for and more.

And to top it off, he had the whole cell to himself. All he needed was his right hand, a little privacy, and the unending possibilities of his imagination.

CHAPTER 56

LOOSE ENDS

The next task on the agenda was simple: sever the one outstanding loose end.

Dylan Ayers.

The young man had, on countless occasions, seen her face from her infrequent visits to the Haversham family home. He was a liability, a threat, and one that needed to be squished. But the problem was the slippery bastard was still alive, like a cockroach.

By the time she'd returned to the estate after abducting Erica, the place had been swarming with police officers, and so she'd snuck away unseen. And when the news had come that Dylan had been arrested, she knew she had an opportunity for Plan B. It was just a shame that Dylan hadn't died during the arrest; it would have saved her a lot of hassle.

Plan B: sneak in, slip past the civilian reception desk and then pay him a visit in his custody cell.

It was simple, but that didn't mean to say it would be easy.

Luck, however, was working in The Cabal's favour tonight. Thanks to Dylan's ineptitude and hangover from the drugs in his system, Darryl and the team needed to keep him in for the full twenty-four-hour custody period. Which meant he was going to be in his cell for the next couple of hours, alone and untouched.

Right where The Cabal wanted him.

Skipping out of her car, she kept her head down as she skulked across the car park and into the building. Usually, she would have dipped her head and acknowledged the reception staff, but there was that Lady Luck again; a drunk civilian had just wandered into the building to pay their respects to the police.

'You know... I... I... I really respect what you lot do for us, you know. I… it's… I… I wouldn't have the balls to do it, man,' the inebriated godsend said, the alcohol fuelling his words.

Avoiding anyone's gaze, The Cabal snuck past the reception desk towards a set of double doors. She scanned her security card and waited until the door beeped and the lock clicked. Then she moved along the corridors. Stopped when she arrived at the custody suite. It was the middle of the night – one of the busiest times in the station – and so the number of bodies, both police and civilian, exceeded her expectation: twenty or so, darting in all directions, paying The Cabal little to no heed.

Invisible, blended in to her surroundings.

Wrapped in a blanket of Lady Luck.

Shuffling to the other side of the room, she scanned her key card and made her way through to Dylan's cell – fourth one on the right. Fumbling in her pocket, The Cabal eventually found the key she'd copied earlier and slotted it into the lock. Waited. Controlled her breathing. Rolled her fingers over the syringe in her pocket.

When she stormed into the room, the sudden disturbance disorientated and startled Dylan. The man awoke in a flash, but the rest of his body was late to the party, offering the perfect opportunity to strike.

The Cabal couldn't afford to dawdle. Couldn't afford to stand and have a chat.

Get in and get out without raising suspicion.

In. Out.

'What—? What's—? Where—?' Dylan babbled as he propped himself up.

The Cabal wasted no time. She was behind him in an instant, her arms wrapped around his neck and head in the chokehold she'd perfected through fifteen years of karate.

After thirty seconds of struggling, Dylan's body eventually turned limp.

Once she was happy he was unconscious – and that he wouldn't wake up in the next thirty seconds – she set him down on the poor excuse for a mattress he'd been forced to lie on. Then she reached into her pocket, pulled out the syringe, and removed the plastic cap on the top. Inside was the drug she'd asked her husband for. Vicodin. High dosage, highly lethal.

Keeping the plastic cap in her grip, The Cabal plunged the needle into Dylan's neck and depressed the plunger until all the liquid was in his system.

Dylan Ayers was already dead by the time she left him for someone else to find.

One loose end down.

Another one to go.

CHAPTER 57

WRONG PERSON

Jake's jaw dropped. For a moment, he became deaf. All comprehensive thought and awareness of his surroundings disappeared, and the words bounced around his head.

Cipriano.

Michelle.

Fourth member.

Luke. Michael. Danny.

Brothers.

Sister.

Then the email correspondence he'd seen in the back of Rupert Haversham's Mercedes appeared in his mind.

Dear Miss Cipriano,

Apologies for the delay in getting back to you, but it's taking me a little longer to find the files you requested. As far as I'm aware, there's nothing to suggest—

He had so many questions he didn't know where to begin.

'It's a long story,' Michelle said.

'I don't care. I want to hear it.'

Michelle cleared her throat. 'I was the first kid my parents had. From what I'm told, my birth mum – Candice – wanted to keep me. But my dad didn't. He wanted a boy, like he was some kind of modern version of Henry VIII. So they put me up for adoption. And then I went into care. When my parents adopted me, they brought me south from Newcastle. My dad held a lot of jobs when I was growing up – journalist, undertaker, mechanic, IT consultant – but he eventually settled down in insurance. My mum, on the other hand, well, she worked in GCHQ. I picked up a lot of things from her. I had a good life. And then I followed in one of their footsteps.'

'No difficulty guessing which one. Is there more? I feel like there's more. Keep going…'

Michelle cleared her throat again.

'My parents told me I was adopted when I turned eighteen. I always maintained that I didn't want to know who my real mum and dad were. If they didn't want me, I didn't want them. But when my adoptive mum died, I was given my birth parents' names, so I decided to go looking for Candice. It didn't take long for me to find her. When I learnt she owned the jeweller's in Guildford, I paid it a visit. Told her I wanted to buy a ring for my partner. When she asked for my name, I told her it was Cipriano. As soon as I said that, she realised who I was.'

'What did she say?' Jake asked, transfixed.

'She was over the moon. Told me to meet her at a coffee shop during her break. So I did. We had a catch-up, and she told me all about what happened with her and my birth dad. That's also when she told me I had three brothers.'

'The Crimsons…'

'And that's where you come into all of this,' Michelle said. 'You helped expose them for what they were. Criminals. All of them. Even my birth dad. He shot countless innocent people and killed even more. I don't even know where he is. Nobody does. For all I care, he could be six feet under.'

A moment of awkward silence fell on the room. Jake took a sip of tea to fill it. But there was something confusing him.

'So what did I do exactly?'

Michelle pointed to the wall again.

'The Cabal. It all leads back to The Cabal. The Cabal's been on my family's radar for a long time now – ever since the late nineties, in fact. My adoptive dad started investigating corruption in the Met back in his journalism days. I was just a kid back then, but he told me all about it. The person behind it had been meticulous. They'd covered their own arse threefold, and he didn't know where to begin. He knew there were bent cops working for The Cabal in the Met, but he just didn't know who. He was hardly able to get close enough, and he stopped as soon as he started receiving these… parcels.'

'We thank you for your service…'

Michelle paused. 'How… how do you know?'

'Because I received the same ones from Henry Matheson last year.'

A bond, a mutual connection only shared between them, now existed. A bond that allayed his fears and suspicions of her.

She continued: 'I worked with my dad in the undertaker's on the weekends when I was growing up. Something to keep me busy and earn me a bit of pocket money at the end of the month. But as soon as I turned eighteen, I got into journalism. I've been following my dad's investigation ever since. But for a long time, I needed a breakthrough.'

She pointed at Jake. '*You* were that breakthrough. After that day in Guildford, I realised who they were – that The Crimsons were my brothers, and that Candice was in on it all along. You gave me closure after I discovered I had a family I didn't want. But when you blew the whistle on Elliot Bridger, and no one listened, I knew I had an opening. I knew that he was part of it all, and then I began my deeper investigations. I've been watching you from the outskirts all along. Drew. Peter. Liam. Martin. Helen. Richard Candy. All of them. And now there's just one more person left to go.'

'The Cabal,' Jake whispered.

'The very same.'

'How do you know he's still out there? How do you know it didn't end with Candy?'

'Call it intuition, but I think there's something else going on. Candy was too obvious, too easy.'

'But the only people above him are the deputy commissioner and the commissioner. It can't get any higher.'

'Maybe we're looking in the wrong direction. Maybe we need to look lower than the top. Someone who's in the midst of the action, someone who can keep an eye on everyone under their control.'

That made sense. The Cabal had been there, fighting against Jake at almost every turn. They were all-seeing, all-knowing, and Jake had often wondered where and how they got their information.

D for Darryl.

'What does Mark Murphy have to do with all of this?'

Michelle leapt out of her chair and moved towards the wall.

'I'm glad you asked,' she said. 'Everyone thought Mark Murphy was dead. Apparently, there was a service held for him that everybody attended. It was a beautiful affair, but it was shrouded in lies and deceit. The Cabal was behind it. Murphy's death was staged so that he could go into hiding.'

'So there was no second funeral threat to me?'

'You work quick, don't you? I found out about that years ago, back when my dad was looking after the investigation. I had to find a way to get you out into the open without raising suspicion. Fortunately, a few of the people my dad used to work with are still in the business. They arranged everything for me. Sorry if it put you on edge.'

Jake breathed a long sigh of relief, his body oozing tension and stress. His name wasn't on the list; he *wasn't* going to die.

'Why Mark? I haven't dealt with Mark in years.'

'Exactly. You knew everyone else was definitely dead. If I'd said it was for Drew or Bridger, you would have suspected something was up.'

'Did you say he'd gone into hiding? Hiding from what?'

'Hiding from his life. Mark's parents were influential in everything he did growing up. They forced him to get into the police force when he didn't want to. They told him that he needed to wait for the opportune moment to come along. And when that time came, he'd be able to slip into the shadows and live his new life, doing whatever he wanted.'

'And the opportune moment was…?'

'Guildford. The Crimsons' final heist.'

Jake had been worried she would say that.

'After he'd done his bit, he was allowed to disappear into the ether.'

'Yes.'

'So he's still alive?'

'As far as I can tell. No idea where, no idea for how long.'

'How's he managed to get himself out of this entirely?'

'It's not what you know, it's who you know. This entire things stretches further and wider than just one police officer, Jake. You see, Murphy's parents were working in conjunction with The Cabal on their criminal empire. Helping with the drugs, the corruption, the money laundering – all of it.'

'How?'

'Mark Murphy's dad was a Freemason.'

'A Freemason… So does that mean…'

'No. The opposite. The Freemasonry was a front, a subterfuge. It was Mark Murphy's *mum* who was behind it all.'

'The Cabal is Mark Murphy's mum?'

Michelle shook her head. 'No, she's dead now – in fact, both his parents are – but she knew The Cabal. I'm afraid you've been looking for the wrong type of person all this time, Jake. The Cabal isn't a man: The Cabal's a female police officer working in the Metropolitan Police Service.'

CHAPTER 58

RESPONSIBLE

As a child, Erica used to be afraid of the dark. Afraid of the monsters hiding under her bed, of the monsters hiding in her wardrobe, of the monsters creeping up behind her when she wasn't looking. She was never able to sleep without a light on or without her bedroom door open so that light from the hallway could spill in. And it wasn't until she was ten that she stopped sleeping in her parents' room.

Eventually, she'd grown out of all the other habits too. The catalyst had been a friend's sleepover at the back of the garden inside a tent. Erica had protested, but it didn't take her long to be convinced. She was going to have to face her fears at some point, and this was it. So after they'd set everything up in the tent, they'd tried to sleep. It hadn't come easily. The noises of the small woodland area behind the house had creeped her out. The sound of leaves rustling, wind gently gracing the flaps of the tent, the sticks and branches and twigs falling to the ground and snapping. She didn't sleep at all that night. But nothing happened to her. She wasn't harmed. She wasn't injured. Murdered. Killed. Abducted. She was fine. And that was when she'd learnt to admire the dark, make it her friend, and that there was nothing wrong with it at all.

It was on that night that she realised to deal with her fears, she needed to face them.

Four years later, that was what she was doing right now. The darkness inside The Box wasn't her enemy – it was her friend. She'd used it to her advantage. By now, she knew the ins and outs of it. Where the toilet was – how far it was from the window. Where the bed started; where the bed stopped; where the seals in the wall were; where the little chips in the floor could be found; where the pieces of dust and debris lay; where the sharp objects that she could use as a weapon were hidden.

The last secret she had discovered first.

And it had happened by accident.

After her captor – she'd decided to call him Jean Paul, named after the Jean Paul Gaultier cologne he was wearing – had threatened to assault her, she'd jumped onto the bed in frustration. The weight of her body had buckled and snapped one of the springs in the mattress. Then she'd lifted the mattress and twisted the spring until it came loose.

It wasn't much of a weapon – in fact, it wasn't really a weapon at all – but it would suffice. There was a sharp point in it that could be used as a dagger. All she needed to do was aim it in the right direction – preferably at Jean Paul's eyes or neck – and then she'd be fine.

It wasn't much of a plan, either. But it was a start.

Overhead, in the distance, a sound echoed through the small hole in the ceiling. She recognised it almost instantly. The sound of soft footsteps, of rubber on metal. The sound of someone approaching.

Was it dinnertime already?

The slit in the wall thrust open and a square of light flooded in, gently illuminating The Box.

'Are you OK?' the voice asked. It was the woman's voice – the one she recognised but still couldn't remember why.

'I'm fine…' Erica said, trying to fill her words with concern and fear.

'Are you missing your boyfriend?'

'I—'

'He won't be bothering you anymore. He's dead.'

Erica opened her mouth but struggled to think of anything to say.

'Why aren't you eating?' the woman asked.

'I… I… I am…'

'Don't lie to me, Erica, please. It doesn't end well.'

'Did… did you kill him?'

'Yes.'

'Why?'

'Because you didn't deserve him. You could have done so much better.'

'Who… who are you?'

'I knew your dad. We worked together.'

Her dad had worked with several women – even Helena the Homewrecker at one point – but still she couldn't put a face to the voice.

The woman continued. 'You've done no wrong in this.'

'It wasn't my idea.' Now her words were filled with guilt and sorrow, and she fought back tears.

'I know it wasn't, sweetheart. I know. You're a good kid, Erica. But you fucked up. I don't want to hurt you… not unless you give me a reason to. You'll get out of this soon. You just have to give it time.'

'How long?' Erica asked. 'What are you going to do?'

'The less you know, the better.'

'I might be able to help!'

The woman on the other side of the six-inch-thick steel chuckled. 'I highly doubt that, dear. Eat. Otherwise I'll be back.'

The woman said nothing more, and the metal lock slid shut, plunging Erica back into darkness. Then came the sound of locks clicking into place, echoing around The Box.

Erica lay flat on the bed and stretched her legs up the wall so that she was at a ninety-degree angle. She should have been mad and angry and upset about what the woman had done to Dylan, but in the time that she'd been locked inside The Box – and the time that the drugs had been out of her system – she'd realised one thing: Dylan had been using her all along. She'd been a pawn in his sick, twisted fantasy. Dylan didn't love her. Dylan didn't want to spend the rest of his life with her. Instead, Dylan wanted her money. Dylan wanted to use her for his own gain. And Dylan wanted to use her to get revenge on Henry Matheson.

Well, fuck Dylan and fuck Henry Matheson.

Dylan deserved to die, and so did the other one.

They were responsible for putting her in this situation. And one way or another, she was going to get out of it.

CHAPTER 59

PINKY

In the dead of night, Jake slotted his key into the lock, twisted it carefully and tiptoed into the house. In recent years, he'd become somewhat of a professional when it came to entering his own home as discreetly as possible. What he hadn't realised was that, while he was learning to make as little noise as possible, Elizabeth was simultaneously learning to listen out for the smallest sound of disturbance. Both playing against each other.

And there she was, waiting for him in the kitchen, arms folded, stern faced.

'You scared me,' Jake said, after letting out a little gasp.

'You told me you were at work.'

'I was.'

Elizabeth slammed her hand on the dining-room table. The sound of her wedding and engagement rings colliding with the wood amplified the noise. 'Don't lie to me, Jake!' she hissed through gritted teeth.

Jake shut the kitchen door behind him, hurried over to her, and placed his hands on hers. Elizabeth flinched and yanked away. Her eyes were puffy and her cheeks swollen. She'd been crying long enough for him to notice this time.

'I'm not lying to you, Liz. I was doing work.'

Elizabeth rolled her eyes. 'It's just lies after lies after lies.'

Jake hated seeing her upset. It made him feel ten times worse. And because he knew that he was the reason, it amplified his guilt exponentially.

'I want you to tell me everything,' Elizabeth said, sniffling. 'I want you to tell me everything, right here. Right now. Otherwise, I'm taking the girls with me and we're not coming back.'

Their marriage had become like a broken record, repeating the same discussions and arguments, replaying the same fights. But this time, it seemed different. Jake sensed a change in her. He sensed that she meant it. And now it was time for Jake to take the record from the player and start afresh.

He looked into his lap. 'OK…' he said. 'OK…'

He didn't know where to begin – where could he? From the beginning? From the last hour when he'd been at Michelle's house?

'I'll tell you everything,' he said, this time looking up at her and staring into her eyes. 'Everything you want to know. From the beginning.'

And he did. For half an hour. He told her about Danny, Michael and Luke Cipriano – all the things she didn't already know about them and everyone else. About Danny and Michael's death. About what had happened to Garrison and Drew and Liam. About what happened to Danika. About what happened to Henry Matheson, Martin Radcliffe, Helen Clements, Reece, Luke, Deshawn, Jamal. About what happened to Richard Maddison, Jermaine Gordon. About what happened to The Farmer and all his associates. About what happened to Bridger and Stephanie and Candy. About what happened to Rupert Haversham and Brendan. About Darryl and Ashley, Erica Haversham and Dylan Ayers. About Candice Strachan and Michelle Cipriano. All of them. All of it. All the people in his life that, for the most part, had made the past four years abject misery.

Jake felt a weight lift from his shoulders as he finished. That was it. It was over. He'd got everything out and laid it out on the table. Now the ball was in Elizabeth's court.

'I know some of it you didn't need to hear *again*, but that's everything…' he added.

For a long while, Elizabeth remained silent as she absorbed everything he'd thrown at her. By now, her tears had stopped. And as he'd been talking and explaining, her expression had gone through the entire range of emotions: fear, shock, surprise, sadness, angst, despair, disgust.

He couldn't blame her for not knowing what to say.

'Is that everything?' she asked after a long silence.

Jake looked at her, incredulous. 'Seriously? After I've just spent the past half hour telling you about everything, you question whether there's more?'

'Well, I'm sorry, Jake, but it's been a little bit difficult to trust you recently.'

Jake placed his hand on hers. This time, she let it stay there.

'It's everything. I promise.' He held out his little finger and wrapped it around hers. Pinky promise. In the beginning of their relationship, such a promise had been sacrosanct. He was aware that it had come to mean less and less over recent months, but he hoped that he'd restored some of its trust.

Jake relaxed as she wrapped her finger around his.

'What happens now?' she asked.

The question he'd been waiting for. The answer had come to him while he was at Michelle's. And his plan had developed on the drive home.

'I need to get you and the girls out of here. Away from it all for a moment. Until I know it's safe,' he said.

Elizabeth wagged her finger in his face. 'No. No, no, no. You said there was no threat. You said the funeral was a hoax.'

'I know, but I need to be one hundred per cent certain.'

She shook her head dismissively. 'You're not doing this to me. Not doing this to *us*.'

'It's for your own safety. You can go to your mum's. She'll be able to look after you. This is so close to being over, Liz. The Cabal hasn't got many accomplices left, only enemies. And when it's over, we can go back to the way things used to be.'

'But what if it's never over, Jake? What if something happens to you? What if next time it's more than just a stab wound?'

Jake leant over and kissed her on the forehead. 'I promise.'

He held his pinky finger in the air again and wrapped it around hers.

| DAY 6 |

CHAPTER 60

DEAD END

'Morning, Jake,' Michelle said as she opened the door.

Jake bowed his head in a nod and entered. He explained to her that he'd just come from dropping Elizabeth and the girls off at Martha's. That he and Elizabeth had spent the early hours of the morning packing emergency supplies – clothes, phones, tablets, shoes, books, colouring sets, puzzles, games, chargers. Everything she would need to keep the kids comfortable and entertained while they were at their grandma's. Again.

'And your wife was all right with it all?'

'I think, for the first time in a long time, she finally understood and trusted me,' Jake said, drawing that part of the conversation to a close.

Michelle made teas for them both, then skipped past him and made her way towards their very own Major Incident Room. The room was well lit, with the early morning sun filtering through the patio doors and warming the walls. The computer on the desk was already switched on, and within a few seconds, Michelle was logged in to several databases and pieces of software alien to him.

'Did you get any sleep at all?' Jake asked with raised eyebrows as he gestured to the computer monitor.

'Who needs sleep?'

Jake moved to the table and set his mug on it, avoiding the papers on the desk. More had appeared overnight and now occupied the entire space.

'I was doing some thinking last night,' he said.

'Sounds like a good sign.'

'I was thinking we need to treat it like a murder investigation. And what do you do when you start a murder investigation?

Michelle looked at him blankly. She stifled a yawn, but then eventually ceded and allowed it to overcome her.

'If you're not making any progress, then you look at things from a fresh perspective. You look at the facts. And if that doesn't help, you start from the beginning.' Jake climbed out of his chair and moved towards the wall, folding his arms. 'And what's the beginning of this *mess*?'

'My family…?' Michelle said as she joined his side.

Jake's eyes searched for the mugshots of Danny, Luke, Michael, and Candice on the board. He found them on the bottom left. Pointing at them, he said, 'What do we already know about them?'

'At the very beginning of their career, they were hired by Liam.'

'Who were their handlers for their first four hits?'

Michelle pointed to a separate section on the wall that was boxed in by white tape. Inside were over a dozen photos of faces Jake didn't recognise. Some of them had large Xs over them.

Michelle gestured to the first image on the top left of the square.

'DI Steve Cooper, Newcastle Major Investigations Team. Along with Liam, he was responsible for delaying the emergency services and helping them change getaway vehicles numerous times. Deceased.'

Michelle then moved across the row of pictures. 'DC Miranda Hartwell, Greater Manchester Police. Helped with their York and Leicester hits. Also deceased.'

She moved to the third image. 'DS Nigel McCann, Reading Police. Supposed to help with the Oxford hit. But he was delayed. And that was when you decided to get involved. Again. Also deceased…'

That rules that out then.

'How did they die?' he asked.

'All of them were stabbed to death. But their killers were never found.'

'So the only people who ever knew about the early connection between The Cabal and The Crimsons are dead…' Jake considered for a moment. Tried to think of who else knew about The Crimsons dealing with The Cabal.

He drew blanks. Everyone he knew about was also dead. Bridger. Danika. Murphy. Drew. Garrison wasn't in the right frame of mind. Liam was still alive, but Jake already knew that was a dead end. Time and time again he'd tried to squeeze information from the book, but Liam wasn't willing to turn another page.

And then Jake's mind turned to Henry Matheson. The cockroach who couldn't be killed or stopped. Did *he* have anything to do with The Crimsons? No, Jake was certain they were completely unrelated to one another. Different arms of the business.

Bringing in the detestables.

Bringing in the desirables.

Bringing in the delectables.

But… He searched his mind further. Considered, contemplated. Transported himself back through Henry's history.

Then he found a correlation.

One, just one.

A splinter, but enough protruded from the fabric for him to grab it and run with it.

'The jurors,' he said.

'What?'

'The jury pools. Several months ago, Henry Matheson tried to pay off his entire jury pool so that the case would fall through. The Cabal had a line-up of people trafficked via The Company who were bribed into replacing them and voting not guilty.'

'But I thought we were talking about The Crimsons.'

'We are.' Jake held a hand in the air to silence her while he spoke and tried to catch his thoughts as they flew past.

'Hear me out. Back when it came to your brothers' trials, their cases fell through. At first, it appeared there were backhanders being exchanged to the CPS, claiming a lack of substantial evidence. But then it later transpired that Danny and Michael had paid off their juries. By the time everyone found out, it was too late because they were already in the witness protection programme. So that means someone high in the food chain was able to leak the names of both juries and give them up before the trials.'

'That someone would have to work in the Home Office, but I'll never be able to find that list. I'm good, but I'm not *that* good.'

Jake shook his head. 'You don't understand. What I'm getting at is: who handed out the bribes? Who paid them off? Someone must have gone round each pool member and given them their money. For Matheson's trial, it was one of the prison guards. But for Danny and Michael's...?'

Michelle paused to think. She had nothing.

'At that time, it could have been a handful of people: Danika Oblak, Elliot Bridger, or Mark Murphy. Those were the three individuals looking after the case in Surrey Police. They're all dead, but I know for certain, from the amount that I've looked into their pasts, that it wasn't any of them. Which means someone else must have done it...'

He was dangling the carrot in front of her now. How long until she realised, he didn't know, but he hoped it would be soon.

Eventually, Michelle's eyes widened as the realisation settled on her. 'You mean The Cabal handed out the bribes to my brothers' jury members herself?'

'I'm saying it's a possibility we shouldn't overlook. And if The Cabal has as much power and influence as we think, then who's to say she didn't manipulate the lists in the first place.'

'What do you mean?'

'Find the list and I'll show you.'

Despite Michelle's doubts, after working her magic on a friend in the Home Office, they had the list they needed. Right now, Jake didn't want to think how illegal and unethical it was. All he was focused on was finding The Cabal. The rest he could deal with later.

'You're not going to believe this,' she said as she turned around to face him.

'Nothing surprises me anymore,' Jake replied.

Michelle focused her attention on the screen and pointed at it. 'Twelve jury members. All women. All of them single mums. All of them have, at some point in their life, had financial struggles.'

'See what I mean?' Jake said as he stared at the faces on the screen. 'The Cabal influenced the list, so they'd have no right to refuse the money.'

'But… get this. *All* of them are dead.'

Jake sighed and looked out of the patio doors.

A dead end. Another fucking dead end.

'Except one…'

Jake's heart slowed. 'Who?'

'Rosie Carter. And she lives in Woking, right round the corner from Guildford Crown Court.'

CHAPTER 61

WARRANT

Bow Green had now become an active crime scene. In all the years that Darryl had been a police officer, he'd never experienced anything like this. Sure, he was aware of the occasional bad egg exercising police brutality on offenders during the eighties and nineties, but he'd never heard of any murders inside a custody cell. It was unprecedented.

But what made it worse was that it was *his* suspect. His victim.

Which, by default, made him the prime suspect. Last one to see Dylan after the interview, last one to handle him back to his cell, last one to close the door on him for the evening – how could he avoid those truths and the finger-pointing that was on its way?

He had to deflect attention away from him. Fast.

A group of SOCOs were huddled around the cell, examining it for evidence. Meanwhile, Poojah the pathologist was bagging the body.

'How long till you know the cause of death?'

'I can tell you the cause of death now. But as to what actually killed him, the usual forty-eight hours. Maybe longer.'

'What do you mean "*actually*"?'

'Dylan was poisoned,' Poojah explained. 'There's a small mark in his neck where the poison was administered.'

'But the guy's a junky. How can you tell one syringe mark from the other?'

'Because it's in his neck, Darryl. How many times have you seen that?'

He didn't care to answer.

'Even the doctor who checked him over yesterday agreed this was the first he'd seen of it.'

'So someone came into his cell, pinned him down and poisoned him?'

'That's my guess. But like I said, I won't be able to tell you explicitly what killed him until I've sent the toxicology off.'

Darryl nodded. He understood perfectly. He thanked her and then ducked beneath the police cordon, disrobed from his oversuit and moved towards the IT room. By now, all the offenders who'd been in holding cells and the officers who'd been on shift during the time of the murder were in the interview rooms, being questioned by MIT to ascertain what they'd heard, what they'd seen and what they'd been doing when the murder had taken place. Someone was accountable for letting it happen, and Darryl wanted their head on a spike. Because not only did they now have a dead body in custody, but they were miles away from finding Erica Haversham. She was still missing, and their only lead was now dead.

That had to mean something. Someone wanted Dylan silenced. Someone close to the Haversham case. Someone desperate and stupid enough to kill for it. Darryl had his suspicions, but he wasn't about to share them openly with anyone. Not yet.

He made a beeline for the digital forensics team, a small unit of computer geniuses and tech wizards in the bowels of the building. They were an integral part of the overall outfit, and were tasked with examining phones and laptops and tablets and any other type of media equipment belonging to victims and suspects. What some of them lacked in social skills, they more than made up for in professionalism and dedication to the job.

Darryl knocked on the door and entered before anyone gave him approval. He was hit with the smell of energy drinks and salted peanuts, and headed straight towards Nick Driscoll, whose seat was furthest from the door.

Nick was Roland Lewandowski's replacement, and in the short time he'd been with the team, he'd impressed. Methodical, patient and thorough, the list of things he couldn't do was thin. Darryl likened him to the Japanese rail service: reliable, precise and on time with everything.

'What have you got for me?' Darryl asked.

Nick spun on the chair. 'I've collated the logs from the key-card scanner by the custody suite from ten last night to about six this morning.'

'And?'

'This is the list.'

Nick's fat finger prodded the return key on the keyboard and displayed a list of individuals who'd entered the custody suite between those times.

Darryl's eyes ran over the names, striking them off in his head.

PC Peter Blythe.

PS Anna Huntingdon.

PC Felix Moutinho.

And then his eyes fell on one that struck him as odd. Very odd.

'DC Jake Tanner,' he whispered. 'Entered the custody suite at 11:31.'

My fucking God, Jake. What have you done?

'What about CCTV footage?' Darryl asked, trying to focus his mind on the investigation.

Nick shook his head. 'It's been wiped. Someone must have been able to hack into the mainframe.'

'How is that possible?'

'I'm looking into it, sir.'

Darryl leant back in the chair and breathed a heavy sigh.

Just as he was about to open his mouth, his phone rang. He answered it immediately, without checking the caller ID.

'Sir, it's Ashley.'

'What is it?'

'I think you need to come down to Interview Room Four,' she said. 'You need to hear this for yourself.'

Darryl shut the call off, thanked Nick for his time, and then raced down to the interview room. The corridor was filled with a flurry of police officers. Some of them were standing around chatting, but as soon as they spotted Darryl pacing towards them, they sprang into action and started work again.

Darryl placed his hand on the door handle, then burst into the room. His abrupt arrival stunned the man being questioned.

'What is it?' Darryl asked.

Ashley rose from her chair and pointed at the man on the other side of the table.

'This is Leyton Cameron, the offender who petrol bombed DS Brendan Lafferty and DC Tanner.'

Darryl knew exactly who the man was – the piece of shit scumbag responsible for putting Brendan in hospital with life-changing injuries. There were serious doubts whether DS Brendan Lafferty would ever return to work again. And the man who'd put him in that position was exactly where he deserved to be.

Following his earlier discussion with Jake regarding Leyton's request for witness protection, Darryl had started to look into the process. But as soon as they'd found Dylan Ayers' location in the Cosgrove Estate, Leyton's only bargaining power had evaporated, and so too had his chances of being entered into witness protection.

The only protection he was going to need was a condom while he was in the showers.

'Leyton's got something he'd like to put on record regarding DC Tanner's professional conduct, sir,' Ashley finished.

Silence descended on the room. Darryl slowly turned his head towards Leyton.

'Go on…'

'That motherfucker beat me up!' Leyton explained, gesticulating wildly with his arms. 'He brought me into my cell and punched me in the stomach and face. He threatened me as well.'

'When was this?'

'When he brought me in.'

'And did you see or hear anything last night?'

The young man shook his head.

Darryl had heard all he needed to.

The evidence was pointing directly to one of the most dedicated, efficient and successful officers in his team; perhaps the best officer he'd ever had the pleasure of working with – Jake Tanner. The man who claimed to have been haunted and tormented by an invisible figure called The Cabal for years. The man who had pulled the wool over his eyes for too long. Well, it was now time to call bullshit on that. Jake had lied to him and deceived them all along. The evidence against him was profound.

All they needed now was Jake's fingerprints on Dylan's body to complete the set. He wouldn't be able to wriggle himself out of that situation.

Not like last time.

Darryl pulled Ashley out of the interview room and leant closer to her, bringing his voice down to a whisper.

'I want you to put a warrant together for Jake Tanner's immediate arrest.'

CHAPTER 62

FRESH AIR

Although he had almost always been surrounded by people in his life – whether on the Cosgrove Estate or stuck in prison with hundreds of other men – Henry appreciated his own company. And the welcoming silence that came with it.

The past few hours of isolation had been bliss – bliss on a whole new dimension. Sitting there on his marginally thicker mattress, staring into the wall, thinking, plotting, calculating, manifesting his dreams.

The dreams that, in the next few hours, would come true.

But for now, he had to wait; the hardest part of all.

A knock came on the door, and the shutter fell down. Standing on the other side, peering through the small window, was prison guard Trevor Dunthorpe. Another one on the take, another one on his and James Longstaff's payroll.

'Step back for us, would ya, Hen?'

Henry obliged at his own pace. He was in no rush. By the very definition of his prison sentence, he was going nowhere fast.

Once he was in position, with his hands pressed flat against the back wall and his legs spread wide, Trevor Dunthorpe opened the door and patted him down. It was physically impossible for him to have received anything in the short time he'd been there, but it was Trevor's job, and the man had to make it look like he was at least doing *something*.

'Sorry about that, Hen,' Trevor said as he stepped back.

'You're all right, Trev. I quite liked it. Haven't felt a touch like that for a long time.'

Trevor feinted, throwing a fist, then dropped it. 'Watch it, you cheeky shit, otherwise I'll get the governor to come and feel you up.'

'What do I have to do for that to happen every time?'

Trevor rolled his eyes and chuckled. 'Freak.'

Then he turned away and headed out of the cell, returning a moment later with a tray of food in his hand. Closing the door behind him, he said, 'Pub lunch on today's menu. You've got your carbs: mash. Your protein: a lovely bit of plain, chlorinated chicken that's been pumped full of water. And your vegetables: a single carrot. Gourmet. Enjoy.'

Henry took the tray from Trevor. 'And what about my Yorkshire pudding?'

'Sorry, yes!' Trevor reached into his trouser pocket and produced a mobile phone – Henry's mobile phone. 'Fully charged and everything.'

Henry switched on the device and logged in using his passcode. As he waited for the text messages to come through, Trevor announced: 'Thought you might wanna know. Matey's in hospital.'

'Oh?' He didn't want to know. There were more important things to think about.

'Ruptured intestines or some shit. Lot of internal bleeding 'n' that. Bloke nearly died.'

Henry was ambivalent to the damage he'd caused Armando. 'He shouldn't have picked a fight he was always going to lose.'

If there was one thing Henry had learnt early on about himself, it was to not let people either step on him or over him. Regardless of who it was. It didn't matter whether they were a friend, a colleague, even a family member. It didn't happen. It undermined his credibility in front of his employees, his competitors, his suppliers, his users and his investors. It didn't make good business sense. But what really pissed him off was that despite the fact he'd been in the business for a long time, and that people were aware of his brutal methods of reprisal, they still continued to undermine him.

Armando and Boris had been guilty of that. And as a result, they'd both paid the price.

'Hopefully, their recoveries are long and painful,' he added.

Next on the list was James Longstaff, but time was a precious thing, and right now he didn't have enough of it left to deal with it himself.

He checked the phone again – nothing. The messages were particularly slow in coming through.

'Is there anything else I need to know?' he asked.

'Reece wanted me to let you know the shipment's scheduled for arrival this evening.'

'Good. And how are we looking?'

'Pukka.'

'What time do I need to be ready?'

'About midnight.'

'And everyone else?'

'I've been reliably informed they're all aware and on board.'

'*Everyone*?' he repeated. 'The guards?'

'Including the guards.'

'You'll be the one paying the price if you're wrong.' Henry paused a beat as the messages finally came through. 'What about the extraction point?'

'All arranged. Set up nicely on the Thames.'

'And the boys?'

'They'll be ready and waiting.'

Henry dismissed Trevor with a wave of his hand, returned his focus back to the food and groaned with excitement as he thought that, soon, in less than twelve hours' time, he would be able to smell the fresh London air again.

CHAPTER 63

KINGDOM OF EMPIRES

Jake's skin prickled as he waited outside the juror's house in Woking. It was mid-morning, and he hoped that she was home.

Michelle rang the doorbell. The sound echoed throughout the house.

Nothing.

Jake took a step back from the door and peered up at the building. The curtains were drawn on both the upstairs and downstairs bay windows, and offered no signs of life.

'Come on,' he said, defeated. 'Nobody's home. We'll have to try again later.'

As soon as Michelle reluctantly stepped away from the front door, it opened. Standing before them was Rosie Carter, the last surviving jury member of The Crimsons' trial. The one who'd somehow evaded the evil clutches of death. And it showed. Her thin frame was hollow, and her collarbones protruded frighteningly from her chest. Something told Jake it was evidence of substance abuse or an eating disorder, both of which could have been linked to the lifelong fear placed upon her by The Cabal. Rosie's eyes moved nervously, and she hugged a thin jumper tightly around her body. In the background, the TV was playing loudly. Jake recognised it as Peppa Pig.

'Miss Carter?' Michelle asked as she stepped towards the front door.

'If this is about the payment, I don't have it. I don't have the money,' she said, wrapping the jumper tighter around her body.

'This isn't about any payments, Miss Carter,' Michelle said. 'My name is Michelle, and this is my colleague, Jake. We're here to ask you a few questions about Danny and Michael Cipriano's trial.'

At the mention of the brothers' names, Rosie's eyes widened and her pupils turned into huge black disks. The colour drained from her blushed cheeks and she grabbed the door, preparing herself to shut it.

'I don't know what you're talking about. I have nothing to say.'

Michelle stepped in just as Rosie shut the door, jamming her foot in the way. 'We're from the Metropolitan Police. We're here to help you. We're investigating the trial that took place, and we have reason to believe your life might be in danger. May we come in?'

It took Rosie all of two seconds to change her mind. Perhaps it was because she knew that the threat against her life was entirely credible. Or perhaps it was because she recognised the harsh honesty in Michelle's voice, even if what she'd said wasn't entirely true. Either way, it worked.

Jake followed them both into the living room and joined Michelle on a sofa opposite Rosie. They declined the offer of a drink and told her that they wanted to get on with it so as not to waste much of her time.

'Where do you want to start then?' she asked just as an HGV roared past the front of the house, sending the patio furniture out front into a dance.

'From the very beginning…' Michelle said. 'Everything you can remember. When you found out you were doing jury service. Who approached you with the money? What do you remember about them? Things like that.'

'You… you know about the *money*?' Rosie asked, her eyes widening even further.

Michelle dipped her head.

'I'm not in trouble, am I?'

'Far from it,' Jake said, hoping the smile he offered her would settle her nerves slightly. 'But like we said at the door, we do have reason to believe that you could be in danger, and it's our job to protect you.'

Rosie looked down at her lap and started playing with her hands, picking at the cuticles of her poorly manicured fingers.

'The rest of them…' she began. 'The rest of them are dead, aren't they? I've been seeing their faces on the news and on Facebook. Does that mean… does that mean I'm *next*?'

Jake choked just as he was about to answer. He sympathised with her on a different level. He knew of the constant fear, the perpetual paranoia that she was having to endure. But they had no proof, no concrete evidence to suggest that she was on The Cabal's radar – that she was next on the list.

'If you tell us everything,' Michelle said, 'we can help protect you.'

Rosie hesitated again. Then she looked up from her lap and began.

'I… I don't even remember when it started. I thought it was normal. I got a letter in the post, giving me the dates of my jury service, but I didn't think much of it. I was pregnant, and I would have been about six months gone when it was supposed to take place. I wasn't working, and I was struggling to pay for this place.

'But then I got a knock on the door a couple of days *after* I got the letter, I think. It was a woman. She told me she was from the local council. She showed me her details and then invited herself in. That was when she offered me fifty grand to give a not guilty verdict if I was chosen. I didn't know what to do with myself. I thought she was joking. But then she showed me a gun and pointed it at my belly. She said fifty grand now, fifty grand after the trial.'

'What did you do?' Michelle asked.

'I took the money. I needed it. Like I said, I didn't have a job. I didn't have any income. I had a baby on the way. And I was struggling to pay my bills and my debt. I didn't have much choice.'

'Did she give you a name?' Michelle asked.

'She did, but I can't remember it.'

'Can you recall what she looked like?'

Rosie hesitated a moment as she searched her memory. 'I think... she was small. Grey-blonde hair. It was short. Sort of like a bob cut. Wearing glasses. Had a small-ish nose.'

Nodding, Michelle continued her line of questioning. 'And can you remember anything else about her?'

'Yeah. I'm not sure if it's important, but she... she told me that she'd had a miscarriage when she was younger. I think seeing my baby bump reminded her of it.'

'Thank you,' Jake said as he made a mental note of everything. 'You're doing great, really great. What happened after she gave you the money?'

'She... Erm, then she handed me a mobile and told me that she would contact me on that. If I needed to speak with her, I should only use *that* phone and nothing else.'

Jake's ears perked up. 'Do you still have it?'

Rosie nodded.

'Can we see it?'

Rosie lifted herself off her seat and moved into the kitchen area in an adjoining room. She shuffled through the contents of a cutlery drawer and then returned a few seconds later.

In her hand, she held an old iPhone 4S.

'It was brand new at the time,' she said as she passed it to Michelle, who was closest to her. 'Probably the most expensive thing I've ever owned.'

Michelle and Jake turned their total attention to the device. Michelle was the one in charge of it, whizzing through the machine so fast that Jake's eyes were unable to keep up. She scrolled through the address book and then the settings, but she was apparently unable to find what she was searching for.

'Did it not come with a SIM? Did she not give you a contact number?' Michelle asked.

Rosie shook her head. 'No. No, no, no. It was different to that. No – instead, she told me to talk to her through an app – *Kingdom of Empires*.'

Jake snatched the phone and scrolled through the app library. His eyes stopped suddenly, falling on the app in question.

'You communicated through a game?' Jake asked as his body turned cold.

'Yeah,' Rosie replied. 'Always the same username too.'

Jake launched the app, moved his finger to the top right of the screen, and opened Rosie's account inbox. There was only one chat in there. At the top of the screen, the name glared back at Jake, pulsating with the beat of his heart.

He stared at it blankly. In disbelief.

'LG540,' he whispered. 'I don't believe it.'

'What?' Michelle asked. 'You know it?'

'Know it? This person's been trying to contact my four-year-old daughter.'

CHAPTER 64

RECORDED ENVIRONMENT

For too long, Jake Tanner, the golden boy, had been running things. Controlling and manipulating them from the outset. Without their realising. And Darryl despised him for it. Worst, he despised himself for allowing it to happen.

He'd been oblivious to it.

But now it was time to take some fucking action.

Darryl seethed with anger. And his driving reflected that: erratic braking, unnecessary speeding, weaving his way around the traffic. There was a long journey to make – fifty minutes according to his satnav – but he was set to do it in almost half that. Riding shotgun with him was Ashley. They'd decided that the evidence against Jake was overwhelming, and that they needed to arrest him. There were too many coincidences, too many fingers pointing directly towards him. And now it was time to put a stop to it all.

But they also had to be sensible, logical, methodical. As far as Darryl was aware, Jake was at home, recuperating from his stab wound. So he would be distracted, restful and relaxed in the comfort of his own home. But if his suspicions were right – and Jake really was The Cabal – then he would also be clever, attentive, aware of his surroundings. And, not least, prone to violence.

Instead, to stop Jake from behaving like a threatened and isolated animal, they were going to have to handle this sensibly and amicably.

Darryl and Ashley. Just the two of them. Against one injured man.

They arrived at Jake's house in Croydon thirty minutes after they left Bow Green. Darryl slowed right down as he turned onto the street and parked a few metres away from the driveway. He'd been to Jake's house on a few occasions – Jake and Elizabeth had even invited him over with his wife for a couple of drinks that last visit. They'd talked, dined, laughed, enjoyed one another's company... and he'd had the headache the following morning to prove it. He'd been happy and excited to unwind and destress. Now, however, he was the complete opposite. His blood boiled with rage.

Darryl erupted from the car and paced towards the house, leaving Ashley to chase after him. He hopped up the small lip of the patio step and knocked gently on the door, the sound echoing up and down the street.

But there was no answer.

He sidestepped past a row of plant pots and peered through the bay windows to his left. The curtains were drawn, and he squinted through the net material in front of them, directly into their living room. A TV sat in the nearest left-hand corner, one sofa opposite on the right, another on the left. The door at the back was closed. There was no sign of life at all. Not even the incessant screaming of one of his children.

'Bitch,' he said as he stormed away from the window and headed back to the car, leaving Ashley behind again.

'Guv,' she called to him. 'Guv, where are you going?'

He gave her the answer as soon as she closed the passenger door.

'Nobody's in. Elizabeth. His daughters. They're all out.'

'Maybe they've gone out for the day.'

'Not if he's meant to be recovering. And his car isn't here either.' Darryl slammed his fist on the steering wheel. 'He's taken them somewhere.'

And then it clicked.

'His mother-in-law's.'

'You sure?'

'They've been spending a lot of time there recently.'

'What about his own mum's?'

'We can try there afterwards.'

It was settled. The only problem now was finding out where she lived.

Darryl reached for the dashboard, grabbed his phone, and dialled the office. Someone on the team answered.

'It's me,' he told them. 'I need you to find me an address. Martha Clarke. She works for the government. She's the housing secretary. I need it in two minutes.'

It was a near impossible task; he knew that, but he made a mental note to hold whomever he'd asked in high esteem if they succeeded – when he finally paid attention to who it was he'd actually spoken to.

Much to his surprise, the team member, Katie Harden, called him back after three minutes and told him the address. He thanked her, hung up, and then sped off down the road.

Fortunately, Martha and Jake lived close to one another, and they were outside Martha's house in the Surrey Hills within minutes. Her property was three times the size of Jake's and dwarfed it in every other sense.

When he arrived at the door, Darryl held his finger on the bell, the sound ringing endlessly inside the house.

Finally, the door swung upon. Standing on the other side was Elizabeth. As soon as she recognised Darryl, her expression changed. Her lips parted in shock. Her eyes widened. The colour rushed from her cheeks.

Gotcha.

'Darryl... Wh-What are you doing here?'

'Jake. Where is he?'

'I don't know. I haven't... I haven't seen him.'

'He's not at your house. Where is he?'

Elizabeth glanced over her shoulder, turned back to face them, and then stepped out of the house, keeping the door ajar slightly.

'Is everything OK? Is he OK? Has anything happened to him?'

'We need to speak with him,' Darryl said calmly, attempting to control his temper.

'Why?'

'We need to speak with him in connection with something.'

'Is he all right?'

'We need to speak with him in connection with something he's been working on.'

Elizabeth placed her hands on her hips. 'Are you just going to keep saying the same thing over and over again in the hope that I lose interest? This is my husband we're talking about. Or have you forgotten that? Now tell me what this is about.'

Darryl glared into her eyes. 'Elizabeth... I'm sorry to have to do this, but do you know where he is?'

'No.'

'When was the last time you saw him?'

'This morning. He dropped me and the girls off here.'

'Did he say where he was going?'

'No.'

'Did you see him last night?'

'Yes.'

'When?'

'In the evening. He came home after the funeral.'

'Funeral. What funeral?' Darryl asked, surprised. Jake hadn't said anything.

'The one for Mark Murphy. He worked with him at Surrey Police.'

Darryl wasn't aware of any funeral. But the name rang a bell. He was sure he'd heard it before. Was it one that Jake had mentioned? Something to do with Elliot Bridger, perhaps? He wasn't sure.

'And then what did he do?'

'I told you: came home.'

Darryl sighed. 'I don't want to do this, but would you be able to come down to the station with us so that we can ask you some more questions in a recorded environment?'

Elizabeth's eyes widened even further. 'Now you've really got me worried.'

'I'm sorry to have to tell you this, but we're looking for Jake in connection with the murder of Dylan Ayers – the man who stabbed him the other day. We also have reason to believe he's been operating a clandestine network of corrupt police officers.'

Elizabeth's hand flew to her mouth, and she let out a little gasp.

'Oh, Jake. What have you done?'

CHAPTER 65

TAKEN THE RISK

The plan, in all its naivety, had changed.

Lying naked in wait wasn't going to work. Nor was pretending to kill herself. There was no way she could have done it convincingly. The ceiling was too high for her to reach, let alone dangle herself from without cutting off her oxygen. There was nothing she could use to poison herself with. And if she pretended to slit her wrists using the bed spring, then she was afraid that she would cut too deep and do some real, irrevocable damage.

No. Instead, she needed to perform a magic trick: making herself disappear.

She'd been crouched beneath the hole in the wall for hours, acutely aware of the passing time and the rising pain in her legs. Her body clock had kept her somewhat regulated, but it wasn't the same as experiencing the comings of night and day. And she was ravenous too. It was some time in the morning, she was sure of that. She hadn't slept much – especially after she'd been told about what had happened to Dylan. But she'd tried to force him from her mind. She knew that these people were capable of killing her. They'd shown that already, but she wasn't about to let them possess all the power.

The door opened in the distance. She steadied herself. Strained her hearing. Listened.

The sound of footsteps on metal gradually grew nearer and then stopped.

She clutched the spring tightly in her hands, her thumb grazing over the pointed end she was going to use as her main defence. She hoped her poor attempt at sharpening it would pay off. The sharper it was, the more blood it might draw, the deeper it might cut.

The window opened directly above her crouched position. She

allowed her eyes to stay open in order for them to adjust to the bright light and craned her neck upwards. A hand appeared.

'Hey!' Jean Paul called. 'Hey… Where the fuck… I don't… Where the fuck have you gone? Hey!'

It took every ounce of willpower in her body to hold her breath. She didn't want to make any sound at all – even thinking about breathing would be too loud.

Then the man slammed the window shut, plunging her back into the darkness. Her eyes hadn't properly adjusted to the void by the time he unlocked the main door and opened it.

Light flooded into The Box, and as soon as she saw his figure distorting the light, she lunged and charged at him. Jean Paul was taller than she'd expected – much taller. Acting on a strand of adrenaline akin to that of the night she'd killed Helena, she stabbed him with the spring, aiming for the neck.

She miscalculated.

The pointed end of the spring buried itself in his shoulder, stopping as it came into contact with the bone. As she tried to pull it out, Jean Paul – still with the faint smell of cologne on him – grabbed her head and flung her deeper into The Box.

She staggered and stumbled to the floor, her ribs colliding with the side of the metal bed. She yelped in pain as an agonising sensation ripped up and down her body, certain she'd heard the sound of one of her ribs cracking. But before she could crawl back to her feet, Jean Paul was atop her.

He grabbed her by the arms and hefted her up. Then he shoved her into the wall. Erica's head snapped back against the steel, sending her into a dizzying wave of despair. Then he dropped her onto the bed. Her eyes were closed, and all she could feel was his hands touching her, grabbing her, groping her.

She lashed out with her arms, clawing at his face as he tried to turn her onto her back. At some point between stabbing him in the shoulder and being thrown onto the bed, she'd lost her weapon – the thing that gave her the greatest chance of survival.

'You silly little bitch!'

She flashed open her eyes and saw his towering, beckoning presence over her – pinning her to the bed, her arms thrust over her head. She wriggled, managing to free one of them. But it was no use. Jean Paul punched the side of her head, sending her in and out of unconsciousness.

He started to undress her, pulling her trousers and knickers off, then started to undress himself, beating her round the face when she tried to break free.

Then he pulled his penis out of his trousers and shoved it into her.

At that point, with his sweat and weight holding her down, she wished she'd taken the risk and slit her own wrists instead.

CHAPTER 66

CONTACTS

LG540. The answer to all of this: The Cabal, the universe and everything. And the account had been right in front of him when Maisie had shown him the game. It seemed so blatant and obvious to him now that The Cabal was using the *Kingdom of Empires* platform to operate her empire. But why had she messaged his daughter directly? The thought worried him: how easy it was for a four-year-old to connect with strangers.

All he needed to do now was find out who had been sitting on the other side of LG540.

After speaking with Rosie, Jake and Michelle thanked her for her time, told her to contact them if she ever needed them, and then they took the mobile phone from her. Hopefully, the device would disclose all of The Cabal's secrets.

'I assume you've got the technological know-how to get the name, right?' Jake asked as he slipped back into the car.

'Not me. But I've got a friend.'

'Let me guess, someone who owes you a favour?'

'They build up in my line of work.'

Jake wasn't sure which profession she was referring to, but he guessed the safe bet was her investigative journalism.

'How long's it going to take?'

Michelle shrugged. 'A day. Maybe two.'

Jake shook his head and looked out the window. That was unacceptable. Too long. A lot could happen in that time – the past few days were already a testament to that fact.

No, they were going to need something quicker.

Michelle started the engine, pulled away from the kerb and started back to her place. As they drove in silence, Jake inspected the phone then started playing with it, rolling it through his fingers, contemplating, thinking, deciding the best course of action.

'There must be more of these,' Jake said, finally voicing his thoughts. 'The Cabal's been running her entire organisation from this app right from the beginning, so she must be communicating with everyone on it. But…' He looked out the window in the hope that the buildings and pedestrians' blurred faces would inspire him.

He began ticking off the names in his head.

'This one dates back all the way to The Crimsons.' Jake pinched the bridge of his nose. 'Danny… No. He didn't have one that we ever found. Nor did Michael. Luke and Candice didn't have anything either. Then there was Bridger… He was under the impression his stepbrother was The Cabal, but either way, his phone perished in the blaze. Danika… Her phone was destroyed and never recovered. Liam… Liam's is locked up in evidence somewhere. Drew… He was too low-level to have any contact with The Cabal.'

Which left only one person.

'Pete,' Jake whispered to himself.

'Garrison?' Michelle added. 'The coma patient.'

Jake nodded excitably.

'The reason Liam tried to get rid of him was because Garrison was working against him, cosying up to The Cabal, and so Liam decided to deal with it. Permanently. But it didn't work.' Jake licked his lips, his excitement making his mouth dry. 'Not only might Garrison know who The Cabal is, but his phone was recovered and is on his bedside table. I've seen it.'

Jake pictured the mobile phone on the table next to Garrison's head, alongside the packet of digestives—

The biscuits.

'I don't fucking believe it,' Jake said as Michelle slowed on approach to a set of red lights.

'What?'

'Garrison's visitor. I didn't think much of it at first, but now it makes sense.' He tried to recall what the nurse had told him. 'He… he gets a visitor out of hours. Early hours of the morning. About 4 a.m. Sometimes earlier. Sometimes later. At first I thought it might be an old lover, or an old friend, or a family member I didn't know about. But what if it's something worse than that: The Cabal checking up on him to make sure he isn't awake and out of his coma? Or, now that he's woken up, what if she's threatened him to stay quiet otherwise she'll put him to sleep forever?' Jake continued without giving Michelle a chance to respond; his mind was running on autopilot now, and he didn't want anything to interfere with it. 'How easy would it be to get footage from the hospital?'

'They don't have any inside the building. Maybe a couple of cameras at the reception desks. Or in the car park.'

'The car park! Yes!' Jake clapped his hands together. 'We need to see that footage.'

264

'But we don't know who we're looking for.'

'If it's someone in the police, then we will. This is someone who's been like a bad smell right up my nose, a constant throughout my career, hiding in plain sight. This is someone who's betrayed my trust, and I will not let them slip past me anymore.'

Twenty minutes later, they pulled up outside Michelle's house. Jake hurried to the building like an excitable child who really needed to use the toilet. They were finally onto something, making progress, getting somewhere.

'I've had an idea,' he said as Michelle slotted her key into the door.

'What?'

'Garrison's phone. I can pay him a visit. I'll take it and we can have a look at his conversations. Find out where they met up for their chats, if any. If they shared any personal details. Rosie's phone isn't going to have that much information on it. Garrison's will.'

'When's visiting hours?' Michelle asked as she entered the property.

Jake checked his watch. 'Soon…'

As Jake followed her into the house, Michelle's phone chimed. She pulled it out of her pocket and stared at the screen… then stopped dead in her tracks, immediately in front of him. He bumped into the back of her and apologised.

'Oh my God,' she said.

'What is it?'

She turned to face him, her eyes wild. 'I've just got a text. One of my contacts in the police.'

'Right, what—'

'He's just told me that Dylan Ayers was murdered in custody last night…'

Jake's mouth fell open. '*What*?'

'And you're the main suspect. They've got a warrant out for your arrest.'

CHAPTER 67

IN THIS LIFE OR THE NEXT

Jake's throat clogged up as his world came crashing down on him. An insurmountable and invisible weight pressed on his chest, making it difficult to breathe. He felt suffocated by the walls gradually closing in on him. And that was all before the panic attack hit.

When that wrapped its claws around him, it amplified the sensations throughout his body exponentially. A blanket of white dropped over his vision and sent him into a delirious state. He reached out for the walls, for stability, for support. But they weren't there. Everything was just out of reach, laughing at him, taunting him. He floated, hovered, lost.

He was being framed for murder – again. His career was in jeopardy. His family life was in jeopardy. His *life*.

The Cabal was determined to dishonour and discredit everything he'd worked so hard for, and make him spend the rest of his life in jail, where he wouldn't last a second.

For a moment, Jake thought death would be a better punishment. But then he snapped himself out of those thoughts and tried to focus. He wasn't going to let that happen. He wasn't going to let any of that happen.

He was going to fight.

He was going to prove his innocence.

And for that, he needed to double down on the investigation. He needed to get to the hospital and steal Garrison's phone as soon as possible. It was the only way.

'Why don't *I* go instead?' Michelle asked.

Jake shook his head. 'They're funny about it. They only let certain people in. Plus, they know me.'

She didn't like the idea of it – and, to be honest, neither did he; he was putting himself at risk of arrest by being out in the open – but it was the only way.

Mercifully, the hospital was only a few minutes' drive away, and he opted to take Michelle's car, to avoid the ANPR and CCTV cameras that would no doubt be looking for his number plate. He'd switched his phone off back at Michelle's house and decided he would only turn it back on in case of an emergency.

As he snaked his way through the car park and reception of the hospital, he kept his head down and turned his face away from any cameras.

The nurse he'd spoken to on his previous visits was in the middle of helping an elderly gentleman walk through the corridor.

'Do you ever take a day off?' he asked her jokingly.

'Do you? You're here almost as much as me.'

Jake chuckled. 'Is he available?'

'Yeah,' she replied. 'He should be. You might have better luck this time. He's remembering a lot more than he did before.'

That was good news. Very good news, in fact. If Garrison was remembering things, then he might be able to help him identify The Cabal so they could prove he didn't kill Dylan Ayers.

Wishful thinking.

Jake thanked the nurse and then made his way to Garrison's hospital room. He hovered outside it for a moment, thinking of what to say and how to approach the situation. Every time he'd tried had ended in disaster, so he decided to try something different this time.

He pulled out his phone and switched it on, despite the risks. If he was going to prove his innocence, then he needed to record the conversation. If Garrison could incriminate The Cabal and tell him everything, then it didn't matter if the police raided the hospital and arrested him – he would have the evidence he needed.

Emergency situations called for emergency measures.

Jake opened the recorder app on the phone and pressed *record* before he entered the room.

'You again,' Garrison said, sitting upright on the bed. He was watching the TV that hung from the corner of the wall. There was a noticeable and surprising change in his demeanour. He seemed happier, vibrant, more full of life.

'Missing me already?'

'Don't flatter yourself, mate.'

Jake pulled the chair out and sat, then removed his phone and placed it on the arm of the chair, face down. 'How you feeling?'

'Sore. Everything hurts, but I'll survive.'

'You always were really brave,' Jake joked.

'What are you doing here, Jake? I don't get many visitors.'

Jake pretended to look perplexed. 'What you talking about? You get loads of visitors. I've seen a couple of people in here talking to you. And the nurses said you have someone come while you're sleeping. Usually in the early hours of the morning.'

'That is the best time for sleep,' Garrison said with a smirk.

How much did Garrison remember? How much was he aware of? Did he know who the mysterious visitor was? Jake decided to probe a little more.

'Do you remember much about the accident?'

Garrison folded his arms. 'Bits and pieces. I remember Drew being there, the little cunt.'

'A lot's happened since then.'

'Oh?'

'Drew... well, he's dead. Liam, in prison. The Farmer's also in prison. Henry Matheson is in prison. Helen Clements is in prison. Elliot Bridger is dead. And, last but not least, so is Richard Candy.'

The more names that Jake mentioned, the more shock registered on Garrison's face.

'It seems you've been a busy boy,' Garrison murmured. 'Good thing I don't have to worry about it now that I'm retired.'

Jake chose to ignore the retirement remark. It was one of the things Garrison had waxed lyrical about when he was on the team.

'Although there's still one person I can't put away,' Jake said slowly, an idea developing in his head.

'Who's that?' Garrison asked, trying to sound uninterested, but the inflection in his voice told Jake that he secretly was.

Jake pointed to the bed. 'The one who put you in this situation.'

'You already did that. Liam.'

'If only that were true. Liam wasn't the one who put you in this bed, Pete. He isn't the reason you've been in a coma all this time. It's The Cabal's fault. She was the one who gave Liam and The Farmer the order.'

Garrison opened his mouth but held himself from saying anything. He was a clever man, probably far cleverer than Jake gave him credit for.

'You might not want to believe it, Pete, but it's true. We've seen the messages she sent to Liam and The Farmer. LG540... that's her username. On the *Kingdom of Empires* app. You know the one?'

Garrison remained tight-lipped. His eyes flicked up at the TV screen and then back to Jake.

'I suppose you're probably wondering why she wanted to put you in this situation...'

Jake paused to gauge Garrison's reaction; there wasn't one. He continued: 'Well, I wondered the same thing for a long time. But then I realised it's because she doesn't like people knowing who she is. We've seen that recently with Rupert Haversham. All of his family are now dead, and she ordered the hit on them because Rupert was one of her closest associates. She's slowly losing the reins on it all. And she can't have you – or anyone who's seen her face, for that matter – get out of it alive. It's too dangerous for her. If you wanted to get revenge on her, you could tell me who she is.'

As soon as Jake finished speaking, Garrison smirked. The smirk turned into a chuckle, then a laugh.

'You sneaky son of a bitch,' Garrison said. 'For a second, I almost believed you. But there were several holes in your story. One: Liam never even knew about *Kingdom of Empires*; neither did The Farmer. And that's the only way the *real* Cabal communicates with you. Two: I've never even seen her face. But I do know her name.'

'Tell me.'

'It's closer to home than you think.'

'And?'

'I can't remember all of a sudden.'

Jake stifled a sigh and fought hard from rolling his eyes. Garrison had clearly sussed him out. He needed to get out of there as soon as possible. The longer he left it, the more susceptible he was to being caught by Darryl and the rest of the team.

Jake lumbered himself out of the chair and moved across to Garrison's bedside table. He pulled out a business card with his credentials on it and scribbled down Michelle's mobile number.

'This is the best number to call me on if you decide you want to talk.'

As he wrote the digits down, he covered Garrison's mobile with his other hand. Out the corner of his eye, he saw Garrison lean across and watch him.

'Just in case you change your mind or if you come to your senses.'

Jake looked up and pointed at the TV. The news was playing. Perfect. 'You can start to believe some of the things on there now. Liam isn't manipulating the coverage like he was before.'

Garrison craned his neck up to glance at the TV, and Jake used the brief window of opportunity to slip the man's phone into his pocket.

'Well, I best leave you to it. I'm sure you've got plenty of resting to be doing – and plenty of thinking to be getting on with.'

Jake pocketed both devices and moved to the door. Mission success.

'See you around, Pete. In this life or the next.'

CHAPTER 68

PROVISIONS

A single surveillance unit, consisting of an unmarked Volvo occupied by a lone figure, had been set up outside Jake Tanner's house. The figure's silhouette was large, and based on the hair, it was a man, but she was sure they didn't know one another – he was probably one of the uniformed officers that came and went on a daily basis. It was unlikely she would have had any dealings with him. But that didn't mean to say she wouldn't know who he was; it was her job to know everyone's names and a small piece of information about them – something incriminating so she could always use it against them if necessary.

Darryl had made the decision to watch the house from afar, awaiting Jake's, hopefully imminent, return. Nobody had seen him all day, and several search teams had been deployed across London and the local Croydon area. Teams from Surrey Police had also been deployed in the area to search for him. But right now, the officer sitting in the car was just waiting for public enemy number one to come home and into the welcoming arms of London's law enforcement.

But she was going to make sure that didn't happen.

She started the engine, pulled into Jake's street and poodled along. As she arrived by the surveillance car, she slowed to a stop. Now the man's features came into view. DC Perry. Thirty-two. Three kids. Sexual harassment case that had been hushed and brushed under the carpet several years back.

Another bad apple.

She rolled down her window. He did the same.

'Afternoon,' she said.

'Afternoon…' There was hesitation and fear in his voice.

She reached across to the passenger seat and flashed the warrant card she'd used on countless occasions to get herself out of trouble. It was forged and made her look like she was also a police constable. She had several more at home. Sergeant. Inspector. Superintendent. Although, the higher she went, the more dangerous it became.

'Darryl told me to switch with you,' she told Perry.

'Already? I've only been on shift for two hours.'

She shrugged. 'SIO's orders.'

'What about me then?'

'He said you can go home. Spend some time with the kids. But he wants you in first thing tomorrow. They've got *everyone* on this case, but I guess they can spare you for the evening. Maybe it's the calm before the storm.'

Perry chuckled, but it wasn't convincing. 'Maybe I should speak to control.'

At the mention of control, her hand flew to the centre compartment beside her. She didn't want to have to kill Perry, but she would if he insisted.

'There's no need for that,' she told him. 'I've got this. Go on. Get home to your family.'

Perry hesitated a moment. His eyes surveyed her, moving over every visible inch of her body.

'I'm not sure. Maybe I should—'

'Ben, what's wrong with you?' she snapped. 'Are you always this insubordinate? Our governor is giving you the opportunity to go home early. When was the last time you spent some proper time with your family?'

There was no response. And if he didn't say or do anything, she was going to release her trump card on him.

Five.

Four.

Three.

Two.

Perry started the ignition.

'Have fun,' she said, 'and we'll see you tomorrow.'

Perry pulled away and left her alone in the street.

As soon as the Volvo disappeared out of sight, she breathed a heavy sigh of relief. That had taken longer than necessary, and she was sure he suspected her of something, but that didn't matter right now. She was just grateful that it had worked. Good fortune had never struck her frequently. She'd had to work hard and deal with various obstacles to get to her position. But when it came to Jake Tanner, things just had a way of conveniently falling into place.

Lady Luck.

Erica was in the boot of the car again, bound, silenced and drugged up to her eyeballs with Vicodin. She didn't know what had happened between the girl and her husband, but when she'd got home, they looked like they'd been in a fight. In fact, no. That was

271

wrong. She *did* know what her husband had done, but she was just in denial about it. He had that smile on his face. The one that he'd had on his face the last time he'd raped someone – the last time he'd raped her. How could she be angry about it when she'd allowed him to do the same unspeakable things to her? He was an animal, but he was also her closest ally. He knew everything about her operations as The Cabal, and so she needed to keep him onside. The only way to get rid of him would be to kill him.

All in due time.

But she couldn't think about that now. It was time to think about the present.

She started the car and moved closer to Jake's house, slowly coming to a stop right outside his door. She exited the vehicle and made her way round to the back to open the boot, glancing up and down the street as she did. It was late afternoon, and soon the streets would be filled with kids making their way home from school – dozens if not hundreds of potential witnesses.

Inside the boot was the semi-comatose girl. Bruises wrapped around her neck from where her husband's hands had pinned her down. The Cabal had done her best to mend Erica's clothes and make her look presentable, but there hadn't been much time.

She reached into the boot and helped Erica to her feet. The girl was weak, and she rested all her weight on The Cabal, who hugged her and struggled with her to Jake's front door, where she produced the key she'd cloned a few months back and slotted it into the lock. Then she lumbered Erica into the property and through to the kitchen at the back of the house.

'No… No…' Erica mumbled. 'Please…'

'I don't want to do this,' The Cabal replied as she moved over to the radiator at the side of the room. Then she produced a set of handcuffs and tightened one of them around Erica's wrist and the other around the radiator pole.

'Please…' Erica whispered. She was weak and disorientated and full of drugs. She'd not eaten anything in a while, and if she wasn't careful, she was going to die.

The Cabal hated her husband for what he'd done to her, and she wanted to help Erica – the maternal instinct inside her was going crazy – but it wasn't the right thing to do. It would be too dangerous.

'Don't worry,' she consoled the girl, stroking the side of her face. 'I'll make sure he doesn't hurt you again.'

That much was true. He had already been sent out on his mission. She just hoped he was ready for the surprise that was about to come his way.

All in due time.

Before finishing up with Erica, she moved the dining-room table and chairs out of reach, and brought the girl a glass of water and a packet of crisps she'd robbed from one of the cupboards.

'I don't know when you'll next see someone,' she told the girl. 'But you've got some provisions. Like I told you, I didn't want to hurt you. I never wanted to hurt you. But things got out of hand. I'm going to fix them. Don't you worry. Goodbye, Erica.'

She headed out of the house, made her way to the car and then drove away, counting down the minutes until Jake Tanner returned and found her – holding back the tears as she went.

CHAPTER 69

ONE GUESS

The decision to return home was not one Jake took lightly. He was a wanted criminal – in the eyes of Darryl and the rest of the Major Investigation Team – but if he was going to go on the run, he needed clothes, provisions, the essentials.

Michelle had offered him the sofa in the downstairs living room, and he'd accepted – he had no other choice. Elizabeth and the girls were off limits. No doubt Darryl had already caught up with them and interrogated her on his whereabouts. The same with his mum, too.

There was no one else he could trust, no one else he could rely on.

'I can get one of my friends to bring some stuff for you?' Michelle asked as they pulled off the M25 and started the final stretch towards his house in South Croydon.

'I'd rather you didn't. I can do it myself fine.'

It was a risk, visiting his own house like this. If he knew Darryl – and he did – then the man would have done one of three things.

One: forensically examine the house from top to bottom.

No. Too much of a pain. Would take at least a couple of days, and there would be no chance of Jake returning if he saw the SOCOs rooting through his belongings.

Two: leave the house and station a surveillance unit outside his property.

Three: leave the house alone entirely.

Jake knew that the last one was wild and virtually impossible. But the second sounded the most plausible. The only problem then was finding a way to get rid of the surveillance team.

'Stop here,' Jake said as they neared his street. 'I'll jump out. You do a recce of the road.'

'What am I looking for?'

'You're a journalist. You should know exactly what you're looking for.'

'And what are we going to do if we find it?'

He shrugged. 'I haven't thought that far.'

'Hopefully, by the time I get back, you'll have an answer.'

Jake stepped out of the car and hovered on the side of the road with his hands in his pockets, feeling like a hoodlum. It was a strange concept, being made to feel like an outsider, an outcast in his own street, his own home, his own family. And it was a concept he hadn't fully grasped yet.

And didn't think he ever would.

Two minutes later, Michelle returned.

'Nothing,' she said. 'There's nobody there.'

'And you're sure?'

'Positive.'

Jake nodded and glanced up at the street sign. 'Park up. I'll meet you at the front door.'

All the lights were off – just the way he'd left it. The front door was intact and didn't look as though Darryl or anyone had forced an entry – just the way he'd left it. And the inside of the house was pristine as well – also just the way he'd left it.

But something didn't feel right. The few nuggets of intuition he had left in the pit of his stomach told him something was *off*.

But he didn't have time to think about it. Time was no longer a construct; now it was a commodity, a trade for his life, and he didn't want to spend longer in his own house than was absolutely necessary.

'What do you need?' Michelle asked.

'Clothes. Toothbrush. Toiletries. My laptop. And my tablet. I'll get the clothes – you get the tech.'

Jake bounded up the stairs and made for his bedroom. His hand was just on the wardrobe handle when he heard a scream, followed by Michelle calling his name.

The shrill sound invoked fear in him. His mind and pulse raced, his heart pounding in his chest like a drum.

Darryl? Elizabeth? The Cabal? Who – or *what* – was down there?

Tentatively, Jake left the bedroom. On the door handle was a metal hanger. It wasn't much of a weapon – his fists would do more damage – but at least it was something. He slowly crept down the steps, through the hallway and into the kitchen.

And froze.

The dining-room table and chairs had been moved, and a puddle of water had spread across the tiles. But the worst thing he saw – the answer to his fears – was nothing he'd expected.

'Erica...' he whispered, his voice choking on the syllables. 'What?

How? Why?'

Erica Haversham was sprawled across the floor, her hand chained to the radiator in the corner of the room. Slumped against the tiles, weak, unconscious.

Michelle looked at Jake. 'What is *she* doing here?'

'One guess.'

'What do we do?'

'We need to take her to yours. There are a few questions we need to ask her.'

'No, she needs medical treatment.'

'And you think that's possible, given the current situation? She might know who The Cabal is. I need her. I need to know what she knows. I need to clear my name of all of this, and she can help me do that.'

CHAPTER 70

FISHERMEN AND HISTORIANS

Nobody knew his name. Nobody knew what he looked like. Nobody knew that he was the husband of The Cabal – one of the country's most notorious and prolific organised criminals. Nobody knew that he even existed. Throughout The Cabal's twenty-year history, Dennis had always managed to stay under the radar. Partly because he was following his wife's advice, and partly because he was naturally good at blending in, and he was capable of doing a good job at hiding when he most needed to. During his school years, he'd always been invisible. Nobody noticed him in the corridors, nobody noticed him in the playground, and nobody even noticed him in the classroom. The same had applied when he'd worked for the security company. He came, he did his job and he went. But along the way, thanks to his ability to blend in seamlessly, he picked up a few handy tips when it came to technology and security, and was now responsible for making sure The Cabal stayed off the grid.

This evening, it was his job to make sure he was the one who stayed off-grid.

Dennis was stationed along the River Thames, just where the mouth of the estuary started to open into the English Channel. In front of him were the towering pillars currently keeping the Dartford Crossing upright. Red and white lights shone brightly from atop the pillars, acting as a beacon for all criminal activity.

Since it had been built in 1991, the Dartford Crossing had changed the drug landscape dramatically. It connected the country's two biggest counties together like never before. In less than two miles, you could be on the other side of the Thames. An hour later, you could be on your way to Dover and out of the country. The construction of the bridge had helped expedite criminals into mainland Europe with thousands of pounds that would be pumped into their homeland economy. Perhaps the biggest change, however, was the influx of drugs that could be smuggled into the country. Hundreds of thousands of shipping containers were brought in on the back of lorries. Few of them were monitored. Even fewer were checked. Sometimes they'd carry humans, sometimes weapons. But mostly it was drugs. And with that influx of drugs came another epidemic.

Foreigners. Romanians. Albanians.

Dennis fucking hated them.

He hated the way they saw England as their playground. He hated the way they thought they could come over with their weapons and their astute business acumen, and completely dwarf the British competition. He hated the way they dominated every aspect of the market and spent their profits in their own country. More importantly, he hated the way the Albanians and Romanians had – only in the past year, in fact – kicked The Cabal, himself and Henry Matheson out of the game.

Twenty years of market domination overthrown by some men in tight jeans and designer clothes.

But that was all about to change.

The meeting was scheduled to take place a hundred yards from his vantage point – Harrison's Wharf, an oil-tanker reserve, situated on the outskirts of the industrial estates nearby. It was way past midnight, and the air around him was nippy, worsened by the sharp gusts of wind that ripped through the Thames.

The dull sound of tyres rolling over the Dartford Crossing, combined with the gentle lapping of water against the shore, disturbed the serene atmosphere. Dennis was lying face down on a small patch of grass. The blades were long enough to submerge him, but it wasn't a perfect cover. If any of the Albanians, Romanians or any members of Henry's crew shone their light in his direction – whether it be headlight, torchlight, flashlight, floodlight, or even the light on a smartphone – he was certain he would be caught. Accompanying him on the stakeout was a twenty-megapixel Nikon 400D DSLR camera with 2x optical zoom, and a police-issued radio surveillance kit. The device was capable of listening to conversations and audio at a distance up to a hundred metres.

In front of him was a row of abandoned white caravans that shone under the moonlight, like teeth littered across the grass. Next to them were a series of blacked-out Range Rovers and Mercedes – the proceeds of drug money. In the centre of the convoy of cars and caravans was a large yellow shipping container that dwarfed everything else in sight.

Dennis knew exactly what it was.

As part of their plans to monopolise the British drugs scene, the Romanians and Albanians used shipping containers for a plethora of other illicit activities. Drug dealing. Prostitution. Gentleman's clubs. Casinos. Business meetings. A place where deals could be done and loyalties either affirmed or betrayed. Something about the situation tonight told Dennis it would be the latter. The container was owned by Yuri, leader of the Albanians. Beside him was Arti, Romanian drug lord, and from Henry Matheson's side was a face Dennis didn't recognise.

Three snakeheads, each with their own venom and fangs, coming to battle it out.

All three gangs stood in a circle, each carrying heavy assault rifles, as though they were to take part in a Mexican standoff. The Romanians stood closest to Dennis, and he observed them from behind, holding his finger down on the shutter and snapping a dozen photographs.

One of them, dressed in a leather jacket and designer jeans – much like the rest of them – lit a cigarette.

Fuck.

The smoke wafted through the air and filled Dennis's lungs.

Fuck, fuck.

He suffered severely from asthma, and the slightest inhalation of tobacco sent his lungs into a chorus of agony. He held his breath, struggling to suppress his cough, but eventually ceded, eyes watering, and coughed into the crook of his elbow.

Much to his surprise, nobody heard, and he returned his attention to the meeting.

By now Yuri and Arti had joined Henry's top boy in the centre of the caravan site. Dennis honed in with the listening device.

'Is everything ready?' Yuri asked.

'Shipment arrived an hour ago,' Top Boy responded. 'Signed, sealed and delivered. Our boys are bringing it down now.'

'You have money?' Yuri asked.

'Money?' Top Boy replied. 'The fuck you talking about? We ain't said shit about no money. Our agreement was for us to bring in the shipment, sell it, and then you get to keep thirty per cent each.'

'There is upfront fee. You don't remember?'

'Fuck off, prick. What you want a deposit for? You man are off your rocka.'

Dennis hadn't realised it – he'd been paying too much attention to the conversation and soon-to-be argument – but the man in front of him had finished his cigarette and was now walking towards him. Dennis's entire body froze as he waited perilously for the man to near him. When he did, the man started to undo his trousers, preparing to relieve himself onto the grass.

And then he noticed Dennis.

The man yelled, reaching for the gun strapped around his shoulder and pointing it at him. Dennis stared down the barrel, petrified. He wanted to breathe, but nothing came out. And for a moment he was sure he felt a warm liquid spreading across his stomach and legs, defeating the cold that had swarmed him for so long.

'Up! Up! Up!' the man yelled.

Within seconds, Dennis was surrounded, thirty or more firearms trained on him, with no possibility of escape – except in the River Thames, where his body would undoubtedly be left for the fishermen or the historians to find.

CHAPTER 71

SO LONG

Henry was discovering all sorts of luxuries during his time in isolation. Not only was he spoilt, he was also treated to silence at night. Night time in the general population section of the prison was usually the scariest – the time when the monsters and fiends came out, when the air was loud with catcalling, insults, wild noises. For fresh meat, it presented a terrifying experience – the first of many.

But here… it was bliss. There was only the sound of his own thoughts, punctuated now and then by a creak in the foundation of the building.

A knock sounded on the door – a single knock, loud enough for him to hear but not quiet enough for him to think it was a distant echo.

Henry assumed the standard position against the wall and waited for the guards to frisk him. This time Trevor was accompanied by another guard – one who wasn't on the payroll. Two versus one. Not that he was preparing to be violent in any way. Tonight, he was at the mercy of the guards as they transported him to another prison. His behaviour over the past couple of days had been nothing short of exemplary. He'd fast-tracked himself a one-way ticket to another one of Her Majesty's finest.

Or so everyone in Wandsworth thought.

The guards cuffed him and ushered him out of the cell, then the three of them wandered the corridor for five minutes, stopping at various security gates and check-out desks, until they came to a large metal shutter. The mouth of the door opened into the prison's exit. Waiting for him was a police van, two burly officers wearing full protective clothing staring up at him.

'Evening, lads,' Henry said gleefully. 'Hope you're decent drivers

– I get a bit car sick if I'm thrown about in the back.'

'In you get,' one of them said, grabbing him by the hand and thrusting him in the back of the van.

Tonight, it appeared, they were taking no prisoners. Henry was a high-profile target, and the governor had decided to move him to Hull's category A prison in the dead of night, where as few eyes as possible would be privy to it. The transfer was supposed to be a secret, but thanks to a handful of bribes and empty promises, Henry's men on the outside had been kept abreast of all the details.

Henry had been privy to them also, and he was pleased to see the number plate of the vehicle hadn't changed at the last minute, as he'd feared it may have. Probably because budget cuts and austerity meant there was only one prison transfer van in the entire fleet.

A fleet of one.

Ushered into the back of the van, Henry made himself as comfortable as possible, kicked off his shoes, and rested his feet against the wall. The space was no more than a toilet cubicle, but he made the most of it.

He had a reason to.

'Any last words?' the driver asked.

Henry opened his mouth, but the driver shut the door on him. 'Piece of shit like you doesn't deserve any,' he heard on the other side.

A few seconds later, the van pulled away, embarking on the five-hour journey towards Hull. They were expected to arrive in the morning, just after sunrise. There were many people he'd wanted to say goodbye to. But upon reflection, he had already said his farewells, in his own way: Boris's feet would mend from the multiple skin grafts the surgeons had conducted, Armando would make a slow and painful recovery, and lastly James Longstaff would eventually recover from the napalm attack he'd arranged to happen the following morning.

So long, fuck you and thank you for everything.

CHAPTER 72

TIME

The van jostled and swayed, throwing him from side to side. He didn't know how long they'd been driving – time became an even more confusing illusion in the box – but it felt like hours. He'd tried, on several occasions, to make conversation with the drivers, build a rapport. But they were tight-lipped, stern. Hardened to the frequent and incessant bullshit that spewed out of inmates' mouths. They were the two chinks in his plan's armour, the two wrongs he couldn't right.

Owing to the short timeframe and massive undertaking of what he was planning, swapping the drivers for known quantities at the last minute hadn't been possible. And so he had no idea how the two men would react.

Whether they'd lie down and stay there. Or whether they'd stand up and fight.

'What's the time, guvnor?' Henry asked, lying in the most comfortable position he could find: on the floor.

'Why do you need to know?'

'I need to say my midnight prayers.'

A chuckle wafted through the holes in the walls that acted as air vents and communication channels.

'Since when has a bloke like you prayed to anyone other than himself?'

'Ever since your mum did that one night we shared together.'

'Fuck you.'

'She didn't tell you?'

'Tosser.'

'What about a piss?' Henry asked. 'Could I go for a piss?'

'Be our guest. We aren't the ones cleaning it up.'

Henry had done some despicable things in his time, but he wasn't about to soil himself. Not when he had a busy night ahead of him.

'You gonna tell me the time, or am I gonna have to look at my phone?'

'The fuck did you just say?'

'Time. I wanna know what time it is.'

'Nah, mate, you said something about a phone.'

Before Henry could respond, the other one interrupted. 'Shut up, Tone. He's playing you. He don't have a phone.'

Henry wished he did. Badly. It would have settled his nerves a whole lot more. Instead, he'd have to make do with the timer in his head.

According to his meticulous plan, he and the two prison guards would be coming to an abrupt stop just outside Cambridge, courtesy of—

Henry's body smashed into the metal wall beside him before rolling back into the middle of his cell. The sound of tyres kissing tarmac and doors opening emanated from outside the confines of his space. Worried shouts and screams erupted from the guards.

His entourage had arrived.

The sounds of the E11 coming to his rescue were muffled behind the metal, but he picked up the gist of what they were saying.

'Get out of the fucking car!'

'Put your hands in the fucking air!'

'Do as I say or I will put a fucking bullet in your fucking skull!'

Their words quickly had the desired effect.

The rear door to the prison van flew open, and standing on the other side were Jerome, Leyton's brother; Harris, the man in charge of the E11's operations; Kudz, the elder who kept a keen eye on the youngers; and Madderz, who was running the gang on the outside.

His seventh, sixth, fifth and fourth in command, respectively. Nobody had yet been able to replace the gaping holes left by Des and Jamal, but they were getting there. Slowly.

'All right, Hen?' Madderz said as he smashed the lock open. 'What you saying?'

'Get me out these fucking cuffs, man, is what I'm saying. We ain't got time to be messing and chatting. Hurry up.'

Time, ironically, was of the essence. In prison, he'd had plenty of it to spare, even waste. But out here, right as he was about to taste the sweet air of freedom, time was a precious commodity he couldn't afford to waste.

The meticulous plan was meticulous for a reason.

After he hopped out the back of the van, he quickly reacquainted himself with everyone, thanked them for getting him out, and then made his way to the first of four black Range Rovers. Each had been kitted out with exactly the same specs and exactly the same illegal number plates. Four carbon copies of the same vehicle. Four ghosts in the country's ANPR systems.

He jumped into the back seat and immediately opened the can of beer he'd requested. Heineken.

The bitter taste quenched his brutal thirst and sent a tingling sensation around his body. Several months without the taste of its sweet, sweet nectar on his lips – he didn't know how he'd managed it.

Now, he wouldn't have to worry about missing it.

Now, he wouldn't have to worry about a lot of things.

His attention remained so focused on the taste of beer on his tongue, however, that he completely missed the violent sound of bullets exploding from a gun in quick succession and two bodies dropping to the ground.

'Right,' he said to the driver after he'd entered. 'Shall we? I've got some foreign friends I'd like to pay a visit to.'

CHAPTER 73

GOOD LUCK

A black bag had been thrown over his head.

A hand had picked him up off the ground and hauled him across the gravel.

A fist had landed right on his temple, sending a white flash of pain across his vision.

A voice had shouted orders, and within seconds everything had ceased, the air filled with silence.

Then another hand picked him up. Pulled the bag from his face.

'Who are you?' the man Dennis recognised as Yuri asked.

Dennis said nothing.

He was surrounded by four individuals – Yuri, Arti, Henry Matheson's top boy and the insignificant man holding his head back. All four of them were locked inside the container, only illuminated by a single light that shone brilliantly in the corner behind him. The light brightened all of his attackers' faces so that he could get a better view of them and remember them for the rest of his life.

What remained of it.

'What you doing here?' Yuri asked again.

Dennis remained silent. His eyes scanned the container – it was like a TARDIS inside, larger than he would've expected – trying to search for an opportunity, no matter how small, to get himself out of this predicament. But who was he kidding? All four men were heavily armed. And then, of course, there were the armies of Romanians and Albanians and East Londoners standing on the other side of the container doors.

He was fucked, to put it nicely. Royally fucked.

'Where you come from, my man?'

'Who sent you?'

'Who do you work for?'

'Why you here?'

The questions were relentless.

Dennis spat on Arti's blazer, the goblet of phlegm sliding down his buttons. Dennis had made better decisions in his life, but right now, that was the least of his worries.

The insignificant man behind him kicked the backs of Dennis's legs, buckling him to the ground, then wrapped his arm under his chin, trapping him in a headlock. He tried to struggle, but soon gave up. It was better to conserve his energy.

Yuri, Arti and Henry Matheson's top boy approached him. They beat him. Punched him. Kicked him. Then Top Boy pulled out a set of knuckledusters that glistened in the yellow light and brought them down on Dennis's chin, breaking his jaw. The pain ricocheted around his skull and exploded behind his eyes, filling his vision with white. Then Top Boy brought them down on him again, this time on his ear. The blow deafened him, and his head lolled from side to side. His mouth quickly filled with blood that then dribbled down his chin. He coughed and spluttered feebly. He'd never felt anything like it.

The final blow was to his stomach, just beneath his ribcage. He coughed, spitting blood everywhere, and then gasped for breath like a dying dog – wheezing, struggling, dying, suffocating on the excruciating pain.

'That's how we used to do it in London during the olden days, gentlemen,' Top Boy said, looking smug and happy with himself.

Dennis's head lolled forward. He struggled to open one of his eyes – the one that hadn't been struck. His internal compass was shocked, unaware of what was left, what was right, down, up, or even where the pain was coming from.

'In Romania we just use guns,' Arti said.

'Nah, fam,' Top Boy replied. 'You gotta be careful with them. They're too—'

Top Boy was cut off by a brilliant sound coming from outside the container – the sound of thirty-calibre bullets raining down on metal. An unrelenting, continuous downpour of ammunition, mixed with screams and shouts and cries for help. Perhaps it was his deplorable wife coming to save him, armed to the teeth like a female version of Rambo.

Yeah, right.

Panicked, Yuri, Arti and Top Boy spun on the spot and pointed their weapons at the container door, retreating from the danger. But all five of them were sitting ducks. It would only take one rapid burst of fire to shoot through the open doors and kill them all.

Dennis just hoped he wouldn't be the first to die. He wanted to watch the rest of them go. A consolation for the savage beating.

Almost as soon as it had started, however, the gunfire ceased, and the sound of the final body falling to the ground echoed outside. Muttered prayers and profanities sounded from Yuri and Arti's mouths. Both men were now standing behind him for protection.

Cautious footsteps approached the container. Slow. Calculated. Measured. All four men kept their weapons trained on the door, though the insignificant man gave him a small shove onto the container floor. Dennis stayed there, perfectly still against the cold metal, pretending to be dead. A glimmer of hope. If he could stay like that for the next few minutes, he might just get out of this alive.

The footsteps stopped. The lock on the container moved and punctuated the still air, reverberating off the walls. Then the doors opened.

Dennis positioned his head so that he could see what was in front of him: nothing. It was empty. Save for the copious amount of dead bodies covered in their own blood.

'Hold your fire!' came a familiar voice from somewhere around the caravan site. 'Hold your fire.'

Then a gun appeared in the middle of the container doors, thrown down on the ground by whoever was outside.

'I'm unarmed. I just want to talk.'

Where did he recognise that voice from?

And then he had it. The figure came into view.

'Henry?' asked Yuri.

But before Henry could respond, several gunshots sounded overhead. Dennis shut his eyes in panic as the sounds raced through his ears, through his skull and out the other side again. As he opened his eyes to find out what had happened, two bodies fell on top of him, and then a third slumped onto his feet.

Yuri, Arti and the insignificant man. Dead.

Top Boy was still alive.

Henry was still alive.

Worse, Henry Matheson was out of fucking prison.

'What d'ya think, Hen?' Top Boy's voice came from somewhere amongst the ringing sound in his ears. 'Impressed?'

'It don't count as good shooting when you're standing two feet away from 'em. That's why they call it point-blank. Anyone can fuckin' do it.'

Top Boy skipped over Dennis and the rest of the dead bodies, and hopped towards Henry. They shook each other's hand and then embraced.

'Who's gonna clean all this mess up?' Top Boy asked.

'You are. Put the bodies in the container and lock it up. Rain'll wash away the blood sooner or later.'

'What about the noise?'

'Better hurry up before anyone finds out where it came from.' Henry paused a moment as his eyes scanned the contents of the container. 'Where's the shipment?'

'They've got it in another lorry at the docks. The boys have gone down there now to get it.'

'And the boat?'

'Sitting pretty on the water.'

'Are we all done here, then?'

It took Top Boy far too long to respond for Dennis to know that he was safe. 'You might be able to help with this one actually,' Top Boy said, turning into the container and moving towards Dennis.

The man hefted Yuri and Arti from his body and lifted him to his feet. It was then that Dennis noticed his body was covered in blood. Whether it was his own or his floormates', he didn't know.

Top Boy dragged Dennis closer towards Henry. The man smiled ebulliently – the smile of a man who'd just escaped from one of the most secure prisons in the country.

'Well, I don't Adam and Eve it,' Henry said. 'You must be Dennis. Pleasure to meet you. I've heard so much about you from your wife. She loves you very much, you know. So much so she sent you down here. Did she ever tell you why you're so far from home?'

'She didn't need to,' Dennis struggled.

'Bit under the thumb, are you?'

'As are you.'

'Not no more I ain't. Things are about to change round here. And your wife's empire is crumbling. It ain't gonna know what hit it. Trust me. They'll be saying my name for years to come.'

'How did you get out of prison?' Dennis left his mouth open so that blood could dribble from it. He already had too much of the taste in his throat.

'Oh, you know. This and that. Here and there. Vis a vis.'

'She'll find you.'

'Whatever helps you sleep at night.'

Henry gestured to Top Boy for his gun. Top Boy handed it to him, and as it passed Dennis's face, the charred smell of exploded gunpowder offered a welcome change to the metallic taste in his mouth and nose.

'You know, a part of me wants to know who your wife is. I've worked for her for so long, done so many things for her and never been given anything in return. I'm a man of principle, and if someone fucks me over, I like to let them know about the consequences. But… when it comes to your wife, I think the biggest punishment I can give her is my existence. As long as I live, as long as I'm out of prison, she will never be able to recoup her business. I know what the two of you had planned. I saw your little camera. I know you wanted to record this so her and her little pals at the police station could arrest us all. And I'm sure that somewhere down the line you even had plans to kill me so you could have all the drugs and the money for yourself, but I'm too smart. And you both underestimated me. Now everything's finished for her. Her empire is nothing, and with Jake Tanner still knocking around, I don't reckon she has much longer. He's a bright boy. I'm sure he'll figure it out soon enough.' Henry checked his Rolex watch. 'Is that the time? Sorry, Dennis, but we must be getting off. Duty calls, and all that. Which reminds me…'

Without saying anything more, Henry cocked the gun and aimed it at him.

Dennis stared down the barrel, his mind devoid of all thought.

'Your wife wanted me to have you killed tonight in exchange for her killing a thorn in my side. She wanted you dead for all the horrible things you've done in your life. Personally, I don't know you, so I can't judge. But I *do* know your wife. And if keeping you alive is a bigger punishment than having you dead, then I'm all for it.'

Henry kept the gun pointed at Dennis, then lowered it to his kneecap.

Pulled the trigger.

The bullet burst from the gun, and pain exploded in Dennis's knee. He crumpled to the floor in agony.

'I said I'd let you live. I didn't say I'd make it easy for you. Goodbye, Dennis. And good luck getting home.'

CHAPTER 74

RIB

It was difficult not to smile, for he had a lot to be grateful for.

The smell of both the River Thames and manure in the air.

A well-executed plan.

A boss with a crumbled empire.

A group of individuals willing to put their lives on the line for him.

A prosperous future filled with those same people and copious amounts of drugs, money and women.

Ever since he and The Cabal had started working together, she'd been afraid of his power and his grip over East London, and had tried to branch out into the different areas of criminality – organised crime, robbery, human trafficking – to prove she was superior. But she'd mastered none of them. She was spread too thin. And she'd always been afraid of Henry taking over. That was no secret. And now that was exactly what he was about to do. But with a little twist.

Henry was driving towards the docks now, heading for the drugs shipment he and the E11 had brought into the country. The drugs were in the back of a shipping container attached to a lorry, and by the time he arrived at Tilbury Docks, they were already being placed into the back of the other Range Rovers.

Henry pulled over to the side of the road and stepped out of the car. His presence was quickly noted, and the twenty-strong crew immediately stopped to applaud him.

'Good to see ya!'

'Oi! Oi!'

'Look who it is!'

'This fucker's come back from the dead!'

Henry hushed them all with a wave of his hand and ordered them to get back to work.

'These drugs need to be in Dover before the sun fucking rises, lads!'

His eyes searched for Reece Enfield, the fifteen-year-old he'd left in charge of organising his transportation out of the Thames.

'Hen…' came a voice. It was deeper than he remembered, yet still carried some of that pre-pubescent innocence to it.

Henry turned. Standing before him was the younger with the highest score on the Leader Board. He'd grown considerably since Henry had last seen him. His hair was long, he was taller, and he was starting to widen up top.

'There you are, soppy bollocks!' Henry said as he wrapped his arm around him. 'Now, where's this boat? I ain't got long.'

'Come with me,' Reece said and started off towards Henry's car.

They drove for five minutes to a jetty right on the edge of the water. It bounced and bobbed as the Thames rippled beneath it. At the end of the jetty was an RIB. Crouched inside it was his captain.

'See you at the safe house, yeah?' Henry asked.

Reece kissed his teeth. 'Course, fam.'

Henry nodded to the young man before hurrying across the jetty and jumping into the RIB. He acknowledged the captain with a nod and then lay flat on the deck.

There was no need to communicate with the captain – he knew where he was going and what route to take, and in exchange, he would be paid handsomely.

The RIB pulled away from the jetty and roared along the Thames, Henry staring up at the sky, revelling in the fact that he'd just managed to break out of one of the most secure prisons in the country. He was ready to begin his new life on the outside. Somewhere quieter, somewhere the heat wasn't too hot, somewhere new that he could dominate and control the same way he had the Cosgrove Estate.

As they passed beneath the Dartford Crossing, a smile grew on his face. If he couldn't supply drugs to his customers, no one could. And now The Cabal, the Romanians and Albanians had been taken care of once and for all.

CHAPTER 75

STEPS

Sleep evaded her for the fifth time in as many nights thanks to the constant battle of thoughts in her mind, the noise, the unending paranoia and distraction. No amount of tossing and turning was able to fight off the paralysis brought by the images she saw in her head.

Jake killing a man…

Jake living on the run…

Jake sitting in a prison cell…

Jake in bed with this Michelle woman…

Jake already in bed with Stephanie Grayson…

Kissing, fucking…

Enraged by the vision, she threw the covers from her body and hurried downstairs, wrapping herself in her robe. The police were still hunting her husband, and there was nothing she could do to help him now. He'd gone past the point of no return. And she didn't want anyone stepping near her family. Not Jake, not Darryl, not anyone. She was even wary of her own mother; the woman kept hassling her, checking up on her, asking if she and the kids had everything they needed.

Well, they did. They'd managed fine when it was just them, and they would continue to manage just fine in the same way.

She stormed into the kitchen and headed straight for the wine rack. Her mother's extensive collection was possibly the best part about the house. And ever since her dad had died, the collection had grown, and grown, and grown. Until it was overflowing in the utility room and garage. For the past five nights, Elizabeth estimated she'd gone through three bottles on her own. In the dead of night. No judgement, no disappointment, nobody trying to stop her from dealing with the stress and anxiety the only way she knew how: a couple of glasses of red.

They also had the added benefit of helping her sleep. Something she needed now more than ever.

Elizabeth poured herself a generous glass and shuffled into the living room – bottle in one hand, glass in the other – fell into the sofa and switched the TV on mute. The images and videos flickered across her face as she stared into the screen, paying it little attention. The thoughts in her mind gradually receded as she finished the first glass.

Then a second.

A third.

Just as she was about to pour her fourth and final glass, she heard a sound. A floorboard creaking above. A footstep. Possibly her mum and her impossibly weak bladder. Elizabeth sat still as she waited for the toilet to flush, grateful she'd had the foresight to put the TV on mute.

When she heard it, she lifted the bottle again to pour that last glass, then realised it was empty.

Three glasses, that was a record. And she'd drunk them in such quick succession she hadn't started feeling the effects of it. Yet. So she decided to hurry herself to bed before the carousel of her world started to spin. And spin. And spin.

Yawning, she switched off the TV, unable to recall a single thing of what she'd watched in the past half hour. Lots of images, lots of people, lots of bullshit for the middle of the night.

Then she lumbered herself off the sofa and shuffled to the utility room at the back of the house. The next part of the procedure required expert precision. A sound too loud and too out of place, and it was game over. The evidence of her sins needed to be buried, just the same as she'd tried to bury and forget Jake's sins.

Delicately, she unlocked the back door, careful not to make a sound, then slid out of the house and onto the patio. At the other end of it was the yellow glass-and-tin recycling crate. There, she set the bottle down as gently as she eased Maisie and Ellie into their beds at night.

She was on the way back to the house when she saw him.

At first, she'd thought it was Jake, her arsehole husband, coming to find her in the dead of night to apologise, beg for her forgiveness, remind her that everything was going to be OK. Like she'd seen countless times in the movies; the hero's secret return before heading off to battle.

Instead, it was the other arsehole in her life – Glen. Climbing through the foliage at the back of the garden, coming towards her.

'What the fuck are you doing here, Glen?' she whispered, the alcohol wrapping its warmth around her, sheltering her from the cold. 'I thought I told you I don't want to see you here ever again.'

'I wanted to apologise for the other night.'

'I don't need your apologies. I don't want to hear them.'

'Elizabeth…'

He took a step closer, and she readied herself. Aside from offering her warmth, the alcohol flowing through her now filled her with the courage to defend herself if necessary – and more violently than the last time.

'I can't stop thinking about you, and I don't want to…'

'There are normal ways of doing things, normal ways of behaving,' she said. 'Being outside my mum's house in the middle of the night is not fucking one of them. Go home, otherwise I'll call the police.'

She hoped he wouldn't call her bluff.

Another step. Slowly, her defence systems sounded the sirens.

'Please don't do that. I want you to understand how great we could be, how much better we can be than you and Jake. I've heard he's not doing very well. His face's been all over the news.'

'What's that got to do with anything?'

'You deserve someone better.'

'And that would be you, would it?'

Another step.

'I swear to fucking God, stay where you are now or I'll call the police.'

His demeanour switched down a gear. His eyes turned darker, and his head dropped lower. 'How? Your phone's in the house. And I'm much faster than you.'

You wanna bet?

Before he could even see it coming, Elizabeth raised her fist and swung a right hook, clattering into his nose. Blood instantly began gushing from his nostrils, but she didn't wait there. She didn't stop. The alcohol was doing all the work for her, and with the amount she'd had, there was no knowing how much damage she could do.

She found out the answer a second later.

After the success of the first blow, she landed another, this time connecting with his chin. The sound of his teeth smashing against one another satisfied her. Then she launched a full-on assault, channelling her inner teenager from fights on the playground as she clawed at his skin, grabbed his hair and yanked it from his scalp, slapped him across every inch of his body, kicked and kicked and kicked him in the legs until she finally connected with his groin. A surprise assault from all angles, a release of months' worth of aggression and resentment – and there was nothing he could do about it.

Once she was finished with him, she dropped him onto the dew-laden grass, whimpering, cowering.

'I've already got one arsehole in my life – I don't need another one. If you ever come anywhere near me or my fucking family again, I swear to God I will fucking kill you. Slowly. And then you'll wish you'd never met me.'

| DAY 7 |

CHAPTER 76

THE CABAL

Erica was asleep in the spare bedroom, Michelle was working in the office like she always seemed to be, and Jake was on the sofa, staring into the ceiling, pretending to be asleep. He liked to think that it was the sound of typing and the irritable noise of shuffling papers that had kept him awake, but he would be lying.

The last thing he'd expected to see when he returned to his vacant home was a missing girl. Yet that was exactly what he'd found – a weak, feeble young woman chained to his radiator, sweating beneath the heat, her arm and wrist badly burnt. The poor girl was in a semicomatose state. Drugged up to her eyeballs, she'd spent the entire car journey back to Michelle's, rolling from side to side. It was only fair that they let her catch up on the sleep and recovery she so desperately needed. Her mind was in no fit state to answer any questions or help with their investigations.

That had been six hours ago, and as the sun began to creep over the horizon and warm the living room through the bay windows above his head, he decided it was time to change that.

Jake rolled his legs off the sofa, shuffled past Michelle into the office, and started up the stairs. He made it onto the third step before she caught up with him.

'What're you doing?' Michelle asked, her hand touching his on the banister.

'It's been long enough,' he replied. 'I need to wake her.'

'Let me do it.'

'Why?'

'The last thing she needs is a man charging into her room, waking her up and demanding things.'

Jake pursed his lips and shot one last look upstairs, as if he could wake Erica with the power of his mind. But he didn't have a counterargument and so allowed Michelle to fetch her. They both returned a few minutes later. In that time, Jake had boiled the kettle, prepared mugs of tea and coffee – he didn't know what Erica would prefer – and a glass of water.

'I didn't know what you wanted,' he said as Erica entered the room with a motherly hand around her shoulders from Michelle.

Erica said nothing as she pulled herself a chair out from beneath the table in the centre of the kitchen. She looked broken. Her hair was dishevelled. Blood vessels had burst in her cheeks, colouring her skin red. Great bags dangled beneath her eyes, almost dwarfing them. And she looked like she'd lost a considerable amount of weight overnight. Her body was shivering, despite the three layers of clothing Michelle had wrapped her in.

'Sleep all right?' Jake asked, setting the drinks on the counter.

Erica shrugged.

'You want something to eat?'

She shook her head.

Delicately, Jake rounded the table and sat opposite her. The distance between them was great – at least six feet. Hopefully far enough so that she didn't feel intimidated or threatened by him, even though they'd already met once before.

'I'm sure you've got a lot of questions,' he began, 'and so have we. Would you mind talking to us about what happened? You're in a safe place. My name is DC Tanner, and this is Michelle. She's—'

'I remember who you are,' Erica said, her eyes falling on Jake.

'Remember?' Michelle asked as she sat beside him.

Jake sighed. He was wondering when this was going to come out. Oh well. Sooner rather than later.

He turned to face her. 'My wife was sexually assaulted at work a while back. I needed a lawyer – someone I knew that would do an almost immaculate job. So I hired Rupert Haversham.' He paused. 'I know. Conflict of interest and everything in that sense, but he agreed. With all due respect to him, I think this was probably the first straight case he'd taken in a long time.'

'Jake…' Michelle started. 'That implicates you in a lot of things.'

'I know. But he was the best in the business. And he was prepared to work pro bono.'

'In exchange for what?'

'It's probably the nicest thing he's done for someone other than himself,' Erica said before Jake could answer. She reached for the cup of tea and wrapped her fingers round it, clearly delighting in its warmth.

The conversation had moved into delicate territory. Jake faced Erica and removed his phone. He asked whether she consented to him recording the conversation, and then they began. If he was going to wipe his name of all the black marks against it, this was the starting point.

'There are just some boring bits we have to go through first. Name. Date of birth. Where you're from. Those sorts of things, and whether you consent to giving this recording freely.'

Once she'd completed the formalities, it was time for Jake to begin. The only problem was finding a starting point. There were too many in his head, and the scope of the investigation was too large. Did his ego want to know more about who The Cabal was? Or was he more intrigued to discover how she and Dylan had managed to kill her entire family and why they thought they could get away with it?

'How about we start from the beginning?' Michelle said soothingly.

'That sounds like as good a place as any,' Jake said, smiling. 'Why don't you tell us about how you and Dylan met and what led on from there?'

Erica inhaled deeply for a long time, held it, and then let it all out in one equally long breath.

'We met online,' she began. 'Through Facebook. I'd seen him around Stratford a couple of times as well. I think he knew a couple of the boys from my school. One day he messaged me, and we just got chatting. He told me he was a musician trying to make it in the game, and that he was going to be the next big thing.

'He had all these fancy things. Like the clothes. The shoes. The chains. The watches. He even had a nice BMW. And he was really nice. It seemed like he was the only one who really *got* me. Understood me. So we started seeing each other. I mostly stayed round his house because I knew my parents wouldn't like him. He was from the other side of the world as far as they were concerned, and they always warned me about going near people like him. But the more time I spent with him, the more I understood how he and his mum lived. They never had a lot of money, so they didn't know what type of life I'd lived and where I'd come from. That was when he told me he needed to front up some money to hire out a recording studio and pay someone to help him produce his songs.

'I asked my dad but he told me no. That was also when they met him for the first time. Probably not the wisest thing to do when you introduce your boyfriend, but it was horrible. Things got heated between us, then they kicked him out and told me to never see him again. I ignored them. I met a lot of his friends. They were all drug dealers—'

'Did he ever force you to take anything?' Jake interrupted.

'No. I smoked a couple of joints because I'd always wanted to. But...' Her head fell, and her gaze dropped into the mug of untouched tea she had cupped in her hands. 'I'm sorry... Yes. Yes, he did. But not at first. After I'd tried a couple of joints, he asked if I wanted to try ecstasy. I told him no and then he left it. But when he introduced me to Henry Matheson, that all changed. We told him about my parents and how they'd treated Dylan, and then he suggested we get revenge, teach them a lesson. At first, we didn't think much of it, but then I heard Dylan talking to Henry a couple of times on the phone. I think after Henry realised who I was, he saw his opportunity to get *close* to my father.'

'Henry was the one responsible for killing your family? He gave the order to do it?' Jake asked, wishing that he'd forewarned Erica that some of his questions might make her uncomfortable. He doubted her fragile mind and body could take much more.

She nodded. 'It was all Henry's idea. Dylan didn't know that I'd overheard his conversations, but I still went along with it. In all honesty, I hated my dad. He was a wanker, and he deserved it. And so did that *bitch*.' Erica didn't need to mention the name – it was clear who she was referring to. 'Before we killed them, I went to Dylan's and pretended to run away. We took a lot of drugs – mostly ecstasy – because I wanted to calm myself down. Dylan said it would make the experience more bearable. And then we killed them. I stabbed that bitch while Dylan did my dad. But when it came to Felicity… I didn't have the heart. I couldn't. She was so innocent. My little baby sister. I couldn't do it.'

But Dylan could. And did.

Jake nodded, chewing and savouring the information she was feeding him. Already five minutes had passed, and they'd only reached the end of the beginning. They were going to be there for a long time, he sensed.

'Why did Henry and Dylan convince you to kill them?' Michelle asked, leaning forward with her arms resting against the table. She had that sympathetic look in her eyes and possessed an expression that suggested she'd been a therapist at some point in her recipe book of careers. Either that, or she was very good at empathising and sympathising with people… for a journalist. The best he'd seen.

'Life insurance,' Erica explained. 'Dylan told me we'd get their life insurance. Mostly Dad's. And that we could use it for his music. But I now realise that was just Henry talking.'

Jake sighed discreetly. The poor girl had been manipulated and lied to, controlled and bullied into doing what Henry and Dylan had wanted of her. All for some life insurance none of them were ever going to see.

'What happened after you got back to Dylan's flat?'

Erica licked her lips and turned shy. 'We… we had sex, got high, had some more sex and then got even higher.'

'Did he force himself on you?' Michelle asked.

'Never.'

'What drugs did you take?'

'All of them. Heroin. I almost died. He gave me too much for my first time.' Erica rolled up her sleeve and revealed the mark in the nook of her arm.

'We'll get you to a medical professional after all of this is over, I promise,' Michelle added. 'But for now, you're safe here. You have nothing to worry about.'

Erica took her first sip of tea. If it was anything like Jake's, it would be cold by now.

'Can you tell us about what happened in the estate with the other girl? Naomi?' Jake asked, conscious of getting as much information as quickly as possible.

Erica breathed another heavy sigh. 'That was Dylan's idea. Probably the drugs making him do it.'

She paused to take another sip. 'As soon as he saw his face on the TV, he panicked. Naomi was from the estate. He said she looked just like me, and that we should stream her face on social media and kill her and make it look like I was dead, and then we could run away somewhere else. It was all fucked up. But I went along with it anyway because I trusted him. For some stupid reason, I thought he could get us out of this because he knew what he was doing. So I picked Naomi up from her flat and took her to Dylan. I waited outside until he was done, but then that… that woman came and knocked me out.'

Jake's interest piqued. 'What woman?' Had The Cabal suddenly entered the conversation?

'Can you describe her to us? Can you remember the details?' Michelle added.

Erica stroked the side of her face as she contemplated. 'It's a bit blurry. But I remember some things. She was wearing Jean Paul Gaultier perfume. I remember that because her husband was wearing his cologne. And she had short, blonde hair. Shorter than mine, but longer than yours' – she pointed at Michelle – 'and a horrible necklace around her neck. It was huge. I recognised her voice as well.'

'Where from?'

'Home. She's come round a few times to speak with my dad. They seemed really friendly.'

'Do you know what sort of things they discussed?'

'Sorry. I never paid attention. But it wasn't always about work. And whenever I walked in, the room went completely quiet. For some reason, it always felt like they were talking about me.'

The paranoid mind of a teenager.

'Are you sure you can't remember what she looked like?' Jake asked.

Erica shook her head. 'Like I said, it's blurry. I never really looked at her. Dad had loads of women round the house asking him for support. They all sort of blended into one after a while.'

Jake recounted the description.

Jean Paul Gaultier. Necklace. Husband. Short blonde hair. A close personal relationship with Rupert Haversham.

Could it be?

'What happened after she knocked you out?' Jake asked, perching himself on the edge of his seat.

'She took me somewhere,' Erica said. 'I don't know where, probably her house. But they kept me in a metal box. It was like a prison. The bed was uncomfortable, the toilet was messy. It was pitch-black. It was horrible. I don't even know how long I was in there for.'

'Two days. Can you remember anything else about it?'

She shook her head. 'I tried to escape. Every meal was brought to me by the woman's husband. I accidentally snapped the mattress, took out one of the sharp springs, pretended to hide and then s-stabbed the man as he came in.' A lump caught in her throat and she stammered for the first time.

Sensing this was a potentially difficult part of the story, Michelle reached across and placed a hand on Erica's. 'Take your time,' she said. 'Take as much time as you need.'

A sniffle started, and she wiped her nose. 'It didn't work. I stabbed him, but it wasn't long enough. And then… and then… he pinned me… he… he raped me.'

What sort of person did that? It was unspeakable, and it made Jake feel sick.

Michelle rose from her chair, moved round the table and placed an arm around Erica, who was now inconsolable. Meanwhile, Jake waited patiently, thinking vividly about the same thing happening to his daughter. How he'd react. How he'd sever the penis and testicles of the man responsible, and then introduce the knife to the rest of his body.

Hello, stomach; hello, heart; hello, eyeballs – I'm Mr Knife.

'We're going to find the people who did this to you, Erica,' Jake said, offering her a consoling smile. 'And we're going to make sure they're brought to justice.'

Erica nodded.

'Is there much else to the story?' Jake asked.

She shook her head, rubbing her eyes with a piece of kitchen roll Michelle had given her.

'After he'd finished, the woman came home and apologised for what her husband had done to me. She couldn't believe it herself. She kept apologising and apologising. But that didn't stop her from drugging me again. The next thing I know, I'm tied to a radiator in a stranger's house.'

That was it. Story time was over. She'd told them everything they needed to hear. She'd exonerated Jake from Rupert's death, Helena's, Felicity's. That part of the investigation was over – he'd cleared his name in that respect. But it was too early to breathe a sigh of relief just yet. He was still being framed for Dylan's murder…

Shit. Dylan.

'Erica…' he began. 'There's something you need to know. I'm sorry to have to tell you this, but… Dylan's dead. He was killed in police custody.'

Erica looked up at him blankly. 'I know.' There was a long pause until she spoke again. '*She* did it. The woman who kidnapped me. She told me after it was done. Said it was because I deserved better. Much better. And that she was sorry I had to go through what I did with him.'

A maternal instinct to protect Erica…

Jake was stunned. His name was in the clear for that, too. But there was still a slight issue. It was Erica's word against a pile of evidence. Not to mention she was as unreliable as they came.

Jake hadn't realised it, but Michelle had left the room. His gaze fell back on the young girl and then down onto the recorder on his phone. He ended the questioning and then ended the recording just as Michelle returned.

'You need to see this,' she said to them both and then disappeared out of the kitchen again.

Jake slipped off the chair and hurried over to Erica, helping her off the seat. They joined Michelle in the office, perched in front of the computer screen, staring at a piece of CCTV footage.

'I'm still waiting for the hospital car park footage to come through, but this is from the estate at the time Erica was abducted.'

More friends, more favours. At this rate, Jake was in a lot of people's debt by proxy.

A knot formed in his stomach as he prepared himself for what he was about to see.

Michelle pressed the space bar, and the video played.

Jake's eyes widened as he watched The Cabal pull up outside the estate, wander through the underpass, into the building, and then return with Erica in her arms a few minutes later. The footage was pixelated, but there was no mistaking who it was.

Staring him in the face was someone he'd come to trust explicitly in the team over the years. Someone he'd thought of as a mother. Someone who'd been right in front of him this whole time, right from the start, right from the beginning…

Lindsay Gray.

CHAPTER 77

NEIGHBOURHOOD WATCH

For the past few hours, Jake had been attempting the monumental and almost impossible task of processing it all. Right from the start: from the very first moment he'd ever met Lindsay Gray, to the latest interaction they'd had. She'd been the first person to speak to him and wish him well on his first day at the office – and, as facilities manager to the building, she'd taken it upon herself to give him the tour and tell him the best hiding places if he ever needed a moment to himself. And she'd never left his side since. Always there first thing in the morning, always there late at night. An unremarkable and almost invisible fixture in the building.

The more he thought about it all, the more it made complete sense.

She'd been watching him from the sidelines.

Running her operation from the sidelines.

Ruining his career and learning everything there was to know about him from the sidelines.

All right in front of him, in plain sight. The perfect disguise.

Following the CCTV discovery, Michelle had used yet another contact to help her bypass the mobile network providers and get all the phone activity in Bow Green at the time of Dylan's death. That way, if they could prove she was there at the exact time he was killed, and that Jake was nowhere near it, they could build a case against her. A watertight one.

Something that he wouldn't have been able to accomplish without Michelle's help. In fact, he wouldn't have been able to do any of it without any of the women in his life. He was eternally grateful for all of them, even if they didn't always see eye to eye.

Elizabeth.

Maisie.

Ellie.

Denise, his mum.

Martha, his mother-in-law.

Danika.

Nicki.

Stephanie.

Ashley.

And now Michelle.

An army of women looking out for him and helping him when he didn't always deserve it and, at times, had gone against their better advice and guidance.

Like now.

There was every chance that Lindsay Gray was currently at Bow Green, pretending to work, safe in the knowledge that Jake would set foot nowhere near it. But there was also a possibility – albeit an admittedly minute one – that she might not be there at all, that she might be in the last place Darryl and his colleagues would think to look to find him: her home.

And there it was, twenty yards away. A plain house in the middle of a plain street in a plain part of London.

In plain sight.

Until the moment he was arrested and taken to the nearest police station, Jake was still a fully serving member of the police force, armed with powers of arrest and the prerogative to exercise them to the fullest.

Something he intended to do.

As he wandered towards Lindsay Gray's front door, he envisaged her face when she saw him, the way she'd react when he arrested her, and the smug smile on his own face as he explained her rights.

At the door, he depressed the bell and waited. To the side was a narrow window that looked into the corridor. Jake leant across and peered through.

When there was no answer, he rang again, this time holding the bell down for longer.

'Can I help you?'

Jake jumped and spun on the spot.

Standing to his right, on the other side of a hip-high brick wall, was Lindsay's neighbour.

'I was looking for Lindsay,' Jake said, feigning a smile, trying to ignore his pounding heartbeat.

'I think she's at work,' the neighbour said. 'I haven't seen her today.' She stood with her arms folded and looked unimpressed, like she'd done this a thousand times before and would do it a thousand times after. For a moment she reminded him of an old headteacher he'd had at high school. Impervious, intimidating, and a complete bitch.

'No problem,' Jake said. 'Thanks for your time.'

'Do you want me to pass on a message if I see her?'

Jake turned his back on the house and started towards his car. 'No. I'm a colleague of hers. I'll give her a call. I just wanted to speak to her in person, that's all.'

Jake thanked her again and jumped inside his car. As he drove out of the street, in his rear-view mirror, he saw the neighbour reaching for her phone and holding it to her ear.

Jake wasn't a genius, but he could work out who she was calling.

CHAPTER 78

MEET

The angry brown river roared in front of her, spitting water into the air and onto the bay. Her world was falling apart and for a very long time she'd contemplated driving into the river's mouth and drowning, letting her lungs and body fill with its toxic water.

She'd been in the same place along the River Thames, at Gallions Point, since the early hours of the morning – ever since Henry Matheson had messaged her in the middle of the night with a picture of him and her living, breathing husband. Yuri and Arti, whom she had started to rely on to bring in her drugs for the past few months, were now dead. And even more pressing still, Henry Matheson was out of prison. That was inexplicable in itself. She'd tried to figure out how he'd done it, but had soon realised it was an inefficient waste of her time.

The facts were the facts.

Henry Matheson was out of prison, and in the short time since he'd escaped, he'd already killed her suppliers and betrayed her in the one thing she'd asked of him: killing her husband. And now he was starting his drug empire again while hers was collapsing. And there was nothing she could do about it.

The facts were the facts were the facts.

Her mobile vibrated on the seat beside her.

'Jean… is everything all right?' she answered.

'You've just had a visitor.'

'Who?'

'Him.'

Her body turned cold and her skin turned to gooseflesh. 'Are you sure?'

'I remember that photo you showed me. Pretty boy. Nice face.'

'Enough flirting. What did he want?'

'Said he wanted to speak to you. Didn't say what it was about.'

Oh, Jake, you clever boy.

He knew her real identity and now he wanted a catch-up.

The facts were the facts were the facts were the facts.

But how had he found out? Where had she slipped up? And why the fuck hadn't he been arrested yet?

'I need a favour,' Lindsay said.

'Oh?'

'Have you still got your contacts?'

'Prison or Parliament?'

'P1.'

'I reckon I can make a few calls. What do you need?'

'Would it be possible to make an inmate disappear for the day?'

'Who are we talking?'

'Contract killer. Highly trained. Highly successful. Highly efficient.'

'Why not find another one who isn't in prison?' Jean asked.

Lindsay shook her head. 'No, no. It has to be this guy. He's the only one who knows me and my methods and my needs.'

There was a pause. A long one. Each passing second filled Lindsay with more and more concern.

'It can be done. But it's going to cost a lot and take a lot of persuading. He'll need to be back before midnight.'

A smirk grew on her face. But it didn't last long; she wasn't over the hill yet. 'Like I said, he's efficient.'

'What will he need when he gets out?'

'A gun. Or two. A car, something fast, but not too conspicuous. A phone. Laptop. Access to my house. You still have the keys I gave you?'

'Of course.'

'Brilliant. Let him in when he arrives.'

'Where are you going to be?'

'Dealing with that other problem.'

'Do I need to brief him when he gets here?'

'Please.'

'And what should I tell him?'

Lindsay explained, hung up the phone and immediately made another call to a number she'd committed to memory years ago. The only number she ever needed to remember.

Her last resort. Her last escape.

And there was no answer.

Lindsay slapped her knee in frustration and let out a little scream, then clenched either side of the phone and started to flex the device. She stopped as soon as she heard a snap threatening.

She tried the number again.

This time, the person she was calling answered. In all her years as The Cabal, Lindsay Gray had only ever met them once.

'You're not supposed to call this number.'

'I need an out. You said to call if I ever needed to disappear.'

There was a brief pause as Lindsay waited impatiently. She shuffled in her seat, and her body shook with nerves. It had only been a few seconds, but it felt like minutes.

'Westminster Bridge. East side. Noon. A black Renault will pick you up. Tell no one.'

CHAPTER 79

A PLAN

'She wasn't there?' Michelle asked, repeating what he'd just told her. 'What were you expecting? Her to just come out with her hands tied behind her back?'

Jake shrugged. 'It was worth a shot.'

A calculated risk that hadn't paid off and could have potentially jeopardised his location and safety. But worth it.

Jake shut the office door behind him, leaving Erica in the living room with the TV remote and a horde of snacks and drinks to feast on.

'What've I missed?' he asked.

'I've got something…'

It was becoming a popular phrase. With each hour there was something new, a new revelation to discover, a new piece of evidence to be used against Lindsay Gray. But something told him this time was different.

'I did what you asked…' Michelle began.

'And?'

'You were right.'

'Are you sure?'

'I checked the records myself, and then I asked someone I know to check them again.'

'And they're saying the same thing?'

'Unequivocally.'

Jake stepped away, pondered.

'How is she?'

'Better, stronger. But I'm not keen on her being here much longer, Jake. It's not good for her health, and it's not safe. In fact, it's probably not safe for any of us.'

'As far as The Cabal's concerned, Erica's still in my house.'

'It's not her I'm worried about…'

'What do you suggest we do with her?' Jake asked.

'Take her to a hospital. Let them deal with her, and when they realise who she is, she'll become the police's problem.'

Jake liked the idea. But there was something that seemed off about it. It put him at risk. If he gave Erica – his only bargaining tool – over to the police, then he would be isolated and vulnerable.

'And what about *this*?' He pointed to the computer screen. 'Do you want to be the one to tell her or should I? Personally, I think it's better coming from you.'

'Why?'

'Aside from the fact you're a woman, you know exactly what she's going through.'

After some gentle persuasion, Michelle finally conceded, and the three of them sat at the dining-room table, a peace offering of a tea each sitting in front of them. In the past few hours, the colour had returned to Erica's face, and she looked almost normal again – she'd showered and changed into some clothes Michelle had offered her, and had been constantly shovelling snacks and biscuits into her mouth since he'd got back.

She popped a Hula Hoop on her tongue and chomped on it. 'Am I going to like what this is about?' she asked.

'We're not sure,' Michelle said.

Jake had given her the floor, so his role in this conversation was to offer support and answer any questions Erica may have.

'There were a couple of things we checked out while you were asleep. Last night, you said that Lindsay, the woman who abducted you, was apologetic and upset about what she was doing.'

'That's right.' Another crisp, tentative this time as she prepared herself for what she was about to hear.

'Well, Jake thought there may be something behind it. Something else going on. So I checked some of my records and my contacts, and it turns out that…' Michelle hesitated as she summoned the courage to say it. 'It turns out that Lindsay Gray is your birth mum.'

Silence.

Erica.

Erica stopped chewing, and the attentiveness and alertness disappeared from her eyes in a flash as she was yanked into her thoughts. The struggle to process the information manifested itself on her face.

'I know what you must be feeling,' Michelle started. 'I went through something similar: I was adopted when I was very young. My birth mum wanted to keep me, but Dad didn't because I was a girl and he so desperately wanted a boy.' She paused, taking in Erica's reaction. 'I know this has come as a bit of a shock.'

'Would you like to understand a little more about it?' Jake asked.

311

Erica nodded slowly.

Michelle had done her piece – now it was his turn.

'When you were born, Lindsay Gray was working as a detective constable for the Metropolitan Police – the same position as me. From what I know, she worked very closely with your dad, Rupert. We've got access to the birth certificate that states Lindsay is your birth mother, and Rupert the birth father.'

What he'd neglected to tell her was that during her pregnancy, Lindsay had been married to Dennis, and Rupert to his first wife. Erica, then, was the result of an affair or a one-night stand, and as soon as Lindsay had given birth, she'd handed her over to Rupert.

'Why did she give me up?' Erica's voice was hollow, lost.

'I couldn't say,' he replied. 'There could be a host of reasons. You have to remember that this was a time when there were very few female police detectives.'

'So she chose her career over me?'

Jake tried to backtrack, but failed. 'She could have—'

'Tell me the truth. Tell me everything. I know you're hiding something from me.'

Jake cast a quick glance over at Michelle. 'I… We… Remember, we don't know all the facts, so a lot of this is theoretical.'

'I don't care. I want to hear it.'

Jake cleared his throat. 'Well, when you were born, Lindsay and Rupert were both married to other people. It's likely they had an affair, and you were the outcome. But when you were finally born, instead of keeping you, Lindsay handed you to Rupert. Ever since then – and this is from discussions I've had with her – she's always maintained that she had a miscarriage. But I think she kept coming round to see you because she loved you. She wanted to keep an eye on you, see how you were developing. She couldn't give you all her love because she was working with dangerous people, building her empire. If anything happened to her, then at least you were kept separate from it all. Meanwhile, your dad raised you and provided for you. Aside from all the bad people he protected, he wasn't a bad man. He was just very good at doing a good job for bad people, that's all.'

Jake took a sip of tea to ease the patchiness in his mouth and throat. He'd given her the Hollywood slant of his theory, the slant where everyone was a hero at the end of the day.

But if she saw right through it, she didn't say. Instead, she asked, 'Where is she? I want to see her.'

Jake stuttered. 'W-We don't know. I don't think that's a good idea.'

'I want to see her. I want answers. Otherwise, I'm calling the police and telling them that you've kidnapped me and you're holding me hostage.'

Jake needed time to think about it all and clear his head. The one thing exonerating him of all the crimes against him, the one thing he had as leverage over Darryl and the rest of MIT, wanted to come face to face with The Cabal. The risks were unprecedented. If anything happened to her, in any way, shape or form, he was looking at a lengthy prison sentence – regardless of the evidence Michelle had been gathering to prove his innocence.

He might never get to see his family again. Elizabeth, Maisie, Ellie. His mum, brother, sister.

But neither would Erica. Her family were all dead. Yes, she was partly responsible, but how was it any different to the way Jake had treated his own family in recent months? His behaviour and neglect and selfishness had been responsible for the death of his marriage and the death of his relationships with those closest to him.

If he could give Erica one last chance to gain some form of closure, then he should.

A knock came at the door. Michelle ushered herself in awkwardly. 'This a good time?'

Jake shuffled aside on the sofa. 'I could do with the distraction.'

Michelle joined him.

'How's she doing?' he asked.

'She's been in the toilet for the past twenty minutes. I thought I'd leave her to it.'

'And you've made sure she hasn't escaped?'

Michelle smirked. 'I don't know if you've paid much attention to the bathroom since you've been here, but the windows are far too small for someone her size to fit through.'

'Of course. How silly of me.'

Michelle allowed a moment of silence to sit between them before she shoved it away again. 'What are you thinking?'

Jake explained that he was torn.

'You want my advice?'

'I don't see why not.'

'Then I think you should take her to see Lindsay whenever we find out where she is. I've been in her position; it's shit. Don't make her suffer any longer. She's been through a lot in the past week, and I think she at least needs some good to come from this.'

'Good? How can finding out that her mum is a corrupt police officer responsible for killing so many people be *good*?'

'Closure. And trust me, when you find it, it's the best feeling in the world.'

Closure.

That was what he needed on this chapter in his life. On his chapter with Elizabeth. On his chapter with The Cabal.

It all needed to come to an end. And a new page had to turn.

Jake switched on his phone and waited for the messages to come through.

'What're you doing? I thought we said—'

Jake waved her away. In the space of a few seconds, a flurry of messages had flooded in from an unlikely contact.

Martha Clarke had sent him twenty messages and seven voicemails overnight.

Immediately, his heart began to panic.

'I'll get back to work then,' Michelle said, her voice filled with disdain.

Jake ignored her as he navigated his way to the call log. He played the first voicemail.

'Jake, I think there's something you need to know. Last night, the man who assaulted Lizzie snuck into the garden. She—'

He stopped the playback and listened to another one.

'I don't know why, but she's adamant about leaving you out of this. You should be ashamed of yourself. This is happening to your wife, and she's more worried about protecting you than she is about her own safety—'

He listened to the rest. Each one was filled with vehemence and verisimilitude. Each one reminded him that he was a total and utter waste of space; that he'd been the luckiest man alive to have Elizabeth as his wife and he'd thrown it all away; that he had no right returning to her home until she felt he'd earned her respect back.

Each word was a dagger laced with poison. A hundred knives piercing his body and heart and soul.

He dropped the phone onto the cushion, dejected. He sat like that for a while, unaware of time passing.

It wasn't until Michelle appeared at the door again that he finally recognised something else.

'What is it?' he muttered.

'Follow me. I have something to show you.'

She led him into the office and sat at the desk. On the screen was another piece of software that looked alien to Jake.

'What is it?' he asked again.

'The evidence is mounting. I hacked into Garrison's phone and logged into his *Kingdom of Empires* account.'

'*You* hacked into it? Not one of your colleagues?'

'I have skills of my own, you know.'

'Skills that your mum, the former GCHQ worker, taught you?'

Michelle fell hesitant. 'I…'

'And each of these *contacts*, have they been *you* all this time?'

'Some. Most… All right, *all* of them. My mum taught me a lot of things, but the most important was that I always needed someone to blame it on. That's why I have my "contacts". They're not real, they don't exist. They're just a loophole for me to deflect attention if necessary. Especially when I'm working with a cop.'

Jake nodded his understanding. There was a darker side to her that he hadn't foreseen – even darker than her invitation to Mark Murphy's fake funeral.

They turned their attention back to the screen.

'What's this we're looking at?' he asked.

'This here is a complete list of the messages from before Garrison was attacked.'

'Oh?'

'Messages incriminating him in Danny and Michael's deaths, as well as in trying to get rid of Liam. I've got printouts and copies and everything.'

'I knew Garrison was a part of it, but I didn't realise he was in *that* deep.'

Or he hadn't wanted to realise it.

Michelle continued. 'I even hacked into Lindsay's account as well. That makes for even more interesting reading. If you can present that in court, there's no chance she'll ever get out.'

Jake smiled, forgetting about the voicemails from his mother-in-law. At last, there was more light amidst the darkness.

But as with all things in life, once things start going well, there's always something to bring you back down again.

Jake's phone chimed. So too did Michelle's. It was a notification from the BBC News app. Jake opened it.

'Henry Matheson… Escape… HMP Wandsworth…' He looked up at Michelle. 'How is that possible?'

'It's not. Not unless he's had help from both the inside and the outside.'

Just as he was about to open his mouth, the computer chimed, igniting Michelle into action.

'What's that?' Jake asked, as he moved closer to the desk, forcing Henry Matheson to the back of his mind.

'*I* set up surveillance on Lindsay's phone. Monitoring her calls, inbound and outbound. And she's just had one. We can listen in.' She loaded up a piece of software on the computer, made a few clicks with the mouse, and within seconds, the recording opened on the screen. 'This is an inbound call she received a few minutes ago.'

Michelle pressed play.

As they both listened to the playback, Jake kicked himself. He knew he should have done something about the neighbour. But instead he'd let it slide.

Jake listened to it again. And then a third time.

'Sounds like Henry Matheson getting out of jail was a surprise to her,' he said.

'Who's the contract killer she's referring to?'

Jake paused a beat to think. 'There's only one person I can think of that she's used in the past.'

'Who?'

'The same person who killed your brothers. He's called The Farmer.'

Michelle swivelled on the chair and began typing furiously on the keyboard. 'The Farmer. Georgiy Ivanov. Russian contract killer. Been in the country – and the business – for years. Very few people know his name, let alone his area of business. He's got contacts high up in the Russian Mafia that have links with the government and other oligarchs.'

Jake placed a hand on the back of Michelle's chair. 'This is beginning to sound like the plot of a thriller. And quite a good one.'

'I can try to get his prison on lockdown. We'll have to locate which one he's in first. But we should be able to stop him from getting out for the day.'

'And if we can't?'

'Then we'll have to hope we can get to Henry Matheson before The Farmer does.'

Another chime came from the computer, halting their conversation. Another recorded voice call. Time stamped two minutes ago.

Michelle pressed play.

'You're not supposed to call this number,' the voice started.

As soon as he heard it, he lunged forward and plunged his finger down on the space bar, freezing the playback.

'Jake... Jake, what is it?'

He froze.

That voice. He knew it from somewhere. It was oddly familiar. Too familiar.

But the feedback and static...

'Play it again.'

'You're not supposed to call this number.'

There it was. That voice again.

'I need an out. You said to call if I needed to disappear.'

'Westminster Bridge. East side. Noon. A black Renault will pick you up. Tell no one.'

As soon as the recording finished, Jake checked his watch, darted out of the office and headed to the kitchen where Michelle's car keys were.

'Where are you going?' Michelle asked, chasing after him.

'I've got a plan,' he said. 'It's crazy, but I think it can work for all of us. But first there's something I need to do. Michelle, this all ends today.'

CHAPTER 80

PACK YOUR BAGS

Henry Matheson had never seen the sea. In fact, the largest expanse of water he'd ever seen – until last night – was in his bathtub. Though he knew the English Channel, separating England from the continent, wasn't technically a sea, it still stretched on for mile upon mile like the ocean did.

As he lay flat in the RIB, traversing the tremendous and tumultuous currents and ripples of the waves, he should have felt excitement, he should have felt a sense of adventure. But instead he'd been wracked with fear. Of drowning. Of losing power and drifting out to sea. Of falling prey to a swarm of sharks. It was completely irrational, but it had been the unending blackness of it all that had frightened him.

He supposed it was the only thing in life that he truly feared. And then he remembered he'd never set foot on a plane...

The journey to the small safe house in Kent took over two hours. The sun was beginning to rise and shimmer on top of the water as they neared their final destination. For the next day or so – until he could get everything in order for his new life in Amsterdam – the cottage on the hills of Kent's coastline would be his home. It was a small cottage, large enough for himself, and potentially another at a push, and it had everything he needed. Which wasn't a lot right now.

A red clock hung from the wall above the sink in the kitchen. Resting on the counter were giant gym bags filled with cash and a combination of jewels and diamonds that hadn't been seized by the police during their investigations. His insurance package. He estimated they were worth at least a million quid to the right buyer.

'Is everything sorted with the house?' Henry asked Reece, who was sitting opposite him.

'Yeah, bruv. All the paperwork's been taken care of.'

'It's all paid for?'

'Except for something small, like ten Gs. But matey didn't seem too fussed about that. He ain't care if he don't get it.'

Henry smirked. 'I'm not surprised. Cheeky bastard charged us way over the selling price.'

Reece shrugged and reached for a packet of cigarettes. 'You wanted someone bent, so that's what you got. You was paying for silence, innit.'

'Since when did you start smoking again?'

'Since you been in the nick. Fucking giving me everything to do, making me your bitchboy.'

Henry grabbed his cup of water on the table and took a sip. 'You know I rate you for what you've done, bro. It wouldn't have happened if it weren't for you. And I don't say that lightly. Does your mum know?'

'About me getting you out of prison or the fags?'

'Both.'

Reece chuckled, but it quickly turned into a chesty cough. He was only fifteen, but he sounded like he had the lung capacity of someone who'd been smoking for fifty years.

'She ain't know nothing about any of it. I ain't seen her in months. Think my teacher once called it being *estranged*.'

Henry set the glass on the table. 'So you ain't gonna miss her when you come with me to Dam?'

Reece's eyes widened. 'You what?'

'You didn't think I was gonna leave you here, did ya? There are still a few things you've gotta learn, but it'll good experience for ya. I'm gonna need you as my right-hand man, my number two.'

'You serious, fam? You better not be messing.'

Henry chuckled. 'I ain't messing, fam. You're coming with on the boat, aight? Although, you ain't gonna be able to set foot in the red-light district until you're eighteen.'

'Fuck off.'

'I ain't messing. Can't have you popping your cherry too young. You won't last two seconds.'

Reece shot him the middle finger.

'You better get your shit together though, fam. Get home and pack your bags. Be here for later on, yeah?'

Reece kissed his teeth, kicked the chair out from under his feet, and then raced to the door. A few seconds later, Henry heard the engine of Reece's lift roaring into the distance.

CHAPTER 81

ALONE

Closure.

Jake was following Michelle's advice and seeking closure. Not for himself, but for the love of his life.

He didn't know when – or *if* – he was going to see his family again. If everything went according to plan, then he had nothing to worry about. But nothing about his crusade against The Cabal had gone to plan, so he wasn't holding out too much hope. Right now, he needed to cross some things off his to-do list. And next up was one that he'd been meaning to sort for a long time. One that he'd neglected for no other reason than his own selfishness.

You should be ashamed of yourself. This is happening to your wife, and she's more worried about protecting you than she is about her own safety.

Jake wandered up to the front door and pressed the buzzer. He didn't know whether the man was even home, but he was prepared to give the message one way or another. If he needed to break in, then so be it.

Much to his surprise, the owner was home.

Standing in front of him was the dweeby little shitbag who'd sexually assaulted Elizabeth, with his long hair, his beady eyes, his oily skin.

And now a black eye.

Glen.

Glen, Glen, fucking Glen.

As soon as he recognised Jake, he tried to thrust the door shut, but he was too slow and Jake caught it.

'I just want to talk,' Jake said as he forced his way into Glen's flat. 'I just want to talk to you about something.'

Glen was too weak for Jake, and he retreated into the corridor, keeping his distance. They were separated by only a few feet, so he was just within arm's reach. And as Jake stood there, staring at the cowering man, he wanted nothing more than to grab him by the collar and beat him into a coma. It was what he'd wanted to do ever since he'd originally found out about the incident. Maybe even strangle him to death. Or was that a step too far?

'Wh-Wh-What are you d-doing here?' Glen asked, panicked.

'I came here to tell you something.' Jake took a step forward. The man stayed perfectly still. Oh, how he wanted to raise his hands…

'Stay the fuck away from my wife. If you ever come near her again, I will find you and make your life a misery. And I will make sure you spend the rest of your days in prison. I've got a lot of friends in certain high places who can make things happen.'

A smirk grew on Glen's face, infuriating Jake even more.

'So have I,' he said, the smirk turning into a sadistic grin.

Anger swelled through Jake. His body tensed. He raised his arm and clenched his fist.

Glen cowered like a baby.

But Jake controlled himself. He didn't want Glen to have any ammunition against him in whatever court cases may happen in the future. He was putting himself and Elizabeth's credibility at risk just being there.

'Have I made myself clear?' he asked through gritted teeth.

'Crystal,' Glen whimpered.

Jake turned his back on the dweeb and hurried out of there before he changed his mind. He raced across the street and hopped into Michelle's car, his adrenaline through the roof. His hands shook as he grabbed hold of the steering wheel and inhaled. In through the nose. Exhaled. Out through the mouth.

In. Out. In. Out.

Until, a minute later, when the tides in his mind withdrew the red fog and replaced it with calming blue swells.

'Finished?' a voice asked beside him.

Jake turned to Michelle, who was sitting in the passenger seat. Erica was in the back. 'Yep, all finished. You were right – closure does feel amazing.'

Jake reached took out his phone and called Elizabeth. The time was 11:30 a.m., and he was just over twenty minutes away from Westminster Bridge. Cutting it fine.

'Jake?'

He sighed pleasantly. It was so good to hear her voice.

'Yes, Nelly, it's me. Are you OK?'

'I'm fine. How are you? Where are you? What are you doing?'

'I don't have a lot of time,' he told her. 'The police will probably be monitoring my phone and trying to work out where I am and what I'm doing. But I just wanted to let you know that… you know the problem you were having? I've taken care of it. I don't think it'll be cropping up any more.'

Elizabeth babbled incoherently down the phone.

'Do you understand what I'm saying?'

'Yes. Yes, I do. But I already—'

'And it might be worth finding yourself a lawyer. If you need help, ask your mum. I might not be able to.'

'Why? Where are you going? What are you doing?'

'I'll speak to you soon, Liz. I love you and the girls so much. Never forget that.'

Jake hung up before Elizabeth had a chance to speak. Then he immediately made another call so that she wouldn't be able to ring him back – and to stop himself from thinking about their rushed goodbye too much. He fought the tear in his eye.

The ringing tone sounded in his ear.

Come on, come on, come on.

'Jake…' the voice said. 'I was wondering when you might call.'

'I think we need to meet, Darryl. I need to clear my name and tidy all of this up. I have Erica. She's alive and safe and well, but she needs medical assistance.'

'Where?'

'Westminster Bridge. Noon. I know it's pointless me telling you to come alone, so I won't bother. But just know that if anything happens to me, Erica disappears for good.'

CHAPTER 82

LINDSAY GRAY

Empty threats. That's all they were. Illusions designed to confuse and panic. Of course, he wasn't going to do anything to harm Erica – she was the only eyewitness who could exonerate him from the crimes he'd been accused of.

But Darryl and the team didn't need to know that.

In their minds, he was a merciless killer, and so long as they believed he was capable of killing Erica at a moment's notice, he had the upper hand. Now was the time to set the record straight.

And he was fired up for it.

As he waited in the back of the taxicab, he constantly checked his watch, observing the time. Counting down the minutes until the meet.

Ten minutes to midday.

Nine.

Eight.

Seven.

As he neared Westminster Bridge, the level of traffic grew. It was almost a gridlock. Stop. Start. Stop. Start. Eating into his precious minutes.

Any severe delays and he could lose The Cabal forever.

Jake drummed his feet on the floor mat and chewed on his thumbnail. Cast his eye around him. There were four double-decker buses on the bridge, two on each side, dwarfing the rest of the traffic from view, making it impossible for him to see Lindsay.

Eventually, with a few minutes to spare, the traffic eased, and the cab turned onto the bridge.

'Pull over here, mate,' Jake ordered.

'You what?'

'Pull over here, mate. I need to get out here.'

'But I—'

'Just do it!'

Jake was already out of his seat belt and opening the door.

As the car braked heavily, the momentum followed through his body, and his shoulder bashed into the plastic partition between him and the cabbie. Neither of them made any apology.

The fair came to £23.50. Jake chucked him a twenty and ten of Michelle's money, told him to keep the change and then jumped out of the car. Cars and taxis and motorbikes and buses whizzed past him from both directions. Continuous, relentless. He was beginning to think he'd made the wrong decision by approaching from this side of the bridge.

He checked his watch – 11:59:23.

Less than forty seconds.

A car horn sounded, and Jake's head darted to the source of the noise. At first, he thought it was the vehicle coming to pick Lindsay up. But as he realised it was a driver manifesting his anger at a cyclist, Jake's pulse slowed a fraction.

The car moved on, the driver still gesticulating malevolently at the cyclist, and that was when Lindsay Gray came into full view on the other side of the bridge. With a gym bag dangling by her side. A light raincoat draped over her shoulders. Hair up in a small ponytail for the first time since he'd known her.

If he hadn't been hyper-vigilant, he wouldn't have recognised her.

Jake stepped forward into the road, keeping his eyes trained on The Cabal. He couldn't afford to let her go. And if running through thunderous traffic would accomplish that, so be it.

Cars continued to rip past him, sounding their horns and slamming on their brakes, until mercifully there was a gap in the traffic. Jake exploited it and sprinted across.

As he reached the metal barricade that divided the two streams of traffic, Jake unlocked his phone and started recording. He then placed the phone back in his pocket, skipped through the standstill traffic that had formed on the other side of the bridge, and hopped onto the kerb. To safety. He kept his eyes locked on Lindsay, who spun from side to side like a lighthouse beckoning to ships, and pounced, adrenaline surging through his body.

This was it.

This was it.

This was it.

The moment he'd been waiting for.

It all ended right here. Right now.

Twenty feet separated them. Fifteen. Ten.

As he drew nearer, Lindsay's head started to turn back in his direction.

Five.

Her eyes widened when she spotted him.

One.

Nowhere to run.

In a panic, she tried reach into her coat pocket, but Jake was too quick, too wired. He didn't know what she was reaching for, but he didn't want to find out.

'Don't do anything you'll regret,' he said, squeezing her arm tightly.

'My whole life is a regret,' she said through gritted teeth.

The woman who was staring back at him wasn't the woman he'd once known. There was no kindness behind her eyes. No warmth, no happiness, no friendliness.

'So you worked it out then?'

'It took me a while. I had a lot of help along the way.'

'You must be proud of yourself. But I'm surprised to see you here. I thought you'd have been arrested by now.'

'I didn't kill Dylan.'

'But it was fun making people believe you did, wasn't it? Where's Erica?'

'Safe.'

Two minutes away, safe.

'I was worried about her. I never wanted to do those things to her.'

'But you were happy to let your husband rape her?'

Lindsay's pupils dilated. 'I'm dealing with that.'

Jake grew increasingly conscious of his surroundings. Of how the traffic was growing sparser and sparser with every passing second. Of how the number of pedestrians wandering past was less and less. Of how isolated they were becoming.

Two figures amidst a vast expanse of tarmac.

If his plan was going to succeed, Erica needed to be here within the next thirty seconds. Which meant he needed to get all of his answers within that timeframe.

'How long have you been The Cabal for?' Jake asked, hoping to get the confession on record.

'The concept of The Cabal's been around for much longer than I have. I've just been lucky enough to carry the baton for the longest time. And after me there will be someone else, someone higher, someone you've never even thought of.'

'Who?'

'That right there is a question you will never find the answer to. Understand that now, Jake, otherwise you're going to be chasing ghosts your entire life.'

'Why did you agree to do it all? The drugs, the human trafficking, the countless lives you've ruined. Why?'

'Every day we all make decisions we don't agree with. Going to a shitty job we hate, waking up beside someone we don't love anymore. I had an opportunity to do something wild, something crazy. And I grabbed it with both hands. What I was doing freed me. You'll understand it all one day.'

Jake caught a figure out the corner of his eye. Erica. Standing behind Lindsay. Slowly approaching the woman that had abandoned her as a baby.

'Was giving your daughter away a freedom? Did that free you to progress through the ranks?'

The colour drained from Lindsay's cheeks. 'How do you…?'

She stopped herself as soon as Erica wandered past her and joined Jake's side.

'Oh, Erica! You're safe. I'm so glad to see you.'

Lindsay took a step forward, but Jake barked at her to stop. She was to come nowhere near them.

A fierce wind ripped through them, and Erica's hair blew in front of her face.

'You've got some explaining to do,' Erica said, her voice calm and strong.

'I've wanted to say so many things to you for so long, darling. I never wanted to give you up.'

'Then why did you?'

Lindsay took a small step closer. Jake allowed it – but any closer and he would have to intervene.

'You have to understand, darling. I was married. Your dad was married. And I was at an age where I didn't think I could get pregnant. My husband and I had been trying for so long and—'

'He raped me.' There were tears in Erica's voice, but she held them back. Tough. Brave.

Lindsay wailed horribly. 'I know he did, my darling. And I'm so sorry. I can never forgive myself, but he won't be a problem anymore. He didn't know who you were to me. He didn't know you were my daughter. When you were born, I told him you'd died. I couldn't raise you and continue with my… my work.' A sniffle, a wipe of her eyes. 'I tried to stay in contact, but it hurt me every time I saw you. You've grown into such a beautiful and wonderful young woman.'

'You don't know me. You know nothing about me. I fucking hate you. I wish you would just die like the rest of them.'

It was as if someone had shot Lindsay in the face. Confusion, despair and agony all morphed into one priceless moment – the worst blow to her ego Erica could have dealt. Forget Jake, forget the arrest. It was Erica's words that had done the most damage.

'Please…' she whimpered. 'I'm so sorry. Please forgive me.'

The once immutable Cabal, begging for forgiveness. Jake never thought he'd see the day. It was bittersweet.

Then he looked up.

In the space of a few minutes, Westminster Bridge had completely emptied. At the other end, by the Houses of Parliament, was a row of police cars setting up a cordon.

At the other end, he saw exactly the same thing. Uniformed officers. Plainclothes officers. Armed response vehicles. Tactical firearms units. He even heard the sound of a helicopter's blades whirring overhead. And in the distance was a black police RIB, floating patiently on the river.

'There's nowhere left for you to go, Lindsay,' he told her. 'It's over.'

'When you've been doing this as long as I have,' she replied, 'it's never over. There's always a way out, always somewhere to go. I like you, Jake. I never wanted to do half the stuff I did, but you gave me no choice.'

'You ruined my life. You destroyed my career.'

'You brought it on yourself. If you'd stayed away like you were warned, none of this would have happened.'

Just as Jake was about to respond, a voice called from over his shoulder, distorting the odd calm that had fallen over the bridge, disturbed only by the wind now gently flowing past them.

'This is DCI Darryl Hughes. Jake, Lindsay, Erica – we want to resolve this as calmly as possible. Please raise your hands in the air and lie down on the ground.'

For a moment – a long, long, long moment – nothing happened. Time stood still. The river. The wind. The birds. The entire city seemed to fall out of harmony. Including Jake, Erica and Lindsay. Neither wanting to make the first move.

'Erica,' Jake said quietly, keeping his gaze fixed on Lindsay. 'Do as they say, please. Get down on the ground and spread your arms and legs wide.'

'But—'

'Do it. *Please*.'

Reluctantly, Erica lowered herself to the ground.

'Now your turn, Lindsay,' Jake said.

But he could already see that she was thinking of something completely different.

There's always a way out, always somewhere to go.

'I'm sorry for everything, Erica! I love you and I always will!'

Her next move should have struck him as obvious, as a slap in the face, but he was slow to react. Without warning, Lindsay dropped the bag and sprinted towards the edge of the bridge. A flurry of cries and shouts sounded from either side of the bridge – and to Jake's surprise, his own mouth. But it did little to stop her. She climbed over the brick wall and vaulted herself into the River Thames.

Then Jake reacted instinctively. He tore after her, and as he reached the wall, he ignored the petrifying chasm of brown and black beneath him and dived thirty feet into the water.

Jake's eyes ripped open as the rush of water assaulted his face. The force of the dive had sent him deep into the cold, the pressure in his head immediate. He exhaled through his nose and swallowed to equalise, surrounded by a wall of black, then searched the murky water for Lindsay, fearing the worst. That she'd been swept away. That she'd been knocked unconscious upon impact. That she'd vanished completely.

Jake allowed the current to carry him, hoping that it would somehow lead him to her. And as his natural buoyancy lifted him to the surface, he flailed his arms and legs about, trying to remain submerged. The clothes on his back weighed him down, but not enough.

The last time he'd done something this brazen and stupid had been in Southampton, jumping into the English Channel after Danny Cipriano. That had been the act that had started this entire saga with The Cabal and police corruption, and it was the act that would end it now. He'd suffered an almost catastrophic panic attack then, but he wasn't going to allow the same thing to happen again. Not this time. Experience had taught him how to deal with it.

But then the current began to drag him deeper and deeper, and he realised he was running out of air. He thrashed his arms violently, kicking out, now clawing for the surface. His lungs were exploding inside his chest, threatening to let go and force water into his body. If he didn't act fast, he would be lost to the depths of the Thames.

Yet the surface was still so far away, just out of reach. He stared vacantly at the sunlight burning through, as the tide overhead rippled and distorted the light.

There's always a way out, always somewhere to go.

Deeper, deeper.

He'd done this once before. He could do it again.

Images of Maisie, Ellie and Elizabeth appeared in his mind. Their happy faces, their happy memories, their happy future forced him to summon the strength and resilience to push himself to the top, to fight against the current.

Eventually, he broke the surface, gasping for breath, choking, gagging, flooding his body with oxygen before he was dragged back down again.

And then he felt something grab hold of him. At first, he thought it was a boat running him over, crushing him. But then he felt a pair of hands wrap around his chest and heave him upwards, breaching into the open. Breathing rapidly, he turned to face his rescuer – an armed officer leaning over the front of the police RIB that had been floating in the river. With a grunt, the man hefted Jake onto the solid flooring of the boat.

For a moment, he lay on his back, catching his breath. Then he opened his eyes. Light flooded into them, and he stared into the sky. In the top-right corner of his vision was a small cloud, thin, delicate, floating through the air.

Lindsay.

He clambered into a seating position and scrambled over the edge of the RIB.

'Where is she? Where is she?' he asked.

The armed officer's response was to wrap a space blanket over him.

'She's gone, mate. We can't find her.'

Jake slumped into the boat, his mind completely devoid of thought.

He should have been happy that The Cabal was gone, but he wasn't.

He should have been happy that it was all over, but it wasn't.

Because there was always someone else, someone higher, someone he'd never even thought of to step into her shoes and carry the baton.

CHAPTER 83

OFFICIALLY

'Quite a situation we've got ourselves in, wouldn't you agree?' asked Darryl from the other side of the table.

Jake, his solicitor Veronica Bateman, Darryl and Ashley were all seated inside one of the interview rooms in the bowels of Bow Green. After spending several hours in the back of an ambulance, where he was warmed, checked over and given the all-clear, Darryl had made the executive decision to bring Jake all the way back to Stratford in the back of a police car rather than interviewing him at New Scotland Yard a few hundred yards from the bridge. It was *his* investigation, *his* autonomy over everything.

'Quite the situation indeed,' Jake said. He still hadn't come to terms with what had happened on the bridge. Nor did he think he would any time soon. 'Where would you like to begin?'

'This is your chance to prove to us you're innocent, so how about from the beginning?'

And that's exactly what Jake did. He laid everything out on the table, right from the start of his career. Bridger and Murphy and how they'd helped during The Crimsons' final heist. Liam and Drew and Garrison and the Stratford Ripper and how they'd been prepared to pin the murders on someone else. Danny and Michael Cipriano's death, Richard Maddison's suicide, Garrison's accident, Drew's murder. Henry Matheson's murder of Jermaine Gordon and Frank Miller. Helen Clements and Martin Radcliffe and their corruption and collusion with Henry. The young boy Lewis he'd helped save. The fraud that had ruined his finances. The human-trafficking ring he'd uncovered and stopped. The kiss he'd shared with Stephanie. The events surrounding Richard Candy's death. The accusations that had been made against him concerning Rupert Haversham. The events of the past few days. All in exquisite detail. He left no secret hidden, no truth untold. Throughout, he explained how The Cabal had been the puppet master and everyone else the puppets in Lindsay Gray's masterful game.

'She was right under our noses,' he concluded. 'She was sitting in the corner of the room all along, following our investigations, knowing everything there was to know about us. She deceived us and tricked us. And she tricked you guys into thinking I was capable of murder.'

Nearly an hour had passed since he'd started speaking, and his mouth was dry. He leant across the table and sipped from his now lukewarm cup of water.

'We're going to need to see the evidence,' Darryl said plainly. He gave nothing away in his voice. Not even a hint that he believed every word Jake had said.

'I have it.'

'Where?'

'I'd like to make a phone call now, please.'

A weight had lifted from his shoulders now he'd said everything on record. But it still wasn't over. There was a lot more that he needed to prove.

At the custody desk, he was given his phone call. Hovering over him were Darryl, Veronica, the custody sergeant and a uniformed officer, all eagerly awaiting to hear what he had to say.

Jake pulled the phone off the cradle and dialled Michelle's number.

It rang and rang. Rang and rang. He begged for her to answer it.

Thankfully, she did.

'Jake?' Michelle asked.

He breathed a deep and long sigh of relief. 'I'm so glad to hear your voice. Did you make it back all right?'

'No one saw me. No one followed me. I'm OK.'

Another sigh of relief. 'I need you to do as discussed.'

'OK.'

'Have you got the copies?'

'Yes.'

'Good.' There was a brief silence. A lump caught in his throat. 'Hey…' he began, finally allowing himself to relax. 'We did it. *You* did it. I just… I just wanted to say thank you. Without you, I'd be running for the rest of my life.'

'You can thank me in person when you see me. And maybe buy me a drink. My order's a Foster's top.'

Smiling, Jake hung up and set the receiver down on the machine.

'And?' Darryl asked, pouncing on him. 'Where is it?'

Before replying, Jake looked at them all, savouring the moment and the look on their faces.

It took them a little over an hour to read through the evidence, absorb it and begin fact-checking it. While he waited, Jake had been returned to his custody cell, where he struggled to find a comfortable position on the supremely uncomfortable mattress.

Typically, just as he'd finally achieved it, the cell door opened.

It was Darryl. 'Hey…'

'Hey…'

'Erica told us everything. The condensed version, at least. She's backed up everything you said.'

'And the evidence?' Jake rolled his legs off the side of the bed.

'Digital forensics are trying to get the recording from the bridge out of your waterlogged phone.'

'Oops.'

'But the rest of it's damning. I had a brief look earlier.'

'And?'

'It's too soon to say, but we can't keep you here any longer than twenty-four hours. And I'm in no position to extend it. I think for now we won't be charging you with anything.'

An ear-to-ear smile flashed on Jake's face. He felt elated. It was over. Officially.

There's always a way out…

Jake rose and wandered up to Darryl, then reached out and shook the other man's hand.

'So…' Jake began, 'when can I come back to work?'

CHAPTER 84

TERRIFIC NEWS

There had been a commotion outside the Houses of Parliament, right on the Westminster Bridge. Fear, laced with a hint of excitement, swept through the building as word quickly spread. In recent years, there'd been a series of terrorist attacks on the bridge – madmen with knives, stabbing people uncontrollably, and even madder men driving heavy vehicles off the road and into pedestrians. The deaths and injuries caused by those incidents were still raw in the minds of every politician who worked there.

But she hadn't been worried. She knew exactly what the commotion was about.

Something had happened. Something had gone wrong for Lindsay Gray – her brilliant escape plan hadn't worked.

She would have liked to say that she was involved in it somehow, but she wasn't. The further removed she remained from Lindsay, the better. For her own sake.

She stalked along the corridors of the Houses of Parliament with her bag dangling by her leg. Some of the other politicians and staff members and bureaucrats nodded to her as they hurried past. They all seemed to be in a rush – either as a result of the earlier incident or because it was the nature of their job.

At the end of the corridor, her mobile rang, bringing her to a stop. She fumbled inside her bag for it and answered the call just as it was about to disconnect.

'Is everything all right, love?' she asked.

'They've dropped all charges against him. He's getting out. He's coming home.'

A smile grew on her face. 'Oh, sweetie. That is terrific news.'

CHAPTER 85

LISTEN

That evening, just as the sun was beginning to set, one thought occupied Jake's mind as he raced along the M25, cradling the speedometer a fraction over the speed limit.

Elizabeth. Maisie. Ellie.

Family.

How he couldn't wait to get home and hold them. How he couldn't wait to give them a kiss and tell them how much he loved them. How he couldn't wait to spend some much needed and overdue time with them.

But first, he'd need to apologise to them all, make amends, restore their love and faith and trust in him.

His mobile rang. He answered it on the dashboard.

'DC Tanner,' he said, feeling weird for saying it. It had been a while since he'd last referred to himself by his title. And even longer since he hadn't felt ashamed to say it.

'It's me.'

'Michelle, I'm so glad you called.'

'How are you feeling?'

'Fine. Cold. In shock. My stab wound ripped open on impact, but they've given me some meds to fight any infections. I'll be fine.'

'Did everything go OK?'

'Perfect. I'm on my way home now. I've got some making up to do.'

'Are they dropping the charges?'

'All of the big ones. There are a few things they said they needed to check over, but they're only minor. Nothing to worry about. But it's done. It's over.' He paused as a lump swelled in his throat. 'Thank you. I mean that. Thank you, thank you, thank you. Without your help… who knows where I'd be. In prison. Dead. But I'm not. And it's thanks to you.'

There was a slight pause, followed by a long sniff.

'I was just doing my job,' Michelle replied.

'Bullshit. It was personal for the both of us, and I hope you got the closure you needed.'

'I did. Thank you. And I couldn't have got *that* without you.' Another pause. 'What's going to happen to *her*?'

Jake moved into the middle lane to allow a Ford Ka to pass him.

'Last I heard, they were still searching for her body. When she fell into the water, she stayed under. The RIB was too late getting to her.'

Michelle hesitated again. 'I don't know what to say.'

'I'm sure you do. It's probably not pleasant though, is it?'

Jake had a few things in mind. *Good riddance. Thank God she's dead. The world's a better place without her.*

As Jake neared Croydon, he told her that he needed to go.

'We'll keep in touch though, yes?' he asked. 'Please?'

'I'd like that.'

'So would I.'

Jake rang off a few miles from Martha's house. Elizabeth was still staying there, and he hoped that Martha was out so Jake could speak with his wife peacefully and in private. He didn't want to hear any more angry voicemails from her any time soon.

He pulled up outside, hurried to the front door, and knocked.

As soon as the door opened, Elizabeth leapt on him, threw her arms around him, and squeezed tightly. It reminded him of the hug she'd given him after he'd proposed. A bear hug.

She released him, then held both sides of his face and kissed him. That particular kiss reminded him of the one they'd shared on their wedding day. In the space of a few seconds, he'd welcomed images of happiness and love and the best memories of his life into his mind, something that hadn't happened for a long time. He'd forgotten what it was like to kiss Elizabeth like that, to hold her like that.

He wanted more of it – and never wanted to let her go.

That evening, dinner had been provided courtesy of Martha on her return from work. He and Elizabeth had spent the past few hours talking, catching up, clearing the air for good.

Jake, still cold from the freezing temperatures of the River Thames, was ravenous. And on tonight's menu was chicken chow mein, egg fried rice, and sweet and sour chicken balls. His favourite. Plain, but his favourite.

'Some might say this is well earned,' Martha remarked as she laid the plate in front of him.

'And you?'

'I'd say it's a step in the right direction. It's good to have you back.'

Was that a smile? A glimmer of light amidst her black heart and soul?

'Well we couldn't be happier,' Elizabeth added. 'Isn't that right, girls?'

Ellie and Maisie cheered, but Jake guessed it was due to the excitement of the Chinese rather than his heroic return.

'We've a lot to catch up on, the three of us,' Martha said, returning to her stern ways.

The respite had been nice while it lasted.

They spent the next hour eating, sharing, chatting with Maisie and Ellie, listening to their stories, the fantasies they'd had throughout the day. Jake had completely forgotten about The Cabal, Lindsay Gray, and everything to do with her.

Until after dinner.

After Elizabeth grew infuriated with Jake's constant shivering, she sent him upstairs in search of one of Alan's thick jumpers. It was the first time he'd ever set foot in Martha and Alan's bedroom, and he hoped it would be the last.

The room was twice the size of his and Elizabeth's, with an en suite in the corner. A giant floor-to-ceiling wardrobe ran along the length of the longest wall, and a dozen mirrors stared back at him. The oversized bed was adorned with multiple pillows, and an ornate bench at the foot of it, complete with a blue throw and another cushion.

But what caught his eye was the dresser near the bookshelf in the other corner of the room.

Numerous picture frames rested on the dresser beside Martha's make-up. A constant reminder of her family. Jake recognised one of the photos he and Elizabeth had given them for Christmas one year. Beside it was a photo of Martha and Alan's wedding day, then another one of a young Alan dressed in a suit, holding a baby in a church.

But the next one…

The next one troubled him and tightened a knot in his stomach.

It grew tighter and tighter as he approached for a closer look, in case his eyes were playing tricks on him.

They weren't.

There, on the right-hand side of the dresser, next to photos of Jake and the rest of the family, was an old and torn photo of Martha and Lindsay Gray at a function, smiling ebulliently at the camera, wrapped arm in arm, glasses of wine in hand.

Jake reached out to touch it, then stopped.

Martha was at the door, leaning in. She looked down at the photo, then back up at Jake.

'The less you know, Jake, the better it is for everyone involved. Please, if you still love my daughter and want to continue to be a part of this family, listen to me on this.'

CHAPTER 86

MR MATHESON

The boy had thought he was a hero. But he'd quickly shown just how brave he really was. It had only taken a few fingernails, and a few broken teeth to extract the necessary information. At first, Reece Enfield, one of Henry Matheson's brightest and best foot soldiers, hadn't listened, but after the pain and the suffering and the torturing began, he'd started to understand. Sit up. Pay attention. And he'd soon relinquished the information with ease. He was still a child at the end of the day. He didn't know how to beat the bullies and defend himself. He was innocent and naïve to the real brutalities of the world that he'd become involved in. And, in a way, he felt sorry for him. It was just a shame that he had to put a bullet in the child's brain at the end of it all.

Henry Matheson was staying in Kent. In a remote part of the county near the Channel, surrounded by fields and cliff faces. Assassinating him wasn't going to be easy. Especially with the clock ticking. Apparently, the woman who'd got him out of prison for the day needed him back within twelve hours. The ankle bracelet around his foot was keeping him honest. Inside the bracelet was a GPS monitoring device, capable of monitoring his position anywhere on the planet to within a metre.

He was driving the car that had been given to him. It was a shitty Ford Escort, but he wasn't one to complain. He knew how to drive it, and it was fast enough that he could get to Kent and back in time. In the back of the car was a sniper rifle. The Cabal and her contact had given him a handgun, but after realising that Henry was holed up in the middle of a field, he'd decided he was going to need something with a longer range. If Henry saw him, a handgun would be no use. So he'd gone to his own safe house and pilfered a sniper rifle from it.

It was one of his prized possessions. It had been with him for nearly ten years and was responsible for his first ever confirmed kill.

After nearly two hours of driving from the Cosgrove Estate in London to Kent, he arrived at Henry's safe house. He switched off the headlights a mile away from the house. Darkness spread across the sky, and the undulating hills in front of him cast giant shadows across the grass. The house was over a quarter of a mile away. The lights inside were on, and through a set of binoculars, he saw movement.

Henry Matheson, alone. Getting his things ready to leave.

He didn't know how much time he had, but he was sure it wasn't long.

He exited the vehicle, hefted the case with the sniper rifle in it from the boot and carried it across the field, climbing over fences and keeping his body low. He found a small patch of grass that was perfect – flat, sheltered from the wind – then set the case on the ground, opened it and started to assemble the rifle. Once the weapon was correctly assembled, he set it on the ground and lay down on the grass, training the optics on the house and adjusting the lens so that the windows occupied the entirety of his view.

Then he reached into his pocket and produced Reece Enfield's phone. He found Henry's number and dialled.

While he waited for Henry to answer, he moved the sights about the house, searching for his target.

He found it the moment the phone was answered. Henry was standing in the kitchen, open, with the phone against his ear.

'What's up?' he asked.

'Do not move,' he told Henry.

'Who is this?'

He flicked a switch. In an instant, a red light shone from the barrel of the sniper rifle and found its home on Henry's chest. Henry noticed it immediately.

'Who are you?' Henry asked.

'A friend of a friend.'

'I've pissed off a lot of people in my time, mate. You're gonna need to be a little bit more detailed than that.'

'No names.'

Henry sighed, eyes darting from left to right, searching. But it was useless. He was covered in darkness, invisible.

'I was wondering when this might happen, you know,' Henry continued. 'But I don't know why it's happening *now*. I've seen the news. Tragic, isn't it? She's dead. You're free. We all are. Whatever hold she has on you is now gone. You don't have to do this.'

'I know.'

'Who are you? I recognise your voice.'

'No names.'

'They call you The Farmer, don't they?'

'No names.' He moved his finger over the trigger.

'You don't have to do this.'

'I know.' A smirk grew on his face. His body relaxed. He held his breath. 'But I want to.'

He pulled the trigger. The gun recoiled into his shoulder, the sound echoing around the fields and quickly losing momentum as it spilt over the hills. Henry's chest had already burst open in an explosion of red, blood splattering across the window and the kitchen around him as his body dropped to the ground.

It was done.

Except it wasn't. Not yet.

The Farmer pushed himself to his feet, disassembled the weapon, set it back in the box and carried it towards Henry's house, with his hand wrapped around the Glock 17 at his back. Reece had assured him that the house was empty, and so far everything he'd told him had been true, but he hadn't got to where he was by believing everything he heard.

The Farmer reached the house, kicked down the door and made his way into the kitchen. Henry's body lay flat on the floor. A pool of blood was rapidly spreading across the tiles, running down the gaps between them. The hole in his chest was the same width as the table leg, and The Farmer could only imagine what it would look like on the other side.

But that wasn't the most interesting thing in the room.

It was the tower of gym bags that rested against the wall to his left. Inside them were heaps of money – bank notes, coins – and pieces of jewellery. And in another one was a shipment of cocaine. Kilograms of the powder wrapped tightly in plastic bags.

He smiled. He'd hit the jackpot.

Before getting to Henry's house, he'd had every intention of returning to prison on time, as per the agreement he'd made. But this changed everything. With the money and drugs, he could escape. He could get out of there. Maybe even head back to Russia. Or start a new career somewhere else.

Before he could dwell on the thought further, Henry's mobile rang. It vibrated loudly on the solid tiles, shuddering and moving with each vibration. The screen was cracked from where Henry had dropped it, but it was still fully functional.

The Farmer picked it up and answered, trying his hardest to adopt a convincing English accent.

'Yes?'

'Your transportation has arrived. Come down to the water in twenty minutes. The lights will be on. If you can't find me, call this number.'

The line went dead.

It was too good to be true.

But the only problem now was the device around his ankle. He was going to have to dispose of it.

Setting the weapon down on the ground, The Farmer lifted his leg onto the chair and inspected the device. The mechanical part was made of metal, but the strap was made from thick plastic. He was either going to need a saw or a pair of shears.

He set about the house, searching for some. To his surprise, at the back of the property was a small room that led into the garden. Inside was a cupboard where he found a pair of cutters. When he returned to the kitchen, he set his leg on the chair and started tearing the anklet free from his skin.

Within a minute, he was done. His leg was free from the device and he was free to escape. But there was no time to celebrate. He didn't know where he was going, and he didn't know how to get there.

He made a quick count of the bags. Four in total – two cash, two drugs. With the added luggage of his rifle case, he was going to have to leave one behind.

The Farmer picked up the bags of cash, holding them both in one hand, and the drugs bag and rifle case in the other. He kept the handgun in his back pocket.

Then he left.

He headed towards the sound of the water lapping against the beach in the distance. After a few minutes of hiking up a steep hill, he found a flight of steps that led all the way down to a beach at the bottom. The patch of sand was small – barely enough to be called a beach. But it was large enough for a couple of people to sunbathe on.

Paying it little consideration, The Farmer started down the steps, jostling his bags against the wooden fence panels that ran beside him.

As he reached the bottom, a boat came into view. It was a small fishing charter that looked smaller than the Ford Escort he'd come in. At the front was a small cabin, and at the back were a couple of benches. The Farmer waited until the boat pulled in closer to the shore, anchored, and then for the captain to hop out. The man waded through the water and advanced to him.

'Henry Matheson?' the captain asked.

The Farmer looked at him blankly. 'That's me,' he said in his terrible British accent.

'I'm Captain Friend. Nice to meet you. Let me take those for you.'

Friend reached across and grabbed the bags of money from him. He put up no fight. If the man was going to kill him and take off with the money, then he already would have done.

No, this was legitimate.

This was his lucky escape.

The Farmer followed Friend to the boat, keeping the rifle case and bag of drugs over his head as he waded through the chilly water. After he climbed on board, Friend grabbed him a towel and wrapped it round his legs.

'Thank you,' The Farmer said.

Friend said nothing as he pulled in the anchor and headed to the cabin.

'So, Mr Matheson, have you ever been to Amsterdam before?'

CHAPTER 87

CLOSURE

Two weeks later

Cyclists everywhere, whizzing past left to right, right to left. Sounding their little bells as they went. For the past few weeks, she'd grown accustomed to them as she tracked her target, monitored his movements. In the city of Amsterdam, cyclists were king. And when it came to mercilessly killing people, her next target thought the same about himself. That he was untouchable, untraceable.

Well, she had news for him…

She stepped into the lift and pressed the button for the top floor. Ever since his arrival in the city, he'd been renting the penthouse suite and had spent most his time between the pubs and clubs and the warehouse on the outskirts of the city. And when he wasn't shipping Henry Matheson's drugs through the streets, he was indulging himself in sin: sex and drugs had already become the mainstay of his time in Amsterdam.

Which made this the perfect disguise.

The lift reached the top floor and opened onto a small corridor, home to the only two penthouses in the building. Before leaving, she checked herself in the lift mirror.

Hair, good. Make-up, good. Outfit, good.

Ready to go.

Exiting the lift, she found the penthouse she was looking for and knocked on the door.

And there he was a few seconds later. The man she'd heard and read so much about. The man she'd dreamt of meeting. The moment she'd been waiting for for a long time.

He was taller than she'd expected and much thicker. His broad shoulders filled the frame of the door, and he was dressed in a sweatshirt and jeans. Casual for a Friday night.

'Yes?'

'It's me,' she replied.

'I don't know you.'

'You ordered me, didn't you?'

'No. You have wrong number.'

The man tried to shut the door, but she surged forward. If she couldn't flirt her way in, she would have to force it instead.

As she did, she reached behind her back and unleashed the Taser she'd bought the other day. The prongs burst from the top of the device and landed cleanly in his chin and cheeks, sending fifty thousand volts through his body. Enough to paralyse him and drop him to the floor.

Without wasting any time, she hurried into the penthouse with her backpack and shut the door behind her.

It was time to begin.

The first thing he noticed was the pain in his face, followed shortly by the restraints around his wrists and ankles. As the bedroom finally came into view, he noticed that the prostitute had tied him up on the floor, arms and legs behind him – his body stiff, his back upright, supported by a pole of some kind.

Then he tried to move his head but couldn't.

'Stuck, are we?' came a voice from behind him.

He tried to see but couldn't.

'It's not nice, is it?'

He tried to speak but couldn't. A gag had been placed in his mouth.

'I imagine this is how some of the people you've come across in the past have felt.'

She finally came into view. Her thin body, her cropped hair, her pink tattoos and make-up. And then there was that outfit; one he'd rather see on anyone else but her.

'Who are you?' he asked, but the words came out muffled behind the gag.

'Do you remember me?' the woman asked.

He shook his head as much as he could.

'We've met before… Well, not *exactly*. This is the first time *we've* crossed paths. But you've met my family. My brothers.'

He tried to recall the names of his victims, the names of his confirmed kills. How many of them had been brothers? It was an unusual connection between targets, but it wasn't uncommon. He could remember two instances. One had been back in Russia, but this woman spoke with an English accent, so it couldn't have been her.

As for the other siblings…

'Cipriano,' he mumbled.

She nodded almost imperceptibly and took a step forward. 'You killed them. And now I'm going to kill you exactly the same way.'

Without warning, the woman yanked the gag from his mouth, tearing the hairs from his cheeks, and threw it to the floor. Before he could catch his breath, she reached down beside him and began pouring a silvery grey mixture down his throat. The particles and dust rapidly filled his mouth and nose, and he began to choke, his chest compressing, his body seizing, his lungs bursting. He coughed and coughed.

'Here, let me wash some of that down for you.'

Then she poured a bottle of water into his mouth, flushing the cement mixture through his body. Images of him doing the same thing to Danny Cipriano flashed in his mind between coughs of pain and fear.

'That's for Danny,' she said, but by now he wasn't paying much attention.

The liquid did nothing to clear his throat; the mixture remained there, lodged, blocking his airways. Oxygen was rapidly depleting from his body, and with each attempt he made to breathe, the world grew a little dimmer.

The woman then raised her fist and punched him in the throat. The force of the blow propelled some of the stodgy mixture onto the tiles, but not enough.

'That was for Michael and Candice.'

He could feel himself growing faint, feel the blood rushing to his face, while the rest of him turned numb. Death was near. And he hoped it came soon.

For the next twenty seconds, the woman hovered over him, watching as he clung to what was left of his life. In his line of work, he'd often wondered what his victim's dying moments were like, but his were a blank.

There was no happiness in his life, no light. Only death and darkness. He'd had a shadow of an existence, and now he was getting the end he deserved.

Before long, his breath turned wheezy, and he began to dip in and out of consciousness.

'And this…' she said, turning her back on him.

When she turned to face him again, she held a pistol in her hands.

For the first time in his life, The Farmer was staring down the other end of the barrel. At that moment, the lives and histories of all his victims flashed through his mind.

'This is for Luke,' she said.

And pulled the trigger.

Closure.

The word had been swimming around her head for the past few

weeks, a concept that had seemed out of reach for so long. But after Erica had found hers, and Jake had found his, it was only fair that she be on the receiving end of some, too.

And now she finally was.

Her body tingled with adrenaline as she boarded the airplane bound for Gatwick. In two hours' time, a call would be made to the Dutch authorities, and the police would discover Georgiy Ivanov's body in a mess on the floor of his penthouse bedroom. By which time she would be back home on the sofa, safe in the knowledge that nothing would ever lead to her.

Safe in the knowledge that the man responsible for the death of two of her brothers had suffered the same fate.

Closure.

After she'd found her window seat and waited for the rest of the passengers to fill the plane, she pulled her phone out of her purse and dialled a number.

The call rang and rang. Rang and rang. Until…

'Hello?'

'It's me. I'm on the plane.'

'Good. And is it all done?'

'Yep. Everything's sorted. I'll let you know when I land.'

'Good work, Michelle. Leave the rest with me. I'll make sure nothing happens.'

'Thanks.'

'Oh, and remember: Jake can never know about any of this. The less he knows, the better.'

CHAPTER 88

WELCOME

Six months later

Just over half a year had gone by since The Cabal has passed away, since Jake had been exonerated and since everything had been put to bed. But there was no cause for celebration.

The investigation into The Cabal's corrupt network was far-reaching and wide. In the past twelve months, the Serious Organised Crime Agency had identified and arrested thirty more individuals who were part of The Cabal's network, ranging from the corrupt prison guards who had allowed both Henry Matheson and Georgiy 'The Farmer' Ivanov to escape from prison (a nationwide manhunt had ensued following The Farmer's disappearance, but there was still no sign of him, and Jake doubted there ever would be), right up to the IT guys in Bow Green and Surrey Police who had helped Lindsay Gray get away with as much as she had. Now that the police knew her name, they had been able to look into her twenty-year career as a police officer. Nobody was safe from the investigation coming their way, including those that were either dead or retired.

Jake had helped as much as he could – he'd given SOCA *almost* everything he knew, keeping the details about Martha away from the investigation – but after that, he'd decided he wanted nothing to do with it anymore. That chapter in his life was over, and he was ready to start a new one.

All in the name of closure.

So when he received an email telling him he was late for a meeting he didn't know he was having, he rushed out of his chair and hurried to the room on the third floor.

Darryl's message had been cryptic and only contained the bare details. He stopped outside the meeting room. Composed himself.

Breathed in. Breathed out. Knocked.

A moment of silence.

'Come in,' the voice on the other side said.

Jake opened the door. Wandering towards him was a man he'd never seen before. Jake shook his hand.

'Detective Tanner,' the man said. He was large – as wide as the door – and tall, clearing Jake's height by a few inches. 'Thank you for agreeing to meet on such short notice.'

'No problem.'

As Jake sat down, he noticed Darryl at the other side of the room, pouring himself a cup of coffee. 'Would you like one?' he asked.

'No thanks.'

Both men sat opposite Jake, and immediately he feared the worst.

'I suppose you're wondering why we've asked you here?' the mysterious man asked.

'You read my mind.'

'Good. My name is Mamadou Kuhoba, Detective Chief Superintendent of SO15, Counter Terrorism Command. We've never met before, have we?'

Jake searched his mind. It seemed impossible that they would have met, but he didn't want to upset the man straight away. 'No, I don't think so, sir.'

'Have you ever heard of me?'

Jake shook his head.

'Well I've heard of you.' Mamadou drank from his cup. 'How are you feeling? How's the stab wound?'

'Pretty much healed, sir, though there's a decent scar.'

'Something to show the grandkids.'

Jake smiled. 'Sure.'

'And how are you settling back in?'

'Not bad. But I'd like to focus on getting more done.'

'I'm glad you mentioned that, Jake. In fact, that's the reason I'm here.' Mamadou leant back in his chair and clapped his hands together. 'Darryl and I have been chatting recently. We've been talking about you, Jake. How dedicated you are. How committed you are to making a change to this city. How you won't let anything, or anyone, get in the way of that. Which got me thinking... there's a new position in my team in SO15 that's opened up, and we think you'd be the perfect fit.'

Jake was dumbfounded. A new position? This was the new chapter he needed. A part of him had always been intrigued by the mysticism and secrecy of counter terrorism. For him, it was one of the ultimate forms of policing – ridding the streets of the worst kind of criminal.

'You'd be on the same wage,' Mamadou continued, interrupting his train of thought, 'and the work would be more physically and mentally demanding. However, we wouldn't have asked you if we didn't think you were capable. You'd have to undergo some physio to make sure you're fit for it, but other than that, we think you're good to go.'

'I… I don't know what to say.'

'You should start by thanking Darryl.' Mamadou turned to his colleague. 'He's the one who put you forward.'

Jake opened his mouth but was cut off.

'Don't get all soppy on me, Jake. You'll be missed in CID, if you decide to take it, but I think you're ready. And I think it's about time you had a change – I think it would be best for you. Everything's been settled on both sides – we just need you to put in the transfer request, go through the usual rigmarole and then, within a few months, you'll be a fully fledged member of SO15.'

'You don't have to make a decision right now. You've got time to talk it over if you want,' Mamadou added.

'Oh, and there's one other particular request as well,' Darryl added.

'What's that?'

'Ashley – she said you have to keep in touch. One of her demands, not mine.'

They all laughed.

Mamadou spoke first. 'So, Tanner – what do you say?'

It didn't take much deliberation. A second later, he had his answer. 'Yes, I'll take it. I'll take the job.'

Mamadou rose and shook Jake's hand. 'Welcome to the team.'

EPILOGUE

Lindsay Gray's body was retrieved a few miles downstream of Westminster Bridge, washed ashore beside the Candy Cleaning Services warehouse. She was pronounced dead at the scene, and her body was later moved to the mortuary. A funeral was held, but nobody attended.

Ashley Rivers treated herself to a singles holiday after the investigation was brought to a close. She'll miss Jake but understands why he chose to leave; she would be lying if she said she didn't have similar plans.

Brendan Lafferty eventually recovered from his burns, but they were so significant he was forced to medically retire from the police. He now lives in Hertfordshire and is getting used to walking again.

Darryl Hughes apologised for his maltreatment of Jake throughout the investigation, and he has now agreed to use what he's learnt on the new faces at Bow Green.

Michelle's help during the investigation earned her a journalism award, which she proudly displays above her computer. She has begun work on her next project, which she hopes will bring her closer to some new people. Meanwhile, she continues to remain in contact with Jake. And Martha.

Erica Haversham, who gained public notoriety following her parents' killings, was charged with murder and sentenced to prison on her eighteenth birthday for twenty years. She and Jake have spoken twice since.

On Jake's behalf, Darryl saw to it that Glen Cooper was arrested for sexual harassment and stalking. He pleaded guilty to the charges and is currently serving fourteen months in prison. To this day, Elizabeth and Glen are the only ones who know that she beat him up.

Dennis Gray's body was discovered a few miles from Lindsay's, in the middle of an abandoned caravan site. He'd bled out from his wounds and was found clutching a camera against his chest. The files retrieved later revealed the story of what had happened and who had been present. The investigation now lies with the Drug Squad.

Pete Garrison later recovered from his coma with no life-changing injuries. He has since been released from hospital and has started a new life away from London, in the countryside, where he can enjoy the beautiful beaches of Cornwall.

Shortly after the investigation was passed to SOCA, Liam Greene passed away from his cancer. He died peacefully in his cell overnight. Jake and several others who knew him from the force attended his funeral. Pete Garrison, however, was not present.

Now that Jake's joining counter terrorism command, Elizabeth is feeling a mixture of happiness and fear. Their marriage has finally turned around, and they're spending more time with one another. On a personal level, she's got back into her photography again and continues to dream of making it a success.

Meanwhile, Jake passed his medical tests and will start working for SO15 Counter Terrorism in a few months.

He returns in *The Wolf*…

Enjoy this? You can make a big difference.

Reviews are the most powerful tools in my arsenal when it comes to getting attention for my books. They act as the tipping point on the scales of indecision for future readers crossing my books.

So, if you enjoyed this book, and are interested in being one of my committed and loyal readers, then I would really grateful if you could leave a review. Why not spread the word, share the love? Even if you leave an honest review, it would still mean a lot. They take as long to write as it did to read this book!

Thank you.

Your Friendly Author,
Jack Probyn

ABOUT JACK PROBYN

Jack Probyn is a British crime writer and the author of the Jake Tanner crime thriller series, set in London.

He currently lives in Surrey with his partner and cat, and is working on a new murder mystery series set in his hometown of Essex.

Keep up to date with Jack at the following:
- Website: https://www.jackprobynbooks.com
- Facebook: https://www.facebook.co.uk/jackprobynbooks
- Twitter: https://twitter.com/jackprobynbooks
- Instagram: https://www.instagram.com/jackprobynauthor

Printed in Great Britain
by Amazon